What We Leave Undone

What We Leave Undone

Johanna M. Selles

RESOURCE *Publications* · Eugene, Oregon

WHAT WE LEAVE UNDONE

Resource Publications
An Imprint of Wipf and Stock Publishers
199 W. 8th Ave., Suite 3
Eugene, OR 97401

www.wipfandstock.com

PAPERBACK ISBN: 978-1-5326-8721-1
HARDCOVER ISBN: 978-1-5326-8722-8
EBOOK ISBN: 978-1-5326-8723-5

Manufactured in the U.S.A.   SEPTEMBER 18, 2019

To Renata

THE SIN OF OMISSION

It isn't the thing you do, dear,
It's the thing you leave undone
That gives you a bit of a heartache
At setting of the sun.
The tender work forgotten,
The letter you did not write,
The flowers you did not send, dear,
Are your haunting ghosts at night.

The stone you might have lifted
Out of a brother's way;
The bit of heartsome counsel
You were hurried too much to say;
The loving touch of the hand, dear,
The gentle, winning tone
Which you had no time nor thought for
With troubles enough of your own.

Those little acts of kindness
So easily out of mind,
Those chances to be angels
Which we poor mortals find -
They come in night and silence,
Each sad, reproachful wraith,
When hope is faint and flagging,
And a chill has fallen on faith.

For life is all too short, dear,
And sorrow is all too great,
To suffer our slow compassion
That tarries until too late:
And it isn't the thing you do, dear,
It's the thing you leave undone
Which gives you a bit of heartache
At the setting of the sun.

—MARGARET ELIZABETH SANGSTER (1838–1912)

Contents

Contents

PART I

There was a blank wall of social and professional antagonism, facing the woman physician, that formed a situation of singular, painful loneliness, leaving her without support, respect, or professional counsel.

—Dr. Elizabeth Blackwell (1821–1910)[*]

---

[*] Elizabeth Blackwell, "Address on the Medical Education of Women" (Public Domain, 1863).

Chapter 1

NEWTON'S CORNERS, NY, 1980

Nori drove her aging Jetta hard, downshifting to slow her descent on the mountain road. The sense of freedom was exhilarating—New Haven had become oppressive, and a series of failures and missteps clung to her. After a few stutters, the car responded to the demands. *Atta girl*, she thought, as she patted the dash. *You still got it!*

After she got her license, her dad had taken her out to some back roads in upstate New York and taught her how to use the clutch. For all her complaints about him, she had to admit he'd been a good teacher.

Through the passenger window, she caught a glimpse of the sharp drop-off with wooded valleys far below; on her side, a river still swollen from spring melt rolled towards town.

After weeks of disaster following disaster, this road trip had restored some sense of control. It marked a new beginning. For a while there, she'd felt her troubles multiply like waves that were in such a hurry to reach the shore that they fell and collapsed on each other.

This road trip was the perfect antidote to despair. She opened the windows to let the crisp pine air fill the car.

She sang along with the country music on the radio—it was the only station she could get up here. A song came on that Kevin had introduced her to last year, when they were still an item. She wasn't going to think about that. Things were going to be all right—the dark days were finally done. The song crooned about love letters. Nori had to laugh at the almost-appropriate lyrics. Her aunt had written her a letter inviting her to come to the lake house, but Nori doubted that anyone had ever referred to Louise as "my darlin'."

Nori's laughter was cut short by the sound of a siren and flashing lights behind her. She pulled over to the shoulder. "Shit, shit, shit," she said, as she thumped the wheel in dismay. *What was the speed limit here anyway?*

"License and registration," the trooper said, as he glanced into the car and then at Nori. She reached for the glove compartment button but it was stuck. "Sorry, sir, it often jams." Nori hit the button a few more times, thumped the door with her fist, until the compartment finally fell open, and with it, out rolled a box of condoms, a package of gum, and a tube of lipstick. Nori could feel her face turning red. She tried to ignore the stuff on the floor and obediently took out the envelope with the registration. Her hands trembled when she handed it to the trooper, who clearly had no sense of humour.

"You were doing fifty in a twenty-five miles per hour zone."

"Fifty?" *Oh no, this was going to cost. And the balance in her account was already so low, this might wipe her out entirely.* "But. . . ."

"Stay here." He walked to his car still holding her papers.

She smacked the steering wheel again. "Idiot!" She quickly gathered up the items from the floor and stuffed them back into the glove compartment.

A few cars slowed down to see what was happening. She wanted to give them the finger, but reminded herself that she was hoping to stay in this town for a while. And it was a very small place where people had very long memories. Everyone knew the names of relatives five generations back. She'd once stood with Louise in the small grocery listening to them telling about cousins and aunts and their di-a-beet-ees.

Nori sat back and tried to practice deep breathing while she waited for the trooper to return. She wanted to get to Louise's house—it was already far later than she'd planned. The day she'd received Louise's letter, she couldn't believe her eyes. The invitation to sort her personal papers couldn't have come at a more perfect moment. Louise explained that Nori would have a better sense of what was worth keeping.

Sooner or later she'd have to tell her that she was currently on academic probation, having failed to meet the departmental deadline for submission of her thesis proposal. That wasn't going to be an easy topic to broach. Louise, after all, had helped her get into Yale and provided additional financial support to cover her costs. She'd almost been more excited than Nori when the acceptance arrived.

When she'd found a summer student willing to sublet her place through the Yale housing office, Nori started to believe that this holiday was really going to happen. "I'm outta here," she'd sung, as she danced around her apartment with Louise's letter.

The trooper returned and handed Nori her identification and her ticket. "You can mail in your payment or go to town hall. Slow down." He walked away.

Nori waited till he left and then drove at a crawl along Main Street. Her rosy colored memories of by-gone summers here didn't fit the shabby reality reflected in the boarded up windows and rippled shingles of roofs that had borne too much snow for too long. Most of the businesses were still closed for the season; the town hadn't quite revived after the endless winter.

No customers lined up for help at the seasonal Ski-Doo and outboard motor shop—mud season didn't allow for either. The ice cream shack and the pizza joint were still closed. On many summer nights, she and Jazz had lined up for ice cream after a day on the beach.

A few pickup trucks were parked outside the Village Inn for the fish and chips lunch special—that, at least, seemed to be a year-round attraction. The handmade sign in the window said, "Bikers Welcome," but the tribes of motorcycles hadn't yet braved the cold. By the time Memorial Day weekend arrived, they'd roar through town, looking for motels or campgrounds to continue partying. A German shepherd yawned from the back of a pickup as he watched her pass—no one else seemed to notice or care.

Making several trips between her New Haven apartment and the car, she'd packed the trunk with a box of books, her suitcase, and her laptop. At the last minute, she'd remembered how much her aunt loved tea; on her way out of town she bought some Earl Grey and English Breakfast tea from a specialty shop on Chapel Street. She didn't have much money to spend, but they wrapped it up in a fancy bag with lavender ribbon.

Nori turned left at the intersection of the two main roads and passed the small library where she'd read her way through the children's and young adult collection on her summer visits, before summer jobs and school kept her away. She remembered the dirty-sock smell of the carpet when campers, desperate for entertainment on rainy summer days, crowded into the small building. The old air conditioner rattled and choked under the strain. Smells of unwashed bodies mingled in the small reading room decorated with bear carvings and fake totem poles. It was just a short bike ride from her aunt's house to the library, making it possible for her to regularly replenish her stack of novels or videos. Louise often commented on Nori's devotion to novel reading in a way that suggested she didn't quite approve—she'd asked Nori about school reading lists. Nori always shook her head no, and contin-ued reading through the Babysitter's Club and Nancy Drew and every series the small library possessed. Now that she thought about it, she'd rarely seen

Louise read novels; she preferred medical journals and books about public health.

As Nori turned onto the gravel road that led to her aunt's house, she felt a jolt of nervousness. It had been quite a while since they'd spent any extended time together. And this time, she had to come clean with Louise about her situation.

Nori hoped the visit would feel like old times and they'd have the chance to do some of their favorite things together. She hadn't been very attentive to her aunt lately, caught up as she'd been in her studies, her part-time job, and her friends.

Two green Adirondack chairs stood side by side on the thin strip of sandy beach. At the far end of the beach, a willow tree spread its roots into the water. That tree had always been her secret spot for reading and playing. Louise would ring a bell when she wanted her to come in for meals. On the right side of the beach, a birch tree leaned with one branch arced towards the water, while the other branch veered towards the land in a carefully balanced arabesque. The thick lawn hadn't been cut since the winter, and light blue flowers were sprinkled like tiny stars throughout the tall grass and weeds. In the center of the beach, the fire pit had fallen apart, and the stones were scattered over the grass.

She smoothed out the knees of her jeans and then rearranged her ponytail into a bun, using her hands to calm down the curls and waves that had a mind of their own no matter how much product she used. Stretching, she took a deep breath of fresh air. It was so quiet—the only sound was the sighing of the wind in the hemlocks. Occasionally, she heard a lumber truck in the distance, shifting gears heavily as it traveled with its load down the main road towards the city.

She swallowed nervously and hesitated; so much had happened, and she wondered how the recent loss of her father, Robert, had affected Louise. It wasn't like they'd been close—they only appeared to tolerate each other for Mary's sake. As far as Nori could remember, Louise had never backed away from an opportunity to argue with her brother-in-law about science, theology, or politics. While Nori had enjoyed watching someone unafraid to question his opinions, she realized that Louise had never openly criticized him in her presence. The adults had presented a solid front to her, and Louise always made sure that Nori knew that Louise honored their parental authority.

She wondered if other families upheld unspoken rules for conversation—she'd often thought it would be lovely to belong to a big Italian family that lived and cooked and argued in exuberant ways, while endless amounts of pasta and homemade sauce appeared by magic on the table. In her family, silences seemed to groan like an old farm table under the weight of things that could not be spoken out loud. Never considered quite old enough to be invited into the full understanding that adults kept for themselves, Nori had chosen to escape into her world of friends and distractions.

For a long time she'd wanted something different that was hard to name. It involved a recognition that she was finally mature enough to be an informed participant in grown-up life. Now, Louise was the only one left to grant her that.

Grabbing her purse, she walked towards the beach, needing a moment to compose herself before she entered. This place held so many memories—the air was as thick with them as it soon would be with blackflies. She wanted to make a cheerful and poised appearance, no matter how messy reality might be. Louise would uncover that reality soon enough—she had a way of seeing through any smokescreen Nori might attempt to create.

Nori pulled her hoodie closer as she shivered in the brisk breeze that crept off the water and moved close to the ground.

Walking towards the house, she noticed that the white paint had peeled off the north side and one of the shutters hung precariously from a remaining nail. Last fall's leaves were still clumped in wet piles where the wind had frolicked with them and then dumped them in damp rotting heaps around the yard. It was disconcerting to find the place in such disrepair; Louise usually hired some fellows from town to do the seasonal clean up.

Nori glanced back at the lake one more time. Flat-bottomed clouds with ominous dark edges were now gathering, throwing deep shadows on the water. A gust of wind created hundreds of ridges and ripples.

She felt dizzy in the face of the shifting light and wind swirling around her. As she turned to the door, wind caught the dangling shutter and swung it wildly against the house before slamming it to the ground. Nori looked at it in dismay before she stepped inside and pulled the door firmly closed.

Chapter 2

NORI leaned her forehead against the door while she tried to catch her breath. When she'd recovered from the smashing shutter, she looked around the porch. A musty cottage smell caused her to sneeze several times. The wicker furniture was covered with dust and stacked in precarious heaps. An aluminum watering can had rolled under the table. Against the far wall, hedge clippers and a rake looked like they'd been tossed. All evidence pointed to a poorly organized preparation for winter.

As she entered the kitchen, Nori gagged at the odor of garbage. Against the left wall, the sink was filled with unwashed dishes. Peering into the fridge, she noticed an unfamiliar assortment of plastic containers stacked haphazardly on the shelves. She shut the door quickly against the stench.

What was going on? Louise usually kept the kitchen immaculate. She walked over to the red Arborite table set under a window with a view of the lake. The table was covered with mail, flyers, and newspapers. In the corner between the fridge and the window, a small corner cabinet was filled with cookbooks—she saw familiar covers: *The Joy of Cooking*, *The Vegetarian Epicure* and *The Silver Palate Cookbook*. Her mother had been the one who loved cooking rich food and butter-laden sauces—Louise tended to focus on healthy and simple dishes. They'd had fun growing sprouts in Mason jars and planting herbs outside the porch door. One summer, Nori had made edible paper using the lavender and nasturtiums from the garden and soaking everything in the kitchen sink.

As Nori tiptoed into the dining room, she wondered if Louise was having a nap. The drapes were drawn, hiding the lake. The room was close with stale air, and the dining table was covered with piles of books, journals, and magazines. She lifted one up and sneezed again at the dust that rose from the cover. This was the treasure trove she was supposed to sort? Maybe she could start a fire and get rid of it quickly.

The living room was furnished with the same maroon couch and armchair that had been there for decades. There was something reassuring about the familiarity of the furniture. The maple coffee table showed the marks left by a few mugs and a candle that had scorched the surface one evening when they weren't paying attention; the fireplace looked like it hadn't been used for a while. Nori glanced at the pile of board games, lining the shelves to the right of the fireplace. In the past, they'd shared some intensely competitive game nights there.

The stormy painting still hung over the fireplace; it was Louise's favorite, even though Nori had never cared for the brooding presence of the clouds. In the painting, the lake was surrounded by mountains that were partially obscured by the falling rain, with the exception of one ray of light that broke through the darkness in the right corner of the painting. Louise had been convinced that the light would triumph over darkness. Nori didn't agree, but the painting really wasn't her taste anyway. It was clear it was going to pour on that mountain, and one ray of light wouldn't change a thing.

She continued down the hall to her aunt's bedroom with a growing sense of dread. Nori peered inside the open door. Louise appeared to be sleeping under a puffy duvet. Her silver hair was splayed over the pillow. She looked tiny in the oak double bed with its carved headboard that she'd purchased from the same elderly patient who'd sold her the house. Nori was startled by how frail she seemed—she hesitated to walk any further into that room. She wondered if Louise was even breathing until she heard a raspy exhalation.

Although the shades were pulled down, sunlight still filtered around the edges. The warm room smelled of furniture wax mixed with something medicinal that she associated with recently washed hospital hallways. A portable oxygen tank stood beside the bed with a green facemask draped on the top. Nori wondered whether to wake Louise or to let her sleep. This was not how she had pictured her reunion with her aunt.

When the floor creaked under Nori's feet, Louise stirred and opened her eyes. "Oh, there you are, dear. Did you just arrive?" She struggled to pull herself to a seated position as the pillows tumbled around her.

"Sorry to wake you," Nori said in a subdued voice, still confused by the fact that the room had been transformed into a hospital room. She walked to the bed and gave Louise a kiss on her cheek, helping with her pillows till she was seated upright and properly supported.

Louise smoothed her fine silver hair with her hands. "I must look a fright. I was just having a nap. Sorry you had to find me in this state."

Although her voice was weak, she enunciated every word clearly as she fixed her blue eyes on Nori.

Nori remembered that direct gaze from when she was a child; it usually left her feeling quite exposed, especially when she tried to get away with some small deception. It was no different now. She felt Louise's sharp eyes assess her physical and mental state. It was intimidating under any circumstances, but now she struggled to look calm, despite the sad state of affairs at the house and the odd circumstance of finding Louise in bed in the middle of the day. This was clearly not the time to confess her recent failures. Not that she was in any hurry to do so. Louise set a high bar for accomplishment—one that Nori had never quite reached.

Nori pulled up a chair and glanced around: a bedside table held a stack of books, a Bible, and a glass of water. She wondered what well-intentioned visitor had dropped a Bible there. Louise might have been too polite to tell her to take it back. A few pill bottles were arranged on a small tray. Beside the table, her walker stood within reach of the bed.

Nori frowned, pointed to the table, and looked at Louise. She wasn't quite sure how to frame the question.

"I've been a bit under the weather. But I feel positively cheered having you here," Louise replied as she paused to try to stifle a cough.

Something about her upbeat presentation felt forced. "Do you want me to make some tea?" Nori asked. "I brought this from New Haven." Nori handed Louise the small bag.

"How lovely. Thank you so much. If you could give me a hand, we could sit in the living room and have some of this tea. I want to hear all about you. It's been too long."

Nori helped Louise swivel to a seated position on the side of the bed. She watched her reach for her walker and realized that Louise intended to do this without assistance. Louise handed Nori the gift bag and stood up, carefully balancing herself before taking a step. She wore a silk bed jacket and loose trousers in navy and gold—she must have chosen her outfit with care, but that didn't change the fact that the clothes hung loosely from her gaunt frame. Nori walked behind her, trying not to hover or hold her breath whenever Louise seemed unsteady. Finding her this way made Nori anxious—absolutely nothing was as she'd expected it to be.

In the living room, Nori helped settle Louise on the couch before going into the kitchen to make tea. While the Earl Grey tea leaves steeped in the brown ceramic pot, she drained the sink of putrid dishwater and replenished it with detergent and hot water. She filled the sink with mugs and spoons. She stared out the window and wished she could take the kayak for a long paddle.

Nori peeked around the corner where Louise sat quietly with her eyes shut. What would be expected of her now? This was not an area in which she had any expertise—Louise knew that she was useless around illness. When Nori's father had suggested that nursing might be a good career for someone like her, Louise had quietly informed him that it wasn't a good idea.

Nori was startled by a knock on the door—her nerves were already on edge, but the thought of company made her anxious. A man of about thirty, in jeans and a flannel shirt, stood patiently on the step with his back to the door. When he turned, Nori's first impression was that he spent a lot of time outdoors as evidenced by his tan and physique. She glanced over his shoulder at the red pickup truck parked beside her sedan.

"Can I help you?" she asked, trying not to notice his brown eyes and friendly smile. She was in no mood for the cheerfulness of strangers—the situation felt unstable and she wanted to sort it out without unplanned interruptions.

"I'm Ben. I'm here to do some work."

Nori looked at him with skepticism. "Work?"

"I just need the key to the shed to get the rakes and clippers." He pointed to the small board on the kitchen wall next to the door. She felt embarrassed by the state of the kitchen and found herself wanting to apologize, all of which made her more annoyed.

"The yard sure looks run down," she said with challenge in her voice. His confidence irked her. He seemed too comfortable in her aunt's house. Like the walker in her bedroom, his presence was yet another unknown variable. Nori felt protective of Louise. People liked to take advantage of the frail elderly; she heard stories about that all the time.

He nodded agreeably without responding to the implied critique. "Time for some spring clean up," he replied. "Have a good day," he said, as he turned to leave. Before he reached the door, a loud crash and a yelp resounded from the living room.

Nori ran into the room with Ben close behind her. They both paused in shock at the sight of Louise on the floor. A lamp had fallen and knocked over some books in the process. Louise was wedged between the couch and the coffee table and couldn't quite get to her feet. She looked at them with an embarrassed smile and held her arms out for assistance.

Ben immediately rushed forward to help.

"I'm so sorry. I got up too fast and became dizzy. I wanted to get that book over there and forgot to use my walker. I didn't fall; I just let myself sink to the floor."

Ben reached over, picked her up effortlessly, and in one fluid motion set her down on the couch. He arranged the pillow beside her. Nori stood frozen in place, then picked up the books and the lamp. She glanced anxiously at Louise.

"Are you sure you don't need a doctor?" Ben asked.

Louise waved at him in dismissal. "Don't call him or I'll have to hear another lecture. I'm fine. Nori is making some tea—if you'd care to join us? You've met my niece?"

Ben looked over at her with a smile. "Indeed. That's very kind, but I need to do some work outside. Winter has scattered branches everywhere, and I'll have to pick them up before the lawn can be cut."

Louise gave him an affectionate handshake. Ben smiled again, nodded to Nori and left.

She watched him go and then turned to Louise with curiosity. "Who's he?"

"Oh, that's Ben. Now tell me about your trip."

"Just let me get the tea."

Nori placed the tray on the table. "Everything went well. It was a smooth ride." Louise didn't need to know how smooth the ride had been. The ticket was hidden in her purse.

Nori remembered her personal resolution to be honest with her aunt. She picked up the mug, but then put it down and moved to sit beside Louise on the couch, taking her aunt's hand in hers. "Auntie, what's wrong?"

Louise took a breath. "I have lung cancer. There's nothing they can do. It is inoperable and has likely spread."

"But . . . you never smoked."

Louise shrugged. "I didn't, but my father certainly did. And some of us were involved in asbestos research long before we knew how dangerous it was." She took a slow ragged breath.

The two women sat in silence holding hands on the couch. Nori blinked away her tears. While the electric clock in the kitchen ticked loudly, the mugs of tea stood untouched on the tray, a simple wisp of steam rising and then dispersing. The scents of bergamot and vanilla mixed with a hint of old ashes from a long ago fire in the fireplace. Nori heard the roar of a chain saw from the side yard.

Nori cradled the mug in her hands. She wished Louise had given her some warning. Maybe Louise had been afraid that Nori wouldn't show up if she knew the truth. She felt so far out of her depth. What if Ben hadn't been here to help Louise when she fell? Who would she call if she needed emergency help? She wanted to run from this, but then felt shame at being so cowardly.

Louise's eyes were closed. Nori tapped her wrist lightly. "Let's get you to bed. That's enough excitement for one day, don't you think?"

They made slow progress to the bedroom, one foot ahead of the other.

Chapter 3

NORI lugged her heavy suitcase up the staircase, pulling on the pine bannister. She'd always loved the bannister and the way it curved gracefully. The second floor was normally closed off unless there were guests; Louise had everything she needed on the ground floor. Nori's laptop bag, draped across her chest, banged into the wall and almost knocked down one of Louise's prints.

She paused at the top of the stairs to peek into her childhood summer vacation room. The bed was still covered with the same quilt and a small bookshelf that contained her favorite childhood books. Louise hadn't changed a thing—Nori felt relieved. It was so much smaller than she remembered; she'd never fit the small bed now. She walked over to the bookshelf and touched the spines of the books she'd loved as a young girl—detectives and adventure stories that she'd lost herself in reading. Glancing back at her suitcase on the landing, the bag looked like it was poised to roll back down the stairs and escape back into the car.

She placed it carefully on a small table in the larger bedroom and let the laptop bag slide from her shoulder onto the bed. A pile of linens had been placed on an old wicker chair. Nori ran her finger over the top of the pine dresser and sneezed twice. She pulled up the blinds that covered the two large windows that offered a view of the lake and opened one of the windows. The whine of a saw echoed up from the yard. Ben was working on the side of the house out of view, and she was glad she couldn't see him. It wasn't just him—it was the whole situation that was making her feel anxious and out of control. She depended on Louise and needed her strong presence right now. Although it wasn't her fault she was ill, the timing was terrible. And Nori hardly dared ask what would be expected of her. Historical research about medicine was fascinating, as long as no one asked her to do hands-on care.

Nori retrieved the vacuum and a dusting cloth from the hall closet. She vacuumed the pine floor and wiped every surface. The smell of furniture polish and window cleaner reminded her of the manse. She made the bed and finished it with a white coverlet. Dumping the contents of her suitcase on the bed, she put her clothes in the dresser and the closet and shoved the empty suitcase under the four-poster bed.

After she placed her laptop on the small desk and arranged her books on top of the dresser, the room felt more welcoming. She ran her hand over the tops of the books she'd purchased last semester. Titles like *History of an Asylum* and *Plagues and Peoples* were reminders of the graduate seminars she'd taken. And her hopes to write on an asylum she'd visited in Connecticut. Until a professor from Pennsylvania had produced an award winning book on the very same topic. She remembered when her friend Jenna had arrived at her apartment that spring day a few weeks ago.

The pounding on the door woke her up and echoed the pounding in her head.

Jenna had marched into the kitchen and pulled the empty bottle of wine out of the sink. "Is this your excuse?" she'd said.

"What do you mean?" Nori replied.

"For not showing up for the seminar presentation. We were counting on you and you let us down. Without even contacting us. You are really pathetic."

Nori groaned. "Oh no. Was that yesterday? I lost track of the day. I'd gone over to Kevin's and found him with that waitress. I was so upset, I came home."

"Oh great. You came home and drowned your sorrows in cheap wine. And left your friends hanging."

"But Kevin. . . ."

Jenna held up her hand. "I don't want to hear about it. Do you ever think that maybe you're responsible for driving him away?"

Nori looked at her in surprise. "Me? How is that my fault?"

"Maybe he got sick of hearing you whine about how someone stole your topic, and how you have it so tough, and how your father just died and left you an orphan."

"That's not fair. All those things happened."

"Yeah, well, we all have challenges. But I bet you don't know about them because you never bothered to ask. Grow up. Get some help. And I don't mean this." She held up the bottle and set it down so hard on the counter, Nori thought it might break.

Jenna walked towards the door and Nori followed her. "Listen, don't call me until you sort yourself out."

Nori watched her unlock her bike and leave without a wave or backward look. She ran her hand through her hair and groaned. Things were even worse than she'd thought. And now the whole seminar group and likely the prof were mad at her too. How was she supposed to fix this?

Nori was startled to realize that she'd forgotten to check on her aunt. She really wasn't used to having responsibility for others, she realized with embarrassment, and she still wasn't sure how much supervision Louise would need. She tossed her laptop bag into the closet and raced down the stairs.

Louise was still sleeping. Nori placed the photograph that Louise had requested from her parent's house on the bedside table. The picture of Louise and her sister, Mary, showed them seated on side-by-side Adirondack chairs smiling at the camera while a young Nori perched between them on the arms of the chairs.

Back in the kitchen, Nori sorted out the mail and took the flyers and junk mail to the recycling bin on the porch. She made a neat stack of the bills and letters and put a rubber band around them. Maybe she could help by taking care of those types of tasks.

Her mother's terminal illness had been of short duration—Mary had been diagnosed with cervical cancer and died a few months later. In that situation, little had been expected of Nori. The church ladies brought more food than they could eat and the team of nurses took care of the rest. Her father's subsequent death had been sudden. At that time, her only responsibility had been to attend the funeral that another minister had organized and then clean out his small apartment. He'd already given away a lot of things when he moved out of the manse. She donated the remainder to a local thrift store much to the surprise of the church ladies. They were so accustomed to suburban life that they couldn't picture living in a tiny apartment with few closets and little storage.

She'd been home from school the summer after her mother's death—the house had felt so empty without her mother. Her father had shut himself in his study and appeared to have lost all sense of direction. He didn't care what time she came home or where she had been. Although she would have given anything for that kind of freedom in high school, his lack of concern made her feel abandoned. She wanted her father to reach out to her despite his grief. Even though she had tried to visit him on special holidays, he wore his sadness like a sweater that he refused to discard no matter how worn it looked. Caring for his wife had given him purpose and direction—this sad man was someone she hardly recognized.

The pipes clanked and complained as the shower water ran. Nori was pleased that her aunt could manage on her own. It would be embarrassing to have to wash her—she'd never given anybody a bed bath. Although the health care aide was due back from a family holiday, Louise had expressed interest in having a shower, so Nori followed her direction.

She leaned against the wall and looked around her aunt's bedroom. The spacious room had pine floors and several windows that looked towards the lake, providing a view of the mountain on the opposite shore.

"Ready," Louise called.

"What's going to happen?" Nori asked at the bathroom door, her voice almost inaudible. She opened the door tentatively and was met by a cloud of steam and the scent of lavender soap.

Louise rubbed her wet hair with a small towel and sighed. She sat on a small plastic bench, dressed in her bed jacket and pajama pants. "I suspect I have a few months."

The rain pelted against the dining room windows, and Nori wondered if spring would ever arrive. Ragged edges of winter continued to bring sharp cold air to the lake. Wearing a wool sweater and sweatpants, she still felt the chill of that damp lake air. Because Louise had been sleeping much of the afternoon, exhausted by the effort of a shower, Nori decided to have a look at the papers that she'd been asked to sort. After all, there wasn't much to do in town—no movie theaters, no friends calling for an impromptu burger or beer. In fact, she felt a wave of homesickness for the cafés and bars that were part of her life at Yale. She often took her books to her favorite café and worked at a corner table, while the tolerant wait staff occasionally refilled her coffee cup. It had been unseasonably warm in New Haven in the week since she left. Her fellow students had probably jumped at the chance to drink beer on a patio. She felt badly about her seminar group and had left town before apologizing. It was inexcusable that she'd missed their final presentation—the grade was assigned to the group and she hoped her absence hadn't affected that grade too badly. They'd probably never talk to her again. Why should they? Maybe they'd heard about her academic probation. Gossip traveled fast among students—they probably felt she got what she deserved.

She sat at the table with her coffee mug and ran her hand over the seat of the chair next to her. Each chair was decorated with a different needle-point pattern—her father had given them to Louise after his wife died with the excuse that he didn't have room for the whole set. Nori thought that it was more likely that he couldn't deal with memories of the many dinners they'd shared sitting on those chairs. Her mother had loved putting on dinner parties with fresh linens and elegant china. She usually crashed afterwards from the effort, but she always loved planning the next one. Although the matching hutch was filled with Mary's dishes, Nori wondered if Louise ever used them—her style tended towards durable white plates that were easy to replace or pottery bowls that she'd found at a local craft fair.

Nori looked around the dining room and wondered what things Louise really valued besides the painting; she wasn't someone who filled her house with all kinds of decorative objects. She didn't even have any photographs around the house except for the one Nori had placed on her bedside table. But she certainly had collected medical books and papers. Nori sighed as she ran her fingers over the cover of a ten-year-old medical journal.

Nori created a discard pile of books—when the tower grew too tall, she moved it to the floor. She'd have to get some boxes. On the floor beside the first stack, she created a second pile of equally dated medical journals, with titles like *Annals of Thoracic Surgery* and *American Journal of Public Health*. Maybe the task wouldn't take very long—none were worth saving. They gave witness to Louise's long career as a thoracic surgeon and public health administrator—but she didn't need that type of testimonial. Especially now.

Nori was disappointed that the entire pile contained so little of interest; she'd hoped for something to distract her from the sad reality of the situation. It was very hard to accept that Louise was terminally ill—it still felt like a bad dream. Somehow she had to find an occasion to talk with her about some of her own dilemmas, but they seemed insignificant in the light of Louise's own life-and-death situation. She'd been too busy getting settled to think about her schoolwork; she welcomed the excuse that caring for Louise gave her to procrastinate on the academic requirements. Yale felt so far away; there were still weeks to deal with that.

She wondered if she could find a new topic and be enthused about it. When she'd visited the abandoned grounds of the psychiatric institution in western Connecticut with her Yale class, the place had totally captured her imagination. It was hard to describe, but she'd been so sure that this was her story to tell. The scale was stunning—seven hundred acres of parkland with buildings placed around the property. Underground tunnels had allowed staff to travel between buildings. Although the concept of the asylum as a self-sustaining city gave patients opportunities to work on the farm or in the greenhouses, the design also enabled countless medical experiments to happen without any oversight or accountability. Their professor explained that shock therapy, experimental drugs, and lobotomies were regularly performed on patients. The beautiful grounds and well-crafted buildings disguised the atrocities committed there.

Nori had planned to explore the idealistic beliefs of the architects and designers that presumed that the Victorian architecture of the asylum would heal the mentally ill. The staggered wings of the buildings allowed patients access to sun and fresh air—something considered important to their eventual healing. The unintended consequences of that design, however, facilitated something more destructive than a lack of fresh air or light. The tension between exterior appearance and lived reality fascinated her—how did anyone know what really went on in the past? The pile of obsolete texts and journals that she was sorting through did not provide any interesting insights into medical history. She threw the last one on the floor and went to look for an empty box.

"I'm finished with the journals and books on the table. I'd recommend sending them all to recycling. I'm sorry there wasn't more worth keeping, but these materials don't have lasting value for libraries or archives."

"Thank you so much, dear. I think Belinda will be happy to have that table cleared up. She's been complaining for weeks about the dust pile."

"I'll see if the library wants them for their next sale, but if not, I'll make sure they go to a recycling depot. How are you feeling?"

"I'm happy for your company."

"Do you want anything to read? I could look in the library for some novels."

"I'm not able to read much these days. But I do have this wonderful view that makes up for a lot." Louise pointed to the lake and to the mountain beyond the lake. "I never get tired of this. Last night I dreamed I was back in my bed on the farm and I even heard a rooster. That creature woke me up, just like it used to do."

Nori looked at her with interest. "I don't know anything about your childhood on the farm. Did you and my mother share a room?"

"We certainly did. And not always peacefully."

"Tell me more," Nori said with a smile.

"Once, when I was about twelve, I decided to stay in bed. I was tired of doing inside work with my mother and outside work with my father.

There was never an end to it. I was jealous. Because she was considered too delicate for the farm work, Mary was often spared the hard tasks. I think Ma liked doing needlepoint and sewing projects with her, whereas I was more of a tomboy. Mary always got compliments for her looks—she took after Ma with a heart-shaped face, perfect skin, and lovely cheekbones. I was plain, with a long face like my father and my hair cut short in a pixie cut."

Nori nodded. She tried to picture the two sisters as children on a farm.

"One day, I refused to get up and do my chores. I was just tired of working. But I forgot that Pa had promised to take me to see a new colt at a neighbor's farm. Although I had planned to stay in bed all day pretending to be sick, when Pa called up the stairs, I got dressed in seconds. I rushed past Ma in the kitchen to avoid any tasks she might think of to keep me from going. I remember how the vinyl seats burned the backs of my thighs, but I didn't care because I was so happy to escape."

Nori looked at her, eager for more details.

"When Pa looked at me, he smiled and asked me if I was on strike.

"I grinned and let my arm dangle out the window, hoping that the breeze would cool it off. I remember the way the tiger lilies along the side of the gravel road would reach their long thin stems up towards the sun. Sometimes I felt like I was reaching along with them, growing up and longing to see other worlds than the small farm with endless work and little play. That day, I wished Pa would just keep driving."

"My happiness was complete as I slipped my feet out of my sandals and put them up on the dash. Like him, I rested my arm on the window and felt the sun warm the skin."

Louise gazed out the window at the lake, lost in memories.

"I can imagine how good it felt to escape for a while. What kinds of work were you expected to do?" Nori asked.

"My mother wanted us to learn to be ladies, so it was important to her that we mastered all the highlights of domestic life. I know that sounds crazy today, but this was in the nineteen-thirties. Mary enjoyed those activities, and she got lots of praise. Sometimes Mother invited a group of church ladies for a luncheon. I don't know if she enjoyed doing it, but she felt it was her duty to put on a fancy lunch. I hated those days. We had to clean and polish and iron and then help in the kitchen. Nothing was ever good enough for my mother."

Louise looked at her hands. "I used to dream of having my own life and meeting friends in a café, where a waiter brought us food and later took away the plates. Instead, I had to peel potatoes and wash floors and scrub the bathroom. Ma also had a garden in the front near the kitchen window. I was expected to water and weed the garden, but Pa did the mowing. By midsummer, only the daisies survived the hot sun—the rest melted away or perished under the pelting rain or hail storms that visited regularly."

"What kind of farm was it?"

"My father had some cows, chickens, and some sheep. It was a hard life that didn't show much, if any, profit. Despite that, he loved it and worked hard to keep it going. I helped with the animals and milking and haying. As a townie, my mother had been raised for a different kind of life. Her father and grandfather were lawyers. The farm was not her dream, and my father never stopped apologizing for it."

"Where did you go to high school?"

"The bus picked us up every morning to bring us to a regional high school. Luckily, I was a year ahead of her so we were in different classes. Still, the teachers regularly reminded me how talented Mary was—she was the lead in school musicals and often sang at church. The only way to compete was to excel academically. Mary was easily satisfied with average grades—she had friends and social events and drama club to distract her. I was pretty much a loner in school, so I put all my energy into my studies. I loved science and math and my teachers encouraged me to think about college. I wanted to get a scholarship because I knew it was the only way I'd be able to attend."

"Did you get a scholarship?"

"I did. And I received some other help that was unexpected. I was so ready to escape that farm. In my senior year, we had just started the fall semester when Mary fell ill with polio. Because Ma couldn't handle any of it, I became the one to supervise her medicine and exercises."

"Your mother must have been terrified."

"Many children with polio were sent to children's hospitals far away from home. Some of those children were in iron lungs and hospitalized for years. Luckily, Mary had a mild case. We wanted to take care of her at home and make sure she would walk again. And I am happy to say that we succeeded. I made her exercise every day to preserve her muscle tone and forced her out of bed to walk. With some tutoring, Mary was able to pick up her school work and graduate a year after me."

"Where did the money come from for college?"

"It was quite a surprise. Ma had kept it secret according to her parent's wishes, but my grandparents had set aside money in a college fund for both of us. They didn't want us to know until we were almost finished with high school because they were worried that we wouldn't work as hard if we knew the money was waiting for us."

"That must have been a great day."

"I was speechless. My teacher told me about the science program at Smith College and that was my first choice. When Mary graduated, she joined me there and we shared a dorm room. It felt like such a luxury to be freed from chores and housework and the endless demands at home. I could read and do my labs and write my reports without interruption. Mary had a great time as well and continued her musical interests along with a degree in education."

"And then . . . you went to medical school?"

"My parents were skeptical about that, but I told them about the women who had studied medicine in order to serve the mission field."

"You thought about being a missionary doctor?" Nori looked at her with surprise.

Louise smiled with a hint of her old mischief. "Not really, but it made the idea more acceptable to them."

"What did my mother do then?"

"She finished her BA and joined me at Yale. She wanted to study education at the divinity school in order to be able to work in a church as a religious educator. We lived in the student apartments for a year and then got our own place near the university." Louise's long fingers smoothed the top sheet of the bed.

"It must have been so exciting to have your own apartment."

"Mary knew how to make a place cozy. She sewed up pillows and drapes from fabrics she found in bargain basements. She loved to cook and bake and entertain, so on the weekends we usually hosted divinity school students who were always hungry. And they argued endlessly about theology—something that didn't interest me in the least. Luckily, they also liked to play chess and board games and we were all pretty competitive."

"Is that how she met my father?"

Louise nodded. "I wasn't sure he was going to last any longer than any of her other suitors, but he surprised me. One evening, she cooked a special dinner and cleaned up the apartment. I didn't realize that they'd become engaged and were planning to announce that to me that night."

"That must have been a surprise."

Louise nodded. "It was a shock. I was so busy with school that I depended on Mary to keep our lives together. I took a lot for granted. When she got engaged, I realized that it was time to figure out where my life was going. I couldn't depend on her to be my roommate forever. She'd found someone that she loved and she was willing to be a minister's wife—I had to be happy for her. I pretended to be thrilled, but there was some heartbreak involved. We'd shared a room for so many years; she'd become my rock."

"It sounds like you had worked out some of the competition from childhood and figured out how to live together."

"I confess that it took me a long time. She always knew what to say and how to be gracious. She surrounded herself with friends and knew how to entertain in a way that made everyone comfortable. I felt awkward next to her, and I knew I lacked both social grace and looks. And Ma always favored her. It was hard to always be on the outside of their togetherness. I think I earned some of my mother's respect when I worked with her during that polio episode."

"I always thought that having a sister would be so much fun, but I guess I never considered how you might constantly compare yourself to someone else or fight over what the other one had."

"Sisters are complicated. They can look like they are fighting to the death, but if someone else attacks either one of them, it's a united front all the way."

"Was my mother competitive?"

"That was the annoying thing—she was generous and didn't seem jealous of anything I did." Louise paused. "Not until later anyway."

"What did you think of my father when you first met him?"

"Robert was a serious Presbyterian clergyman in training. I had pictured Mary with a different type of person, but she was so smitten with him, I kept quiet. Over time, Robert proved that he was a man of integrity. He was solid and reliable and loved your mother. I learned that he was a rock in times of trouble. We gave each other lots of room to disagree on matters of science and religion, but he was always there when I needed help and he certainly stood by Mary."

"I love hearing your stories, but I hope it's not too tiring." Nori helped Louise take a sip of water.

"I'll rest for a while, but it's wonderful to share stories with you. There's one thing I really wanted to talk to you about. I don't want my illness to interrupt your studies. It may not be an ideal setting, but I hope you can use the time when the aides are here to do your own work. Nothing could make me happier. Use my study if you need more space. If you need any introductions to people in the community, I'd be happy to make some calls for you. My friends in the historical society can be very helpful. Don't be fooled by the gray hair and gloves—they are graduates of some very fine colleges."

"I'm sure they are fascinating people." Nori felt guilty. Although she needed to talk to Louise, was this the right moment? After hearing about how her aunt had longed to go to college, how could Nori confess that she'd taken it all for granted? And once there, she'd screwed up so badly. She decided to wait to confess her failures. Maybe there would be a better time. After all, she didn't want to upset Louise.

"Sometimes I worry that you have too much faith in me and that I won't be able to live up to your expectations."

"It's my job to have faith in you. I can stop once you have faith in yourself."

"In that case, please stick around for a long time." Nori helped her arrange the pillows and pulled up the covers. She kissed her cheek. "Rest well. I'll make tea when you wake up. And I definitely want to hear more stories."

"I've got quite a collection," Louise said, "and there's nothing like having an audience to inspire the storyteller."

Later that afternoon, Nori helped her aunt into the chair. "I was thinking about your stories," Nori said, "and I realized something. I'm really sorry that I didn't know my grandparents."

Louise nodded. "That is unfortunate. My father would have showed you how to do things and taken you to the barn. He was a quiet man, but he would have been proud of you. My mother was complicated, but I have a feeling she would have had a soft spot for you. You might have had to learn how to do needlepoint and quilting, but perhaps you would have enjoyed that."

Nori grinned as she tried to imagine herself in a farm kitchen putting up preserves and doing quilting. "You always had the feeling that she preferred Mary?"

"I did. But maybe I misunderstood her ways of showing affection. I was jealous of Mary, and that affected how I saw things. I realized much later that Ma could be honest and direct, and her wisdom was helpful throughout my life."

"Can you give me an example?"

Louise closed her eyes to remember and then began to speak.

ROLLING BROOK FARM, 1941

Ma and I had to bring food to an elderly farm worker on a farm down the road. While he'd been sick, various neighbors took turns to check on him and bring him dinner. Mary had recovered enough from her polio that she could read on the couch in the living room.

"We're going out for a little while. You stay right there till we get back," Ma said. She poured the soup into a glass jar and then washed her hands. "The soup for dinner is on simmer, and you don't need to do anything to it."

"Where are you going?" Mary asked.

"It's our turn to bring Mr. Nordhoff some food. He's been sick for two weeks."

"What am I supposed to do while you're gone?"

"You can do your homework. And if you finish that, you can study your catechism. Reverend Moore will be coming next week to examine you. You won't be allowed to do your public profession if you don't pass."

Mary sighed. "It's not fair."

"I don't think you're in any position to decide what's fair. You have responsibilities and I expect you to fulfill them."

I was a bit surprised that Ma was standing up to Mary. She'd been so spoiled while she was sick.

"But Louise doesn't have to study her catechism."

I rolled my eyes at her. Did she have to revert to being a ten-year-old just because she'd been sick? Mary rolled her eyes back at me, but I turned my back to her. I was not going to engage with her when she was acting like a spoiled brat.

"That's right. And that's because she already is a member."

Mary fell back onto the pillows and knew she was defeated.

I was happy that Ma didn't indulge her. It was time that Mary stepped back into life. I was tired of caring for her and everything else too. I picked up the basket with jars of stew and soup, while Ma took the apple crumble.

When I glanced back at Mary, her head leaned on the crest of the couch like a forlorn puppy. I didn't let her see my smile, but she was overdoing the pathetic act. I imagined the minute we left, she'd get up to look in the mirror and brush her hair one hundred strokes.

The screen door slammed behind us.

"Put the food on the floor in the back. There's a cardboard box on the floor. You can drive."

I smiled with surprised satisfaction. Although Pa had given me driving lessons on the back roads, Ma had never been willing to be a passenger. We travelled slowly down the gravel road and took the first concession north to a small shack. I drove with care, checking the mirrors and keeping well under the speed limit. I didn't even try to turn on the radio in case Ma would think I wasn't taking this seriously.

When we entered the one-room cabin, I held my breath at the smell of tobacco and urine. Mr. Nordhoff sat in a reading chair, next to the wood stove, smoking a pipe Despite the heat, he wore a woolen flannel shirt. A pail beside the stove was filled with expelled chewing tobacco. When he coughed, I could hear the congestion in his lungs. I longed for a stethoscope so I could try to listen to his breathing the way our family doctor did.

"How are you, Mr. Nordhoff? We've brought you some food."

"That's so nice of you. And who's this with you? Is it Mary?"

"No, I'm Louise," I said, while staying close to the door. Not only was the cabin disgusting, the old guy needed a bath. I wondered what he'd done with his teeth. They were probably in some bowl in the tiny kitchen at the back of the cabin. I handed Ma the food but stayed near the door, ready to escape.

"We have some chicken soup, stew, and some apple crumble. The stew is still warm, if you want some now. I could put it in a bowl for you."

"Sure. I'll take the stew now and save the soup for later."

My mother filled a mug with the stew and brought it to him with a spoon. "How are you feeling?"

"Not too bad. Got this cough. Haven't been sleeping much."

"Do you need to see the doctor? I can call and ask him to come out."

"Nah, I'll be all right. Just gotta get through this." He coughed again and spat into a crumpled handkerchief.

I wondered if he had something infectious. I hoped Ma wouldn't touch him.

"You eat your food. There's dessert on the counter when you want it. I'll come back tomorrow and pick up the dishes."

Mr. Nordhoff nodded as he hungrily spooned the stew to his mouth. I wondered how he was going to eat without his teeth, but he chewed and chewed and then swallowed. Because the sight of him eating made me queasy, I opened the door, waved goodbye, and sat in the car to wait for Ma.

She joined me a few minutes later.

"That place is disgusting. It reeks. Does he even have a toilet?"

"He's got an outhouse out back and he probably pees in a pail at night."

"Ugh. No wonder it smells in there." I started the car and accelerated a bit too hard as the tires slipped on the gravel.

Ma grabbed the dash. "If you don't learn to care for people and to see who they really are, you aren't going to be worth a dime as a doctor."

I was startled by her vehemence and glanced at her.

"You think he couldn't feel your disgust? People know those things. He was only sixteen when he left Europe and came to work as a farm hand. He had no formal education but he still learned to read and write. He loves birds and knows everything you might want to know about them. He's done wood carvings of local birds that people love to buy."

I tried to take in what Ma was saying, and I immediately felt guilty. "I just . . ."

"Never mind. Just remember what I said. Compassion is just as important as brains. Make sure you have both."

I kept both hands on the wheel like Pa had taught and looked straight ahead as the heat shimmered over the gravel road and disappeared into the dust kicked up by the car. My face burned with shame—Ma was right, and I was too embarrassed to admit that to her.

Chapter 4

LAKE HOUSE, 1980

THE next day, Louise sat in a chair next to the bed, while Nori smoothed out the wrinkles on the bottom sheet.

How could it be noon? It would be a big relief when the aide helped with some of the care. Louise had accidentally spilled water in the bed, so Nori had to start over with fresh linens.

She kept putting off telling Louise about her problems at school, but the secrecy was making her sick. She had to do it, no matter what Louise would say. Nori perched on the edge of the bed and explained the whole story.

Louise listened quietly until she was done. "Sometimes things don't work out," Louise said. "It can be a matter of timing. Research can hit a dead end. Being creative means taking risks and sometimes failing."

Nori nodded slowly. She was relieved that Louise had taken the news so well.

Louise continued. "You have to believe that you can do this—it really doesn't matter what others think. I know you'll find another topic. But remember it's important to listen to your advisor. She's seen a lot and knows how to move students through the system. Don't be too proud to take her advice."

Nori looked at Louise and felt such a lump in her throat that she had trouble speaking. She impatiently wiped away a tear. "I felt like such a failure, and I was too ashamed to tell you. I wasn't sure I deserved to be in that program."

Louise patted her hand. "Nonsense. One dead end doesn't equal failure. Research involves trial and error. Dealing with some adversity prepares you for the rest of your career and even for life."

"Thanks for being so understanding . . ." Nori stopped when she heard the porch door slam followed by footsteps in the kitchen. She looked at Louise with alarm. Who would enter the house without knocking?

"Sounds like Belinda." Louise said with a smile. "We'll talk more later."

Nori stood up and attempted to finish sliding the fresh pillowcase over the pillow. A heavy set woman in her late fifties sauntered into the room wearing blue scrubs with white running shoes. Her plastic ID from the home care agency was clipped to her chest pocket. Throughout her red hair, gray roots were visible and she sported elaborately penciled brows that made a high arch over her eyes. She ignored Nori and turned her smile on Louise. "Well, don't you look nice?"

"I'd like you to meet my niece, Nori."

Belinda shook Nori's hand and put her hands on her hips as she studied the corner of the bed and then looked back at Nori. "I know you. You used to play with my niece."

Nori squinted at her nametag. "Johnson?"

"Yeah, Jasmine Johnson. Every summer you guys got together."

"Jazz is your niece! I haven't seen her for years."

"Well, she's around. She runs the café in town, and I'm sure she'd love to see you."

She hadn't seen Jazz since her senior year of high school, and she wasn't so sure that Jazz wanted to see her. In the old days, they used to hang out every summer. Jazz had been crazy about that guy, Jake, and Nori had warned her he was no good. She realized that she'd probably been jealous. After all, they'd been friends for years when he showed up, and Jazz found better things to do. Nori had felt betrayed. But it wasn't just that. She also didn't trust him, but Jazz didn't want to hear about it. They'd had a fight and drifted apart. She probably should have kept her mouth shut—after all, people had warned her about Kevin too, but she'd been too stubborn to listen. And that hadn't turned out very well. Maybe she had really poor judgment when it came to men.

"You gotta learn how to do this right." Belinda meandered over and picked up the other case and the pillow. "You start with the case inside out and then you pull it over the pillow in one smooth motion. Now let's get that bottom sheet a bit tighter. We don't want wrinkles, because wrinkles lead to bedsores, and that's the last thing Louise needs." She looked at Louise. "And I bet you're tuckered out from sitting up and want to get back to bed?" Belinda went to one corner and waved at Nori to take the other and they lifted the mattress and pulled the puckered linen tightly around the corner until the bottom sheet was completely smooth. "That's more like it," she concluded. "She'll catch on," she said to Louise as she stood in front of her, helped her to her feet, and then deftly turned her so she landed on the bed.

Nori was annoyed. She felt like Belinda criticized her efforts, but forgot that she was not trained to work as a health care aide. The woman's familiarity with her aunt was irritating—she chatted nonstop like they were best friends. And she seemed to accomplish all the care so effortlessly.

"I'm going to do some errands now," Nori said, as she leaned forward to kiss Louise's cheek. She felt a need to get out of the house; the grocery store seemed like a reasonable destination. With everything in town still closed up, there wasn't much else except the library, so maybe she'd head there as well.

From the kitchen, she heard Belinda's loud laughter as she told Louise a story about her vacation. Nori put on her rain jacket, took her purse and keys, and grabbed the list on the fridge door. She left the house, letting the screen door slam behind her. She really needed a break from all this. It had been raining for a few days, and the damp cold was really depressing. She wanted to be there for Louise, but the whole thing was a bit overwhelming. Why couldn't Louise fight harder and not give in to the disease? She'd heard that people did visualization exercises and managed to shrink tumors or heal themselves. It was worrisome to see her aunt so accepting. Couldn't they do something? She could have years of life ahead of her.

Chapter 5

As Nori turned sharply into the parking lot of the library, she heard the groceries roll around in the trunk. Luckily, it was cold enough to leave them there for a while—one advantage of the cold spring weather. Behind the library, a one-storey brick building served as the community health center, and a few cars were parked outside the front door. A small hospital was located halfway between Newton's Corners and Hagerstown. Trauma victims or serious cases requiring complex surgery were generally referred to a larger medical center almost an hour away.

Entering the small library, Nori felt like she was back in kindergarten—the room was filled with rows of children's books, games and puzzles. A few people sat in the reading room with newspapers and magazines, and the two public computers were occupied. The librarian smiled at Nori and returned to her typing.

She wandered into the back room, past the shelved videos, CDs, and adult fiction. and CDs. Fortunately, no one was back there. A round maple table and matching chairs stood in the corner. Four quilted place mats with pictures of evergreens and bears decorated the table. Three walls were covered with modest bookshelves and one wall had windows looking over the backyard towards the health center. Someone had made a hand-painted sign over the shelving that said "Welcome to the Adirondack Collection."

She'd never been interested in local history when she'd visited in the past—she was more drawn to mystery novels and adventure stories and hanging out with her friend Jazz. Realizing she needed to broaden her interests, she decided to browse through the local history collection.

The shelves were filled with books on Adirondack cooking, handmade furniture, bird life, cabins and camps, and histories of the state park. She flipped through a memoir written by a woman who had been a wilderness guide, built her own cabin, and survived alone in the bush. How did people manage to do such heroic things?

She still had an hour before she needed to relieve the health care aide. She selected a few books and carried them to the table by the window.

Nori was surprised to realize that the Adirondack State Park was the size of Vermont and totaled six million acres. She remembered passing signs that indicated that she was entering the park, but she'd never thought about the fact that the town of Newton's Corners was actually within the park boundaries. Many of the towns were located near bodies of water, as people settled along early transportation routes. With names like Long Lake, Blue Mountain Lake, and Raquette Lake, Nori remembered hiking with Louise in some of those places.

She picked up a heavy book with a burgundy leather cover that provided a survey of institutions in the area—schools, churches, clubs, hospitals, and other organizations. She stopped flipping through the pages when she saw a picture of a sanatorium in the nearby town of Saranac. From humble beginnings, it had apparently grown into an almost completely self-sufficient health care institution and community. The fresh mountain air, superior research and treatment facilities, and excellent medical staff had apparently allowed the sanatorium to become world-renowned for tuberculosis care.

Elaborate stone gates marked the south entrance to the institution. From the original rustic log structures, newer buildings demonstrated increased sophistication of design and materials. The buildings represented diverse styles ranging from neoclassical, colonial revival, and Tudor styles.

According to the book, the sanatorium had covered more than sixty-three acres of land on the northeast corner of Saranac Lake; a total of thirty-six buildings populated the sanatorium village including a chapel, library, farm, doctors' cottages, nurses' residence, administrative building, and research labs.

How could she be completely unaware of the presence of an institution located so close to her aunt's house? Apparently the institution closed in the 1950s after drug therapy eliminated the need for residential tuberculosis care. Nori tried to remember what she'd learned about tuberculosis. The disease had always seemed like something out of a Dickens novel—she pictured Victorian consumptives who coughed discreetly into their handkerchiefs.

Nori checked her watch and realized it was time to go. Although Louise had promised she wouldn't try to get up without having someone nearby, she didn't like the idea of Louise being home alone. Nori stood up and straightened the place mats. She'd sign out some of the books that were allowed to circulate and read whenever Louise was asleep, but it was handy to know that there was also a quiet reading corner in the back of the library.

Nori carried the books to the front desk and handed Louise's library card to the librarian.

The woman looked at her and then studied the card. She shook her head. "You're not Louise."

"I'm her niece. I'm visiting for the summer."

"You better get your own card. Fill this out, please."

Nori provided the necessary information and waited impatiently while the woman typed up a card. She hoped Belinda wouldn't mind if she was a few minutes late. She shifted her weight from one foot to the other and read all the notices on the community bulletin board advertising local events such as the spring book sale and a flea market in the area.

Driving back to Louise's, she passed the café that Jazz owned. She'd have to make a point of dropping by soon. Would Jazz even talk to her? She hoped she could mend the rift. It was going to be pretty lonely up here without at least one person her age—they'd always had so much fun together. If only she hadn't ruined that friendship.

She resolved to talk to Jazz soon, no matter how uncomfortable that might be. With any luck her café would also sell decent coffee—the stuff at the gas station was toxic. She missed the iced coffee that her favorite café in New Haven served all summer. With Louise confined to home, and Nori's time cut into chunks of caregiving with short intervals of respite time, she was lucky to have a research project to distract her.

Despite the nostalgia she'd felt about coming up to the lake house, she realized she didn't have connections with the life of this community. When Louise was gone, she wondered if she'd have a reason to return. Jazz was lucky—she had friends and family in the area that kept her rooted.

Chapter 6

NORI set a tray for Louise on the bedside table and then helped her transfer to the chair next to the bed. She'd learned to do it more smoothly after watching Belinda. As annoying as she'd found her initially, she had to admit the woman knew what she was doing and took good care of Louise.

Belinda had borrowed an adjustable table from the home care office that made it easier for Louise to take her meals. Not that she had much appetite. Nori tried to offer her homemade soups and milkshakes, but she needed a great deal of encouragement to eat. When swallowing triggered her cough reflex, Nori rubbed her back and anxiously waited for her to catch her breath. It was hard to watch.

Nori carried a tray with a bowl of vegetable broth to the bedside table. "I would love to hear more of your stories, if you feel up to it."

Louise smiled. "I can't believe you find an old woman's reminiscences interesting."

"There are whole chapters of family history that I don't know about. But I don't want to tire you out. Just tell me if you're not up to it."

Louise took a drink of water and pushed away the bowl of broth. "I'm not too tired to talk, but I'm really not hungry. I'll try in a little while."

Nori sat in the chair beside the bed. "You graduated from Smith and then attended Yale Medical School, right?"

"That's correct."

"I remember hearing about the anniversary of women's admission to Yale College in 1968. When did the medical school admit women?"

"Around 1916, I think there were three women. In the nineteenth century, there were many women physicians, but once a degree was required, women were excluded. By the time I arrived, it was old news."

"Old news or not . . . I can't imagine that it was easy."

Louise shook her head. "The road was never easy for any of us. We had to work harder to prove ourselves and ignore the perpetual commentary on everything we did. The jokes, the pranks, and the constant scrutiny were tiring."

"But you loved it, right?"

Louise smiled. "I'd wanted to be a doctor since I was a girl."

"Were there ever times when you doubted yourself?"

Louise took a breath. "There were challenges. One night, I was sleeping in the room reserved for on-call doctors when one of the nurses asked me to check a post-op appendectomy patient. After I assessed the patient and wrote orders, I ran into the chief of surgery, who'd been doing an emergency surgery. He pulled me aside and asked if I was interested in being a surgical resident. I'd been hoping for that, but I still asked for some time to consider. There was something that didn't feel quite right about it. I think that annoyed him greatly."

"He wanted you to be grateful?" Nori asked.

Louise smiled. "A few days later, I went to his office to talk about another matter. I had noticed that many of the fellows were scheduled for far fewer night calls than I was, and I was upset. I wanted to register a complaint through official channels. Before I could say anything, he sat down on his couch and assumed I was there to sign up for the residency. He was planning to enjoy the moment of being a benefactor to this poor woman student." She took a sip of water.

"To his great surprise, I told him about how I thought the schedule was unfair. He thought that was ridiculous and told me that I should consider myself lucky to have the work. I was lectured on following the chain of command, and then he moved closer and tried to kiss me. I was horrified. I pushed him away, and he tried again, telling me that no one would disturb us because he had locked the door. When I protested, he became very angry. He returned to his desk, picked up his reading glasses, and started to read a journal without another word. I was shaking with anger, but I knew I had to be careful. I was so close to finishing, and I couldn't risk being expelled from the program."

She stopped for a few moments.

Nori perched on the edge of her bed and hoped she would finish.

"I walked up to his desk and told him that I had once respected him. He said nothing and ignored me. I'd been dismissed. There was nothing more I could do, so I left his office. I fell apart in the washroom down the hall."

"Ooh, that's terrible. What did you do then?"

"I didn't have much choice. No one would have listened to me if I'd dared complain about him. I'm fairly certain it happened regularly with him. After all, what hope did the nurses have of reporting him and keeping their jobs? In the remaining weeks, he made fun of me, refused to call on me, and told nasty jokes at my expense in the operating room. I kept my mouth shut, but I knew I'd have to find another location for a residency. It was one of those times when I doubted my vocation. I'm not sure things have changed that much for women, but I truly hope things are better."

Nori nodded. "I haven't experienced any of that, but some of my friends have. I think people are still afraid to report such harassment."

Louise sighed. "I was relieved to graduate and leave Yale. I wasn't sure how vindictive he might be, but I didn't want to give him a chance to ruin my career. When a recruiter visited the university representing a volunteer program organized by a coalition of northern churches, I attended the meeting. They needed volunteer doctors, nurses, and teachers to work with people in the rural south. They offered to cover my travel and provide me with room and board, so I decided to go. I took a long bus trip to a tiny place in Mississippi and started my doctoring, fresh out of school. I was terrified. Because I was the only doctor there, I didn't have time to think. I worked flat out for the whole summer and it was an incredible experience. It confirmed for me what I wanted to do. I realized then that there would always be obstacles, but it was important to keep my goal in clear sight."

"Where did you stay when you went to the south?" Nori asked.

"I was billeted with an older white couple on a farm. They were happy to receive a small allowance for my room and board and they minded their own business. I was so tired when I got home at night and it was so hot, I usually ate a light supper and went straight to bed. On the weekends, I tried to write letters home, but it was so hard to describe my life."

"What kinds of medical care did you provide?"

"I did prenatal care, delivered babies, immunizations, checked blood pressures, and prescribed diabetes medicine. Many people had never seen a doctor, and certainly not a woman doctor."

Nori nodded and tried to imagine what her aunt had experienced.

Louise continued.

One day, very early in the morning, I heard a rap on the window outside my bedroom.

Bessie, my nurse from the office, wanted me to come to the clinic because her brother had been injured. When we arrived, it was still dark and no one was around. An older black man was propped up against a tree with two friends standing guard. I checked him and decided we had to take him inside for treatment. The guards helped us put him on the stretcher in the examining room. He was Bessie's brother, Cal, who served as a minister in town. Some troublemakers had shot him during an evening service the night before. They'd been too afraid to transport him because the police were on the street till late, arresting anyone who moved. They kept him hidden in the church until Bessie came to find him.

I worked to clean his facial cuts and a gash on his neck.

"Why'd you come here?" he asked.

"You mean to the South?"

"Why doctor in a place like this? Don't you come from some fancy school?"

"I wanted to volunteer. Get some practice in the real world, not just my fancy school."

"You better be careful. Cops aren't happy you Northerners are coming down here telling them how to run this town. This real world can be too real for anyone."

"I try not to get into the politics," I said. "I'm here to practice medicine." I drew up some topical analgesic into the thin glass syringe, flicking my nail against the glass to dissolve a small bubble.

"It's all politics. When people can't be in church praying together, it's politics. When our people can't read and can't vote—that's politics. You can't get away from it. Maybe you people think you can divide up politics from life, but stay down here long enough and you'll see it different."

"No talking now, I need to work on this cut. You'll feel a sting when I put in some lidocaine, but then you shouldn't feel the rest."

"That's gonna be the hardest thing—to get him to stop talking," Bessie said. She took his hand and held it tightly.

I slowly injected the lidocaine into the skin around the cut on his forehead and sponged it with clean gauze. "Bessie, I'll need more light. Can you shine that flashlight on his forehead? And then you'll have to cut the sutures with your other hand."

"Can I help?" Cal asked. "Seems like you need some more hands."

"Just be still." I had to smile. "We women know how to make do." Using a fine surgical thread, I carefully sewed up the cut with twenty sutures.

Then I looked at my work. "You're good as new. If I had some ice, I'd put it on your eye, but as it is, you're going to have quite the shiner."

"That's all right. They'll know Bessie has been swinging her fists again. I think the ladies feel sorry for me."

I stepped back to evaluate him. "What else hurts?" I asked Cal.

"My ribs are sore. They kicked me when I was on the ground."

I examined his rib cage and listened to his lungs.

"They got no right coming in church and disrupting our services."

I didn't comment while I continued to assess him. "You really need to take a few days to rest, let those ribs heal, and stay off that leg."

"No time for vacation—no rest for the wicked," he said as he tried to sit up.

"I'll tape up those ribs and I've got some pills for you. I'll check on you tomorrow."

"Don't let the cops see you visiting. Church starts at ten so you can come before or wait till after. Now how much do I owe you?"

Bessie helped him put his shirt on and then washed his hands and face while I put the pills in an envelope and wrote the directions on the outside.

"I'll come before. And this is a free clinic. Sponsored by some of those Northern types." I smiled as I handed him the envelopes. He tucked them in his chest pocket.

"You a churchgoer?" he asked me as Bessie helped him into his sleeve.

"Used to be," I said. "When I had to."

"Maybe someday you'll want to. You're welcome to worship with us."

"Thank you. Bessie, can you get the men to come help?"

Bessie found them slumped in chairs in the waiting room. She touched the shoulder of the taller one and he immediately sat up. "Take him home now."

The tall one nodded and pushed the arm of the other man who stood up before he was even fully awake.

The sun now filled the sky with brilliant morning light that spilled around the edges of the clinic's blinds.

"Thanks for helping, Bessie. I'll come and see him tomorrow early."

"You want me to walk you home?"

"I'll be okay. You be careful. Let me know if you have any problem with him."

"I always got problems with him, but what's a brother for?"

I didn't know what having a brother was like, but I thought often of my sister, Mary, and missed her. I tried to write to her on the weekends, but it was hard to describe what life was like down there.

As I walked back to the farm, the fields were lit up with the golden light of August. The heat slithered over the road in silvery filaments that disappeared or moved on whenever I seemed to get close. Maybe my landlady wouldn't mind if I had a nap. I wasn't even hungry—I just wanted to sleep for a few days.

On Sunday morning, I walked to town. Dressed up in Sabbath still-ness, the town seemed to have no one about. I carefully made my way to the parsonage. I knocked on the back door of the parsonage and admired the garden until I heard Bessie's steps.

"Come on in. He's sitting in the parlor. Can I get you some lemonade?"

"Please." I followed her into a formal parlor furnished with a tapestry-covered love seat and a matching wing chair, one lone chair from a dining room set, and an antique standing grandfather clock. A bookshelf against the far wall was filled with rows of books.

Cal sat in the formal chair in his preaching suit with his injured leg elevated on an ottoman. Although a Bible rested on his lap, his eyes were shut and his head tilted back. He looked tired and bruised, but his good eye opened as soon as he heard footsteps.

"Resting just like I told you?" I asked.

"The Sabbath is meant for rest. Please sit down."

I sat on the love seat.

Bessie brought two glasses of lemonade and put them on the coffee table. She was wearing a simple blue dress covered with a floral apron. Her hair was pulled back into a bun at the nape of her neck. She wore no jewelry except a small silver cross on a chain around her neck. She looked to be a few years younger than her brother but I estimated they were both in their late fifties. They shared the same broad noses and high cheekbones.

"How are you feeling today?" I asked.

"Like I was in a car accident. And these stitches are pulling and itching."

"Sounds like you're on the road to healing. What about the leg?"

"Feels pretty good. I'm trying to stay off it but you know how that goes. Bessie is strong but she can't carry me around." He closed his Bible and set it carefully on the table.

"I'll have a look at your leg before I leave. What will you tell the faithful this morning?"

"You ever heard of Howard Thurman?"

"No." I took a sip of the lemonade.

"He was a professor at Howard and he wrote a book called *Jesus and the Disinherited*. You should read it. He tells us about what makes us lose our inheritance and how to get it back."

"Blessed are the meek for they shall inherit?" I asked.

"Sometimes the meek can realize the strength they got and they rise up and say, 'Enough.' Some people think meek means being timid, but meek means being humble enough to know where your strength comes from so that you can the oppose the bullies."

"And how does the congregation feel about rising up?"

"They're ready."

I glanced at Bessie who was sitting on straight-backed dining room chair. Bessie was quiet and expressionless but listening carefully. I finished my lemonade.

"Do you mind if I check your leg?"

"Go ahead. Bessie checked it this morning." Cal rolled up his pant leg and I checked the dressing and touched the skin around it to see if there was any heat or swelling.

"I don't see any signs of trouble. Are you taking those pills?"

"Yes, ma'am. I don't mess with Bessie. She never learnt the word 'meek.'"

I smiled and sat back down. The antique clock ticked loudly in the room.

He straightened out his pant leg and winced again as he leaned forward and then remembered his injured ribs.

"Did you all grow up here?" I asked.

"We sure did. My daddy was preacher in the same church. Sent us away for school, but we came right back."

"And neither of you are married?"

"I was. Georgia died having our first child. Bessie was away at nursing school." He paused.

"I'm so sorry," I said.

"When Bessie finished school, she came back to care for our father. I'm so glad to have her help, even if she can sometimes try a man's patience. She might still marry if she doesn't scare all her suitors out of town."

"I'll try to read that book you mentioned."

"Bessie, can you reach that yellow book on the top shelf? Thanks." He lifted his arm to point, but then winced again.

Bessie handed the book to me.

"I'll return it to Bessie at the clinic. Guess I better be going now. Looks like you could use one of those pain pills before you start your preaching."

He nodded. "Maybe we'll see you in church one of these times. Thanks for dropping by."

I smiled as I shook his hand. "Stay out of trouble," I said. "Rest."

"Same to you," he countered with a smile. His eyes were warm with humor, and he held onto my hand. "You're a fine doctor. When you go back north, don't forget my people. The poor you'll always have with you. Don't get so used to seeing the poor that you forget they're there."

I nodded. It felt strangely like an anointing, but I'd be leaving in two weeks and I'd probably never see him or Bessie again. I hoped I'd never forget them. The thought brought unexpected tears of sadness that were mixed with muddy-eyed fatigue. I hoped they would manage to keep each other safe while they carried on the struggle. I had no illusions that my small contribution had made much difference. It would take armies of volunteers and thousands of hands to build a new city where all were counted. But I did know that my brief encounter with the likes of Bessie and Pastor Cal would go with me, challenging and calling me to have courage where there seemed to be none.

Louise closed her eyes for a moment and caught her breath.

Nori reached for her hand. "Wow, that was some experience. So you left two weeks later. Did you take a bus back to New Haven?"

"I slept for two days on that bus. Mary picked me up at the station and shared her big news that they'd eloped while I was away."

"They did? How did you feel about that?"

"It was difficult. I tried to be excited for her, but inside, I felt like I was losing her forever. I was grateful that I wouldn't have to parade around in some awful bridesmaid dress, but I felt sad that I hadn't been part of her special day. Mary had always planned to sew a gorgeous dress and throw a big party with dancing and lots of food. But with one more year of school, it made more sense to have a simple wedding. Robert moved into our apartment."

"Didn't you feel like a third wheel sharing your place with newlyweds?"

"I wanted to move out, but my options and my funds were limited. Luckily I had applied to a fellowship just before I went south. When I returned home, a letter of acceptance was waiting for me. I didn't know much about the place, but it seemed like a good chance to get some more experience, do some research, and acquire some references for an application to a residency. My long-term goal was to be admitted into a prestigious surgical program and I would have to do that without a reference from the chief at Yale. I was ambitious and willing to spend the time doing a fellowship as an intermediate step."

"Where was the fellowship?"

"The surgical fellowship was sponsored by the sanatorium in Saranac that had a reputation for excellent tuberculosis treatment. Since I'd done a fair bit of thoracic surgery, I thought it would be a good chance to build on my experience. I needed to have a strong application to be competitive for some of the top academic hospitals."

"And you decided to go there. I still can't believe I'd never heard of the place."

"When drugs promised to eradicate tuberculosis, the san closed in the mid-1950s. The building stood unused for a long time and there were fights over what to do with it. I think it's boarded up and abandoned, but there's always talk of developing the property. The land offers marvelous views of the water and the mountains. Some developer will get his hands on it and carve it into a subdivision filled with detached houses."

"And you worked there for a year?"

Louise nodded. "A little less than a year."

"I'd love to hear more about your time there. We discussed TB in my sociology seminar, but I don't remember much about the treatment regimens, other than rest cures."

Louise sighed. "Why don't we pick up there next time? I think I hear Belinda coming for her shift."

Nori took the tray and rolled the table out of her way. "After you are settled, I'll go out to do some errands. Anything you need?"

"I've had a craving for some ice cream. Vanilla or butter pecan, if that's not too much trouble."

"Not at all. I'll pick up dessert and also find something for dinner. Maybe we can have dessert first?" Nori helped her transfer to the bed, straightened the sheets, and kissed her cheek.

With a wave to Belinda, Nori grabbed her purse and left the house. She couldn't believe she was excited to go to the grocery store. Sometimes she just needed that bit of space to try to get a handle on all that was happening. The past and present were so entwined, that she felt like she was living simultaneously in multiple stories.

The next morning when the aide arrived for her shift, Nori decided to visit Jazz at the café. She'd put it off long enough. Belinda had probably told her that Nori was back so it wouldn't be a surprise—she was probably waiting for Nori to make the first move. Even though time had passed, she knew that Jazz would not have forgotten. She really wanted to make this right.

The café was located in an older frame house painted blue with bright yellow shutters. The former sun porch now served as a gift shop and was filled with scented candles and throws and pillows and children's toys. The café contained a few tables and chairs and a coffee bar facing the back wall. Racks of children's books and gift cards lined the walls. A blues track filled the café with infectious sound.

Nori sat at a small table and studied the menu. She ordered a stack of pancakes and coffee. She looked up gratefully when the waitress filled her cup. Packs of coffee beans were for sale near the counter.

"Is Jazz around?" she asked the waitress.

"She's doing paperwork in the back. You want me to get her?"

"I'll check in with her after breakfast."

After she finished her pancakes, Nori took the notebook and pen out of her bag and nodded when the waitress offered her a refill. She decided to record the stories Louise told. This was family history, and if she didn't take care of it, no one else would.

She was so absorbed in writing that she didn't see Jazz until she was standing right across from her.

"Slumming today?" Jazz asked.

"Nice place you got here," Nori said. "And very good coffee." Jazz looked the same. She'd always been tall and lean with a runner's physique. Her dark hair was a mass of red curls that she'd stopped trying to tame. She wore a floral dress from the fifties with a boxy blue cardigan and combat boots. Nori envied her sense of style—she'd always been unafraid to put together vintage items with new accessories to create a unique look.

Jazz stood with her arms crossed over her chest, appearing to be ready for a fight if necessary. "Looking for a job? Too bad, 'cause I'm not hiring."

"Nope. I'm kind of busy right now. But thanks, anyway."

"That's weird, 'cause I hear you got thrown out of some fancy graduate school."

Even though she still had a verbal edge, there was something softer about her look. Knowing Jazz, she wasn't going to let her off easily.

"If you listen to all the gossip that flies around here, you'll be very busy, and quite misinformed," Nori replied.

"I heard you were looking for me? Was that misinformation?"

"You got a minute?" Nori pointed to the chair across from her. She held her breath to see if Jazz would join her or if she would walk away. She realized how much she missed her.

"I'll ignore the lineup outside." She signaled to the waitress to bring her a coffee, and she pulled out a chair. "How's your aunt?"

Nori sighed. "She's getting weaker every day. She's as sharp as ever, but she gets tired so easily."

"I'm sorry. She was always really good to me. Even after. . . ."

Nori looked at her sharply. "After what?"

Jazz shrugged. "She kept in touch and said she was sorry we'd fallen out. She helped me, later, when I . . . well, when I got stuck."

"I didn't know." Nori felt the gap between them.

They were both silent. Jazz stirred some cream into the mug the waitress brought.

Nori knew she had to make the first move. "Look, I wanted to talk to you. I feel really badly that we've lost touch. I'm so sorry for how things went. I mean it. I was an ass and you had every right to tell me where to go."

Jazz glanced at her and then played with the wooden stir stick, snapping it in half. She still said nothing.

Nori pressed on. "I had no right to mess with you. I knew you had a thing for that guy, and I was jealous. We'd been friends forever and suddenly he was all you could see. I didn't trust him. And then that night, I just wanted to show you that you shouldn't trust him either. Nothing happened between us. I wanted to see what he would do. I promise you . . . nothing happened. But I realize it wasn't right to get between you. I am really sorry."

A long silence hung over the table.

"Well, it doesn't make much difference now."

Nori looked at her trying to figure out what she meant. "Why not?"

"He's gone. Moved to North Carolina. Said he was going to work with his cousin in construction."

"Oh, geez, I'm sorry."

Jazz shrugged. "Don't be. Good riddance."

"You got someone new?" Nori asked.

"Yep. I got a new man. He's three now."

"What?" Nori grabbed her arm. "You have a kid?"

"I do. He's great. We call him J. J. but he's really John Joseph after my dad."

"Where is he now?"

"He's in a nursery school in town. The rest of the time, my mom helps when I'm working and my sister does too. When he was younger, he came to work with me, but now he takes everything apart and I can't run the place and watch him."

"And his dad?"

"Doesn't want anything to do with him. In fact, he left town about the time I told him I was pregnant."

"What a jerk. Can I see J. J. sometime?"

Jazz gave her a long look. "Maybe."

Nori looked at her. "I've missed you."

Jazz took a breath. "What's going on with that graduate school? Did they really toss you out?"

Nori shook her head. "Nothing quite that dramatic. They put me on probation. I screwed up. Things piled up after my dad passed, and I didn't finish my work and now I have till September to get things in order."

"What are you doing about it?"

"It's not that easy. I have to find another topic and write a proposal and bibliography. And with my aunt sick.. . . ."

"Don't use her as an excuse. She would hate that. I hear she has aides coming to help. You can work first thing in the morning or whenever. If you want it, you'll find a way to do it. You could stay up late at night. I'm sure she goes to sleep early. Don't make excuses."

Jazz wasn't cutting her much slack. Nori looked around at the café and changed the subject. "This place is really nice."

"I had some help. It gets really busy in the season with all the tourists. My sister has a real estate office in town. We've been buying up houses one at a time and fixing them up."

"Do houses sell up here?"

"Lots of retired folks and people from the city want a place in a small town. We pick small houses that are easy to maintain. I do the country casual or the cottage chic look, and people eat it up."

"That's amazing. What else do you do?" Nori couldn't believe it. Jazz was someone to be reckoned with. She felt like a wimp by comparison.

"I run."

"What?"

"Seriously. I took up running again. You can join me if you want. Every morning."

"Now I'm really impressed. I remember you used to do track and field." Jazz nodded.

Nori glanced at her watch. "I gotta get going. I don't like to leave Louise for too long."

Jazz stood up, pushed her chair back in place and looked at Nori. "You wanna get a beer sometime? My sister loves any excuse to take J. J."

"I'd love that."

"How about Saturday night at the lodge? I'll whip your butt at shuffleboard."

"It's a deal. Let me make sure there's coverage for Louise. Early evening is probably better for me."

"Me too. Let's say five o'clock then."

Chapter 7

THE kitchen was tidy and the laundry was folded in the basket. Having the help of the aides kept the house running. Nori checked a recipe, and someone knocked on the door. Ben, wearing jeans and a black shirt with a priest collar, stood at the door. She stared at him in confusion. Why would a landscaper wear a collar?

"I'd like to visit your aunt, if this is a good time?"

Nori's face showed her disbelief. "But you're the gardener."

Ben chuckled. "That happened to Jesus too. A case of mistaken identity."

Nori looked at him. "What do you mean?"

"Sorry, Biblical reference. After Jesus left the tomb, Mary Magdalene didn't recognize him and thought he was the gardener."

"Thanks for the Bible lesson. But . . . what are you doing here?"

"I serve the Episcopal Church in town. Louise is a member there and I'm here to do a pastoral visit at her request."

Nori looked at him. "I wasn't aware my aunt was a member of any church. I'll check and see, if you don't mind waiting for a moment."

After checking with Louise, she pointed him towards the bedroom. Nori remembered how quickly he'd jumped to help when Louise had fallen that first day.

She chopped up the leeks and boiled the potatoes in a separate pot. As she sautéed the leeks in butter, their fragrance filled the kitchen. While she cooked, she thought about how different Louise's childhood on the farm had been from her own childhood in the manse. Louise had been expected to work hard; by contrast, Nori had it very easy. But it meant she had few skills to bring to the work of caregiving.

She burned her fingers peeling the skins from the hot potatoes and realized that it would have been better to let them cool first.

45

"Mind if I sit for a moment?" Ben asked.

She put down her knife and placed the colander in the sink. "Sure, please sit down. Tea or coffee?"

"No, thank you." He waited until Nori took a seat across from him. "This must be very difficult for you," he said. "Louise told me that you spent many summers here. I'm really sorry that this time is so different."

Nori looked down at her hands, and her eyes welled up with tears. "I never expected it to be like this. I just lost my father and now this."

"I can imagine that it's overwhelming. I'm willing to help in any way you might need. Just let me know. People in the church are ready to help but they don't want to impose. If you need food or garden work or people to sit with Louise, we have willing hands to help."

Nori nodded. "Thank you. I really appreciate it. I'm not a nurse, and I really don't know how to cook," she said, jumping up to turn off the leeks before they burned. "I don't have any qualifications for this job but here I am."

"You're doing just fine. Louise is really grateful that you're here."

"I think she's getting weaker," Nori said anxiously. "When I arrived, she was still able to get up and walk around. Now she just sleeps."

"She may have been pushing herself till you got here."

Nori looked down at her hands. "I'm afraid. . . ."

Ben nodded. "I will do my best to be here when you need me. But it might help to know that Louise is ready."

She looked at him in surprise. "But I'm not," Nori said.

"I understand," he said quietly. He sat for a few more minutes and then left.

Nori felt the weight of the silence in the house. She added some stock to the leeks and potatoes. She'd let it simmer, while she sat with Louise. She hoped Louise would feel up to some more storytelling.

Chapter 8

NORI pulled on her jeans and a light gray merino turtleneck, then ran a brush through her hair. Jazz would arrive soon, and she didn't want to keep her waiting. The dress code at the lodge tended to favor flannel shirts and work boots, so she didn't want to overdress. Belinda had promised to stay until Nori returned from her evening. It seemed she was happy that the girls were patching up their friendship.

Nori hurried to give Louise a kiss and then grabbed her leather jacket and purse.

When she heard a horn, she ran out to the waiting car.

"You ready to rock and roll?" Jazz asked.

"Bring it on," Nori replied with a smile.

They drove the short distance to the bar on the outskirts of town and found a parking place between two large pickup trucks; Jazz's car looked like a toy by comparison.

"I hope they're not too drunk to notice my car when they leave."

"I hope *you're* not too drunk to drive me home later."

"I'll be the designated driver so you can let your hair down. I'm sure it's been a while. Not that I want to see you as a sloppy drunk."

They found a table near the shuffleboard. Country music played over the speakers and the hum of conversation circled round the room. The bar stools were already fully occupied and the waitress carried large trays of draft beer to the tables around them. They ordered a pitcher of draft and looked around.

"I guess you know everyone here," Nori said. She envied the ease with which Jazz moved through the crowd, joking and hugging people she knew.

"Pretty much. Selling the only decent coffee in town puts me on the map. How's Louise?"

"Same—just getting a little bit weaker by the day."

"Tell me about your project, what is it, a thesis?"

"It's a PhD thesis and they want to see a proposal before I can get started. I'm interested in the history of design and health care."

"How can the design of a building affect care? Unless the halls are too long and nurses get tired of going to the very end of the hall to answer a call bell?"

"I started doing research on an asylum in Connecticut. We went on a tour of the buildings after the place had shut down for good. You've never seen such a creepy place in your life."

"In what way?"

"It felt like everyone walked out one day and didn't come back. Beds were still in place, medical equipment filled the treatment rooms, and patients' art hung in the lounge. I had the feeling that they might come back at any moment and ask what we were doing there."

"Why did they close the hospital?"

"Somebody decided that mental health needed to move into the community, so they decided to de-institutionalize all those people and put them in rooming houses and group homes."

"That must have been rough. I suppose some people had been there for a long time."

"For decades. It was all they knew. Their families were long gone, and their stories were forgotten."

"What did you plan to write about all that? It's not like they could tell their stories."

"I wanted to look at the architecture and make an argument about the kind of care that resulted. It was organized like a small town with buildings distributed over acres of parkland. Despite the beauty, people did things that weren't right to the patients."

"Like what?"

"Medical experiments and cruel treatments."

Jazz groaned. "That is so sad. Why would you want to work on that?"

"Because it's important. Sometimes you have to dig up those stories to make sure that things like that can never happen again. Patient rights are more protected now by consent laws, and they have a right to information. When the design allows people to keep secrets, you have to be vigilant that people aren't abusing their power."

"Can I buy you ladies a drink?" a fellow asked them. His eyes were bloodshot and he smelled like cigarettes and beer.

Jazz looked up at him. "Get lost, Joe."

He was surprised and backed away from the table. "Dykes," he muttered. "They're everywhere."

"Asshole," she replied and then turned back to Nori. "You were hoping to get an exclusive on the story. Then what happened?"

"Some professor from another university got there first and published a book that's getting excellent reviews. My advisor told me to forget it. If I tried to do anything similar, it would look like I was copying him. And the university doesn't look kindly on plagiarism."

"Sounds like she knows what she's talking about."

Nori nodded. "I guess so."

"Either you trust your advisor to know the ropes or you think you're smarter than she is. Maybe you're so smart you don't need this degree."

"Stop it."

"I'm serious. The whole point of having a mentor is to trust them to give you good advice and to learn from them. If you're too smart or too stubborn to listen, you're just throwing away your time and money."

"Easy for you to say. I planned to find another topic, but then so much shit happened, I couldn't focus."

"Shit happens to everybody. I bet you went into cry baby mode wanting sympathy and then when you didn't get that, you decided to bail on the whole thing."

"That's not fair."

"Am I right? You felt sorry for yourself. I'm not saying you don't deserve to feel sorry and you had a whole lot of stuff happen. But you probably threw up your hands and gave up."

Nori looked at her beer. She knew if she tried to defend herself, Jazz would counter every argument she might make. Compared to Jazz or to her aunt, maybe she was too willing to give up. The worst thing was, she didn't really believe she could do a doctoral thesis that would pass her advisor's critical evaluation. Maybe Yale had made a mistake accepting her into the program. She just didn't have the right stuff.

"Here's what we're going to do. First, we're going to play shuffleboard until I win, and then we're going to figure out a plan. Don't expect me to stand by while you sabotage your chance to get a fancy diploma from Yale University. Let's go play." She pushed her chair out and walked towards the shuffleboard. "You guys almost done?" she asked.

The two fellows looked at her in surprise. "Yeah, I suppose so. Can we buy you gals a drink?"

"No, thanks. We just want the board."

After a few rounds of shuffleboard, Nori and Jazz sat and ordered another round.

"Now we're going to make a plan," Jazz said. "I'm sure Louise would agree that you didn't come this far to fail. And she wouldn't be happy to be used as an excuse for failure."

Nori nodded. "She's already made that clear."

"Talk to me. What kinds of places have you thought about? Let's stick with your original interest in design and health care. Are there other types of health care settings you might want to research?"

"The typical acute care hospital doesn't interest me. There were fancy spas in the mountains where people could take advantage of fresh air and sun. None of that gets me very excited."

"What else?"

"I really don't know for sure about this one idea . . . I've haven't really looked at it yet."

"Stop with the excuses and tell me what you're thinking. This is just a conversation, not a commitment. Brainstorming. No judgment." Jazz seemed genuinely interested.

"I was in the library in that reading room in the back looking through books on Adirondack history and culture and I found a health care institution located about an hour from here in Saranac. Although it closed in the fifties, it was a big deal in its day. Louise has been telling me stories about her past, and it turns out she spent a year working there."

"Why don't you go up there and take a look at whatever is left? I remember my mom talked about it sometimes. I think some cousins were in that place. Anyway, you can talk to locals. Check it out. You could ask Belinda to stay till you get back, just in case it takes longer than you planned. Seeing the place might get you motivated. Even if there's nothing left, you can still get a feeling for the setting and the town."

Nori nodded. Jazz was right. She already had a connection to the place through Louise, and it was close enough to drive there and back.

"Do you know what it looked like?"

"I've seen pictures."

"Some of us just understand things better visually."

Nori nodded. "That's true. I still feel guilty when I work on the project. It doesn't seem right to do that when she's so sick."

"I think it's healthy to have some other focus and it doesn't mean you aren't fully concerned about her. You know that she'd be really pissed if you put aside your project to worry about her. All you can do is have a look and start the investigation. If it doesn't go anywhere, we'll come back here, drink more beer, I'll whip your ass at the board again, and we'll dream up something else."

"You make it sound so easy," Nori said.

"You make it all so bloody difficult. Just get on with it. Being over-whelmed is no excuse."

Nori nodded slowly and took another sip of her beer. Maybe she'd start doing some background research to see when the place was built and how many patients were treated there. She needed to get a feel for the scope and size of the institution. That would be one way to start the conversation with-out making a big commitment.

"One more thing—if you have time, I sometimes go to flea markets to collect things for my store. Anything we don't use, I can sell at the summer market at the fairgrounds."

"That would be fun."

"The next one is next Sunday. My sister sometimes comes over on Sundays to make pancakes with Jesse. We'd have to leave really early; it's up in Massachusetts so it's about an hour's drive. We'll probably be home by mid-afternoon. Just let me know. I'll be going anyway, but it would be more fun to go with someone else."

"I'll give you a call." Nori finished her beer and checked her watch.

"Let me take you home now. You need a good night's sleep so you can start your project in the morning."

"Easy for you to say," Nori said as she slipped on her leather coat and grabbed her purse.

Chapter 9

BERKSHIRE HILLS FLEA MARKET, 1980

Nori and Jazz wandered along the long rows of tables where vendors sold lamps, tablecloths, old farm tools, and vintage clothing at the state's largest outdoor flea market. With the sun up, it was a lot warmer than it had been earlier that morning. Nori took off her hoodie and tied it around her waist. The smell of fried dough and coffee filled the air. Professional collectors pushed their way past the tourists, choosing items that they knew they could sell for profit in their shops.

Nori waited while Jazz admired some of the vintage hats and gloves, checking her reflection in the mirror with every new item. Nori wandered a bit further, checking regularly that she could still see Jazz—she wasn't planning to lose her in this crowd.

Stopping at a table covered with old books, maps, records, and photos, she flipped through an album filled with square black and white photos with white borders kept in place by photo corners. In one picture, a couple held a baby in a christening dress; in another, a young child smiled proudly over the handlebars of his first tricycle. Nori studied a picture of a young man standing in front of stone gates. In the next page, the same fellow rested in a reclining chair. The photos depicted the same young man making a leather belt. He looked to be in his early twenties—a smooth shaven fellow with his hair oiled and carefully parted to one side.

"Do you know this person?" she asked the vendor, holding the album up for him to see.

He shook his head. "Just picked it up at an estate sale."

"Do you remember where?"

"Sure. I was fishing in the Adirondacks, somewhere near Saranac."

"How much for this?"

He looked at her carefully. "Twenty-five."

"Twenty?" she offered.

He shrugged. "Sure."

She handed him the money and he put the album in a plastic bag from a local grocery store. "Thanks."

She walked over to where Jazz was still trying on hats. "I thought we were here to buy furniture to stage your houses."

"I love these vintage hats." Jazz looked at the bag she carried. "What did you get?"

"A photo album. I'll show you later."

Jazz returned the hat to the table, sighed and walked away. "How about a coffee and some donuts?" she asked. "There's a couple down there who make apple cider cinnamon ones."

When they were seated at the picnic table with their snacks, Nori pulled out the photo album and passed it to Jazz.

"Who is this guy?

"Don't know who he is, but look at this one. Those are the south gates to the sanatorium. If you look at that car, it must be the late nineteen-forties or early fifties."

"What are you thinking?"

"I just hate to see people throw out albums like this."

"But if you can't identify the people, can you use the photos?"

Nori nods. "It would be ideal to know their names, but you can still learn a lot from looking at the photos. Look at this one of the guy at a swimming party. You can see the scars on his chest and the sunken left side. He probably had some ribs removed along with part of the lung. Some of the surgeries left people with life-long deformities."

"They really got butchered," Jazz commented as she studied the picture.

"I'm sure the patients weren't given much choice other than to comply."

"That's awful. You have to do something with this."

"You mean like write my thesis?"

"Well, that too, but no one's going to read that. It'll be stuck on some library shelf. Maybe you could do another project once you graduate using these materials. Make it accessible to local people and invite them to identify people in the pictures. A lot of people are still reluctant to talk about that place and there's bad feelings about what was done there. At least that's what my mom said." She ran her fingers over the photo corners that held the picture in place. "Maybe it's time to bring that into the open and let people tell their stories, if they want to do that."

Nori looked at her in surprise. She'd never considered anything beyond getting her thesis finished. She'd supposed after that she'd try to find a job and teach in some small college, where she'd spend her nights and weekends trying to write something that would get her tenure.

"Didn't you ever learn to think outside the box?" Jazz asked.

"Who would want to hear about this stuff? It's an old story with old diseases."

"Many local people worked there or had family that were patients. Should the whole thing just be forgotten? Don't you have an obligation to think about a broader audience?"

Nori looked at the album and the back at Jazz. "Why should that be my problem?"

"You have an obligation to try. You went to a fancy school and people are trusting you with their stories, including Louise."

"That's not fair. I've got enough to do here with trying to pull together a thesis and care for Louise. I can't be responsible for educating the whole community—especially about a history that some want to leave covered up."

"Relax. I'm not saying you have to do this right now. And I'm not telling you to educate them. I think they're already educated, but they might need help getting their story on paper or film. I'm just suggesting you keep an open mind. Unless you plan to never come back and forget all this once you're back in Connecticut. Which, now that I think about it, is probably what you'll do. Because we know you usually choose the easy way out."

Nori looked at her in annoyance. "Don't be ridiculous. Of course I'll come back."

"Settle down. I just think you need to keep focusing on the bigger picture. Maybe you were meant to do this. You need to link into your greater purpose." She smiled at Nori.

Nori shrugged. Jazz could talk all she wanted but she didn't need a bigger picture or a more demanding purpose. This summer was challenging enough.

They finished their coffee in silence.

Nori didn't feel comfortable with leaving things like that. "I gotta say, I'm glad you took me to the flea market. I was happy to save the album. It's hard to think about all this when Louise . . ."

Jazz interrupted. "You know that Louise wants you to do this. She'd feel badly if you stopped on her account. Maybe she's waiting for you to make a plan."

Nori looked at her. "Do you really think so?"

"I bet that Louise picked you to tell the story. Maybe she invited you up here hoping you'd get interested in it. But she's never going to tell you what to do or force you. She's thrown you a challenge and she thinks you're up to it. Don't make it more complicated than it is."

"I'm not making it more complicated; I just don't see my way through at the moment."

"Can I say one more thing? Since you're already annoyed with me?"

"Just go ahead," Nori said, "you know you'll say it anyway."

"Anything you try is going to have some failures attached to it. Do you think I got everything right when I started my café or when we decided to renovate and sell houses? I could write a book on the mistakes I made—not that anyone would want to read it. But I believed I could learn. Now you have to start believing. And get moving."

Nori sat and looked out the window. She didn't know what to say. Was that really what she was doing—avoiding a decision because she was afraid and using Louise as an excuse to do nothing?

Jazz glanced at her. "I've said too much. I'm sorry; it's none of my business. I have a big mouth—as you know."

"No, you're right. I'm afraid to start. I keep making excuses and I'm getting tired of myself. I'm afraid I'm not smart enough to do this and soon I'll be exposed as a total loser."

"You gotta fix that. Nobody else can."

They drove the rest of the way in silence.

Chapter 10

"I'D like to search the photographic files for pictures of the Saranac Sanatorium," Nori explained to the clerk.

The woman looked at her blankly. "What do you want them for?"

"I'm doing research for a thesis at Yale."

"Here's the finding aid. Go through this and then request the ones you want using this form. And use a pencil, please."

"Can I restrict my search to specific years?"

She shrugged. "You can try."

Nori tried a different approach. "Do you know if the archives have any letters or diaries from people who were patients?"

"I don't know. Seems like that might be restricted." The clerk was tapping her fingers on the desk impatient to get away from Nori.

"Could you tell me how I might check?"

"Like I said, you can go through these finding aids and see if you find anything and then I'll look it up."

"Thanks," Nori said as she carried the binders to the table. She rolled her eyes at Jazz who had agreed to come with her on this research trip.

"Wow, that's a lot of help," Jazz whispered to Nori.

Nori sighed and handed Jazz a binder. "Look for anything about the San or Saranac or TB and see if they catalogued anything by location."

They scanned the books and made a list of requests and handed them back to the clerk.

"I don't know if those are available," she said.

Jazz stood up from the table. "Could you give me the name of your supervisor please?"

The woman looked confused. "She's in a meeting."

"I'm an assistant to this researcher, and we drove up here, taking time away from a dying relative. This brochure welcomes the public to use the archives, so we're here to use it. Now it is possible to retrieve these items, or do I need to speak to your supervisor?"

The woman sniffed and turned to go to the storage area. Jazz winked at Nori.

Nori glared at Jazz. "You'll get us thrown out."

Jazz shrugged. "We don't have time to waste. She needs to step up and do her job. That's all I got to say."

The woman came back and loudly placed the items on the counter. "You can't copy these letters. They're too fragile."

"Camera?" Jazz asked.

"No flash."

"Great, thanks." Jazz picked up the items and brought them to the table. She took her camera out of her bag and set up a stand. As the camera clicked, Nori pored through the other items.

They worked for two hours without speaking, taking pictures, photocopying, and transcribing the materials.

"We have to get going," Jazz said as she checked her watch.

"I think we're done with this stuff." Nori exhaled and stretched in her chair. "I can't wait to see what you found."

Jazz smiled. "Can't wait to show you."

They carried the books and envelopes back to the desk.

The clerk had little to say, especially when Jazz gave her an exaggerated thank you.

They could barely contain themselves, but they made it outside before they both burst out laughing.

"I'm an assistant to this researcher and she will need access," Nori repeated, mocking Jazz, putting one hand on her hip in an exaggerated posture.

"Being nice doesn't cut it when you're trying to run a business. Let's get rolling; I have to be back in an hour. We can pick up some sandwiches in town and then get on the road. What are we doing next? The research is cool—like those old Westerns, where you walk into a saloon with the guns blazing . . ."

"I never quite pictured it that way."

"Watch and learn, girl. In the future, they'll wonder how you manage to publish a book a year. Without me, you'd still be begging for permission."

As Jazz drove, Nori watched the countryside flash by. She was happy they'd collected so much information. Once she sorted through it, she'd have to start making selections. It was a bit intimidating to think about all the photocopies and scans and photographs she was collecting. She needed to be very careful to identify her sources and document each item. Some things also required specific permission if she wanted to quote them. She'd never worked with this much information, and she wasn't sure she had the organizational ability to manage it.

"What are you worried about now?" Jazz asked glancing over at her.

"How do I keep track of all this stuff?"

"Sometimes a few shipments of stuff arrive at the same time, and I have to check the contents to make sure it's what I ordered. Then I put it on the shelf and keep track of when it sells. Those are basic inventory skills. I can't imagine it's any different for you."

"But how will I know that I've got enough material? I already feel like I'm drowning in information and I don't even have a thesis argument yet."

"I don't think you can have that at the start. Seems like at the beginning you collect information broadly and then you narrow it down. I use a spreadsheet to track the inventory. I can search by the date I ordered something, when it arrived, how much I paid, and when it got sold. Once a spreadsheet is set up, you add the data as you get it. It would be a good idea to get all that sorted before you get much further into it."

Nori groaned.

"Tell me how you track things now."

"I use colored file cards and I also write things in a notebook."

"Are you kidding? That's not good enough. And forget file cards."

Nori held her head. "I don't know what I'm doing."

"Don't be such a drama queen. This is no different than running a business. Sometimes things grow fast and you have to create systems to keep up with it. I told you I would help and I will. Now let's just enjoy the ride, 'cause when I get home, I turn into mommy." She turned on the radio and sang along with the country music.

Nori looked at her in disbelief.

"You got something against country?" Jazz asked.

"I didn't know you were a fan."

"You'll catch on. It's the only station we get up here."

Nori grimaced but picked up the chorus. As Jazz skillfully drove the car over the winding road, the two sang and harmonized and occasionally laughed at the lyrics.

Jazz pulled into the laneway and stopped beside Nori's car. "You'll see. This music is perfect for you. It's all about failing and trying again."

"Great. Thanks for coming with me," Nori said.

"Say hi to Louise. I'll get those documents off my camera and send them to you. I can make some time Friday morning to set up the database with you and then you can start entering the items. If you could get to the café around ten, we can work on the office computer."

Nori nodded. "I owe you."

Jazz smiled. "I know."

Nori waved as Jazz pulled out of sight. She stood for a moment, breathing in the fresh air.

Nori was dusting shelves in Louise's study and sorting more books to send to the library sale. One had an intriguing title: *Stories from the Fight against the White Plague.* She flipped through the book and saw a photograph of the familiar gates to the san. She sat at Louise's desk and went through the pages more slowly.

The book was filled with photographs of people learning crafts or working on the farm. Some sat in long wooden chairs covered with blankets as snow blew into unheated porches. Another group was gathered with tennis rackets. Nori chuckled at the photo of women and men on a winter hike, clothed in fur coats that almost reached the ground. The personal stories expressed nostalgia for the days and years they'd spent in the san—something that Nori found a bit surprising. She'd assumed that most people felt isolated and confined there, but perhaps the truth was more complex.

Nori was startled to see a picture of a familiar woman standing in front of a small cottage with three men. The camera had caught them laughing at a joke. One of them was a tall African-American fellow, the second one was swarthy man who looked Italian, and the third one was a foot shorter than the first two. All of Nori's attention was focused on one person. Wearing a lab coat over scrubs was her aunt, smiling at the camera. The caption merely said "Rose Cottage," and didn't provide their names.

What it had been like for Louise to leave Yale and go to Saranac? The geographic isolation had to have felt so different from her previous location at an academic medical center. Why had Louise ultimately chosen to settle near that small town? She must have had opportunities to work in urban centers that offered more prospects for research and social life, and yet, she'd chosen this town in the Adirondacks. Nori had to go see this place, or whatever was left of it.

The next day, Nori ran into Ben at the public library.

"Do you have time for a coffee?"

Nori checked her watch. "I have an hour."

"How are you doing?" Ben asked after the waitress brought their coffee.

"I'm doing all right. Louise seems to get a little bit weaker every day."

"Are you getting some work done at the library in between taking care of Louise?"

"She made me promise that I'd keep working on my proposal. I've been reading about the sanatorium that used to be up in Saranac. It's such a weird connection that she worked there."

"Interesting. Getting your feet wet?"

"The water feels cold," she said with a smile.

"Some of my elderly parishioners have mentioned being there."

Nori looked up in surprise. "You know someone who was a patient?"

"There's a lady in the retirement home in town who must be in her eighties and is sharp as a tack. Her sister was a patient there."

"Do you think she'd agree to talk to me?"

"I'll ask her."

"I hope she wouldn't mind a conversation. I want to be cautious with a topic that might be painful for people."

"There was definitely a sense of shame and stigma related to that disease and patients were made to feel like untouchables at the time. But I'm sure she'd love to talk to you."

Jazz walked by their table. "Hello."

"Join us," Nori said pulling out a chair for her.

"I've got to place some orders or we'll run out of coffee."

"You two know each other, right?" Nori asked, as she looked from one to the other.

Ben smiled. "Jazz lets us use the café some Saturday nights for youth group meetings. The kids feel more relaxed in a café than in the church basement. And of course, J. J. is a star student in the Sunday school."

Nori looked at Jazz. "You take him to church?"

"Maybe not church yet, I think he would be too disruptive. But yeah, he goes to Sunday school. See you guys."

Nori checked her watch. "I have to go."

He nodded and picked up the check. "I'll try to drop by before the end of the week. Louise asked me to bring communion."

Nori shook her head. "I never knew my aunt to be a church person. But clearly there's so much I don't know."

Ben smiled but said nothing more.

Chapter 11

SARANAC, 1980

N ORI drove past the barricaded road that had served as an entry point for the san, marked by stone gates that were now falling apart. She parked on a gravel road that ran along the far side of the property. The lake was visible at the bottom of the road and "No Trespassing" signs were posted around the perimeter.

Nori hiked into the property from the side where a snow fence had fallen over, offering her easy access. Although the windows were boarded up, she recognized the administrative building from the photos she'd seen. All the doors were secured with huge padlocks and chains. Broken glass, discarded beer cans, and charred logs testified to past campfires and drinking parties.

Behind the main building, the grounds opened to a park space lined with small cottages. Shadows of former walking paths crisscrossed the field to the assorted buildings. Nori imagined patients taking their daily exercise or scurrying through the cold to go to the cafeteria. She turned left and walked towards the nurses' residence. Although locked and boarded up, she pictured nurses coming and going for their shifts in uniforms and capes. The two-storey dwelling had been home to many women over the years—now the windows were boarded and the front door sprayed with graffiti.

She turned to look at the water and the view of the mountain across the lake. It was amazing to think that Louise had looked at this same view. Although it was a lovely setting, it felt so isolated—she wasn't sure she'd want to be a patient or staff in a setting like this.

At one of the small cottages, she peered into the window from the front porch, stepping carefully to avoid the broken timbers. A sign over the front door said "Rose Cottage." Although the furniture was gone, the structure of the house was largely intact. She tried to imagine patients passing their time with occupational therapy and social events. Birds darted in and out of the pine trees around her.

Nori jumped as something moved in the bushes at the edge of the property, but she was relieved to see that it was only a herd of wild turkeys, making their slow progress across the property. She checked her watch; she only had half an hour left to explore before she had to drive home.

The scale of the place was astonishing—it was more like a village than a hospital. Where had all the patients and staff gone when it finally closed? It must have been strange to be the last employee to close the doors.

She walked to the front porch of another small cottage named Birch Cottage and sat on the front step, trying to imagine the people who'd lived there. She pulled out her notebook and drew a map of the grounds based on the remaining buildings.

She shivered again and decided to get moving—the atmosphere had started to feel oppressive. There was something about this place that felt so sad she could hardly bear it.

To warm up, she walked quickly around the green and peered into windows. Some cottages contained simple furnishings, but vandals had cut up and burned most objects. She took pictures of the sleeping porches, the abandoned gardens, and the boarded up windows.

It seemed like a strange thought, but she wondered if places like this retained something of the spirit or the suffering of the people who had passed through. Ghosts, she thought, and shivered again. She'd never entertained the thought of ghosts or spirits inhabiting places, but she couldn't deny that something here was unsettling. She wondered what Jazz would think about all of it.

There was a story here—she could feel it. And unless some enormous obstacle arose, she hoped to be the one to tell it. Just knowing Louise had been here made it seem more personal and more necessary. Jazz was right— she needed to stop worrying about whether she had the ability to do it, and just get on with the work.

The project was more complex that she'd originally thought. It would take enormous skill to weave together the design argument with the patient experience. She hoped her advisor would share her enthusiasm for the topic. Although she turned the car heater to high, she still shivered all the way back to the lake house. How had people slept in those unheated porches at the san?

She'd have to work hard on a well-organized proposal. She'd start with something about how the institution represented an important chapter in the history of medicine. Then she'd focus on the question of design related to healing. She'd have to scan images and architectural drawings of the lay-out of the buildings to provide visual support.

Maybe Jazz was right—she needed to finish her thesis, but also to think ahead to a project that would speak to a broader audience. Even if her advisor rejected the proposal, she knew she had to do it. Obstacles just made one jump higher, Jazz had once told her. If she could get Louise talking about her time there, it might help her to understand how the design worked from a physician's point of view. And in the process, she'd learn more about Louise's life and choices. There was a lot more to uncover than she'd ever realized. Only a child assumed that older people's lives were uncomplicated; she was getting the feeling that her aunt and her parents had dealt with a lot while attempting to keep her life untroubled and coherent.

Chapter 12

WHEN she returned from her visit to the sanatorium, Nori was relieved to find that Louise had rested during her absence. The medications seemed to take the edge off her pain without making her sleep all the time. It was a fine balance, as the nurse had explained to Nori.

As Belinda prepared to leave, Nori handed her a bottle of gin as a thank you gift.

"You didn't need to do that," she said with a huge smile.

"I really appreciate your willingness to stay late."

"I'll save this for summer nights on my porch. Hopefully, I won't have to wait too long for those."

Nori knew she never would have managed any of this without her help. Some of the other aides who covered shifts were much less proficient. She appreciated the fact that Belinda had a strong sense of loyalty to Louise. They'd known each other for a long time and Louise had helped her when one of Belinda's children had been very ill. Nori had been so threatened by Belinda when she first arrived. In retrospect it now seemed silly.

Nori sat with Louise and told her about her visit. "You should have seen the place. It was so creepy. I walked around and peeked in windows. Vandals had painted stuff all over the walls and there was broken glass everywhere. The way the wind moved through the trees there—it's weird, but I felt like I heard people sighing."

She gave Louise a sip of water.

Nori continued. "It was so amazing to know that you had worked there. And you lived in that nurses' residence?"

Louise smiled. "I'm glad you got the see what was left of the place. The views were splendid and most of the buildings were designed to take advantage of the setting. As a woman doctor, I wasn't allowed to have my own cottage like the male doctors, so I lived in the nurses' residence. We had to ring a bell at the door and wait till the superintendent let us in. Despite the supervision, nurses escaped through the back fire escape."

"Some of the literature referred to a 'healing environment.' Did you encounter those ideas when you were there?"

"The original founders believed that the building itself and its setting would facilitate healing—an idea that was shared by similar institutions around the world. Having nature and fresh air promoted curing."

"But modern hospital design shifted the focus to efficiency instead?"

Louise nodded. "Efficiency became one of the primary values, and in the case of the operating room, those improvements were welcome."

"When you first arrived at the san, did you believe that the environment of care could have a healing influence?"

Louise gazed at the window and was silent for a while. "When I arrived at the san, I was completely convinced that science would bring about the desired cure."

"But something changed?"

"I never lost my faith in science. But I did find it hard to account for patients who experienced healing without scientific interventions—no surgery, no medications. Whether it was the fresh mountain air, the beauty of the setting, or something else, I had to admit that there was something mysterious about healing that could not be attributed to science."

"And there were other sanatoria located around the world?"

"There were institutions in Finland, Switzerland, and Holland. Patients also went to tent camps in the desert to get the benefit of dry air. I believe notions of a healing environment were included in the hospice movement.

"I've had time to think about all that. From my bed, I see the same view that I have loved for years and that gives me great peace. We both know there's no hope of curing my disease—but even when confined to this bed, I feel the possibility of saying goodbye to the things I love. That is much better than a hospital bed. Maybe our ideas of healing were too narrow. I think that the job of science is to explain how medicine works, whereas the job of faith or theology is to explain why—why we suffer, why we can still hope, how healing happens. They are two different languages that sometimes tango and sometimes dance alone. Although I chose to work in science, when I learned the language of faith, I became a better doctor. But I never gave up my first allegiance to science."

Nori felt frustrated. Why did Louise speak in such riddles? She'd always been so practical. It was frustrating to have both Louise and Jazz talking about religion, and she felt excluded. She wanted to accuse them of selling out as a weakness, but she had to admit that if there was strength, it was to be found in both of them. They had an unblinking way of facing the world that was enviable. She sometimes felt like a child in comparison. And not just a child, but an overindulged one.

She looked at the view and wondered how she would feel in Louise's place. "When my mother was sick, she refused to be transferred to an inpatient facility."

"I can understand that. I hope I can stay here till the end."

Nori took a big breath. Louise talked easily about the end—but Nori still felt anxious about it every time it was mentioned. She briefly wondered if her own fears about the topic made it difficult for her aunt to feel heard, but she brushed that thought away.

"Now, let me see the map you've drawn," she said as she pointed to the paper in Nori's lap.

Nori handed her the page and watched as Louise traced her long finger along the pathways that crossed the central green.

"There was a library over there. And some of the doctors had residences along this road. I can't remember exactly, but there were some more buildings here. A research lab and the administration building stood there."

"I'll show you the final version when I've finished adding all the buildings. It still surprises me that the whole history seems to be largely forgotten."

"Things change quickly. The belief that tuberculosis had been eradicated meant that the whole chapter could be closed. Until drug resistant TB emerged."

"I probably need to discuss drug resistant TB in my proposal to underline the relevance of the topic. I had the strangest experience while I was there." Nori looked at Louise and hesitated. "I sat on the front steps of a cottage, Birch, I think it was. And I had this strange perception of pain that felt as if it were my own but also someone else's. I know that sounds really weird. Maybe my imagination was working overtime."

"I have a great deal of respect for that kind of intuition. Most of us don't have the capacity to listen well enough."

"You don't think I was imagining things?"

"You felt what you felt. No one else should tell you what that was."

The next day, Nori knocked at Ada's apartment, where she'd been invited for tea. She was met by a frail, but alert, woman, wearing a sweater and skirt and comfortable walking shoes. She poured tea from a Brown Betty pot into china cups that had been set out on a tray.

"I understand your sister wrote letters to you while she was a patient?" Nori asked.

"She did." Ada passed her a cup of tea followed by a plate of homemade shortbread cookies. "Would you like to see them?"

Nori looked up in surprise. "I would love to see them."

When she left after tea, Nori carried a packet of Maggie's letters.

As soon as Louise was settled, Nori sat at the kitchen table to read.

Christmas 1952

Dear Ada:

Yesterday we had a Christmas party at the lodge. We dressed up and did each other's hair and makeup. You wouldn't have recognized me—I looked so sophisticated. A driver took us to the lodge in a fancy car where they had reserved the main room for us. When we walked into the room, I felt like a princess in a magical winter wonderland. A huge Christmas tree stood in front of the window and a fire crackled in the hearth. While we sampled appetizers and drinks at an open bar, a man in a velvet blazer played carols on the piano. Many of the doctors there were already inebriated and singing along to the carols; some of the girls wasted no time catching up.

I met one man who worked as an inspector for hospitals. Although based in Albany, he travelled all over the state. His wedding ring was enough to make me move away quickly.

I'll never forget what it felt like to dance in that room with the lights sparkling and the music playing. I saw the snow falling heavily outside and I hoped we'd have no trouble getting back tonight because I wasn't planning to spend the night.

The whole thing is very hush-hush. We've been warned to keep quiet about our "privileges" or we'll lose them. I have no idea whether we are part of the san gossip and I can't imagine how we might not be, but no one has said anything to me. We're lucky at Birch Cottage because the road runs right behind the cottage and we can slip out the back door without anybody seeing us leave. The front is pretty private with birches and evergreens. I don't care. It's not like we can get in any trouble when it's the boss who's throwing the party.

Some of the girls got louder and sillier as the evening went on. You asked me in your last letter if anything serious happens. It's mostly a lot of flirting, but the guys often have rooms at the lodge and sometimes couples slip away. I figure it's not my business. You also asked whether the men are afraid of kissing the patients from a san. The joke that the girls tell is that the men don't kiss them, but they'll do anything else you want. If you ever tell any of this to mother, I will personally come and hang you from the rafters with your bed sheets. I know that it sounds pretty risqué and some of these girls have had some pretty wild lives before they got here. But if you were stuck in that san for months on end, you'd be happy to get a chance to feel special, to put on a nice dress, and to have some fun.

There was one thing that did upset all of us and I wasn't sure whether to tell you about it. That girl from New York that did my makeup, she was discharged suddenly and was taken to the train station. We weren't sure why she had to leave so abruptly. She told one of the others that she was pregnant and that one of the men had given her a hundred dollars and told her to go home to her family.

And I know you're going to ask why doctors can't make sure that the girls don't get pregnant, but in her case, something went wrong. But don't worry!!! I am nowhere near taking that leap with any of these guys. I just want to have some fun. I don't think people on the outside realize what it's like to live in a world where the angel of death hovers over us and our job is to pretend that it won't happen to us.

I'm planning to save myself for whatever life is waiting for me, but if I'm honest, it does make you wonder sometimes about what kind of choices you'd make if you really knew you were going to die soon. Not that I plan to!

I am so determined to get home and get my studies started. I hope you are enjoying your courses so you can get a fancy job. If you get an apartment, then maybe I can come and live with you when I get out of here. After all, I don't really want to go home again. I'm older now and I don't think I want to go back there. I know that if you get your own fellow, you won't want me as roomie, but hopefully that's not going to happen before I get out. You have to tell me if you have any secrets in that regard!

I think of you so often. Thanks for writing to me and sending me the care package. I loved the skin crème and the lipstick and I sure hope you didn't spend too much. Because the air is so dry here, I worry that my skin will crack in the cold. When I come home, you won't recognize me because my face will resemble an old pair of leather hiking boots. Write me soon.

Hugs,
Maggie.

Chapter 13

Nori carried a pot of tea to the table and offered Ben some banana bread—there seemed to be numerous loaves of it in the freezer. People were very generous with food offerings. Although she knew she should make some attempt to keep track of donations and write thank you cards, dishes were dropped off anonymously on the porch or in the mailbox. Because Louise had little appetite and Nori couldn't eat all the food all by herself, she shared with Belinda and the other aides.

"Tell me about your research. How are things going?" Ben asked.

"Thanks for putting me in touch with Ada. I had a good visit with her and she gave me some letters that her sister wrote while she was a patient at the san."

"Anything useful?"

"She described secret parties that doctors gave at an off-site location. Some of the young patients were loaned fancy dresses to wear to a lodge where the administrator brought together influential people from government and health care agencies. Although Ada's sister seemed happy to leave the san for an evening's entertainment, it still seems like such an abuse of power to me. Those women were vulnerable."

Ben shook his head sadly. "I agree."

"Ada gave me permission to use the materials. Her sister passed many years ago and there's no other family members. Am I wandering too far from the question of design?"

"I guess it's a reminder that the design was just part of the puzzle. Beliefs about the rights of patients, the power of consent, the control of institutions, and the role of professionals were all embodied in the design. I think the building symbolized the rules of the relationship. I'm not sure those young women had much choice."

Nori nodded. "In that case, Ada's sister's story might be one example of how that design allowed such practices to be unobserved?"

"The design seemed to encourage secrets. Why don't you talk to me about what you have so far and I'll sketch it out? Sometimes it's helpful to see a diagram of your thinking."

Nori passed him some paper and a pencil and tried to collect her thoughts. "I have to give some overview of the historical background of the disease and methods of treatment. The san has to be placed in historical context."

Ben wrote that down and then waited quietly for her to continue.

"I need to describe the building and how the setting was perceived as contributing to healing. People left the cities, which were considered unhealthy, for this mountain location because they believed it could cure them."

Ben nodded. "Good. Keep going."

Nori gazed at the lake as she gathered her thoughts. "An exploration of the patient and staff experience might give some insight into how people functioned within the design. After all, it's not just the design that interests me, but how design affected behaviour."

"Patient and staff experience," Ben echoed as he added that to the page. "What else?"

"This next part is hard. There's something I need to discuss about how society isolated those patients. I'm not sure how to put that into a sentence, but it relates to the stigma of the disease."

"What if you call that the broader ethical questions? It wasn't just the building that led to the isolation, but the whole system took away the rights of patients and treated them like children."

Nori nodded. "One of the other questions seems to be about adapting or resisting change. But maybe that's too far outside the topic?"

"Could you say that those who stood to benefit from the system worked hard to keep it from changing?"

Nori nodded. "I think so. I'll have to see if that can be substantiated, but it seems like such an elaborate infrastructure wouldn't adapt well to changes in the disease treatment. You couldn't easily turn such an enormous institution into an outpatient treatment facility."

While Ben worked on his diagram, she didn't interrupt.

He held up the page and used the pencil as a pointer. "You start with the introduction, review the literature on infectious diseases with a focus on tuberculosis, provide a case study of the san, give an intensive look at the patient and staff experience based on primary sources like diaries and let-ters, and then finish with a critical evaluation of the design and care model with its ethical implications. I think this would be a very interesting study. I'd read it."

Nori was surprised. "Fantastic. Would you like to write it?"

He shook his head. "I'll leave the writing to you. I get enough practice writing sermons." He seemed pleased. "You really think it works?"

"You're good at this. This helps me to picture the structure. My problem is I try to include everything and then I get overwhelmed."

"Don't do more research than you need to do. One of my professors used to say that the only good thesis is a completed one. Keep a file for future projects."

"That's funny. Jazz told me the same thing. If you don't mind me saying, you're one hell of a priest. I might have to start going to church."

"You're always welcome. Our coffee hour is particularly good because Jazz supplies us with fresh roast." He stood up. "I must get going. I have a new mom and baby to visit."

"Why don't you take her one of these pumpkin loaves? She probably doesn't have time to bake, and I can't eat it."

"Thanks. I'll be back next week and I look forward to seeing your progress."

"The pressure is on. I think you've really given me a framework."

She watched from the kitchen window as he backed up his car and drove away.

Later that evening, when Louise was settled for the night, Nori sat at the dining room table. Although she was excited by Ben's map and by Ada's letters, she knew that it was time to let her advisor know what she was doing.

While the house was quiet, Nori wrote a brief description of her research to date. She attached it to an email to her advisor. Although she thought about leaving it until the morning, she decided to send the draft right away.

The next morning, Nori put the mug of tea on the tray that fit across the bed. Her mind was still on Ada and her sister's experiences at Birch Cottage. She wondered if they'd deliberately transferred young and attractive women to that cottage. The administrator seemed to know how to manipulate people to get the information or access he wanted.

When she brought tea to the bedroom, Louise seemed alert and comfortable.

"You've known Ada for a long time, right?"

Louise nodded. "Her sister was at the san when I arrived, but I didn't have any responsibility for their cottage because they had their own doctor. I only got to know Ada when I moved to town years later and we realized I had overlapped with her sister's time at the san."

"She let me read through letters that her sister wrote from the san. Did she ever talk to you about those?"

"Not really. By the time we met, we had moved on with our lives. I know her sister left the san when it closed and became a teacher. Ada moved to town and married a man who was employed by the public works department. When he died, she sold her house and moved into the senior's residence."

"In those letters, her sister described private parties sponsored by the san for the doctors and for state health officials. A group of young women were regularly driven to a lodge to party with the men. They were given party clothes and free drinks. All this was apparently arranged by the administrator."

Louise shook her head. "I had no idea. But there were many retreats and events that involved the male doctors to which I was never invited. It was irresponsible for those men to take advantage of those young women."

"When you took the fellowship there, what did you expect your duties to be?"

Louise put her mug on the tray, but kept her hands circled around its warmth. "The fellowship was advertised as a surgical one. I was expected to do rounds, be on call, admit patients, and develop a staff education program. As the first fellowship holder, they weren't always sure what to do with me."

"The program wasn't as developed as you thought it would be?"

"They were proud of their reputation for providing advanced care, but it seemed like they were resting on their laurels. They were very satisfied with themselves and had little interest in learning anything new. When you think you're the best, there's not much room for improvement."

"But you believed that change was necessary?"

"Change was long overdue. Tuberculosis had become an industry. Companies made blankets and sleeping chairs and spittoons and all kinds of accessories and people worked in and around the sanatorium to keep it running. The town itself had a booming hospitality industry that provided supportive lodging and food for visiting families. Even the state benefitted from keeping things as they were."

"And what about the administration?"

"I think the management worked to resist any change. The board seemed to be in complete agreement and I believe they were well compensated to stay that way. People can become complicit in evil while maintaining a sense that they are doing good."

"They must have been annoyed when you marched in and told them they should do things differently."

"I think 'marching' might be overstating it," Louise said with a smile. "It seemed to me that people deserved to benefit from the most recent developments in care."

"But for those men to be challenged by a young woman doctor. . . ."

Louise looked above Nori's head at the window and the lake. "I just did what I thought was right. It wasn't anything unusual."

"I sometimes worry about digging up things that people would rather keep quiet. Perhaps there are some who might want to suppress the story? Or am I being paranoid?"

Louise paused. "There's no doubt that many have mixed emotions about that place. To tell the whole story, you'll need to explore those contradictions or at least suggest they existed. The very design that was meant to bring about healing also allowed a variety of abuses to occur—and for some, that's still a painful legacy. I'm not sure that keeping silence about that time has facilitated the healing of all those troubled people."

"It's quite a responsibility."

"I agree. But if you choose to do this, I have complete confidence in you."

"I feel like it's a story that has to be told."

Louise smiled at her. "Excellent," she said. "In that case, let me tell you something. I've been trying to recall where I have stored something that might help. When I had construction done to remodel the downstairs, things were moved around to keep them safe. Now I'm not sure where they ended up."

Nori looked at her. "What kinds of things?"

"I kept a diary that year at the san. I didn't want it to fall into the wrong hands because it was deeply personal. But I also didn't want to impose it on you, in case you thought I was putting pressure on you to work on a particular topic."

"I'd love to read your diary. Would you mind if I looked around for it?" Nori asked.

"Be my guest. I apologize for the mess in my study. The spring-cleaning project ended prematurely when I got sick. You can look in the attic too, but take a flashlight and be very careful up there."

"I'll check it out."

Louise smiled. "Good luck. I'll have a nap while you look around. I certainly hope it's worth the trouble. I haven't read it for years—it's not easy to revisit that time. Just because it was a long time ago doesn't mean it isn't still tender." She paused. "But if it's helpful to you, use the diary in whatever way you see fit."

Just before Nori went to the attic, she checked her laptop and found an email from her advisor. She read it quickly and then reread it more carefully. Dr. Carver sounded surprised and even somewhat irritated by the direction that Nori had taken and reminded her that if she was planning to work with living subjects, she would have to follow the departmental and university guidelines on ethics review.

Nori had hoped she might be excited, but instead, Dr. Carver expressed concern that Nori was taking on too much. She had attached the guidelines for writing a proposal and sternly advised Nori to follow them literally or the committee would reject her proposal, no matter how exciting the topic might sound.

Nori felt utterly deflated by her lack of enthusiasm. She should have waited to send the email. Perhaps Dr. Carver hadn't realized that it was just a rough draft of her current thinking, not a proposal.

Should she apologize or retract the email? How bad was it? In a worst case scenario, she'd have to offer to withdraw from the program. If her advisor was annoyed now, what would she be like when she saw the final product? All of her familiar anxieties and doubts rose to the surface. Perhaps the topic *was* beyond her abilities. She sat at the table and held her head in her hands. Why had she let Jazz talk her into believing she could do this? She hadn't even been that good of a student in high school. What was she doing at Yale?

Nori slowly got up and went to the door of Louise's room. She appeared to be resting quietly, so she didn't disturb her. How long would she still be with them? Nori hated to think about that day when Louise would pass. She desperately wanted to show Louise that she'd been worthy of her support. In order to do that while she was still alive, Nori knew she had to push on through obstacles. Louise had trusted her with her diary and believed that Nori could tell the story. There was just no room for doubt now.

There was no point in overreacting to Dr. Carver's email. Perhaps she'd read Nori's email late at night when she was tired from the day. Maybe if she could write to reassure her that she was still in the early stages of research and was merely testing the topic. And she'd refer to the proposal guidelines to let Dr. Carver know that she'd read them and would comply in her final proposal. She wished they could talk in person, but that simply wasn't possible.

Chapter 14

Nori located the flashlight in the kitchen cupboard. She'd already searched for the diary in the filing cabinet and on the shelves of Louise's study with no luck. The attic was next on her search list.

Although the flashlight beam was fairly weak, it was better than nothing. Nori pulled down the staircase that folded up into the hall ceiling. She'd seen Louise go up there occasionally in the past, but she'd never climbed up herself. When she flipped the wall switch, a single light bulb cast a weak and flickering light over the third floor attic. Two small windows on either side provided additional light. Nori hesitated at the top of the stairs—the place felt cold and unwelcoming.

As she used the flashlight to swat away the long silky threads of spider webs that reached across the room, the beam from the flashlight scrolled over the floorboards and beams. She directed it into the corners, trying to orient herself to the space. In one corner stood a cedar chest and a table; in the opposite corner, a metal clothing rack held several plastic moth bags. The odor of mothballs wafted from the bags and boxes.

Nori rooted through one of the boxes that contained Louise's shoes. She admired a pair of black suede heels in mint condition. The box also contained well-scuffed penny loafers, walking shoes, and a pair of leather hiking boots that Nori recognized from past hikes together—it was a compilation of her aunt's life. She closed the box and pushed it against the wall and then placed the flashlight on the oak table. She unzipped the moth bag and ran her hand with admiration over the soft and curly texture of a Persian lamb jacket. The smell of cedar and mothballs mixed together and infused the attic as she opened bags. She pulled out a black chiffon dress with a matching silk slip and held it up against her to see if it might fit. She tried to imagine a younger version of Louise wearing dresses and heels to an event. Although her mother had always described her sister as anti-fashion, these pieces were classic.

She opened the lid of the cedar chest and felt around in the piles of soft piles of sweaters and scarves. "Bingo," she said with delight when she felt the leather cover and bound spine of what appeared to be a handcrafted journal in soft brown leather.

After closing the cedar chest securely, she made sure that all the moth bags were zipped up. She pushed the folding staircase back up and carried the light and journal to the living room. She couldn't wait to start reading.

Just as she opened the cover of the journal, Louise cried out. Her voice sounded high-pitched, and the sound of it gave Nori chills.

"Mary," Louise called.

Nori went to check, still carrying the journal she'd just opened in one hand. It was impossible to put it down. "Mary's not here," she reassured Louise. "It's me, Nori. Were you having a dream?" Nori touched her aunt's forehead. Her skin was clammy and her respirations were rapid. Nori wiped her forehead with a cool cloth and sat next to her. "Are you having any pain?" she asked.

"I think I was dreaming," Louise replied in a more normal voice. "Did I wake you?"

"Not at all. How about a sip of water? I'll sit here till you go to sleep."

With Louise settled, Nori opened the journal again. When the forced air furnace came on, it sounded like a train running through the room. Nori kicked off the lap blanket as the room warmed up and began to read.

PART II

A tuberculosis patient should cultivate outdoor pleasures whenever possible and, as soon as his condition permits him to move about, a wide field is open to him. On the porch, however, many take up bird study and with the aid of opera or field glasses it is remarkable how many birds a patient can come to know even while in bed. Botany, too, may be begun in a similar way, for many patients or friends willingly bring strange or common wild flowers to anyone whose field of action is strictly limited. It must be fully appreciated, however, that the bird life and plants of any locality are so great in number that at first the bewilderment of riches seems overwhelming. Photography is now made so easy that little experience is needed to take a fairly good photograph, but much study and interest can be aroused by pursuing such a hobby further, and for these color photography has perennial charms.

—Dr. Lawrason Brown[*]

---

[*] Lawrason Brown, *Rules for Recovery from Pulmonary Tuberculosis* (3rd ed. Philadelphia: Lea and Febiger, 1919), 104.

Chapter 15

LOUISE, SARANAC SANATORIUM, 1950

WHEN I drove through the south gates, I thought I had entered a country estate, but once I'd parked the car and looked back, it felt more like an enclosure.

I was amazed to see that the place was far more extensive than I'd realized. Numerous buildings backed up to the parking lot, and, beyond them, mountain peaks. It was a gorgeous setting for a sanatorium, surrounded by mountains, water, and trees, built into the slope of Mt. Pisgah, looking out over the Saranac River Valley and Mt. Baker beyond.

With a gentle slam of my car door, I stepped back to admire the car that Robert had helped me purchase secondhand from a parishioner in his congregation. I'd finally given up the old rust heap that had seen me through medical school. This car filled me with an extraordinary amount of pride. Even after the long trip on dusty roads from Albany, the chrome and beige paint still gleamed.

Pa would have enjoyed driving through the mountains in a car like this—he might have commented on the changing scenery and hung his head out of the window to breathe the fresh air. Even though his favorite reading on the farm had included an atlas and several ancient National Geographic magazines, he'd never had the opportunity to leave the county where his farm stood. If he had aspirations to travel, he'd never spoken them out loud. In fact, his one defining feature was a desire to stay in place on the land he owned. There were times I envied him that sense of place. Not that I wanted to be stuck there—it had been a huge relief to leave the farm to go to college. Of course, I had traded the familiarity of the farm for a string of anonymous and inhospitable dormitory rooms. I could only hope that the san would offer me something slightly better for my accommodation, but I warned myself to keep my expectations low.

I left my bag in the car while I checked with the front office. The letter of acceptance had been short on details. Because I'd written to let them know that I would arrive on Sunday afternoon, I hoped that they were ready to welcome me. I'd only ever worked in hospitals before this, and I sensed this would be different.

Walking slowly towards the administrative building, I admired the combination of stone and wood used to build the structure. Night likely fell quickly here—afternoon shadows had already begun to angle long fingers between the buildings and across the lot. I shivered and buttoned up the mohair cardigan that Mary had knitted for me as an early Christmas present. "You'll need it," she'd said. "That mountain air will get very cold."

I wondered how patients felt when they were taken through these gates. Were they reluctant to enter—unsure and afraid of what awaited them? Did they experience the kind of homesickness I was feeling?

A man in a security uniform slouched on a bench near the door. His half-opened eyes watched me cross the parking lot. Although his expression was sleepy, he reminded me of the barn cats at the farm that crouched motionless, but ready to pounce on the hapless barn mice. Actually, I doubted his ability to pounce because his belly hung over the waistband of his pants, and the buttons on his shirt strained. If he were the welcoming delegation, I mused, then I wouldn't blame anyone for running in the opposite direction, right out of the gates, and down the gravel road.

Passing by the bench, I nodded politely in his direction; he responded by exhaling a cloud of cigarette smoke. He seemed like a sullen fellow, and I felt an instant dislike. I especially didn't like the way his eyes travelled over my dress. I was still wearing the Sunday clothes that I'd worn to church with Robert and Mary in the morning. I wasn't a churchgoer, but it seemed rude to enjoy the hospitality of a clergyman and not attend his church. Robert certainly put many hours into crafting his sermons. Although they didn't capture my imagination, the congregation seemed to appreciate him and his preaching. It was unusual for me to have an idle hour and I often found myself daydreaming through most of the service. This morning I had pictured myself in rugged clothes and hiking boots, leading a group of avid hikers up one of the high peaks of the Adirondacks.

At the reception desk, the switchboard operator answered and transferred calls. Between those calls, she looked at me with curiosity. She wore a cotton cardigan over her floral dress and her reading glasses were tipped halfway down the bridge of her nose. Her graying hair was curled in a permanent wave, bobby-pinned back behind her ears. A packet of cigarettes was visible inside her purse, open on the chair beside her. I caught a hint of mint gum that didn't disguise the smell of smoke.

"Can I help you?" she asked, looking over her reading glasses.

"I'm Dr. Garrett." When she gave no sign of recognition, I explained further. "I'm here to do a fellowship in surgery."

The receptionist continued to look at me blankly. She checked her clipboard. "I don't see anything here about a fellowship."

"Dr. Clarke sent a letter of confirmation." I passed the letter to her. What could have gone wrong? I'd notified Dr. Clarke of my expected arrival.

The woman shrugged. "Well, he never told me and now he's off for a long weekend."

I tried to control my impatience. "A room is apparently reserved in the nurses' residence for me, according to this letter of confirmation." I tapped the letter to underscore my point.

"You're a doctor?" she asked, looking at me with curiosity.

I nodded. Had she never seen a woman doctor?

"Let me check with housekeeping."

While she called housekeeping, I studied a glass case in the foyer that contained historical photographs and a variety of awards. In one picture, four men sat on an open porch with lap blankets draped over their legs. They looked cold and miserable. Beside the photograph was a plaque that acknowledged the sanatorium as the best facility in North America. Another picture showed a factory owner from town receiving an award for service. His factory produced the wooden lounge chairs that were standard furniture in the sanatorium. I silently hoped that they didn't persist in putting the patients out in the cold as a cure. As far as I knew, that practice had ended decades ago.

I heard the jingle of a set of keys and walked back to the desk.

"Here you go." The receptionist slid a key toward me. "You're in room 202 in the nurses' residence next door. The superintendent will let you in— just ring the front door bell. Jack can help you with your bags." She tapped on the window to get the attention of the guard. "Come and help," she yelled in a peremptory way.

"Will I also receive a key for the front door?" I asked.

"The superintendent will let you in. There's someone assigned to be there round the clock."

Before I could question that, the guard sauntered inside.

He looked me up and down and then asked, "Where's she going?"

"Nurses' residence," the receptionist said. "Help with her luggage."

He turned and headed out the door and I followed him. He took the suitcase out of the trunk and carried it to the lobby of the residence. Without a word, he turned and left.

"Thanks," I called to his back, but he was already on his way.

The superintendent, wearing a blue dress uniform and sensible shoes, reviewed the rules of the residence with me and handed me a note from Dr. Clarke with instructions to be at the operating room by nine in the morning to meet the head nurse. I felt relieved that some preparations and plans had been made for my stay. It was strange to come all this way and to have no one expecting me. Dr. Clarke's original letter had suggested that I had been carefully selected for a prestigious fellowship.

Prestigious was not the word that came to mind as I looked around the second floor room that resembled every other dorm room I'd inhabited throughout my medical studies. The humble furnishings included a single bed, dresser, and a small desk. The curtains and bedspread were sewn from faded green and beige plaid cotton. The tile floor had been carefully waxed and polished, and a hint of wax still hung in the air. Behind a door was a narrow closet containing some hangers. On the shelf above the metal bar, an extra blanket was folded for cold nights. I placed my hand over the radiator but felt no heat. Mary would groan if she saw the room, I thought, and I wasn't far from groaning myself. But I told myself to smarten up and be grateful for what I had. Driving that fancy car had given me "notions," as Ma might say.

I put my clothes in the drawers and hung a few things in the closet. Mary had taken me shopping for a few basic items. She said my clothes were a disgrace, so she insisted that I buy new pajamas, underwear, and a good dress.

I lined the windowsill with the apples and pears and a few bags of tea that I'd packed at Mary's house. With any luck, I could make tea later in the small kitchen at the end of the hall.

I hoped that my room would have a view of the mountains, but instead, I had a perfect view of the parking lot. At least I could keep an eye on my car from my vantage point. Maybe there'd be time to locate the hiking trails and parks in the surrounding countryside. And I'd see the mountains every day while I worked in the infirmary. I was trying hard to cheer myself up but I felt gloomy, and the room didn't help.

I hoped the clinical experience would be exciting and challenging. Hopefully it would be within my capacities—after all, I'd had a fairly rigid internship at Yale and had carefully brushed up on diseases and surgery of the chest before I arrived. I know they'd all be watching so I wanted to reassure them that I was the right candidate for the fellowship. If they weren't used to women doctors, I needed to establish myself quickly.

My gray mohair blanket on the foot of the bed added some personality to the room. Eager to get outside and walk the grounds before dark, I locked the door and headed outside. The sun was dipping below the mountains, and the temperature was plunging along with it.

I walked towards a central green behind the main administration building and followed the road past a series of buildings that included a schoolhouse, a series of small cottages, the library, and a stone chapel. Although the road continued beyond the buildings, I didn't want to go too far—I had to find something to eat before the cafeteria closed for the day. The superintendent had warned me that food services were limited on Sunday.

As I passed the small stone chapel, I saw a group of people leave the building and continue their conversations outside. A tall black man told a story to three other men—he had broad shoulders and stood a foot above the rest of them. I estimated he was in his sixties as his hair was completely gray. He looked like someone's kindly grandfather, and he seemed to have a natural authority to which people responded. He reminded me so much of Pastor Cal in Mississippi that I had to look twice. He nodded politely to acknowledge my presence and then focused on the circle of men around him. The group burst into laughter at something he said.

I turned around to locate the cafeteria and followed the smell of chicken soup that lingered in the air. A sign advised that the table was reserved for medical staff, so I obediently sat there. I happened to be the only person. As I unwrapped the sandwich, I imagined Mary and Robert sitting down to a proper Sunday meal—roast beef, potatoes, and vegetables. I would call her next week when there was more to tell. Sitting alone in a darkened cafeteria with a stale sandwich didn't make much of a story. The place felt a bit somber but perhaps it was just my mood—I'd expected a warmer welcome. I looked forward to immersing myself in the work and leaving my uncertainties behind.

The next morning I went to the operating room to introduce myself to the head nurse who gave me a tour and a brief orientation. Reading the list of scheduled surgeries for the day made me feel more confident—the list in-cluded standard surgical procedures that I'd done many times. I was slightly disappointed in how routine it all seemed, but I told myself not to judge so quickly.

Yawning with increasing frequency, I obediently read the policy and procedure manual in the staff lounge while waiting for Dr. Patterson, the chief, to finish his surgery. I was tired—the new room and the silence of the night had kept me up till all hours.

I hoped the chief would clarify what was expected of me. Sitting in the small waiting room drinking tepid coffee did make me wonder what I'd gotten myself into. Although I didn't enjoy being idle, I told myself to be patient in this new situation and I tried not to compare everything to Yale. I was pretty sure that they didn't want to hear about my Yale experience, and I didn't want to come across as an ivy-league know-it-all. For men, that kind of behaviour was considered normal, whereas for women, it was considered bad manners.

I read the procedure manual, with its endless list of patient rules. Ev-ery moment was controlled and monitored, including regular temperature taking and enforced rest time. The recommended nutritional standards included three meals a day and four glasses of milk. By that standard, I was likely malnourished. I usually ate on the run between patients and surgeries. Patients who were ambulatory were allowed to do jobs around the san and reside in the small cottages with roommates.

I felt sorry for the patients on bed rest. Although various entertain-ments and handicrafts were provided for distraction, the boredom had to be overwhelming. When Mary had been confined to bed while she recovered from polio, she'd been so grumpy, that it had been a relief for all of us when she became mobile. Did extended bed rest actually effect cures? I told myself to stop judging until I figured out the lay of the land, but if the manual was any indication, the prescribed regimen was an artifact of an earlier century. I only hoped that the operating room and surgical wing were more modern, or I'd never last.

Dr. Patterson invited me into his office near the operating room. A few African violet plants thrived on the windowsill. The clouds that hung around the distant peak of the mountain distracted me, but I forced myself to focus on the doctor. Although a nice looking man in his fifties, his face suggested he had lived a hard life. His skin was deeply lined and his eyes seemed flat. I noticed a fine hand tremor when he moved some papers to the side of his desk. He seemed uncertain about where to begin the conversation.

I tried to fill in the gap. "This is really nice," I said, waving my hand over the office and the view.

He nodded. His name was embroidered in blue thread on the chest pocket of his white coat. His hair was almost completely gray and parted sharply to one side, with edges trimmed up the sides like a soldier.

"Are you finding your way around?" he asked me and then quickly looked away.

"I'm ready to get to work if someone can clarify what I'm expected to do."

"Dr. Clarke is away but he'll see you on his return. Here's the on-call rotation and the Operating Room schedule. I could really use some help. We have an admission coming in this afternoon. Could you take that?"

I felt relieved. This was familiar territory. I hadn't come all this way to read policy and procedure manuals. In fact, there was no time to waste if I hoped to do some research while here. With any luck, I'd be able to produce a publishable paper before I left that would strengthen my applications to residencies.

I had thought about asking Dr. Patterson about research possibilities but decided I'd better meet Dr. Clarke first and get some idea of his expectations. Dr. Patterson seemed weary and overworked and I wondered if he had any interest in research. It was important to set the right impression and neither act too aggressive, nor too relaxed.

"Before I go, could ask one thing? Most of the procedures on the OR list are standard thoracic ones. Are you doing any new procedures here as well?"

He continued to look out the window. "That's the bulk of what we do here. If it's not what you expected, I'm sorry. If you don't mind some advice from someone who's been here for a long while, it would be wise to go along with what you're told to do. You'll be here for less than one year and hopefully you will find the experience useful. But don't be disappointed if the surgeries seem routine. In an academic setting, there are always new procedures to learn that keep one challenged. You will no doubt have a brilliant career ahead of you and someday you might be grateful for this experience. But I don't want to hide the reality of the situation from you."

I felt a twinge of alarm. "But . . ." and then I told myself to be quiet. Was he suggesting that his own career had been less than impressive or was he simply trying to prepare me for a year of drudgery?

"Focus on your research and writing. That will make our administrator very happy and will ensure that you'll move on to your next position with ease."

I nodded slowly, trying to take in what he was telling me. "At Yale we observed that some of the more traditional thoracic procedures for TB seemed to do more damage than provide any cure or relief."

He looked out the window and said nothing.

He wasn't interested in what was happening at Yale. Why did I think I had to bring that into the conversation?

"As I said, I would recommend that you adapt to the program—it is part of what the san promotes as its claim to be an active treatment hospital. If you hope to succeed here, do what you are asked to do, write some papers, and all will be well."

I sat back in my chair and looked at him, but he refused to meet my eyes. I wasn't going to get anything else out of him.

He cleared his throat. "Perhaps it might help to picture the san as a grand old lady. There is still so much life and beauty to respect, but. . . ."

A grand old dame, I thought, who didn't like to change a thing about how she'd set up her claustrophobic living room. That was a bit depressing. I wanted to tell him how committed I was to excellence, but I realized my words were wasted.

He stood up. I took the hint, shook his hand, and left.

A grand old dame, I thought again, as I walked through the halls and saw the patients resting on wooden lounge chairs in the sunroom. I hoped they were getting more treatment than reclining in nineteenth-century chairs.

Chapter 16

LOUISE, SAN, 1950

WALKING down the long hall of the surgical ward, I paused to take another look at the amazing beauty outside the window. The infirmary had been designed to maximize those views for the benefit of the patients on bed rest. There was something to be said for that design, compared to the four-to-eight-bed post-surgical wards that I had worked on in other hospitals that offered no natural light and no beauty. Patients often became disoriented in such settings.

Even though it was only September, the maples were already turning color. Winter promised to be a challenge, if I could believe those who'd warned me about the incessant winter storms in the area. Once the inclement weather arrived, I'd probably use the tunnels under the building to get around. Till then, I was grateful to walk outside as much as possible. The fresh air was truly invigorating.

The janitor at the end of the hall washed the floor with slow rhythmic strokes, leaving glistening floors in his wake. He nodded to me as I tiptoed over the wet tiles. I was starting to recognize some of the cafeteria and maintenance staff, and they were always courteous. It was harder to get to know the nurses in the residence, even though I saw them every morning in the small bathroom at the end of the hall. In the evenings, they relaxed in the lounge and made toast in the kitchen—sometimes burning it and filling the halls with smoke. Although they were polite, it was clear that they did not expect me to join their evening pajama parties. Because I wasn't much for practicing dance steps or fixing makeup, I spent my evenings catching up on professional reading.

As usual, I wore a lab coat over my surgical scrubs. My hair was gathered into a ponytail with several bobby pins keeping it in place. I went to the nurses' station on the surgical unit to admit a new patient. The surgical head nurse wore a fitted white cotton dress uniform. Her white nurse's cap perched on top of her stylish bob. Nurse Benoit was clearly proud of her slim figure and striking looks. Her gold graduation pin was positioned over her name-tag. Her Oxford lace-up uniform shoes had recently been polished with white shoe polish that showed bluish-white streaks where the liquid had dried unevenly.

As I approached, I overheard her say in stern tones, "Miss Reynolds, come back here, please."

I felt sorry for the student nurse who slowly returned to the nursing station.

Nurse Benoit moved close to her face. "Your hair is too long and it's hanging over your uniform collar. I trust you'll take care of that by tomorrow. Or don't return to the ward."

The student nodded and scurried away as fast as the chipmunks that were ubiquitous on the grounds of the san.

"Are you ready to examine the new patient?" she asked. She was all business, but that was fine with me—I wasn't here to build friendships. Based on first impressions, I wouldn't expect much kindness from her. I was determined to give no cause for trouble, but I also had no intention of being bullied by a head nurse.

She indicated that I should follow her with a tip of her head. Carrying her clipboard like it was a private treasure, she marched at a good clip down the hall. Maybe she'd been a military nurse, I thought, as I tried to catch up.

When I followed her into the four-bed male ward, I was temporarily blinded by sunlight streaming in from the back wall windows. The beds were arranged in each of the four corners of the room and were equipped with an over-the-bed table and a bedside cupboard. Narrow closets took up the middle back wall of the room. Only three of the beds were occupied, whereas the fourth was neatly made and empty. Three men rested on the beds wearing institutional pajamas. One patient read an automotive magazine and another listened to a ball game on his transistor radio. When he saw Nurse Benoit, he immediately turned down the volume. The room smelled of pine soap, aftershave, and stale coffee.

Nurse Benoit approached the patient closest to the door and waited for me, with a shift of her shoulders to indicate I was wasting her time by being so slow.

I made a conscious effort to tune her out and to focus on the patient. I glanced at the name above the bed. "Mr. Anderson? I'm Dr. Garrett."

The man nodded and looked at me with evident mistrust. I was used to having patients mistake me for a nurse. I tried to give each patient a moment to get used to the idea that I actually was a doctor. Although once or twice a patient had refused to allow me to examine him and had requested a male doctor instead, usually patients adapted.

The head of his bed was elevated to help him breathe easier. He occasionally fiddled with the nasal oxygen cannula, and I could tell it irritated him to have it on his face. His long, sun-tanned arms rested on the bedrails, and a white band of skin surrounded his left wrist where his watch had been. The watch was on the bedside table—a reminder of his previous life.

I lowered the bed rail and counted his respirations—he was short of breath even while resting. Nurse Benoit pulled one edge of the privacy curtain around the bed. Privacy was an illusion, though, as every word could be heard through the curtain. I was pretty sure the other lads in the room were intensely curious about their new neighbor. One didn't need to study them for long to know they were bored out of their minds.

"How are you feeling?" I asked. Not that I couldn't guess, but I wanted to hear it from him. Assessment required a quality of attention that couldn't be rushed, no matter how many non-verbal hints Nurse Benoit was sending my way. I almost told her she was welcome to leave, but I knew the nurse in charge was obliged to accompany doctors on their rounds. I had no doubt she could make my work difficult if I went out of my way to irritate her now.

I reached over to take his pulse—it felt rapid, and his skin was very hot and dry. His cheeks were flushed.

I unraveled the stethoscope from my pocket and put the rubber tips in my ears. I rubbed the chest piece to warm it up before placing it on his chest.

"My back hurts," he pointed to his back, "and it's hard to catch my breath. Seems pretty stupid when all I do is lie here."

I slid my stethoscope inside the front of his shirt and over his chest hair. "Just breathe normally." The room was quiet—the other men were pretending not to listen and talked to each other in murmurs.

"When did you first start feeling unwell?"

"About two months ago, I got so tired and was up at night coughing. When I started coughing blood, the wife said I should see the doctor and he sent me to this place." He looked up at her. "How long will I be here?" He dropped his guard for a second and I had a glimpse of the naked fear beneath his weathered exterior.

"Hard to say," I said, not wanting to raise his hopes unnecessarily. I listened to his back and then carefully folded up my stethoscope. "We're going to run tests, do an X-ray, and see what kind of treatment you need. It will take a while to sort it all out."

The head nurse pulled back the curtain. As I turned to leave, he grabbed my wrist and spoke with quiet intensity. "Doc, I gotta get home. My business will go under."

I felt his desperation and paused at the bedrail without immediately pulling back my hand. I could tell that Nurse Benoit didn't like the fact that I was spending "unnecessary" time talking with him. "What kind of business?"

"I run a garage that does bodywork and repairs. A small place—I got a young kid to run it while I'm away." He let go of my arm.

I touched his wrist lightly in an attempt to reassure him. "I'll do my best. But we have to get you well before you can go anywhere. As soon as the tests are done, I will return to start an IV. For now, drink as much as you can."

He looked down at his hands on the white sheets. His cuticles were outlined with car grease that no amount of hospital soap would erase.

I turned as I left the room. "See you all tomorrow." They waved good-bye. I tried to imagine my father in this place, confined to bed and kept away from the outdoors that he loved. At least the surgical patients were either scheduled or recovering from surgery and knew that some kind of active treatment was in the plan.

I needed more information before I could diagnose Mr. Anderson, but I already knew that he was a very sick man. I ordered an immediate chest X-ray and blood work. I started the IV and hoped that the oxygen would help his breathing, allowing him to rest more comfortably.

Nurse Benoit marched ahead of me back to the nursing station. I wondered if she disapproved of me personally or if she didn't believe in idle conversation. Whatever it was, I worked to control my irritation.

After finishing rounds, I walked to the cafeteria for an early lunch. On the whole, the food was surprisingly good. With a small dairy operation and greenhouses on site, the cafeteria offered plentiful fresh food, as well as fresh baked bread and muffins. I had never understood why hospitals served such notoriously unappetizing food to patients with depressed appetites, but fortunately, good nutrition was believed essential to curing at the san. I was hungrier here than I had been for a long time.

Because the lunch hour rush hadn't quite started, the cafeteria was quiet. A few nurses sat at a table by the window having an early lunch. I chose the shepherd's pie with peas and mashed potatoes and carried my tray to the table in the corner.

A nurse came to the table carrying a tray. "Mind if I join you?" she asked. "I'm Penny." She wore a white uniform and a nurse's hat. Her blond hair was dangerously close to hitting the collar of her dress—a violation of the uniform code that would no doubt offend Nurse Benoit. Penny wore bright red-orange lipstick that outlined her lips perfectly. Her blue cardigan matched her eyes and introduced some color into the room. I wondered how she got away with wearing it instead of the regulation white cardigan that was part of the uniform. She didn't seem to be too worried about the rules, in fact, she showed no hesitation at sitting down at a table clearly marked as reserved for medical staff. I was just grateful for the company.

"Nice to meet you. I'm Dr. Garrett. Have a seat."

Penny sat across from me and shook my hand.

"What floor do you work on?" I asked.

"Today I'm on One West, but I float."

"Is the ward census up at the moment?" I asked.

"At the moment all the beds are full. It's hard to predict. Sometimes we'll have a flurry of admissions and then nothing for a few weeks. That's why they like to have floaters like me who can fill in the gaps. I don't mind because that way I don't get stuck on one floor."

I nodded and took another bite of the shepherd's pie. Suddenly, the public address system announced "Paging Dr. Garrett stat for One West."

Glancing with dismay at my uneaten lunch, I knew I couldn't afford to ignore an emergency page.

"I'll take care of the tray. So sorry," Penny said. "See you around."

When I arrived on the floor, the nurses' station was empty, so I hurried down the hall until I reached Mr. Anderson's room. He was lying flat on the bed with a CPR board under his chest. There was fresh blood on the floor and on the top sheet. His complexion was gray and he was nonresponsive. The airway in his mouth was connected to an airbag that a nurse was squeezing to give him air.

"What happened?" I asked as I moved towards the patient.

"He rang for help because he felt dizzy. He coughed, threw up blood and then lost consciousness."

"Pressure now?" I asked.

"Fifty over palpation."

I checked the IV. The vein had collapsed, and the fluid was leaking in the tissues. It would be hard to start another but I had to try.

I felt a practiced calm as I navigated the crisis and gave the staff quiet but firm orders. Once the fluid was running, I adjusted the flow and continued my assessment.

The men in the other beds glanced anxiously at Mr. Anderson. A nurse pulled the curtains around their respective beds. I could only imagine how anxious they were inside those shrouded cocoons.

Turning to Nurse Benoit, I said, "I'll need an OR immediately. Get the anesthetist on call. Transport him to the OR stat. Is the chart ready?"

"Consent is signed and blood work is done. He is typed and crossed for six units. Dr. Ridley is on call for anesthesia."

"I'll go scrub. Get him there fast and find Mr. Anderson's wife as soon you get a chance—she might be in the cafeteria."

I ran up the stairs up to the OR and changed in the dressing room. While scrubbing, I saw them bring the patient on a stretcher and transfer him to the operating room table. In my mind, I rehearsed the upcoming surgery. The primary challenge would be to find and control the source of bleeding. This fellow was in poor shape, and I didn't want to make any bets on his chances for survival.

The scrub nurse stuck her head out of the OR. "Pulse is faint, and the BP is around fifty."

I nodded. "Keep the IV infusing. Any word from Dr. Ridley?"

"He'll be here in five. Not too happy at being called. Dr. Clarke and the board are on an off-site retreat."

"Retreat? But he's on call."

"They hate to miss it. I've heard it's kind of a luxury golf weekend."

"What a shame," I replied with sarcasm.

Dr. Ridley finally arrived just as I was finished scrubbing. "What's so important?" he asked as he began to scrub.

"Male, forty-five, positive for TB a month ago, think he's bleeding out, lost consciousness on the ward, pressure around fifty."

After scrubbing, Dr. Ridley strutted into the operating room like one of the roosters on the farm. I ignored him while I checked the instrument tray and the setup.

He looked at the patient. "Poor bloke doesn't stand a chance." He smiled at the scrub nurse. "Remember your Latin . . . mor-i-bund, means bound for death."

"Let's open him up before we write him off," I cautioned.

Dr. Ridley shrugged. "Whatever you say, doc." His casual attitude irritated me. I wondered if he'd been drinking. I took a moment to watch his hands, but they seemed steady enough.

The IV fluids were dripping steadily into the patient's arm as the anesthetist took readings and administered drugs. I studied the patient's chest and mentally rehearsed the first cut. The nurse held out the gloves that fit me perfectly. I pulled them on with a snap and moved towards the stretcher. Dr. Ridley continued to monitor the anesthesia.

"What are you all waiting for?" he asked as he smiled to the other nurses in the room. "My golf game needs me."

I ignored him and focused on my task. I painted the patient's chest with brown antiseptic paint and then picked up the scalpel. At that moment, I focused only on the surgery. I no longer heard any of the chatter around me as I made the incision, assessed the bleeding, and did what I could to stop it. He'd lost so much blood, I didn't think it looked good, but I tried to repair the damaged lung. He'd probably delayed getting help because he was afraid of being admitted. There wouldn't be a miraculous intervention on my part. Here was my first patient, and unfortunately there was little I could do except sew him up and let him pass.

Dr. Ridley muttered something under his breath. I wasn't sure what he said, but I thought it was something like "I told you so."

I felt a slow anger rise as my cheeks flushed. I peeled my gloves off and left the OR without saying anything. He'd probably be back playing golf within the hour, whereas I had the sad task of informing his wife. This was part of the work that I really dreaded. I'd never become adept at delivering bad news to the family, and I was certain that his wife would be blindsided.

Chapter 17

LOUISE, SAN, 1950

I ROLLED my neck to release the tension in my shoulders as I left the operating room. I mentally reviewed the procedure I'd just completed, and then I rehearsed what I'd tell his wife. There was no way I could have saved Mr. Anderson—his situation had been grave and he'd delayed treatment. I slowly approached the woman who sat on the couch in the lounge, resting her head against the back of the chair with her eyes closed and her hands folded in her lap. Suddenly my rehearsed speech seemed inadequate.

Her eyes flew open as I cleared my throat. I put a restraining and comforting hand on her shoulders, to keep her from jumping up.

"Mrs. Anderson, I'm very sorry. Your husband did not survive the surgery. There was nothing we could do. He suffered a massive hemorrhage due to the advanced stage of his illness."

Her face crumpled. "But . . . I thought you could help him."

"His disease had progressed too far and one of his arteries gave way. We tried to repair it in surgery, but it was too late. I'm so sorry."

Mrs. Anderson put her face in her hands and wept quietly.

I stood awkwardly and didn't know what else to say. I wasn't a religious person and didn't feel comfortable saying the usual words of comfort. I was very relieved when one of the floor nurses, who had been caring for the patient, arrived and put an arm around her.

I escaped, sorry that I couldn't have intervened earlier. Mr. Anderson reminded me of my father—a hard-working man with no time for illness. Even if I could have diagnosed him earlier, there was no guarantee the outcome would have been different. I wish his odds had been better. Although I'd missed lunch, I'd lost my appetite. Sensing the nurses whispering as news travelled down the wards, I wanted to escape. I knew it wouldn't look good that I'd lost my first patient. If I thought I might dazzle the administration with my surgical skills, I was mistaken. Logically, I knew that I had handled the situation to the best of my ability, but a sense of failure followed me down the hall.

I walked across the green towards the chapel that I'd noticed on my first evening. I needed to get out of the infirmary for a few moments and away from the nurses who eyed me with a combination of sympathy and skepticism.

Constructed of rough-hewn barked spruce logs, the chapel sat on a fieldstone foundation with a gabled roof. As I entered the quiet space, light streamed through a stained glass window above the altar and reflected the colors onto the gleaming wood floors.

Sitting in one of the wooden pews, I took some big breaths and tried to calm myself. The loss of my first patient distressed me, compounding the sense of dislocation I'd experienced since I'd arrived. Being an outsider to both the nurses in the residence and the doctors who shared their own housing with their families, I knew it would be complicated to make myself at home here.

One of the stained glass windows depicted Jesus praying in the garden. He had agonized alone that night, and even his companions couldn't stay awake while he prayed to be spared the inevitable. I'd always read weakness in Jesus' submission, but perhaps I missed some signs of strength?

The rich colors of the glass reminded me of some of my sister's sewing projects—she had an eye for color and design. I missed our time as roommates and the conversations we had over long dinners. Mary had filled the empty spaces in my life and allowed me to focus on my career while still benefiting from the stability and the warmth of a home life. Her unwavering belief in me gave me courage I should have realized was a gift.

I hoped my life in future would offer more than this endless sequence of dorm rooms and cafeteria dinners. I wanted to be rooted somewhere and know that I had found my place. But that still felt so far away—I was overcome with sadness and homesickness. I covered my face with my hands and cried quietly.

I felt the pew shift as someone sat at the end of the row. I looked up and saw the man I'd noticed the other day outside the chapel.

"Everything all right?" he whispered.

I looked at his kind face. "I think so," I said. "Are you the chaplain?" I quickly wiped my eyes, reluctant to be seen in such a vulnerable state.

"I'm a patient. My name is Jimmy. I don't want to disturb you, but if you need to talk, I'm always around."

"Thank you," I said. The chapel was quiet. I felt embarrassed to be caught crying. I'd learned long ago to mask any emotion lest my male colleagues interpret it as weakness. I glanced at my hands, scrubbed red from the recent surgery.

Jimmy sat quietly with his hands folded, and his eyes closed. I looked away because it seemed rude to invade his privacy. My emotions calmed, and I took some deep breaths. I was grateful for his silent presence.

After a few moments, he shifted slightly in his seat and turned to me with a reassuring smile before he stood up to leave.

I nodded to him and hoped he realized that I appreciated his kindness. With few words, much had been communicated.

I imagined how I might describe my first day to my father if he were still alive. He would listen quietly and then remind me that the farm also experienced unplanned losses—lambs that didn't make it to stand on their feet or calves that weren't strong enough to feed. I missed his gentle wisdom. I'd have to find it somewhere inside myself in order to deal with whatever this place had in store for me. I had a feeling it wasn't going to be easy.

Chapter 18

LOUISE, SAN, 1950

"How are you? Have you started your work?" Mary asked.

I sat in the phone closet at the end of the residence hall with the pocket door pulled firmly closed. I'd never been in a confessional booth, but I imagined it felt like this—dark and claustrophobic and filled with the echoes of people's private conversations. Still, it was lovely to hear Mary's familiar voice; I closed my eyes and listened closely. I could usually read her mood by listening to her. Mary seemed reluctant to talk about herself and asked me questions about the san instead. I tried to give her enough details to satisfy her curiosity, but I wondered why she was deflecting my questions. It felt more like an interview than a conversation.

I told her about my first days at the new job, the patient I'd lost, and the people I'd met. I described my room overlooking the parking lot and the natural beauty that surrounded the san. When I had given her all the details, I asked her how she was feeling. There was a long silence on the phone line.

"I've had a miscarriage." She kept her voice neutral, but I could hear a tremor of emotion.

I wanted to hug her through the phone lines and let her know that I was so sorry. "How far along were you?"

"Enough to feel good and pregnant. The doctor said to recover and try again in a few months. If one more person says that this baby will be another of God's little angels, I'm going to hit her."

"People say stupid things. How is Robert taking all this?"

"He went on about how this was God's will. I told him to shut up."

I was surprised. "You didn't!" I'd never seen Mary rebel openly against any of Robert's pronouncements.

"Sure did. I apologized later but told him to save the sermons for his congregation."

I bit my tongue—I was no expert, but I was pretty sure that God's will did not include babies dying. Besides, the whole idea was ridiculous—how could any human presume to know God's will? That was one of those things about which Robert and I would never agree. Mary rarely criticized any of her husband's theological opinions; I felt secretly pleased to hear she'd pushed back at his certainty. Not that I wanted to promote conflict between them—but it was healthier for Mary to express herself honestly.

After I hung up the phone, I sat in the phone closet for a while. I felt so sad. She'd be a wonderful mother. My complaints seemed so insignificant by comparison with her loss. I promised myself that I would try harder to make things work during my fellowship. How little I knew about what was to come.

Chapter 19

LOUISE, SAN, 1950

"Are you settling in?" Dr. Clarke asked. He put down the report he'd been reading when I entered, leaned back in his chair, and lit a cigarette. On the wall to the right of his desk hung a certificate in hospital administration. To his left was a wall of windows overlooking the mountains. Behind him was a tall bookshelf with books and photographs. The large desk took up a great deal of the room, and it was covered with piles of paper.

I shook his hand and sat in one of the chairs facing him. "Everyone's been very helpful." I couldn't put my finger on what it was exactly, but I was uneasy in his presence. I had the feeling he wanted me to be impressed by the power his office and furniture represented.

"I've been busy with a board retreat. But in the meantime, you've started orientation and work. What happened with that new admission? You lost him in the OR." Dr. Clarke looked at me, waiting for an explanation.

There was something about his tone that felt accusatory, so I paused to collect my thoughts. I wanted to answer his questions, but not say more than necessary. And I wasn't sure how much he knew about thoracic surgery.

"He waited too long to come for treatment and as a result, he hemorrhaged from advanced TB. There wasn't much we could do."

"We'll examine the case in our morbidity conference, and we'll let you know if we need any more information from you. I trust that won't happen again. I'd hate for the state to make a connection between your arrival and increased mortality rates."

I wondered if he would also question the anesthetist's tardy appearance or my suspicions that he'd been drinking. "The patient's condition was grave and the only option was to open him up and see if there was anything we could do. Patients will die during or after surgery. If the disease is too advanced or if there are unforeseen complications, they will die. No surgeon can prevent that."

I took a breath. He probably resented being lectured to by me but there was really was nothing anyone could have done for the poor man. Maybe he had a better idea. "Was there something else you might have done in that situation?"

"Well, that's neither here nor there," he said, cutting short any discussion.

This interview was not about my clinical decisions, but more likely a general attempt to remind me who was boss. This man was a bully—I needed to be vigilant around him. He wanted people to be compliant to his direction. I might have cooperated that way once, but I had learned a few lessons along the way, like standing my ground.

He looked at his watch. "I want you to organize some teaching events with the staff—maybe on an afternoon when you can attract both day and evening shifts. Find some topics that are relevant and post signs around the wards."

"When would you like the classes to begin?"

"Soon as possible. The state wants us to offer more staff education."

"Fine," I said. I hadn't seen any evidence of rounds or educational events at the san, but I wisely kept that observation to myself. There was a vast difference between the san and the daily educational activities of a teaching hospital. I wasn't surprised that the state found them underperforming in professional and continuing education. Complacency was a dangerous thing at any level of professional practice.

"Good." He took a drag of his cigarette and then placed it on a huge, cut-glass ashtray. "There's one more thing. There's a patients' council that meets and reports concerns to the administration. We need a physician representative on that council."

"I'd be happy to do that."

"They are a total pain in my backside. That Jimmy guy gets the patients all wound up, and then they start demanding this and that. They keep pushing for the san to hire a full-time chaplain, but there's no way the state is going to pay for that and neither will I. Keep your ears open for any trouble and report back to me." He twirled his cigarette against the edges of the ashtray and the ashes fell into small heaps while the end of the cigarette glowed. "Any questions?"

Was I being conscripted to spy on the patients' council for him? "Just one . . . I've noticed in the journals that TB care seems to be shifting away from these large institutions and into the communities where patients live. New drugs are showing a lot of promise." I wasn't asking to irritate him—I genuinely wanted to know. It would make a big difference in how I carved out a possible research topic.

He waved his hand as if to swat away a nasty fly. "Nonsense. We provide the best care, with fresh air and different therapies or surgeries that cater to our patients' needs. Your fellowship is intended to concentrate on surgery in addition to any special assignments I give you. Those other things are fashions that won't last. What we have here works well and has made us famous around the world. I hope you realize how lucky you are to be here."

I nodded but said nothing. I wasn't feeling particularly lucky at that moment. Perhaps he hadn't seen the literature. I decided to keep my mouth shut. I really needed this fellowship to work out.

"As part of your contract, you'll give a lecture to the board and other invitees at the end of your term. You can start your research by describing the surgical advances we have here. I am pretty sure I can get your paper published in the *Journal of TB Care*. I have friends on the editorial board."

I didn't want him to see how much that idea appealed to me. I would love the opportunity to be published in that well-known journal—to boost my reputation when it came to residency applications. But so far, I hadn't seen much evidence of advanced surgical care at the san. Never mind, I thought. I'll do the research and see where it ends up. His connections could help me in future.

"We could consider sending you to the international meetings of the TB society. I think they're meeting in Switzerland in the spring."

Switzerland! I couldn't believe my ears. I'd always wanted to go there. If they paid for my trip, that would make all the difference. Maybe this fellowship would turn out to be a great opportunity. I had to keep an open mind. "That would be interesting," I said, trying to find a balance between showing interest and being cautious of appearing too eager. What if Mary could come along? We'd always dreamed of doing a European tour.

Dr. Clarke stood up, and I realized that I'd been dismissed. "Call my girl to get an appointment next week. As long as you realize that there's a chain of command in place, you'll fit in just fine."

I looked at him but he was already rifling through some papers on his desk. Chain of command, I thought to myself. Had I joined the military?

"Damn it, where's that memo?" he muttered. "Carole!" he yelled to his receptionist.

I felt sorry for his secretary who entered the office as I slipped past her.

As I walked back to the infirmary, I wondered how Dr. Patterson managed to work with him. I wondered if Dr. Clarke had chosen me because he thought I could be intimidated. What was his ultimate purpose in hosting the fellowship? It was apparently the first time they'd offered it to anyone.

I told myself to stop fretting and to focus on the work. If the final result included conferences and publications, it would all be fine in the end.

As I walked away from the administration building, I took the outside path to the infirmary to get some fresh air. I stopped for a moment to watch the dark clouds racing overhead. I was beginning to see the outlines of how complex relationships and expectations were at the san, and I felt some trepidation at the thought of navigating them.

I knew I'd have to be very cautious around Dr. Clarke. I didn't appreciate having my judgment questioned by those who really didn't know what they were talking about. I wondered how much clinical experience he had. Mary would warn me not to aggravate Dr. Clarke—stop poking a hornet's nest with a stick. I was going to have to keep myself under tight control—Dr. Clarke was not only a keen observer, but he knew how to find a person's vulnerable places. I wonder if underneath all that bluster, he was, in fact, a deeply insecure person.

When I returned to the surgical suite, I ran into Dr. Patterson in the hall. "Could I bother you with a question?"

"Of course," he said.

"Dr. Clarke suggested that there might be an investigation into the Anderson case. Should I be worried?"

Dr. Patterson shook his head slowly. He appeared weary and unshaven. "Keep in mind that Dr. Clarke is not a surgeon. The autopsy report stated that your patient suffered a pulmonary artery hemorrhage, and his disease was far too advanced for any surgical intervention to be successful. Unless you know how to provide a patient with two new lungs or a replacement artery, there wasn't anything else you could have done. A committee will review the case and follow up with questions, but I don't think you have cause to worry."

I exhaled slowly with relief. "That was my first case here."

Dr. Patterson nodded. "Don't let anyone undermine your confidence. I understand you studied with Dr. Graham at Yale?"

"You know him?" I was surprised. Perhaps they'd contacted him for a reference.

"We trained together in Edinburgh. He was a brilliant surgeon. I can't imagine he created a pleasant atmosphere for a woman.. . . ."

Although I waited for him to say more, he left it there. The surgical training world was a small one—and people had long memories. I felt relieved that Dr. Patterson seemed to support me.

The next day, I rushed straight from surgery to the room where the patients' council was scheduled to meet. My eyes scanned the crowded room to find a vacant chair. Jimmy sat at the head of the table and smiled when he saw me. When I walked over to shake his hand, I tried not to think of Dr. Clarke's order to spy on this group.

The fact that he seemed genuinely pleased to see me made me feel better. Compared to Dr. Clarke, Jimmy was hospitable. I wondered how the rest of the patients felt about having me there—judging by some of their frowns, they were not pleased.

"Who's she?" one male patient asked in a loud whisper.

Jimmy looked around the room. "I think everyone's arrived, so let's get started. In case you haven't met her yet on the wards, I'd like to introduce Dr. Garrett, who is doing a surgical fellowship here. Dr. Garrett is our medical representative to the patients' council. Let's go around the table and introduce ourselves."

I tried to remember the blur of names and faces. As the meeting progressed, we moved through the printed agenda, and I was impressed by the way that Jimmy kept the meeting on track. He was clearly accustomed to a leadership role. People accepted his authority—something that would probably irritate Dr. Clarke to no end.

He was careful to not let the meeting stall or fall into pointless argumentation. Wearing a neatly ironed blue oxford shirt and khaki pants with loafers, he was freshly shaven except for a thin moustache. His resonant voice carried easily through the room. There was something comforting about him.

Patient representatives voiced complaints and made requests for more social events and film nights. Jimmy reviewed a list of the institution's complaints about patient behaviour and infractions of the rules and they discussed disciplinary matters. I had seen how the san expected patients to comply with an endless set of rules and viewed them as children who needed disciplinary reminders, and I was not surprised to see how that annoyed them.

When the meeting concluded, I chatted with a few patients. Jimmy spoke with the person who had volunteered to take minutes and they exchanged information. When I started to leave the room, Jimmy asked me to stay for a moment.

"Do you have any questions?" he asked.

"No, not really. I'm not sure why I need to be here, but thanks for making me welcome."

"I appreciate you taking the time," he said politely.

We walked towards the cafeteria without having agreed on the destination.

"You seem to be quite used to running meetings."

He laughed. "I've done my share. I work for the YMCA and we love to have meetings."

"I'll have the meat loaf," I told the dietary aide.

"Me too," Jimmy said.

The dietary aide smiled at Jimmy and ignored me. "You'll have to wait a minute while I get some more out of the oven. If you'll just step aside and let the line pass, I'll be right with you," she said.

"You're obviously one of her favorite customers," I teased.

He patted his stomach. "I appreciate their work. And I let them know."

We took our trays and stepped to the side to let others pass. When we had our meals, I paused and glanced at Jimmy. I wasn't sure whether he intended to sit with me or if there were conventions in the cafeteria that made that taboo. The medical staff table was at the far back of the cafeteria and I glanced at it, wondering what I was supposed to do.

He saw me look in that direction and immediately sensed my hesitation.

"I'm going to go sit with the patients over there. Thanks for coming to the meeting. Enjoy your lunch."

I was grateful that he sensed my discomfort and indecision. Although I would have been happy to continue the conversation and meet other patients, I wasn't sure about the rules. And it seemed like every situation in this place had rules. When I heard the patient group erupt in laughter in response to something Jimmy said, I wished I could join them.

The following afternoon, I sat in a small conference room behind the nurses' station and reviewed a pile of charts. I used a small notebook to keep track of some of the details, but there was so much information to process while I tried to acquaint myself with the patients and their medical histories.

"Hello, Dr. Garrett. Working hard?"

I looked up from the chart and saw Penny, the nurse I'd met in the cafeteria. She pulled out a chair across from me and sat down.

"Are you on this floor today?" I asked.

Penny nodded. "I'm on afternoons. And you?"

"I'm trying to get to know the patients. I can't believe how long some of these patients have been here."

"It's quite amazing. And some of them are as cheerful as can be. I would have lost my mind with all the rules, like lining up for temperatures four times a day. Speaking of which, I gotta go monitor vital signs." She made a face.

"Have fun," I said with a smile.

Penny started to walk towards the door and then paused. "I was sorry to hear about Mr. Anderson."

"Did you know him?"

"I was here when he was admitted. What brought you here anyway?" Penny asked with curiosity.

I shrugged. "I needed a job."

Penny looked at me and laughed. "Me too."

While we were chuckling together, Nurse Benoit appeared at the doorway and glared at us. "It's time for report, and we've got an admission coming to 211. If you're not too busy, that is."

"I'll be right there," Penny replied. Penny gave me a mock salute as she headed to report.

Chapter 20

LOUISE, SAN, 1950

I PILED some of the charts to one side and tucked my notebook on the shelf in the conference room. "I'd like to keep these charts here for now," I said to the head nurse, pointing to the heavy charts on the side of the table.

"I've put a note on the chart rack, but I expect you to return them to their place when you're finished," Nurse Benoit said. "Our charts are very important and they are not allowed to leave the floor."

"I'll take care of it after I see the admission," I said. Her attitude was grating to say the least. And she was still relatively young—give her a few more years and she'd truly be a battle-ax. She sniffed, picked up her clipboard, and marched down the hall expecting me to follow yet again.

I entered the single patient room, surprised by how different this room was compared to the average patient ward. Reserved for affluent patients, the private room had luxurious drapes and a fine-quality wing chair in the corner with a wooden end table. A young woman in her thirties sat on the bed wearing a patient gown. She watched proudly as her husband sat on a chair beside the bed and held a sleeping infant in his arms.

"I'm Dr. Garrett. How old is your baby?"

"She's two months."

"She's lovely. I'll need to examine you." I turned to the husband. "Perhaps you'd like to wait in the room at the end of the hall, and I'll come and get you when I'm done?"

The husband nodded and left the room carrying the baby like a football in his arms. Nurse Benoit closed the door behind him.

I loosened the ties of the patient's gown. "How long have you been feeling unwell?" I noticed the dark circles under the woman's eyes. Her skin seemed very dry and she exhibited some shortness of breath on resting. My instincts were telling me that she was sicker than she likely realized.

"While I was pregnant I had night sweats and back pain. I wasn't very hungry and I had trouble standing. When I went to see my doctor for a well baby visit, he did a test and said I had TB so he sent me here." Her eyes filled with tears at the memory. She twisted her wedding band round and round.

"I'm going to listen to your lungs and order some blood work. We'll also do X-rays. Once all the tests are in, we decide how to proceed. Lean forward, please, so I can listen."

I unfolded my stethoscope and listened to her lungs. I tapped her back and ran my hands along the spinal vertebrae. "Does it hurt there?" I felt her wince and tense.

"Yes, right there."

I retied her gown and helped her ease back onto the pillow. I stepped away from the bed as I wound my stethoscope back into its oval form and figured out what to say. This was not going to be welcome news for a new mother. "You're breast feeding?"

She nodded.

"How far away do you live?"

"About two hours."

"I'm going to admit you, and you'll need to be here for a while. Will your husband be able to manage the baby?"

"He's really good with her, and his mother will help. He'll be driving home soon."

"It's going to be a bit uncomfortable for a while till your milk dries up. The nurse will give you compresses. He'll have to give her bottle feedings."

Mrs. Collier began to cry silently with big tears rolling down her cheeks. "I really have to stay here? For how long?"

"I don't know yet. I'm sorry. Do you have any other questions?"

Mrs. Collier shook her head.

"I'll go and talk to your husband. I suggest you feed the baby when she wakes. I'll round up bottles and formula from the utility room for the ride home."

She nodded tearfully.

Nurse Benoit moved forward and put a meal card on the bedside table. "Fill out this card and we'll make sure you get a supper tray. No crying now. There's no point in being a baby."

I couldn't believe my ears. I shot her an angry look while keeping my tone even. "Nurse Benoit, why don't you order a light supper to be sent up and sandwiches for her husband with some coffee?"

"But we can't. . . ." Nurse Benoit stopped when she saw my face. She left the room in a barely disguised huff.

I ignored her and focused on my patient. "This is going to be difficult but you're going to have to be brave for your little girl. We'll do our best to get you better and back home as fast as we can."

Mrs. Collier blew her nose into a lace handkerchief. "I've never been away from her for even an hour."

"When will he be back to visit?"

"Next Sunday is his day off."

"I'll go talk to him. You rest up and try to eat something when the food arrives."

Mrs. Collier clutched her handkerchief in her fist. She leaned back into the pillow with her eyes closed as silent tears ran down her cheeks and onto her nightgown.

In the lounge, Mr. Collier slept in a rocker with the baby in his arms. His head was tipped slightly to one side but he held the baby securely against his chest. I hesitated for a moment and then touched his arm. He startled awake and pulled the infant even closer with an instinctive protective gesture.

"Mr. Collier, I need to talk to you about your wife," I said. I explained to him that I needed to admit her in order to do further tests. "You'll need to get some help with the baby."

His eyes filled with tears, and he blinked rapidly. "I'll do whatever it takes. Just get her well."

"I'll do my best." My instincts told me that Mrs. Collier was going to need surgery, and it would take a while for her to recover. I hoped that he would be up to the task of caring for the infant. Although I had a pretty good idea of the surgery she would need, I preferred to wait for the test results before I shared my thoughts with them. They needed time to absorb the news that she would be admitted. The rest could wait.

Chapter 21

LOUISE, SAN, 1950

After finishing my charting, I left the infirmary to browse the fall craft fair. The days were getting noticeably shorter. It would soon be difficult to get any exercise unless I managed to slip out of the building during lunch hour.

The schoolhouse was a frame building, shingle-clad with hipped roofs over the main section, and angled in such a way to provide a splendid view of the mountain. As I made my way inside through a crowd of patients, I saw tables covered with crafts and baked goods.

Decorations and strings of brightly colored lights decorated the windows. The fragrant scents of mulled cider and freshly baked cookies filled the air. At the table closest to the door, two patients stood proudly beside their handicrafts: macramé, crochet, and needlepoint objects. I ran my fingers over an embroidered tablecloth with floral patterns that reminded me of the linens my mother had decorated.

Other tables were covered with brass work, baskets, photography, and bookbinding. What really caught my eye was a hand-bound leather journal—the work was impressive, and the color of the tan leather would slowly deepen with time. A small flap kept the book closed, and a leather lace provided extra security. As my finger ran along the gilt edges of the pages, I thought about buying it for Mary, even though she wasn't a journal keeper. On the other hand, I'd often thought about keeping one, but the thought of Mary reading it had stopped me. Could I justify buying myself a present and, even more important, would I commit to the discipline of daily journaling? I decided that this was the time to try.

The patient in charge of the table wrapped it in brown paper. Further down, I located a handmade chess set that would be perfect for Robert.

While sipping my cider, I spotted a woven table runner in green and mauve and gold that would fit Mary's dining room table.

I wandered along holding my purchases in a shopping bag. Since I had arrived at the san, I'd spent no money, preferring to save as much as I could. Still, I felt excited to find such perfect gifts and was happy to support the auxiliary. I admired woodworking projects that included animal carvings, birdhouses and lamp stands, but I had no place for those kinds of objects. The curved inlay on one of the cutting boards extended through the full thickness of the wood so that it was visible on the top, bottom, and both ends. Someday I'd have a place of my own that I could decorate in the style that I wanted—nothing fussy, but still cozy.

Patients sat proudly near their creations and talked to each other, looking up with anticipation when potential buyers stopped to admire their art. The Ladies' Auxiliary continued to do a brisk business selling apple cider, coffee, as well as homemade cookies and cupcakes. I bought some cookies to store in my room for late night snacks.

Towards the back of the room, several easels had been set up to display a series of paintings. The canvases ranged from abstract to traditional and on the left side, a variety of watercolors were grouped together depicting nature scenes that appeared to be painted around the san. I was completely intrigued by an oil painting that depicted a storm gathering over a lake. Against the darkening sky, the wind whipped up white caps on the water. In the far corner of the painting, a ray of light penetrated the darkness and cut through the landscape. The tension in the painting was remarkable; I felt like I was holding my breath as I studied it. Although the darkness and the impending storm seemed to have the upper hand, I liked the resistance offered by that one ray of light; it seemed to suggest that there was always hope, even in the darkest of circumstances. The paint had been applied thickly, giving the canvas a texture that helped capture the movement of wind and wave. I looked around for the artist but no one stood nearby.

"Can I help you?" one of the patients asked when he saw me looking around.

"Is this artist here?" I asked pointing to the painting.

"That would be Jimmy." He looked around. "Nah, he's not here. You'd know if he was. He's hard to hide." He laughed at his own joke and then started coughing.

Could the artist be the same Jimmy from the patients' council? I took one last look at the painting before I walked away. I would ask him about it the next time I ran into him.

The next afternoon, I stood quietly in the corner of the classroom and watched as doctors and nurses showed up for the scheduled class. I had arrived early to rearrange the oak desks into small semi-circles. I didn't want them sitting in rows like in a traditional classroom. I hoped to get the participants talking to each other. Although I'd prepared everything and made lists, I still felt nervous. There had been complaints on the wards by staff that felt they were being forced to take classes when they had other things to do. Penny was my eyes and ears among staff, and she said it had remained a grumble, not a full-scale revolt.

I knew I had to be confident and well-prepared or they would take over the class. I had no intention of allowing that to happen. It was unfortunate that they were given little responsibility for maintaining and upgrading their professional knowledge—it wasn't helpful to impose such events on unwilling learners. The general tone of the place didn't encourage inquiry or learning. I'd encountered a lack of curiosity among some of the staff that amazed me. Teaching hospitals offered daily opportunities to learn. With any luck, I could motivate some of them to be willing to learn new things. Since attendance was more or less mandatory, I had a captive, if resentful, audience to work with.

Penny stood at the door to make sure that everyone signed the attendance sheet. She'd been a great help in getting word out to the nurses and encouraging them to attend. The nurses seemed to be happy to have an occasion to chat with those they knew from other floors. One young doctor arrived and slouched in the desk with his eyes closed, making it clear that he was too tired to be bothered with a class. Another doctor came in and started to light up a cigarette.

"No smoking here please," I told him.

He looked at me in disbelief but I did not back down. He reluctantly put the cigarette back in the cardboard package and shoved it into his lab coat pocket.

I ignored the sulking doctor and nodded to Penny to make sure the first slide was ready to go. Because the antique projector had the capacity for only one slide at a time, I really hoped I had put them in the right way. There were always things that would go wrong, but I reminded myself to face any obstacles with humour and tact. I took a big breath. If this class failed, it would be hard to get a second chance.

When the room was full, I stepped to the lectern. The chatter stopped as they looked at me with mixed expressions: some in irritation, some in expectation. I tried to focus on the latter.

"Welcome to the first of our clinical education series. Please take your seats." I paused while everyone sat down; I was sure they could hear my heart pounding. I'd done plenty of lectures in my time but usually to attentive audiences. This crowd was tough.

"I'd like to thank you all for coming and I'd like to thank Nurse Shaw for her help in organizing this event. During the next four sessions we will use case studies to examine different aspects of TB care. If you'd like to suggest topics or volunteer to present, please talk to Nurse Shaw or me afterward. Let's get started."

When I switched on the projector, I felt the participants shift their attention away from me to study the projected X-ray. I wanted them to feel like detectives while they studied the case and practiced some diagnostic skills.

"Our case today is Mrs. C., a thirty-two-year-old mother of a two-month old infant. She developed symptoms during pregnancy, including night sweats, anorexia, and back pain that she attributed to the pregnancy. Her PPD test was positive. Her blood work showed leukocytosis and an elevated sedimentation rate. Here is a slide of her chest X-ray on admission. What do you see?" I paused and waited for someone to speak. The room was silent except for the sound of the slide projector. I kept quiet although my nerves were jumping and wanting to fill the space with words.

One doctor raised his hand. "The anterior vertebral body has deteriorated and there's an enlarged psoas shadow with calcification. Combined with the other symptoms, I'd have to say Pott's disease."

"Good. Who can describe Pott's disease?" I asked. I projected the second slide and the room was silent as participants studied the picture.

"Isn't it a form of TB of the spine?" one of the nurses said.

"Correct. What part of the spine is most frequently affected?" Some faces were blank, others were wondering whether to risk answering. I could tell the nurses were intimidated by the presence of the doctors, but I felt it was important that they be educated together.

"The lower thoracic and upper lumbar vertebrae?"

"What do we need to look for?" I looked at them with challenge and kept up the pace of questions so they wouldn't lose their focus. They stared at the image and I could sense that despite themselves they were engaged in solving the puzzle. I suppressed a smile and waited for their replies.

"If two vertebrae are involved, the disc doesn't get the necessary nutrition and deteriorates. This can lead to a collapse of the spine and back pain," said one of the doctors.

"Treatment?" I asked.

"Surgical treatment to drain an abscess or stabilize the spine. Analgesics for pain. Immobilization of the affected area."

I nodded agreement. "What else?" I really enjoyed teaching and watching people work out a puzzle placed before them. I could have lectured to them on Pott's syndrome, but this allowed them to become more engaged. The mood shifted as people interacted with the case study and forgot their irritation about being forced to attend.

"There was an article in a journal last month about some new drugs."

"Good. Name them."

"Uh . . . I don't remember." The doctor looked sheepish.

"How about you look it up and report to us at the next conference?"

He nodded and wrote a note in his black notebook.

"Anything else?"

"You said this patient had a baby? I guess it would be important to immobilize the spine and caution her to be very careful when lifting the baby or feeding it."

"What would be the benefits of that?" I asked.

"I suppose having the baby would motivate her to get well," one of the nurses replied.

"True, but what else?"

"Maybe the baby will provide a form of physical therapy so that she'll get stronger as the baby gets bigger," another nurse said.

"Excellent. What about her emotional state?" I observed the slouching doctor roll his eyes but I ignored him.

One nurse put up her hand. "Being separated from her baby for any length of time will be really hard on her. I'd expect she might get depressed. Maybe she'll need occupational therapy for distraction."

"Very good. Our patients are more than a disease or a surgical site. They have worries and concerns that can affect their overall health." I looked around to see how they responded to that.

The slouching doctor looked skeptical and then spoke. "It's none of my concern whether she had one baby or triplets," he said. "My job is to do her surgery and monitor her post-op recovery. You nurses can do the other stuff."

"Does everyone agree?" I asked. A thick silence hung in the room. I held my breath and waited for someone to speak, but the nurses were hesitant to contradict the doctor.

Penny spoke up. "Fear or depression might slow down the healing."

The truculent doctor sat up and shook his head dismissively at her comment. "Irrelevant. The healing happens whether or not the patient is in a good mood. It's a process that is independent of mood."

I caught Penny's eye and watched as she tipped her head towards the door. I noticed a shadow of someone standing outside the door; I guessed that it was Dr. Clarke. Why was he eavesdropping on the class? Didn't he trust me to run a class in a professional manner? What on earth was he so worried about? It was merely a case study and hardly radical content. I shrugged and turned back to the group discussion. He could do what he wanted, but I planned to carry on. I focused on the discussion that was becoming more heated as it progressed.

"I don't agree," said one of the older nurses. "I've seen people make amazing recoveries or stall at a certain point of healing and I've always felt the exact reasons were beyond what one could know." She looked at the doctor defiantly, daring him to contradict her.

"Are you talking about science or about religion? Because I'm here to do science," said another doctor. "If you want to talk about healing, call a chaplain."

I checked my watch. "We have some differing opinions. Let's explore those ideas more closely in small groups. In the time remaining, I'd like each table group to write up a treatment plan listing the priorities for this patient—paper and pens are on the tables. Include the management of physical, emotional, and perhaps spiritual needs. You have ten minutes to do this. I'll give you a two-minute warning when it's time to wrap up. What are your questions?" I paused and then stepped back to let them organize themselves. I heard the voices rise and fall as people took turns to contribute to the treatment plan. I pulled up a chair and sat with the first group without inserting myself into their discussion.

"You need to stop interrupting," one of the older nurses chastised the young surgeon. "Everyone has something valuable to contribute and we do more than just cut up people in this place."

I glanced at Penny who was sitting with the next group. She rolled her eyes. After a few minutes, I moved to sit with another group who were engaged in discussing the potential dangers of physiotherapy for the patient.

Finally, I moved to the front of the classroom and recorded some ideas in my notebook for the next session. When the time limit had been reached, I interrupted the groups who were still engaged in noisy discussion and debate.

"Each group can summarize their discussion in the time we have left. Could I hear from the first group?"

One of the nurses from Two West raised her hand. "We spent a lot of time trying to figure out the priorities for this patient's care. I'll try to summarize our discussion." She gave her report, and then one of the doctors in the other group gave his summary. Finally all the groups had finished their reports.

"We are unfortunately out of time for today, but we'll pick up the discussion next time. Thanks for your excellent work. Although each of us is trained in our separate professions, we bring those skills to the ward as part of a team. Please move the desks back in order and sign the attendance sheet before you leave if you didn't do so on your way in. Our next seminar will be in two weeks. I have a short quiz for you now, and when you're finished, you're free to leave."

The room was quiet while the participants took the test, and then one by one they dropped their papers on the front desk and left.

I gathered my papers and books and felt a huge wave of relief.

I pulled aside one of the young doctors who had seemed to be engaged in the discussion, unlike some of the others. "What's your name?" I asked.

"Dr. Cullen."

I shook his hand. "Glad to meet you. I was wondering if you'd be willing to give me a hand with these educational sessions. Apparently the state has mandated them and I think you'd be an excellent person to help shape the content of these."

He looked surprised and then pleased. "Well, I'm kind of busy, but I'd be happy to hear what you have in mind."

"Why don't we have lunch next week and we can talk about it? Would Wednesday at noon work for you?

He scribbled a note in his agenda and then left.

"That went well," Penny said.

I nodded, more than grateful for her support. "What a relief. Hopefully next time they'll have a better idea of what to expect. By the way, what was Dr. Clarke doing out there?"

"Who knows? Just being nosy. We should celebrate. There's a place in town if you'd like to get a drink some night. Just to get away from here and relax."

I looked up. "When?"

"Tonight?"

I laughed. "Do they welcome people from the san?"

"This joint is happy to take cash from anyone. They don't ask questions. Although it's a real dive, they pour generous drinks. And the jukebox has some decent songs." Penny smiled. "We need a break from this place—it's too easy to lose perspective."

"Sounds great. I'd love to."

"I'll knock on your door around eight."

I looked around to make sure the room was in order, turned off the projector, put the slides in a box, and gathered up the tests. I noticed the pharmacist waiting outside the door. He was wearing a white lab coat and a blue oxford shirt with a bow tie. His round glasses gave him a scholarly appearance.

"Dr. Garrett. I'm Doug Belken, the pharmacist."

I shook hands with him. "Happy to meet you. I didn't realize you were waiting for me."

"I didn't want to disturb the class."

"How can I help you?"

"I just wanted to talk to you about something."

"Do you want to get lunch at the cafeteria and we can talk there? I just need to put this stuff in my office."

"I'd prefer to talk in your office," he said glancing over his shoulder.

I wondered why he was so cautious.

When we were settled in my office, he cleared his throat. "I've been keeping up with the pharmacological literature on TB. There are many interesting developments."

"I agree," I said. "The field is changing rapidly."

"I know someone who works at Anderson and Smith in New Jersey, and they're willing to send us a small number of doses of their new meds to do our own pilot study. They would be very interested in our results."

I looked at him in amazement. "You could get us a small number of doses? How many? How soon?" This was really good news.

"He wants to test our initial interest in running a limited trial of about four. It's not much but they said they would produce more soon. You'd have to get set up to run a small trial with consents and protocols, but you could eventually publish the results."

I nodded thoughtfully. "I'm pretty certain that Dr. Clarke won't support this. I'll mention it to Dr. Patterson first. Don't tell anyone else. I'll get back to you as soon as I can."

He stood up. "Thank you."

I stood up as well. "Thanks for telling me. I'll see what can be done."

He nodded and quietly disappeared to the east wing where the pharmacy office was located.

Four doses wasn't much, I thought, but on the other hand, it might open the door to more possibilities. If we could show concrete results, there would be opportunities to publish and discuss our findings. But somehow we had to find a way to work around Dr. Clark—that obstacle seemed as unmovable as the mountain outside the window.

Chapter 22

LOUISE, TOMMY'S HIDEAWAY BAR, 1950

"Well, look who's here. Nurse Penny. Your usual?" The bartender smiled at both of them. "And who's your friend?"

"What's the usual?" I asked.

"Gin and tonic."

I nodded at the bartender. "Make it two. Hi, I'm Louise," I said as I shook his hand.

The bar was dark except for a light over the bar and one over the shuffleboard. A dartboard hung in one corner but no one was playing. A pink fluorescent sign in the window advertised a popular beer. The air was heavy with a combination of stale beer, cigarettes, and fried food. Two patrons played shuffleboard, and one sat hunched over a drink at the other end of the bar. The place was dingy, but at least no one knew us. It was like a well-deserved holiday to be outside the gates. In fact, I felt almost giddy with relief at escaping the san and surviving the first education seminar.

The wind howled outside the bar and the windows occasionally rattled. They'd predicted snow flurries for the night.

The bartender put two drinks in front of us. "I take it you're a regular?" I asked Penny as we clinked glasses.

"Working and living at the san . . . it gets to be too much," Penny said with a sigh. "A girl has to have a night out once in a while."

I took a sip of my drink. "You're single?"

"Been dating a patient for the last year, but we don't get out much." She smiled wryly.

I looked at her in surprise. "A patient? Is that allowed?"

"Not officially, but if they tried to stop it, they'd lose half their staff."

"No!" I said in disbelief. "Staff and patients?"

"Or patients with other patients. Who knows, maybe you'll meet someone?"

"No, thank you. I'm just here for a short while and then I plan to move on." To change the subject, I asked about Penny's beau.

"His name is Joe and he's in Rose Cottage."

"I'll be doing rounds there next week. Tell me, how can you date when he can't leave the place?"

Penny chuckled. "There's lot of stuff going on, film nights, concerts, chapel services, and games. And then, if you know your way around, there are always ways to find some privacy." Penny flashed a mischievous grin.

"Seems like there's eyes everywhere. I bet Nurse Benoit would enjoy tracking you down with a patient in the bushes behind the residence."

Penny laughed. "If you ever need privacy, I'll tell you where to go."

"I think the library is good enough for my social life."

Penny smiled. "How about you? Never married?" Penny asked, glancing at my hand.

"Never. Have you always wanted to be a nurse?" I asked, trying to change the subject. It wasn't like I felt I had any interesting personal stories to share. I had dated in college and in medical school, but nothing had been life-altering or worth talking about. I never felt comfortable with the ways women would tell each other everything about their relationships. In this case, however, there really was little to tell. I'd had my encounters, but I couldn't honestly say that I'd felt in any way changed or deeply committed to anyone so far. The fellows I'd met were as career driven as I was, and that seemed to be an unlikely combination for long-term commitment. Love didn't seem to be part of the picture.

"I was a candy striper at the local hospital and my mother was a nurse, so it all fell into place. What else was there? I couldn't see being a teacher, especially since I'm not big on discipline."

"Where did you train?"

"In Buffalo. Worked on a surgical floor after graduation and then I heard about this place. I really wanted to get away from home for a while and try something different."

"What is it with Nurse Benoit? Does she dislike me or everybody?"

Penny smiled. "Don't take it personally. She's bossy, and she loves being in charge. Dr. Clarke gave her an award last year for the best nurse and it went to her head. Some say she wants to be director of nursing, but who knows?"

Before I could ask any more questions, one of the patrons waltzed by unsteadily and tried to wedge himself between us, I drew back, repulsed by his beer-breath.

"Would either of you ladies like to dance?" he asked with a shaky bow.

"No, thank you," I replied. We turned our backs to him, hoping he would go away. Undaunted, he continued to waltz behind our chairs with an imaginary partner, making comments about how lovely that partner looked. It was hard for us not to giggle, but we didn't want to encourage his presence. When he'd had enough of being ignored, he moved on to the men at the shuffleboard table.

"Finally!" I said with relief.

Penny looked at me. "You really weren't interested?"

We both burst out laughing.

Chapter 23

LOUISE, SAN, 1950

I WENT to the waiting room after surgery to report to Mr. Collier about his wife's operation. He sat on a green couch, beside a bouquet of plastic flowers. In a matching chair, the baby slept in her grandmother's arms.

"Everything went well," I said. "I drained an abscess on her back and did some corrective surgery on her spine. She's going to have to be very patient because it will take a while to recover, and she may need to wear a brace. But I'm pleased with the progress she has made."

"When do you think she can come home?" he asked anxiously.

"It's still too early to say. Let's see how she does. How's the baby?"

"She's gaining weight on the formula. She misses her mom though."

"I can imagine. If you want to get something to eat in the cafeteria, you'll have lots of time while she's in the recovery room. The nurses will come and get you when they get her settled on Two West. After lunch, just go to the waiting room on that floor and they'll look for you."

"Thank you," Mr. Collier said as he stood up and shook my hand. I nodded to the grandmother, who smiled at me.

"Please get her well. We need her."

I looked at the exhausted father and the concerned grandmother and nodded. "I understand," I said. "I'll do my best."

Sitting outside Dr. Clarke's office for yet another meeting, I tried to be patient. As I listened to the receptionist typing, I was reminded of commercial class in high school—all of us sitting in neat rows, typing the same letter over and over accompanied by the irritating ding of the bell when we reached the end of the line. Ma had wanted me to learn to type so that I could always get a job. I had other ideas about what I hoped to do with my life.

I felt increasingly irritated at being kept waiting; I always tried to be punctual, and I expected the same from others. It wasn't like I had nothing to do—two admissions needed orders, and one pre-op assessment was waiting. Why on earth did I have to report every week to the administrator? Even as an intern, I hadn't been subjected to this much oversight. He was trying to manage me and control my every move—but I couldn't figure out why. There was nothing unusual about the work I was doing.

Because I'd been busy with surgeries, I hadn't made any progress on figuring out what he wanted me to write about the surgical program for publication. The pharmacist had no further information on the possible drug trial, so I had to let that go for now. But I did my best to understand the institution and continued to read through histories of current patients, not sure exactly what I was looking for.

The other medical staff seemed to avoid me, unless they wanted me to cover for them. Penny had told me that Dr. Clarke hosted retreat weekends at a resort and regularly wined and dined with physicians and state officials. I wasn't going to say a thing about any of it. After trying to argue for some equality at Yale as an intern, I had learned that it was better just to do the work and keep quiet. I knew why I was there and I wasn't afraid of working hard. In fact, I hoped it would make the time pass more quickly.

It was so strange that the institution didn't really seem to value research or development of new ideas, content instead to preserve the status quo. But perhaps I judged too quickly—Mary had often told me I was too critical.

The patients deserved good care, and I would do my best to provide that. The notion of spying on the patient organization was distasteful to me, so I needed to be very careful in how I responded to that directive. And I planned to continue my own research into the new pharmaceutical options for TB care. There was no excuse to keep the benefits of scientific progress from patients.

Although the door to his office was closed, I could hear Dr. Clarke's angry voice. When the door finally opened, I was surprised to see Jimmy emerge. He nodded to me but didn't linger. I wondered why Dr. Clarke was so upset with him.

I leafed through a golf magazine on the table. Next time I'd remember to bring a medical journal to read. As I flipped through the magazine, I was startled to see a picture of Dr. Clarke in front of a golf cart with his arm around the shoulders of the state commissioner of health. Beside the cart were two doctors I recognized from the sanatorium. This was how business was done—I wondered what kinds of conversations they had together over the post-game dinners. I put the magazine down when I heard my name called.

Dr. Clarke came to the doorway and waved me in with impatience, as if I was the one who had kept him waiting. He sat in the chair behind his enormous desk and lit a cigarette. His face was red with anger, and his fingers trembled slightly as he inhaled deeply on the cigarette. He flicked the ashes into the large glass ashtray on his desk. I wondered about his blood pressure.

"Damn patient association. They think they run the place, and their demands are endless. I'd love to get rid of that Jimmy. You get him ready for discharge—I want him out of here!"

"I see," I replied. I hadn't yet evaluated Jimmy or reviewed his chart, but I planned to do so in the days ahead. That decision would depend on medical criteria, not on Dr. Clarke's orders, but I refrained from saying that out loud. If I aggravated him any more, he might have a stroke.

"Where do they get the idea that patients can make demands? We look after them, and they should be grateful that we do. Where would they be without this place?"

I decided it was best to let him vent. While he wrote something angrily in his notebook, I glanced at pictures on the credenza behind him. In one photo, his arm was wrapped around an elegant, gray-haired woman; it was probably his mother. In another photo, he stood against a wintry landscape with his wife, two children, and a golden retriever. I wondered about his life outside the san. Unlike the other doctors, he didn't live on the grounds. I'd heard he owned a huge house on the river near town, and he liked to entertain there.

He closed his daybook with a slam and focused on me as if trying to remember what I was doing there. He crushed the butt of the cigarette against the sides of the ashtray and rolled up his sleeves.

"You started the education series?"

I suppressed a flash of irritation and clasped my hands together in my lap. He knew that I'd done it because he'd been eavesdropping outside the classroom. "Yes. We had good attendance for the first class, and the next one will be held a week from Thursday."

"They better appreciate they're getting time off the job to learn. I wasn't in favor of it, but the state has been breathing down my neck about staff education, and we have to keep them happy. I don't want you wasting more than an hour on it. And take attendance. I want to know who is showing up and who is not."

I nodded slowly and held up a paper I'd brought along. "I have the attendance sheet here as well as the test scores."

He waved his hand to dismiss the offer. "I don't have time for that. And the surgeries?"

"We've been busy with a variety of procedures. Dr. Patterson has given you the OR stats?"

"I'm not asking Dr. Patterson," he said. He lit another cigarette with a silver lighter on his desk, took a puff, and looked out the window as a dark passing cloud cast a shadow into the office. "Every time you come here, I want you to bring a list of the surgeries you've done. Maintaining an active surgical roster is an important part of our mission."

"I have a question. I noticed that some of the patients have an extended length of stay without an automatic review of their case or an updated treatment plan. Is there a process in place to regularly review long-term stays?"

"That's not your concern. We have a very well-qualified chart audit group that regularly reviews such things. You're here to do surgery and provide care on the wards—not to review patients, unless it's to determine if they need more surgery. We need to show the state that our beds are full and we are running an active surgical program. We don't want to be reclassified as some chronic or long-term care place. Now, do you have any other questions? Otherwise, I need to get going." He seemed distracted and looked at his watch.

He was the one who insisted on the meetings and now he was acting like he had more important things to do—never mind that my work was piling up while I sat here in a useless meeting. "There's one more thing I wanted to ask you. When I read the recent TB journal, there was an article about the effectiveness of certain new drugs."

"I am well aware of the variety of drugs and treatments. Let me remind you that such matters are not part of your job description. You're here to do surgery and to initiate educational programs. Am I making myself clear?"

"But . . ." I began to tell him that I had never actually seen a job description.

"Listen to me, Dr. Garrett. I heard you caused some trouble at Yale. I hope you don't plan to do the same here. I will not have that kind of nonsense on my watch. You might find yourself back on the farm feeding the pigs."

I was shocked. Who had he been talking to at Yale? I knew I had to be compliant because I wasn't ready to give up this fellowship. For one thing, it might take months to find something else and I simply couldn't afford that. But more important, I knew I had to finish this fellowship to have some solid achievements to show after leaving Yale. I took a breath. "I see."

"Keep reporting to me. You don't make a move without my approval. Just call my girl for a time." He stood up to indicate the interview was over and turned his back to me.

I marched out past the administrative assistant and went out into the cold air. The leaves were blowing around the grounds, defying any attempt to rake them into piles. The trees looked sparse as their bare branches reached up towards a cloud filled sky. The wind cut right through me. The late fall was somber—with so few hours of daylight, I felt like I was waking up in the dark and finishing work in the dark.

Chapter 24

LOUISE, SAN, 1950

A FEW days later, I bundled up and walked over to Rose Cottage to meet the male patients who lived there and to update their charts.

Their cottage was a one-and-a-half-storey building with a cobblestone foundation, clapboard sheathing, and a steep octagonal roof. Two dormers interrupted the roofline. On the ground floor, the floor space was expanded by the presence of two sleeping porches. The cottage design was charming—I admired the cut-stone foundation. I would love to live in a cozy cottage like that.

Although it was cold, with snow forecast for later in the afternoon, at the moment the sun was out, and it felt good on my face. Many patients were reclining in sleeping chairs or walking on the paths across the green.

I knocked on the front door of the cottage.

When a man answered, I held out my hand. "Hello, I'm Dr. Garrett, and I'm here to do rounds."

"Hello, doc, come in. I'm Joe." He was a tall, slender man with brown eyes, wearing a flannel shirt and jeans and slippers lined with sheepskin. He was handsome, with kind eyes and a ready smile. I could see why Penny was attracted to him.

"I thought I'd talk to each one of you and update your charts."

"We heard you were coming, so we did some house cleaning. It's hard though—my roommates are slobs."

He smiled and waved her towards one of the two upholstered chairs. A brown couch lined the back wall of the room facing the fireplace. A pack of cards and a few sports magazines were scattered on the coffee table. Beyond the living room was a modest galley kitchen with enough room for a square table and four chairs. The house looked tidy and well cared for.

"Do I smell something baking?"

"With company coming, I thought I'd try out my mother's date square recipe. They'll be done in a little while, but I'll put the kettle on now."

I smiled and sat on the couch while Joe turned on the stove and then sat in one of the upholstered chairs. From my vantage point, I could also look into the sun porch where two sleeping chairs stood.

"There are three of you living in this cottage?" I asked.

"That's right. Jimmy and Dan will be back shortly. We lost one last month. We usually have four men here. There's two bedrooms upstairs and one down here. I usually get the sleeping porch because I snore."

"You lost one? He went home?" I was confused.

"Home as in heaven. He died."

"I'm sorry. That must have been difficult for all of you."

"We don't talk about it. That's the rule in this place. Just pretend death doesn't happen. But of course it does—it can happen to any of us."

"And how have you been feeling?"

"I feel pretty good. I just keep testing positive, so they won't let me out, but I'm ready to go."

"Let me listen to your lungs and take a few notes. Where is home for you?" I stood up while Joe stayed in the chair. I applied my stethoscope to his chest and listened to his breathing. I had wondered if it might be awkward to examine these men away from the more clinical setting of the infirmary, but Joe was clearly accustomed to the drill and seemed comfortable with the questions and examination.

"I'm from Buffalo. Used to be a math teacher."

"Do you hope to go back to teaching someday?"

"I stopped hoping a long time ago. Just taking it one day at a time."

I sat down across from him. "Your lungs sound good. Any shortness of breath, trouble sleeping, cough?"

Joe shook his head.

"And you're involved in the occupational therapy classes?"

"I try to keep busy. I like building things and fixing things, so there's always work for me around here. Do you have any idea about when I might get out?" He looked at me hopefully as he stretched out his legs.

"I'm going to have a look at all your history and I might need some updates on your lab work and X-rays. I'll have a better idea once I gather all that information."

Joe nodded. We both looked up as the front door opened, and a slim, light haired man entered, followed by Jimmy.

"You've probably met Jimmy already," Joe said grinning, "but it's Dan you really got to watch out for."

I shook Dan's hand and then turned to Jimmy. "If it's convenient, I'd like to speak with each of you individually to do an assessment and update your charts." I wanted to be as professional as possible.

"What are you baking, Joe?" Dan asked. "Trying to sweeten up the lady doctor?"

Joe smiled. "Date squares will be done in a few minutes."

I turned to Jimmy. "Do you have a moment now?"

"Certainly. I'm not going anywhere," Jimmy said. He turned to Joe. "There better be some squares left for me."

"Let the doctor do her work, and then I'll serve up some tea."

"Can we use the sun porch?" I asked.

"Sure." Jimmy stood back to let me pass and then followed. It was chilly on the porch despite the sun. I couldn't imagine sleeping in an unheated place, no matter how many blankets I had, but the san maintained that sleeping in unheated spaces was effective therapy.

"As I mentioned, I'm trying to update the treatment plans for patients in my care. I just need to ask you a few questions and do a brief examination. Let me start by asking you, how are you feeling?"

"I feel good. I'm just not sure why I'm still here."

I nodded sympathetically. "I'm sure you're anxious to get home. How long have you been here?"

"One year, but I haven't seen a doctor for months. Have they all given up on me? Is there something I should know, like I'm incurable, and no one wants to tell me?"

"I'm sure that's not the case. What kind of work do you do at home?"

"I was the northeast regional director of the college-based YMCA movement. It's now an integrated organization, but in the past we had our own colored Y's. I used to travel all over the south visiting colleges and organizing events."

"You probably need to get back to the job?"

"If I still have one," he said. "That sort of thing carries little weight around here. Once you're admitted here, family and work responsibilities count for nothing."

I felt badly for him. "Tell me about your family."

"My wife also works for the YWCA in New York. She's very busy with that and with taking care of her mother. We've been married forty years."

"Any children?"

"No."

"I know you've probably told your story many times, but I was wondering if we could briefly review your medical history. When were you first diagnosed?"

"I was up at my camp, Cedar Island, a few hours north of here, and I was worn out. I'd been travelling nonstop throughout the winter and spring and I had hoped that some vacation at my camp would get me back to normal, but then I got sicker. I was coughing and had fever. I was worried that I would get so sick at my camp that I wouldn't be able to get out of there."

"What did you do?"

"I paddled myself out. I still don't know how I did it, but I was pretty determined that I wasn't going to die alone on that island. When I got to town, I collapsed. The local doctor checked me over and sent me here. This was the closest sanatorium, and I wasn't in any shape to protest. Been here ever since."

"What treatments have you had since you arrived here?"

"They did some surgery when I first arrived, cut up my lung, and then tried collapsing it. Didn't seem to do any good, really. Then they stopped doing anything. I think the food and rest likely were more useful than any treatment, but I'm getting impatient to go home."

I put down the notebook where I'd been recording his history and pulled out my stethoscope. "I'd like to listen to your chest."

Jimmy shrugged and unbuttoned his shirt.

As I listened and instructed him to inhale and then exhale, he looked out the window. I noted scars from previous surgery. I wondered how this place could just let people languish here. This man had important work to do and no one was giving him any answers. I couldn't imagine how alone his wife must feel.

"I want to get an updated X-ray of your left lung, and once I do some tests we can discuss next steps."

"I was afraid there was no next step," he said with quiet honesty.

"We can discuss which options have the best chance of success. My goal is to get you well and send you home. You've been here long enough. Has your family been to visit?"

"They wouldn't come near here." Jimmy said. "They're terrified of these places. My people still think of this as a place to die. I can't blame them."

I nodded. "Let's get the tests done and then we'll talk. Is that all right with you?"

He nodded. "Thank you. I'll make sure he's making the tea."

I stood up, and we shook hands. Again I thought of how much he was like Pastor Cal in Mississippi.

He was almost out of the door but paused and turned back. "Thank you for seeing me," he said. "It would really help me to know what my prospects are. It's very hard on my wife to have me away for so long with no idea when I might return."

I nodded.

"Should I send Dan along?"

"Yes, please." I watched him walk away and thought about the miles he had travelled for the purpose of visiting colleges, speaking to young people, and urging them to give themselves to a cause. Without active treatment, it made no sense to keep him here. No matter what Dr. Clarke said, these patients were experiencing hardships being away from home for so long.

Dan entered the sun porch. He had a light step and easily hopped onto the sleeping chair.

"As you know, I'm reviewing all your treatment plans. Let me start with asking how you're feeling?"

"I feel good."

"Are you eager to be discharged as well?"

Dan shrugged. "Not really. This is my home now. I really don't know where I'd go if I didn't live here."

"I see." I stood up. "Would you mind if I listened to your chest?" Dan undid his shirt. I listened to his breathing and took his pulse.

Dan fastened the buttons on his shirt while I jotted down a few observations in my notebook. "What kind of work did you do before this?"

"Mostly odd jobs. Since I've been here, I've learned how to be a clown." He looked at me with a proud smile.

"A clown?" I was so surprised I stopped writing. He was a small slim man, quite unremarkable in appearance. I couldn't imagine him with the makeup and costume of a clown, but he seemed to have an athleticism that would serve him well.

"The patients put on entertainments every month. I often host those, and I visit patients who need some extra cheering up."

"Good for you. What a wonderful contribution. I'd like to update your chart with some new blood work and tests. Once I gather that information, we can talk. Do you have any questions for me?"

"I'm in no rush to leave this place. I know some of the others are, but I don't really know where I'd go. There's nothing waiting for me out there."

"I'll keep that in mind," I said. How many others, I wondered, had made this their home? How would they fit back into situations that had changed in their absence? If what Penny had said was true, many people had formed new relationships while they were here and those at home had perhaps done the same. I had to be careful not to assume that leaving the san would be the best solution for everyone—some might be devastated to leave.

I gathered up my notebook, pen, and stethoscope and followed Dan into the living room where Joe invited us to sit at the dining room table.

He carried a teapot on a tray with cups and saucers and a plate of his date squares.

"This looks really nice," I said. "Is this standard Rose Cottage hospitality?"

"According to the patient manual, we're not allowed to entertain the ladies here, so our hospitality is limited. We're making an exception for you."

"I appreciate it." I took a bite of the square. "These date squares are as good as my mother's. I'm impressed."

"We keep telling Joe to open a restaurant when he gets out. He can work the bar, cook, and do construction when the place falls apart. He's a perfect one-man show."

I didn't notice the time pass as we drank tea and they asked me questions about my life in New Haven. Jimmy told us about the work he'd done there with the college YMCA. He had a strong dedication to his people that made me hope I could discharge him as soon as possible so he could return to work.

I checked my watch and realized I had to go see some patients. As I walked away, I waved to the guys who had gathered on the front step. Dan did a few front flips across the yard and then bowed to his audience. They applauded and whistled and then went back inside.

I hoped that I could clarify their health status by updating their files. The absence of directive about discharging people struck me as odd. Most places I worked had clear guidelines about post-operative patients and transfers, discharges, or rehabilitation plans. Using the TB test as a marker of readiness for discharge wasn't reliable. But people were afraid even when the disease was inactive.

Mary had been worried when I told her I was coming to work here.

"What if you get the disease?" she'd asked me.

"I've been exposed to many TB patients already," I tried to reassure her. She would not be comforted to know that there were several doctors and nurses, some from New York, who were patients on the ward. In fact, one of the doctors had been discharged and had set up a practice in town. Some luck, combined with a healthy immune system, helped staff avoid the disease. I knew I'd been lucky, but I also practiced scrupulous hand washing.

I wondered what kind of welcome the men from Rose Cottage would receive when they finally went home again. When I had returned to my parents' farm after a year at medical school, I expected to find things the same as they'd always been. In fact, my imagination had painted a romantic picture of farm life. While I'd been away, my parents neglected to tell me that my father had had a stroke. They said they didn't want to worry me. Instead of the active man he'd always been, after the stroke he sat in a chair and said little. Tenants had taken over the farming. Ma seemed to do little besides take care of him and cook. Their bodies had shrunken to fit their worlds. They looked at me like I was a stranger intruding on their routines. I felt guilty at my eagerness to return to school.

I hadn't known what to talk about with them, and they seemed completely uninterested in my life and work. Before his illness, my father had always been eager to hear my stories. I'd resented the change that had taken over their lives. I hoped the men in the cottage would find their way back to the lives they'd left behind. I planned to do what I could to help them on their way and hopefully not cross the administrator by doing so.

Chapter 25

LOUISE, SAN, 1950

I WAS in the library reading medical journals and puzzling over my findings when I was startled by a banging door.

Penny shook the snow from her navy wool uniform cape. "I thought I'd find you here." She took a place at the table across from me and looked at the pile of charts and notes. "Should I ask how things are going or just be quiet? You look beat."

I sighed. I looked at my notes and at Penny and made a decision. I pushed my notes towards her. I couldn't possibly do all this by myself; I was going to have to trust someone. I hoped I wouldn't regret this, but my instincts told me that Penny would not betray me. "I'm not sure what I've taken on, but it's definitely more than I can handle by myself."

"What exactly are you looking for? Do those numbers represent the length of stay?"

"It's a bit sensitive, and if it fell into the wrong person's hands, I would be in very serious trouble."

Penny nodded. "You can trust me."

"It's hard to know who to trust around here."

"I know. You need to be careful."

"I'm trying to investigate medical records of different patient groups to see what kinds of treatments they've had, how long they've been here, and what the chart says about their status when they are discharged. I'd like to compare those numbers to the statistics in the board reports."

"Let me see if I understand. You're selecting a certain number of cases, tracking their status during their stay, and sorting out where they went when they were discharged, whether that was to home, or to the morgue?"

I nodded.

"I'm happy to help, and I'm very good at keeping my mouth shut. Oh, by the way, did Nurse Benoit come to see you in the residence the other night?"

"No, why?"

"That's weird. You know she has a suite on the ground floor and rumor has it that she doesn't even pay rent. Dr. C. lets her stay there for free."

"Really? I've never seen her upstairs."

"I came to ask you something and she was standing close to your door. When I said hello, she completely ignored me and hurried away."

"That's strange. I didn't know she lived in the residence. And hanging around my door. That's just creepy." What would she be doing? Acting on Dr. Clarke's orders? "She probably has keys to all the rooms as well. We need to be very careful. Don't leave anything lying around in your room that you don't want her to see."

"She has the perfect opportunity to spy on us—she knows our shifts and when you're booked in the OR. She can just slip upstairs without anyone seeing her."

I shook my head. We needed to be careful.

"Let me show you what I'm trying to do." I held up a chart. "This patient was a forty-five-year-old female. The discharge status noted on the front of the chart shows that she left the san last July to return home. But if you read the nursing notes, which most people don't, it's pretty clear that she died here at the san in April. Why doesn't the discharge status and date match what really happened? If this chart was altered, who did it and why?"

Penny looked closely at the chart and then flipped to the final nursing notes. "Somebody could have altered the chart *after* the doctor had signed off, but it would still have to be someone with access to the medical record once the chart was disassembled. When the doctor signs off the chart, it becomes the property of medical records archives, and that's a restricted area."

Penny and I looked at each other.

"What would be the rationale for changing the death date?" I asked.

Penny massaged her temples and looked around to make sure no one was within earshot. "It might have to do with pushing the reputation of the san, you know, boasting about cures. Or it might be about state funding and patient census. There's clearly something to gain and something to lose. We just need to figure out what, but first we need to be very clear on what it is that's being done. One thing might lead to another."

"Maybe if they demonstrate a high cure rate and cover up the mortality rates, it would be a good rationale to pursue donations."

"But it's still fraud, right?" Penny looked at me for confirmation. When I nodded, she leaned across the table and whispered, "How can I help?"

"You need to keep this completely secret, even from Joe."

Penny nodded. "I swear."

"I'm starting to drown in all this information. I need a way to sort it so I can see patterns, but it also needs to be coded in case someone finds it. We need a credible cover story."

"I'd be happy to help with any of that. You want to be able to see an identifier that's neither a name, nor a medical record number, and also the admitting diagnosis, treatment, and length of stay."

"Exactly, and if they're still here as patients, make a note of that too. We'll both be fired on the spot if Dr. Clarke hears about this. Watch out for that guard. He's snooping around all the time. He keeps turning up on the wards and around the grounds. I don't trust him at all. And now we know that Benoit has some kind of access, so keep an eye on her too. There may be others who are involved, so don't trust anyone. For now, let's keep this between us, and if we find some solid evidence, we can sort out what to do with it."

Penny nodded in agreement. "Yeah, that's a good idea. That guard is definitely a creep. He's not a security guard as much as Dr. Clarke's paid bodyguard. By the way, you might want to consider giving some chocolates to the records clerk who brings you all these charts. You really need to stay on her good side. When do you want the compiled information?"

I shrugged. "Whenever you can get to it. Start with these first ten patients. I have notes here that summarize their stay. This is going to be a long-term project—there are tons of records to go through. But if you can help with the sorting and organizing, I'll keep digging through archived charts and collecting the information. Most of the chart notes can be read quickly—they're very repetitive. But we want to track any major surgical or medical interventions or deaths that don't match what we see in the record."

"I'll start right away. If anyone asks, what should I say I'm doing?"

I held my head as I tried to think of a rationale. "Let's think. What's our alibi?"

"Something that would bore people to tears so they wouldn't be inclined to ask more."

"We could say we're comparing surgical to medical treatment of patients for a paper to be submitted to the *American Journal of Nursing*."

"Good enough for me. Most people think all nurses do it take temperatures and make beds, so they won't be interested."

"Have you ever heard of chart audits being done here?

"No, why?"

"Just wondered. Dr. Clarke mentioned it once in a meeting and said that somebody or a group of people did chart review."

"I haven't heard anything about that, but I'll keep my ears open."

"I'll try to ask some of the doctors as well, but again, watch your questions because you don't want to raise any alarms."

"Are you by any chance hungry? Do you want to get dinner tonight?"

"What time is it now? How can it be four o'clock? It's pitch dark. How about at five so I can finish up this chart? If there's anything you don't understand in the data, just ask me. It might be hard to decipher some of my writing."

"I'm used to reading doctors' handwriting. I think penmanship should be required in medical school. See you later." Penny left with the notes carefully folded inside her navy blue nursing cape.

I spent the remaining time tracking the data from the charts I had on the table. Once I finished taking notes, I put the charts on the cart reserved for that purpose. After tucking my notes into a brown envelope to give to Penny later, I rolled the cart to the space behind the librarian's desk for safekeeping. The evening clerk was reading a romance novel, and she briefly looked up before returning to her book.

Tomorrow I would be in surgery all day so I wouldn't be able to do any research, but it was easier to store the records than ask the medical records clerk to hold them and have to deal with her displeasure. Penny was right. I should pick up some chocolates for the librarian and the records clerk on my next trip into town. I sincerely hoped they didn't bother to talk to others about the number of hours I spent there. I was just fortunate they kept the small library open in the evening and even luckier that no one on the staff had any interest in reading the latest journals or medical texts. In this case, their lack of interest in professional development was a factor in my favor. The less people knew about the time I spent digging through archived charts and records, the better.

In this case, being an outsider to both the female nurses and the male doctors gave me some freedom. Although my surgical work was closely scrutinized, probably because people still didn't believe women could actually do that work, socially I was invisible. That was nothing new for me, so I accepted it and focused on my work.

I was grateful to have one person who supported this research, and I looked forward to having Penny's insights into this problem. She was quick, and she liked a challenge—if this project expanded, she'd have that and more. I just hoped I could keep both of us from any suspicion or observation; it was important to have access to this material without scrutiny. If the san was a bit lax about records, it would be helpful for our research.

The doctors apparently had better things to do than worry about charts and discharge notes. What exactly they did for entertainment, I wasn't completely sure, but they seemed to spend as little time as possible in the clinical areas. The whispers I overheard suggested that there was a great deal of socializing. Spending my evenings with Dr. Clarke and the rest of his cronies was not my idea of fun anyway, so I thanked my lucky stars they ignored me.

Chapter 26

LOUISE, SAN, 1950

A FEW days later, Penny knocked on the door of my room to collect me for the patient talent show.

"Did I wake you?" Penny asked.

I groaned and rubbed my eyes. "No, I was just trying to make sense out of some of these numbers." I closed my notebook and put my thoracic surgery text on top with a thud of frustration.

Penny sat on the bed. "Get ready. The show's about to start."

I brushed my hair and grabbed a sweater.

"That's it?" Penny asked.

"What do you mean?" I asked, looking down at my black pants and gray sweater. Penny was skilled at combining vibrant colors and applying eyeliner and rouge. I however felt more at home in scrubs and a lab coat. I'd never been comfortable drawing attention to myself, especially growing up with Mary, who had the same kind of ease with her looks.

"Do you even own lipstick?" Penny asked.

"Of course I do." I looked at the top of the bureau and then searched through a small cosmetic bag. "See?" I said as I held up an unused tube.

"Put it on! And some blush too. Wear that blue sweater that your sister made for you. That color looks good on you."

"When did you become so bossy?" I asked. "You remind me of my sister. What difference does it make?"

"Sometimes you need to remember you're a woman as well as a doctor. You don't have to choose one over the other."

"I wasn't aware I was choosing anything. How's this?"

Penny looked up and down. "Much better. Leave your hair loose," she said, as she saw me start to pull it into a bun. Penny stood up, smoothed the bedspread in one experienced flourish and headed for the door.

When we arrived, the auditorium was filled to capacity with patients and staff. Although curtains were drawn across the stage, feet could be seen running back and forth. Noisy chatter filled the room as the audience waited in anticipation for the show to begin. Some patients in wheelchairs lined the sides of the hall. Penny and I took the last free seats in the very back row as Penny waved to a group of nurses across the aisle.

A small orchestra played as the curtains opened. The audience clapped and cheered loudly. Dan emerged dressed in a tuxedo. I would not have recognized him—his presence commanded the stage and his voice carried easily over the crowd. I looked at Penny in surprise and Penny smiled back.

"Ladies and gentleman, welcome to another musical evening. This one promises to be better than ever. We rounded up some fine talent tonight."

The crowd whistled and clapped.

One patient that I'd recently seen raking leaves on the green went up to the mike and taught the audience a well-known song. The auditorium filled with the sound of voices. A small choir of ten people performed two folk songs. A woman who had a voice like Patsy Cline wowed the audience with another song. I had the feeling that these same acts had been performed many times before and were well known to the audience, but that didn't diminish their enthusiasm. In a place with few distractions, a variety night was greatly appreciated.

When the skits and musicals were done, Dan introduced the last act. Jimmy came out wearing a white shirt and dress pants. As he looked at the audience, they became quiet. The mood in the hall changed to anticipation. Jimmy was well-known, Penny whispered to me, for his performances in chapel services and musical evenings. He was unhurried as he took a breath and nodded to the pianist. She played the first lines and then paused and his rich baritone filled the hushed room. I felt goose bumps on my arms as his voice swelled, and I pulled my sweater tighter. "Deep River," he sang, "my home is over Jordan." He evoked a longing for home, and I had to wipe my eyes. I was not alone; many were crying and some patients had their arms around each other. When finished, he nodded to the pianist and bowed to the audience. There was a moment of complete silence before the audience cheered and clapped.

"Pretty amazing, right?" Penny said.

"Wow, that's quite a voice," I whispered. "And he's probably not even working with full lung capacity."

We shuffled out of the auditorium with the rest of the crowd.

"Do you feel like joining the party?" Penny asked.

I hesitated and looked out the window towards the lake. A campfire was already burning and patients were gathering round it.

"Come on . . . it'll be fun," Penny said.

"You're going to be warm enough out there?" I asked, as I looked at the jacket that Penny was wearing.

Penny smiled. "Yes, mother. And I'll have help."

"You have fun. I'm going to turn in. I have surgery early tomorrow." I turned away and bumped into Jimmy.

"So sorry," I said. "That was an amazing performance."

The hallway was noisy with crowds leaving the auditorium. He leaned forward so that I could hear. "We had to sing in church. My mother insisted."

"Well, you can thank her. She was right. You have a gift."

He smiled. "I'll tell my mother once you discharge me."

"I'm working on it," I said.

As I walked towards the nurses' residence, I smelled the smoke from the campfire. A full moon rose over the lake and spilled a circle of light. An elderly patient had told me to watch for this week's "beaver moon." According to him, trappers and old timers used the moon as a reminder to set their beaver traps before the swamps froze, ensuring that they would have a supply of winter furs. The Indians called it the "first frost" moon. We were long past the first frost now and had already had several snowfalls, but I loved the idea of naming the moon. I stood for a moment to watch its translucent glow on the water before the cold sent me inside. The sound of a guitar drifted up from the campfire and voices sang "Michael, Row the Boat Ashore." I was surprised that the patients were allowed to break curfew. Either the authorities had a night off, or they had decided it was better to allow people to let off steam once in a while. I wasn't sure where the medical staff went on a night like this—perhaps they were wrapped up in family comforts in their cottages or having their own parties off-site.

A few lights were still on in the residence, but most people were either working their shift or attending the campfire. The administration building was completely dark. Dr. Clarke had been away all week with no explanation. His receptionist said he was attending a conference. Perhaps the patients knew he was away and assumed it was a good time to throw a party.

The radiator was working hard and making lots of noise in my room, but I was grateful for the warmth. Part of me wished I were at the bonfire singing along with the people there.

It was confusing at times to sort out how I was expected to act. The rules for social engagement were different than other places I'd worked. Living in close proximity with patients and in isolation from the rest of society meant that alliances and friendships were formed; it was unrealistic to expect otherwise. But I couldn't tell how deep those relationships went. Penny certainly had a better overview of what was happening because she moved through different parts of the san. In my case, Dr. Clarke had been quite specific about which wards and which cottages I would visit. It would have made sense to use the only woman doctor to supervise the women's cottages, like Birch Cottage, but he was adamant that I was not to be involved there.

I knew that I needed to keep some distance from patients in case I suddenly needed to make decisions about their health. On nights like this though, it felt lonely.

I changed into my flannel pajamas and went to my desk to find a book that might help me sleep. I ran my finger along the edges of the thoracic surgery text. Suddenly, I realized that my journal was now sitting on top on the text, whereas I was pretty sure I left it tucked under the book earlier. It was an old habit that harked back to sharing my room with Mary—I never wanted her to read anything on my desk, because she would pass it on to Ma. It was a form of self-preservation that had become a habit.

I walked around the room to see if anything else was out of place or missing—had someone had been there without my permission? What did they think they'd find? I had nothing worth stealing. I flipped through my clinical diary but it only contained numerous clinical observations, such as blood pressures and other metrics. I didn't comment on any larger questions about patient care. My heart was beating loudly at the thought that someone might have me under surveillance.

I needed to be very careful, I told myself, and not assume that anything in this room was private. Unseen people had keys and could easily access the room while I was in surgery or on the ward. I was usually away all day and it wouldn't be difficult to track my movements; the operating room schedules were printed and distributed throughout the hospital. I looked around the room and wondered where I could put things I wanted to keep private. There was a simple bookshelf and the small hanging closet—few hiding places presented themselves, but I couldn't afford to keep my journal where someone might locate it. I decided I would tuck it under the mattress in the hopes that someone was too lazy to turn the room upside down, but it still seemed like a pretty obvious choice.

My personal diary also needed a hiding place. I looked again at the hanging closet, but it offered no loose floorboards or unseen cupboards that would protect my writing. I stood in front of it, frustrated by the lack of options, when I spotted the blue box of sanitary napkins on the top shelf. Of all the places in the room, I doubted that anyone would bother to look there.

I stuffed the leather journal inside the box and pushed it away from the edge of the shelf so it was still visible but not as accessible. I couldn't quite believe it had come to this, but clearly someone was interested in keeping a close watch on me. There was no point in reporting it to anyone since I had no idea who could be trusted.

I tried to distract myself from the unsettling intrusion by reviewing what I'd learned that day. As I got into my pajamas, after checking the door lock twice, I thought about the research I'd done.

Before going to Rose Cottage, I'd requested the archived medical files of the three men and was surprised at the stack of charts each had accumulated. When they'd recovered from surgery done during their first months, they had been allowed to move into the cottage. After that, their medical treatment seemed to be almost non-existent, other than token monitoring for temperatures and required attendance at occupational therapy sessions.

Some things didn't add up. A male patient, forty-six years old, originally a resident at the cottage, was marked on the chart as "discharged to home" as his final discharge status, even though Joe had told me that his roommate had died. That made no sense. Joe had been quite clear about the man's death, even though he said people avoided the topic. Avoiding the topic was one thing, but changing the status on the chart was quite another. So why list him as discharged? I needed to check other names against the discharges and see if there were discrepancies—it might explain why the statistics in the annual report didn't fit with my findings.

I sat in my bed, huddled under the blankets, and stared at the wall. The murder mystery book I had selected earlier from the stack in the common room was still on my bedside table. I couldn't concentrate on fictional mysteries when there was a real one right under my nose. I had a sense that there was something strange going on, but I couldn't guess how many people were involved in it. I sat on the bed with my arms around my knees, trying to think over the pounding of my heart.

When my patient, Mr. Anderson, had died in the OR, I had briefly wondered how they tracked mortality rates in the operating room, as opposed to deaths that happened on the wards or in the cottages. If I were expected to write a paper on the effectiveness of surgical treatment in this population, it would be difficult to do so without some reference to the mortality rates. But that might be a tricky subject to undertake if someone was altering the numbers. Was I willing to risk my future on something like this? If something irregular was happening, I was pretty sure that Dr. Clarke was involved. He probably assumed I was so naïve and eager to please that I would never raise any questions. Perhaps I had once been that pliable—but it seemed that turning a blind eye was not an ethical option. I felt a deep and unsettling anxiety in the pit of my stomach as I contemplated a future where I was an unemployable troublemaker. I had already invested so much time and resources in my education and training. Was I really prepared to threaten all that for the sake of some altered statistics?

I propped my pillow up against the wall and folded my hands across my belly. Was surgery effective only for certain types or stages of TB? If so, which types of surgery were most effective? If a patient died a few weeks after surgery, how could anyone isolate the cause of death? Complications from surgery had to be distinguished from infection or other pre-existing conditions, like diabetes or heart conditions. I realized it would be safer to commit my thoughts to memory instead of keeping it in my clinical journal. For once, I was grateful that we'd been expected to memorize huge swaths of Bible texts and poetry as children. I had almost photographic recall—something that had been very handy in the past. I would let the clinical journal be the decoy for anyone looking, and I would keep my private journal hidden in the closet. If I planned to pursue this, I had to be willing to face the consequences if anyone found out. Was I ready and willing to do that?

If the numbers were being altered to indicate higher cure rates and to mask mortality rates, that would be fraud. I wondered what they hoped to gain. I sat back against the wall and sighed. I'd never been involved in reimbursement issues—the operating room was traditionally located far from the accounting department of hospitals, and I'd never had the slightest interest in learning about that aspect of health care. But I could see that the statistics were essential to the bottom line. If these actions were deliberate, the perpetrator would likely go to great lengths to keep it secret.

The radiator no longer emitted heat, and I was chilled to the bone. It often took a while to get heat generated in the bed—I missed the warm bricks my mother put in our beds on cold nights on the farm. There was still laughter coming from the campfire. Hopefully Penny would be safe and sound in the residence before the superintendent or anyone else reported her. Maybe she'd figured out a way to sneak past the superintendent to get to her room.

The place was part summer camp and part reformatory. Despite the campfires and laughter, I felt a dark undercurrent. Both staff and patients participated in a drama that seemed to deny that death was one possible outcome. Such a possibility was kept out of sight and not discussed. Bodies were whisked out of the place in the dark, and some patients had no family to claim them or mark their passing. I could imagine that a certain amount of fun and partying was a distraction from the vulnerability that patients experienced. Wouldn't it be healthier to confront and discuss this in an open manner? Perhaps it was simply too uncomfortable for all concerned, especially the staff, who were perhaps not skilled in such conversation. I knew from my own experience that I felt awkward in those situations, having never been schooled in such honest dialogue. But I believed it could be learned, if only the mentors and teachers were willing to create those opportunities.

I had to stop and get some sleep or I would not be able to function in the morning. I turned off the light and burrowed into the bed, trying to warm up my feet by rubbing them together.

Chapter 27

LOUISE, SAN, 1950

As I walked to the ward, I was amazed by the diligence of the house-keeping staff that managed to dust and scrub every inch of this place. Perhaps they operated on the Victorian assumption that the tuberculosis bacillus lingered in the dust and needed daily eradication. I wondered if the laundry department still burned used handkerchiefs like they did in the previous century.

I was in the middle of a pre-operative assessment when the intercom called me to the nurses' station. I carefully helped the patient to lie down again after listening to her chest and excused myself.

"Someone looking for me?" I asked at the desk. "Sounded urgent?"

The head nurse pointed to the phone that was lying on the desk. "Dr. Clarke," she mouthed silently.

I picked up the phone. "Dr. Garrett here."

"Can you get over here immediately?" Dr. Clarke asked abruptly.

"Would ten minutes be sufficient? I'm in the middle of an examination."

"Fine." He hung up without saying goodbye or thank you. I put the phone back on its cradle and returned to the patient. What on earth was the emergency? I reviewed everything I'd done in the past week. I thought of my journal tucked away in a blue box in my cupboard. I tried not to worry, but the abrupt summons had rattled me. That was the problem with having secrets.

Fifteen minutes later, I walked to the administrative building. Because the wind was bitterly cold, I hugged my lab coat around me. I would need to start using the tunnels or learn to wear a winter coat. Although adding layers was a nuisance, I preferred to get some fresh air between buildings, rather than be confined in those narrow tunnels.

The receptionist nodded me in.

Seated in a chair near Dr. Clarke's desk was a blond woman wearing a blue cashmere twin set and a gray wool pleated skirt. The outfit was perfectly accessorized by a pearl choker and matching earrings. Mary would approve, I thought. Despite her elegance, she seemed nervous as she folded and unfolded her hands in her lap.

"Dr. Garrett, glad you could finally come," Dr. Clarke said not without some sarcasm. "This is Michelle—she does fundraising for us and she's a personal friend." He got up to close the door.

"Nice to meet you," I said. I shook the woman's hand and then sat in the free chair that faced the desk. I waited for them to tell me why I'd been summoned from the ward.

"We have a problem and need your help. Michelle's been diagnosed with TB by her family physician who recommends admission here. She'd like you to be in charge of her care."

I looked over at Michelle to confirm this and Michelle nodded slowly.

"I have a referral from Dr. Brown." She handed an envelope to me. "I hope I won't need to be here very long."

"We'll do a full assessment first," I said cautiously as I accepted the envelope.

"I guess I don't have much choice." Michelle played with her pearl earrings and glanced nervously out the window. "I'm not happy about this."

Dr. Clarke interrupted. "I've checked with admitting. The only private room available is on Two West. I expect the very best from you, Dr. Garrett. You're dealing with someone important to the mission of this institution."

"I give my very best to every patient," I replied looking directly at Michelle. "Are you ready to go to the ward now, because I can walk you over? We'll stop in admitting and make sure they have your information."

"Let's get this over with," Michelle said, resolutely picking up her bag and following me out of the office.

"I'll check on you in a while," Dr. Clarke said to her. "I've got some calls to make. I just need a word with Dr. Garrett."

After Michelle had left the office, he leaned over his desk. "Get her well. That gala she organizes supports this place and your fellowship."

I looked at him carefully. His concern for Michelle's wellness was primarily related to her job as fundraiser.

Michelle carried her white suitcase as she walked beside me down the hall.

"Can I help with that?" I asked.

"I'm fine. Not an invalid yet. I must apologize for Dr. Clarke. He can be a real ass, but he is completely dedicated to this place. Not that many people know that he's also devoted to his family and his mother. He visits her in a nursing home several times a week."

I was startled. "I hadn't heard that."

Michelle looked at the hall they were passing though. "I've spent lots of hours fundraising for this place, but I never thought I'd be a patient here. Sure makes everything look different."

"What kinds of events have you organized?"

"I'm chair of the annual gala—this year we're having some trouble finding a headliner to replace the one who just cancelled. We raise money for the Free Bed fund that supports patients who can't pay and for special projects."

"That sounds worthwhile. Are there a lot of patients who can't pay?"

"There are but I don't really get involved in that level of detail. Our patients and supporters range from very wealthy to very humble. The state provides a certain amount, and we work to meet the shortfall. The Ladies' Auxiliary supports special projects as well."

"If I understand correctly, supporters or former patients donate money, and then you use that fund to support the cost of care or other budget items?" I asked.

"We cover individual cases based on need and we also undertake special projects to improve the facilities. There are wealthy people who vacation in their camps up here and they're often willing to make donations to the cause. This place has a worldwide reputation for TB care. Local people are proud of that. And they benefit because they run small hotels for patients who are recovering or for families who are visiting. The san offers many secondary benefits to the community as a whole, so they usually support my fundraising efforts. It's good business for everyone. Sad to say, of course, but true."

Michelle and I stopped at the admitting desk. The clerk, who was chatting on the phone, looked up, recognized Michelle, and cut short her call.

"Miss Wagner will be admitted to Two West," I told the clerk.

"Why don't you come in and sit down? I'll take your information," the clerk said deferentially.

I walked to the waiting area and flipped through magazines while Michelle gave her information to the clerk, who typed it carefully into the record. Although I had lots to do, I knew that Dr. Clarke expected VIP treatment for Michelle, so I tried to be patient.

When she was finished, Michelle joined me in the waiting area. She looked even more distressed than she'd been in Dr. Clarke's office—the ID band on her wrist was a powerful reminder of her changed status. While we walked to the ward, Michelle was silent, and I did not interrupt her thoughts. I tried to imagine myself in Michelle's place and thought about what it would feel like to be admitted; it was a truly frightening thought.

I stopped at the nurses' station. "Miss Wagner will be admitted to a private room on this floor."

The ward clerk nodded. "I just got a call from admitting. We don't have her chart assembled yet, but room 108 is ready."

"I'll take her there. When a nurse is free, could you send her down to help her settle in?"

Michelle's steps slowed noticeably as we got closer to the room.

"Do I have to wear those horrible hospital pajamas?"

"I'm afraid so. The nurse will help you with that. I'll be back in a while to examine you. I know this is hard but we'll do our best to sort this out as quickly as possible."

I walked to the nurses' station to write the admitting orders and to read the letter the referring physician had sent. This wasn't going to be fun— I dreaded looking after one of Dr. Clarke's friends while he scrutinized my every move. I'd have to be careful not to give him any reason to criticize my work. I wrote orders on the chart and passed it to the unit clerk for processing. No matter what the family doctor had already done, I preferred to run my own tests. I hoped for Michelle's sake that she might respond quickly to treatment and get back to her life and work.

Chapter 28

LOUISE, SAN, 1950

WHILE I was reading the referral letter from Michelle's doctor at the nurse's station, a nurse from the other floor called about Mrs. Collier. She'd been running a low-grade fever and wondered if I could come and see her.

After finishing Michelle's admitting notes and orders, I ran downstairs and took Mrs. Collier's pulse and felt her forehead. She seemed lethargic and answered questions with a yes or no—this was so unlike her that I was concerned.

Her husband followed me out of the room. "What's going on?" he asked, with a deeply furrowed brow.

"She has an infection that we'll treat with medications and fluids. I'll probably start an IV." I looked at him and felt badly that I couldn't give him better news. He was unshaven with dark circles under his eyes. "I'll have them bring a cot into the room. You need to get some sleep, and you can use the shower in the hall when you get up. The nurse will make sure you get a tray for dinner."

He nodded and then walked back into the room.

I didn't want to let on how much I was worried about her. Mrs. Collier had been making such good progress; it would be a shame if she ran into complications now. With her immune system already compromised, perhaps she just didn't have the resistance to fight a post-operative infection.

Later that day, while I wrote a progress note on a chart at the desk on Two West, the clerk took a phone call from admitting and immediately started assembling a new chart.

"Dr. Garrett, we're getting an admission shortly into 221, the private room down the hall. If you have time to see her before your OR, then I can process the orders."

"Certainly." I glanced at my watch and grabbed the stethoscope from the counter. "Where's Dr. Smith or Bennett today?"

"They're away for a few days."

I nodded. I wasn't going to comment on that, but it certainly seemed that many of the fellows had a pretty casual attitude towards their work.

"Apparently she's a nun from Mercy House," the clerk told me.

"Where's that?"

"It's a convent and farm almost an hour from here."

A short time later, a stretcher carrying a young woman was wheeled off the elevator by the orderly. The nun was wearing her habit and her face looked gray. Following the stretcher and the orderly was an older nun who also wore the same habit with a coif, wimple, veil, and a tunic that reached the top of her laced up black shoes. I waited till they transferred the patient from the stretcher to her bed and then walked into the room followed by the head nurse.

"I'm Dr. Garrett," she said. "And this is Nurse Moore."

The older nun shook her hand. "I'm Mother Maureen. The younger woman opened her eyes briefly but seemed to be too exhausted to care who was there.

"How long has she been sick?" I asked the older nun.

"We thought she had the flu. She had a fever and was coughing for a few weeks and we put her in the infirmary. But then she just didn't get better. She couldn't seem to take in any food and we were worried about that. The local doctor, who makes house calls when needed, suggested we bring her here. I'd say she's been sick about three weeks."

"If you'd like to wait while I do my assessment, there's a cafeteria on the main floor and a chapel as well."

Mother Maureen looked with concern at Sister Claire and seemed reluctant to let her out of her sight. She took her hand. "I'm going to leave you for a little while so that Dr. Garrett can examine you, but I'll be back."

Mother Maureen nodded and left the room. I walked to the bed. "Sister Claire, we're going to sit you up, so I can listen to your chest." Together we propped her up, because she was too weak to cooperate. She was listless and had trouble focusing on my questions.

I turned to the head nurse. "We'll need a chest X-ray and blood work stat. I'll sign the routine orders but I want to know what the results are as soon as they come in. We'll need to start an IV."

The nurse nodded and took some notes on her clipboard. She returned with the IV tray, and I carefully inserted the needle into Claire's left arm. She seemed unaware of the process as I regulated the fluid drip and pulled the bedrail up.

"I'll be back to see you later." I turned to the nurse. "I'll write the orders, but keep a close eye on her."

After my surgery, I stopped by Claire's room. Mother Maureen was sitting in the corner with a prayer book while Claire appeared to be sleeping. I indicated to the older nun that I would like to talk with her outside.

"I'm glad you brought her here," I said, "because she has acute TB. When I see the X-rays, I'll have a better idea of how extensive it is and whether or not she'll need surgery. We also need to keep an eye on anyone at the convent that was in regular contact with her. Perhaps you can arrange with your local doctor to test the others."

Mother Maureen nodded.

"You'll need to leave her with us for a while. We'll take very good care of her. The nurses are excellent, and we'll make sure she has everything she needs."

"Any idea how long that might be?"

"I don't know. I won't keep her a day longer than necessary. Do you have any questions or concerns?"

"Can I visit her?"

"I'll give you a brochure with the visiting hours and information. We have a priest on call that can bring her communion if she wishes. I'll give you a number where you can leave me a message, and I will get back to you as soon as possible. She'll be on strict bed rest for a while."

Mother Maureen's brow furrowed. "We tried so hard to care for her at the convent. But she looked like she was getting worse."

"You did the right thing. Please keep an eye on everyone else, including yourself."

Mother Maureen nodded thoughtfully. "It's very hard to leave her here. She's one of our youngest sisters and she is an important part of the community. She's our nightingale in chapel."

"I'll do my best," I said, "and hopefully she will soon be back to full health. Did the head nurse have you sign all the consents and papers?"

"Yes. But if you take her to surgery, please let me know."

"I will."

"We will be praying for her—and for all of you doing the work here. Thank you. I'll say goodbye to her now, and then I'll be on my way."

"Did you drive here?" I asked with curiosity.

"I've always enjoyed the open road." This was the first time she smiled and I caught a glimpse of the young woman she'd once been. "Some have even called me a speed demon, though I don't know what they're talking about," she said with fake innocence.

I smiled as we shook hands. "I'll do my best," I said, as I realized how many times I'd already promised other patients the same thing. These days, I felt less confident that my best was good enough, but there was no need to shatter the illusions of patients and their caregivers.

"God bless you," Mother Maureen said.

A few days later, I reviewed the blood work and X-rays before I went to talk to Sister Claire. As I approached the room, I heard a man's voice.

"Illness is punishment from God. It is important to confess your sins so that you can be made well again."

I gasped in shock and pushed the door open. An elderly priest stood by the bedside. Claire had her eyes closed.

I moved forward. "I'm sorry, but I'll have to ask you to leave. I'm her doctor, and I need to consult with my patient."

The priest looked at her with some disdain. "I have to talk with her first. It's her soul that is in peril."

I stood my ground. "I need you to leave now, please. Your message is not helpful for my patient. Or for any others I'm sure."

The priest glared at me, then left in a huff. Claire opened her eyes and gave me a small smile.

"I can still call him back if you like," I said in a low voice.

"No, thank you," Sister Claire replied.

I sat down beside the bed. "I have your results here, and I'd like to review them with you so that we can make a plan for your treatment. You can thank your superior for bringing you in. If she hadn't, you'd be in serious trouble."

I consulted with Dr. Patterson and Doug to see if there was anything else I could do for Mrs. Collier. When Doug suggested a different antibiotic and intravenous administration, Dr. Patterson supported his recommendation. I also assigned a special duty nurse to stay with her.

After I changed her medications to stronger ones that could be administered by IV, I spent some time talking with a very worried Mr. Collier. He had left the baby at home with his mother; they didn't want her exposed to any infections. Although I tried to reassure him, it was clear to all of us that this was a setback. I requisitioned another series of lab work and blood cultures to see if they could determine the cause of the infection. After recovering so well from her surgery, it was just unfair that her condition would deteriorate so unexpectedly. I needed her to recover—she was such a young person and so important to her small family. Tonight I would review all my research again to see if there was anything I was missing. I also needed to get back to the library to read through some of the archived medical records. There weren't enough hours in the day to do the research I wanted to do. I felt this rise of anxiety, and acid burned the back of my throat. This situation was not sustainable, but I had no choice but to persist until I found some answers.

Chapter 29

LOUISE, SAN, 1950

WEARING my winter jacket and snow boots, I carried a file with notes over to Rose Cottage. The evergreens provided some color in an otherwise gray December landscape. Several days had passed since we'd seen the sun—it was either overcast or snowing. The cloudy days contributed to a subdued mood. Although I was too busy to allow my mood to get in the way of my endless task list, I could tell that the patients were listless.

I had an appointment with Jimmy to discuss the results of his lab work and X-rays. I'd reviewed his treatment since his arrival at the san.

The walkway to the front door of Rose Cottage had been freshly shoveled but the wind had blown the snow to cover it again. When I knocked on the door, Jimmy answered with a big smile.

"Come in from the cold," he said. "The kettle is on in case you'd like some tea."

"That would be lovely," I said as I followed him into the kitchen. The cottage was quiet—Dan and Joe didn't seem to be around. I sat at the kitchen table and placed the file on the table in front of me. Jimmy poured boiling water over the tea and carried an old-fashioned teapot to the table with two floral china cups and saucers. The cups reminded me of the ones that the Ladies' Auxiliary used for coffee hour at our church back home.

"Milk or sugar?" he asked.

"Just clear."

Jimmy joined me at the table. "Looks like you have news. Let's hear it."

I opened the file folder and took out an X-ray that I held up to the overhead light. "First, it's a good thing you were sent here when you got sick. If you look at this X-ray, you'll see that the disease had compromised your lung in serious ways." I pointed to the shadows on his lung. "And I believe you were right—if you'd stayed on your island, you would have died there. Now here are the results of your current blood work." I passed him the lab result sheet. "If you look at the values I circled, most are normal. Because you have pernicious anemia, I think we should address that immediately. I will arrange for you to get B12 shots. Why don't you take a moment to read this summary of your reports, and then we can discuss them?"

I sipped my tea and looked around the kitchen while he read the file. The cupboards were painted white and a lace valence hung over the window. The floors were covered with white and black tiles. The counters were tidy and the fridge and stove gleamed. Someone had been diligent in house-cleaning. I wondered if the men shared the chores or if one person did all the work. Joe had told me that the administration expected cottages to be kept spotless or their tenants would be evicted and sent back to the infir-mary. If there ever was a strong motivation to clean, that was it.

He finished reading and then closed the file. "Perhaps you could trans-late all this to me?"

"I researched your medical history since you first arrived, and I think there has been overall improvement. My priorities are to address the chronic effects of the disease on the left lung and to correct your anemia. The anemia is easy to fix, and we will work on that immediately. The lung is a bit more complicated and there are some treatment options. You're still testing posi-tive and there's a cavity on your left lung. One surgical option might include a pulmonary resection where we cut away part of the lung but try to keep as much of the functioning tissue as possible." I sketched a lung on the page and drew a diagram of what I might need to remove.

Jimmy studied the drawing without comment.

"A different surgery involves creating a window between the third and fourth ribs in order to allow for the creation of a space between the lungs and the ribs and which would then be filled with sterile paraffin. This is a more traditional treatment that I don't recommend. The space that is the upper lobe collapses under the paraffin." She drew another illustration of the lung and the ribs. "Those are some of the surgical options."

"I see." Jimmy stared at the diagrams without any expression on his face. "So, you either cut up my lung or you choke off part of it with hot wax. Lucky me."

I truly wished I could give him better news. I took a sip of my tea and looked out the window at the gusts of swirling snow. I caught a glimpse of someone's face wearing a tuque and a parka. "Who's that?" I asked, thinking that it might be Joe or someone from another cottage, checking to see if anyone was home.

"Where?" With remarkable speed, Jimmy got up and looked out the kitchen window. He couldn't see anyone so he opened the back door; the wind blew snow all over the floor. "There are some footprints." He pushed the door closed again. "What exactly did you see?"

"Somebody in a parka and a hat but I couldn't see a face. I didn't recognize the person."

"Let's assume it was just someone nosy. You know how people are around here."

"I know. I've been getting jumpy." I looked at him and wondered if I should say anything to him about my suspicions. Because he seemed so solid, I decided to trust him. "I sometimes wonder . . . well, how much we are under surveillance?"

"What have you seen that makes you wonder that?" Jimmy asked.

"Please don't repeat this, but I had the distinct feeling that someone searched my room recently."

Jimmy nodded and seemed unsurprised. "Trust your instincts and be careful. And if you ever need anything or feel unsafe, tell us and we'll do what we can."

I nodded and took another sip of my tea. It was cozy in the kitchen, especially with the wind gusting outside. The clock on the stove ticked loudly. "When you were in Dr. Clarke's office the other day, why was he so angry?"

"We've been pushing for some changes and he doesn't agree. We've requested a full-time chaplain and better communication with the patients about their treatment plans. Some people haven't seen a doctor for months."

"He thinks you're a troublemaker."

"I know . . . but someone's gotta do it," he said with a smile. He refilled her teacup. "About my case." He pushed the file back toward her. "You're the expert. You decide. I trust you."

There was something so comforting about sitting at the table, drinking tea, and talking about things—it reminded me of what a normal life was like. There was so much I wanted to ask him about his life and his work, but I needed to remember my role as a professional.

The snow had accumulated into a thick white blanket that obscured all the buildings and trees. It was the kind of storm that made people disoriented. Farmers had died making their way from the house to the barn in that kind of weather. Just a few feet away, they might have found warmth, but instead they perished, frozen in place.

"In my opinion, I suggest that we delay just a little while longer on the surgical option. I may have something else to offer, but I am not at liberty to say at this moment."

Jimmy nodded. "I need to know that I am working towards getting discharged."

"I promise I won't make you wait any longer than necessary, but I can't discuss it yet."

"I'm willing to wait if you think it's going to be worthwhile, but if that doesn't work out, I'll choose whichever option allows for the quickest recovery. I trust you to suggest the best options."

I realized I had to get back to the ward. "I should go. Thanks for the tea." I gathered up my papers in the file and carried my cup to the counter. "I'll be in touch as soon as I know more about this other possibility, and otherwise, we'll pick the most effective option and get it underway."

He shook my hand formally and watched as I walked back to the infirmary. I truly hoped I could find a solution for him that would return him to his home.

A few days later, I went to my weekly appointment with Dr. Clarke only to find he was away again.

The receptionist had little to say. "Might be away for a bit," she said.

"Oh, sorry to hear it. Do you happen to know where he is?"

"Nope, he doesn't tell me. But he calls regularly."

I thought it was very odd for him to be away. I'd heard some rumors about his absence, but no one seemed to really know. I was relieved, however, to miss another meeting with him—I could do my work just fine without his direction. We ran several more education sessions for which the young doctor took the lead, and the staff were enthusiastic about the content. I had asked several of the nurses from the surgical floor to teach a lesson and they were pleased to do a team presentation.

The light had already faded from the sky when I arrived at the medical library reading room; the days were so short now, I felt darkness greet me in the morning and waiting again in the afternoon. A winter storm had raged for two days, driving snow across the fields and up against the buildings. No patients took their outdoor exercise—even the birds had taken shelter.

I continued to accumulate statistics on each chart for the length of stay and the discharge status within a selected population of the san. I noted each patient's admittance date and discharge date and calculated the total length of stay, keeping track of the discharge status so I could track whether the patient had died, gone home, or transferred to another institution. Some patients also went to a care cottage in town as a transitional step between the san and returning home, if indeed they had that option. While I did my own investigations, I tried to imagine how to write the paper Dr. Clarke had requested without crossing into territory that would land me in trouble with him.

My main challenge was to keep from being overwhelmed by the sheer quantity of information. It wasn't just the length of patient stay that contributed to that density of information, but the charting by nurses of every single detail of a patient's life added to the bulk. Such senseless charting as "up in the chair," and "tolerated well," added little to the chart, but it seemed to be required of nurses.

When a chart indicated that a patient had been discharged, I tried to go back to the doctors' orders and nursing notes to see if the patient notes fit with the recorded discharge status. Sometimes I was so tired after a full day of surgery and seeing patients that I wondered why I even bothered to do this research. No one would care if I went to my room and spent the evening reading romance novels. There were enough of those paperbacks stacked on the shelves of the small kitchen/lounge on my residence floor to last me for the year. Who would care if I just let this all drop and walked away? By the spring, my fellowship would be over, and I could leave. I could present a paper on surgical outcomes that would offend no one and still satisfy the final requirement of my fellowship.

I stared at another chart without seeing and allowed myself a moment to reconsider all this. I wasn't sure why I made this my problem—sooner or later it would come out and any wrongdoing would be uncovered. My eyes were tired from all this reading, and I usually went to bed with itching and burning eyes. I was nervous about leaving any kind of evidence and felt increasingly edgy about someone finding my research notes. The anxiety and fatigue were affecting me in a variety of ways—I sometimes wondered if I was getting an ulcer, and I had also recently suffered my first migraine in years.

What would Dr. Clarke do to try to get me out of his way? It wasn't merely physical harm I dreaded; it was his ability to undermine my reputation and my future as a surgeon. The anger he displayed at Jimmy's attempts to bring patient issues to his attention was likely only a small fragment of what he might unleash towards me. Was this really worth the risk?

As I gazed into space, I thought of Jimmy's painting of the storm over the lake. It was one of those times when the darkness threatened to consume and dominate everything around me. I thought of my father who been a faithful steward of his land and animals, not complaining or questioning, but doing the best he could with limited resources. And then I thought about Jimmy who seemed to have such a strong moral code. Maybe the small ray of light in his painting represented people with courage who stood up to evil. It made me wonder what I stood for. It was one thing to have professional ambitions, but underneath that, did I really have the courage to stand up to evil? People thought I was brave to take up surgery, but in fact, I was doing exactly what I wanted. Was that courage? I doubted it.

I opened the next chart on the pile and began to read. Being faithful in small things, I thought, meant putting one foot ahead of the other, even if the final destination wasn't clear. I'd promised to do no harm, and that meant that I couldn't turn away if I suspected wrongdoing.

How could I confirm whether these discharge notes were accurate? If I could compare the san's files to the town's record of vital statistics, then discrepancies would reveal themselves fairly quickly. I'd have to try to get to town on my next day off.

Of course, I'd added to my workload by pursuing this investigation in my free time, so I only had myself to blame for the resulting fatigue. Not that there was a lot of choice; it was too cold to think about outdoor recreation— the temperature had fallen way below freezing and I'd finally had to resort to using the tunnels. I had been warned that frostbite could happen in a matter of minutes. There were always patient entertainments at the san, including film nights, theatricals, and craft activities, but I didn't feel comfortable attending too many of those events. None of the other doctors seemed to attend; even the patients might be uncomfortable to have me there.

A week later, I finally managed to get a day free with reasonable weather to visit the town hall. I hoped the weather would remain calm; I didn't relish the idea of having my car slide off the road into a ditch. In fact, I dressed very warmly and put a blanket in the back seat just in case.

I had prepared a story in advance for the clerk at town hall and I hoped that I could make a credible case for gaining access. The clerk, an elderly woman who seemed burdened by the amount of work waiting for her, didn't seem to care in the least why I might want such information. I supposed if I spent my days registering births and deaths, I might have little curiosity left as well.

To prepare for the town visit, I selected ten patients who appeared to have died at the san but whose charts I suspected had been altered. I passed the clerk the list and waited for her to do her search. When she handed me the papers, I sat at a small table in the corner and read through them. I took notes hurriedly because I still had some shopping to do, and I wanted to drive before dark. When finished, I returned the papers to the clerk and thanked her for her help.

"I might be back to do some more research, but I don't want to be a nuisance."

"Oh, don't worry dear. It's nice to have some company. Not too many people drop by this time of year."

"I was worried about driving on those country roads."

"You have to be careful. You work at the san, do you?"

"I do."

That seemed to be enough information for her, and she shifted her attention to the backlog of paper on her desk.

I stuffed my research notes into my bag and put on my coat. The door had a Christmas bell tied to it that rang out cheerfully as I left.

It was odd to see the seasonal decorations in the windows of the stores. I hadn't paid much attention to Christmas. I needed to post the presents I had for Mary and Robert that I'd purchased at the craft fair. Even if I got a few days off for Christmas, I couldn't imagine driving to Albany in this weather.

Maybe Penny would want to celebrate in some small way. I wondered if I could find some small gifts for the guys in Rose Cottage and for Penny. I stopped at a candy store to buy chocolates for the medical records clerk and the librarian. Walking down Main Street, I felt energized by my outing.

After an hour of shopping, I'd found some presents. For Dan, I found a book of magic tricks; for Joe, an apron made of industrial strength denim that said "Top Chef;" and for Jimmy, a book on Adirondack and Hudson River landscape painting. I hoped he would like it—the style seemed very close to some of his work. I spent more time searching for something for Penny; knowing how she loved color, I'd finally settled on an Irish shawl woven of soft mohair that used all the colors of the earth, sky, and sea. It would match her blue eyes perfectly. Penny could wrap it around her shoulders when she sat at her desk in her room. And for myself, I bought two pairs of wool bed socks. It wasn't exciting, but I knew it was a perfect solution to my ice cold feet. I bought some face cream at the apothecary and threw some lipstick in my basket as well. Luckily, the department store offered free wrapping for my presents. It was a wonderful expedition, and I felt like I'd been on a week's vacation by the end of it.

I was still deep in thought as I walked towards my car feeling the exhilaration of a successful shopping trip. I'd stopped earlier at a small coffee shop for a bowl of soup but now it was time to get back. The shadows were lengthening along the main street as I left, and the shoppers were beginning to return to their homes.

I was surprised to run into Dan on the sidewalk outside the department store.

"Fancy seeing you here," he said. "Been Christmas shopping, I see."

I pulled my bag closer. He didn't need to know about my surprise gifts. "How about you?" I asked.

"Just did some errands. Seemed like a good day to come in."

"I guess so," I said, noncommittally. "You have transportation?"

"I have a car."

"See you around." It seemed odd to me that he just happened to be in town that day. I wondered what kinds of errands he had to do. I also wondered if he was following me but that seemed so unlikely, I pushed the thought out of mind. The sun had already slipped away. It was time to get back—especially if I hoped to get supper before the cafeteria closed. I sang along with the Christmas songs on the radio—it had been a while since I'd felt this free.

The next morning, I visited Michelle who was sitting next to the window wearing her institutional pajamas and reading a fashion magazine. A generous arrangement of flowers stood on the bedside table. I sat in the extra chair on the opposite side of the bed.

"You don't need to read about fashion—you are the embodiment of high fashion."

She laughed as she looked down at her patient gown. "This old thing?" she said.

I took a breath. "I just got some of the tests back, and I thought you'd want to know. They're all negative. There's a shadow on your lung and that's what your family doctor saw, but it is not active TB. We'll keep an eye on it, but I think it's an old infection."

"You mean I can leave?" Michelle asked in disbelief as she sat up in her chair and closed the magazine.

"No reason to stay. You can go home and start working on the gala."

Michelle groaned. "The gala. What am I going to do about that? I still need a headliner."

"I was talking with some of the patients who had some suggestions. I can take you to meet the men at Rose Cottage when convenient."

"How about right now?" Michelle said, as she hastily threw her things into her small suitcase and looked for her street clothes. "Discharge me, doc, I'm going home."

I smiled. "Give me a few moments to finish the paperwork. I just wanted to make sure that you were ready to go home—seeing as you're having such a nice vacation here."

"Oh, please. . . ."

"You pack up. I'll be back shortly to walk you over to Rose Cottage."

"Hurry back. I'll be waiting."

Chapter 30

LOUISE, SAN, 1950

THAT night, Penny brought a stack of papers to my room in the residence. "Did you have a good trip to town?"

"After I did my research at town hall, I visited the stores. I never was that much of a shopper, but I have to say, it was delightful to shop instead of figure out length-of-stay numbers. I did some Christmas shopping and mailed a package to my sister. It's a bit of a surprise to see there's a normal world outside of this place."

Penny sighed. "I can't wait to go shopping—it feels like it's been forever since I was out in the world."

"I ran into Dan in town. He just appeared on the street and said he was doing some errands."

Penny looked surprised. "That's strange."

"Maybe I'm just getting paranoid, but I did wonder if he was following me."

"Let's hope not. How did the numbers at town hall compare to what we had?"

"There's definitely something off with the official stats."

"So we need to keep digging. It still bothers me that Dan might have been following you. We really need to be careful. I can talk to Joe."

"It might just be a coincidence. Just tell Joe to be careful. We don't know exactly who is involved in all this, and you can't explain much to Joe."

"Before I show you my charts, I have something for you."

She handed me a note that had been folded into a handmade envelope. On the card was a lovely rendering of Rose Cottage in pen and ink that showed a Christmas tree in the front window. Over the cottage roof hung a banner that read: "Christmas Party." Inside the card was an invitation to attend the Christmas Eve service at 5:00 p.m. followed by an Italian dinner at Rose Cottage.

"They have an early service so that patients can get to bed on time."

"I'm think I'm free on Christmas Eve and then on call Christmas Day—that would work out perfectly. Can I bring anything?"

"Joe will have it all under control. He loves nothing better than to cook up a storm at Christmas. Do come—it'll be fun. Now, let me show you my charts." Penny pulled out two pieces of paper on which she'd drawn a graph with a number of columns. She also had a separate index so that her chart wouldn't reveal the patient's name. "Here is record number 000123, and this is the admitting diagnosis, list of surgical procedures, total length of stay, and discharge status. I left a column for miscellaneous notes. Some of the patients have remissions and then acute episodes making it important to track their transfers from ambulatory or cottage status back into full inpatient status, otherwise your numbers will be off. Anyone who is here less than thirty days we'll eliminate from the study."

"You're right. I hadn't thought of that. Some patients get discharged and then return, or they move to the cottage, but then have to be transferred back to the infirmary." I studied the graph and marveled at how clearly she'd managed to summarize the information. "You're right—it's not enough to track admissions and discharges. We have to keep the bigger picture in mind. By the way, you're really good at this."

Penny beamed with pleasure at the praise. "My dad was an accountant. He showed me how to make graphs when I was a kid. I used to enter numbers for him all the time." She sat on my bed, grabbed one of the pillows and hugged it. "I heard some gossip today."

I looked up from the chart. "What?"

Penny enjoyed her moment.

"You know how Dr. Clarke has been away?

"Yes."

"Apparently he's going to be away longer. There's lots of gossip, but no one knows exactly why.

"What?"

Penny jumped off the bed. "Some say his wife is sick, but who knows?"

"Who's in charge?"

"Dr. Patterson will be acting chief."

I was shocked. This would change everything. I stared at the chart without seeing it as my mind raced ahead. Would Dr. Patterson be willing to approve a trial? Dr. Clarke would be furious when he returned and found out; I really didn't want anyone to suffer adverse consequences for being involved in this. But if we had enough time to get some results, it would be worth some risk.

I wished I could just initiate it on my own, but it was essential to follow policies and procedures. Everything we did would eventually be subject to scrutiny. I'd already worked on the consent forms and protocols in case we got a chance. As far as I could see, the infrastructure was in place and ready to be tested, as long as Dr. Patterson was still willing to be the principal investigator and the patients were willing to be trial subjects. He didn't seem bothered by the idea of doing a trial. Perhaps his job was so secure he didn't need to worry. Or maybe he'd just blame the whole thing on me. It was hard to tell.

I turned my attention back to the charts and numbers.

"So the length of stay is not always justified by either the diagnosis or the treatment. Some patients are just kept here for no particular reason, other than to prop up the census?"

"Technically, if they test positive, they have to stay. But in other locations, TB patients are gradually leaving institutions and being treated at home. Domiciliary care is cheaper for the state to maintain. But the problem here is that the criterion for discharge requires a negative test, and we know that patients can test positive and not have active disease—like Michelle."

"Why would they keep some of these folks here for years, if they are well enough to manage at home? That seems cruel."

I shrugged my shoulders. "Perhaps they want to keep a baseline census, either to maintain a certain classification, such as an active hospital designation for purposes of the state, or to keep a per capita funding formula that allows them to collect state subsidies. I don't know enough about the reimbursement side of things. I think the pressure to do surgery has something to do with wanting to be seen as an active treatment hospital rather than a chronic care institution. It's a lot more complicated than I ever realized, and there's probably a degree of risk involved with trying to uncover the truth."

"I've always been told that this place is supposed to be the best in the world for TB treatment. We offer so many programs here—it's hard to imagine that so much of that is window dressing."

I shrugged. "Even though the programs are useful, there are things that might prove to be more effective and provide cures in a shorter amount of time."

Penny looked at me gravely. "Do you think that new drugs and treatments will eventually close this place?"

I nodded slowly in agreement. The radiator clanked and shuddered against the wall.

"Do you think our cover story is still credible?" Penny asked.

"I think it sounds boring enough. I'm not even sure who would be interested in our findings—it's a bit tricky to figure out whom to trust, so continue to trust no one. I've been thinking of asking Doug to store some of our data in the pharmacy safe. It might be a safer place than our rooms or my office and I don't think anyone would look there. What do you think?"

"Great idea. Just don't be seen talking to him because that might trigger someone's interest."

"I have to say, with Dr. Clarke on leave, there are opportunities."

"Like what?" Penny said, as she slid off the bed and put the pillow back and smoothed the bedspread.

I hesitated. "I hope you won't be offended. There's part of this that I need to keep secret right now. It's not that I don't trust you, but it may involve someone you know and I don't want you to get into trouble. It's safer if you know nothing."

Penny nodded in agreement. "I don't need to know. I'll keep working on the numbers. By the way, I almost forgot. I was talking to the medical records person and she said some of the records might not be available because they're currently signed out to the chart review."

"Now that's interesting. Did she say who was in charge of that?"

"You'll never guess . . . Nurse Benoit."

"Oh boy. Don't ruffle anyone down there and keep telling her you're working on a nursing project. Thanks for your hard work. See you tomorrow," I said.

"Good night," Penny whispered as she opened the door, checked the hallway, and quickly made her way to her room.

I studied the charts. It was dark now, and the wind howled outside my window. Someone said there might be as much as two feet of snow by the weekend and the temperatures were supposed to drop well below zero overnight. I shivered and put on another sweater.

While doing rounds on the surgical ward, I ran into Mother Maureen at the nurses' station. She leaned on the counter for support; her skin looked drawn and there were dark circles under her eyes. I knew she was spending long hours at Claire's bedside.

"Could I speak with you for a moment?" she asked.

"Certainly. Let's use the conference room." I followed her into the room and closed the door.

"Are you feeling all right?" I asked.

Mother Maureen shook her head. "I'm fine." She took a breath. "Although I'm thankful for the care that Claire is receiving, I don't feel that she is making enough progress. I'm very concerned."

I explained that I felt Claire's condition had stabilized. Although she wasn't getting worse, the challenge remained to choose the best course of treatment. "Stabilizing her so she'd be a better surgical risk has been the main goal."

Mother Maureen thought for a moment. "How long do you think she'll be here? If there's no active treatment on the horizon, then I'd rather take her back to the convent infirmary."

"I urge you to give it a bit more time. There are some possibilities I am exploring, however, I'm not at liberty to talk about those at the moment."

"Yesterday I spoke with a patient in the cafeteria who'd been here for three years. I really don't want that to happen to Sister Claire. She is an integral part of our community."

"I understand that you're eager to have her discharged, and I want to reassure you that that is my goal as well. If I could just ask for a bit more time—this is a time to heal.. . . ."

"A doctor who quotes Ecclesiastes." Mother Maureen looked at me carefully and then nodded agreement.

She had decided to trust me—for now. I knew I needed to show some improvement soon or Mother Maureen would discharge her against medical advice. She was a formidable person. I hoped I would not fall short in her estimation.

The next day, after performing my morning surgeries, I dropped by Dr. Patterson's office.

"You haven't moved to the main building yet?" I asked.

"I'm quite happy to stay here. They know where to find me if I'm needed."

"Do you know why Dr. Clarke is away?"

"He's on leave. He's long overdue a sabbatical."

I studied him carefully and waited to see if he would say more, but he did not.

"I brought the protocols for your final review."

While Dr. Patterson read the final draft of the research protocol, I studied the snow clouds gathering. Yesterday, a storm dropped a foot of snow on top of the piles that had accumulated in the past week. I'd never seen so much of the stuff, and it just kept coming down. Hills of shoveled snow were piled up in various corners of the property. I was beginning to long for winter to end. Many of the patients seemed listless in the cold weather, and even the hardiest of walkers had trouble being outside for any length of time.

I studied Dr. Patterson as he read the file. He looked tired. I wondered why he chose to continue to work at the san. I wanted to ask him, but he didn't seem to encourage that kind of conversation. I also wondered why he would take the risk of running this drug trial. Penny told me that his family had settled in the area and didn't want to move—his wife liked her home and two of his children were on a high school ski team. Surely he realized that doing the trial would aggravate Dr. Clarke to the point of firing people? Why did he think the trial was worth the risk when nothing else was? It wasn't my place to warn him of the obvious risks. Maybe he was bored with the endless rounds of surgeries that promised little lasting relief for the patients. Although I had less to lose with only a few months left to the fellowship, I worried for others who might be adversely affected by the fallout when Dr. Clarke found out.

"Let's go over this once more. You have enough of the trial medication for four people to start?" he asked.

"That's all I could get, but Doug assured me he'll obtain more soon. Although the company can't keep up with the demand, he has friends there who might move us up the priority list—especially if we agree to be a test site and publish results. It's good advertising for them and gives them credibility."

"I'd like to have the contact information for the drug company in the next submission please. This drug has already been tried in other locations in England and the States, correct?"

"Reports are very good from a variety of trial sites."

"And you'll be involved in the daily monitoring?"

"I plan to do regular blood work and vital signs."

"How long will this test run?"

"We'll administer a fourteen-day course of the meds, and the company says we should see some improvement. They've studied the use of mono-treatment with Streptomycin, but we'd like to do a combination treatment with Isoniazid and Streptomycin. I've discussed this with Doug and with someone from the company, and they think it's a promising strategy."

"How will you know when there's improvement?

"I expect to see that the patient will be afebrile, feel better, and have gained weight with no side effects. There should be a decrease in coughing or sputum and X-rays should show improvement. Bacteria might still be present in the smears, but they'll become more difficult to culture. We'll monitor through X-ray and sputum and blood work."

"How will you choose the subjects?"

"I'll take two of the longer-stay patients in the cottage and then two new admissions in order to compare the effect on acute and chronic phases of the disease."

"Good. How many staff will know about this?"

"You and Doug so far. Penny knows a little. I told her I needed to keep her out of the trial for her own well-being due to her friendship with one of the subjects."

"How will you know if things aren't working?"

"If the X-rays or other lab work don't show improvement or if symptoms like cough and fever return, then I'll know. If there are any adverse reactions, we'll discontinue the drug immediately and try to come up with other options. We need to keep the patients' expectations reasonable. They should know there are no guarantees."

"If they are willing to take the risk, then we have to hope for the best. Sounds like you've covered it. If this succeeds, it may eradicate TB and the need for the san altogether. We'll both be out of a job. Make sure you get signed consents on file, and swear them to secrecy until we see how this goes."

I wondered how he felt about putting in motion forces that could make the san obsolete. I felt strongly that there would always be a need for surgery and for care facilities that expanded the mission to other lung diseases and surgeries. "I think surgeons will always be needed. There are still two hundred thousand known cases of TB in the States with one hundred fifty thousand unknown active cases, and one hundred fifty thousand new cases annually. But there'll be other challenges, even when TB is eradicated; chronic diseases, like emphysema and asbestos lung, are going to increase. If people keep smoking, we'll have a plague on our hands."

Dr. Patterson nodded as he looked out the window. "We'll just have to see how things go."

His affect troubled me—he seemed committed to the project but somehow detached as well. He showed neither excitement nor fear; I would have expected one or the other. "There's one other thing—I'm pretty sure my room was searched after the patient concert when someone knew I'd be out."

Dr. Patterson nodded. "Keep me informed, and be very careful. I don't think we need to bring in the police at this point, but we can do that if it's necessary. If you feel any level of personal threat, call me immediately or call the local police." He wrote his number on a prescription pad and passed it to me. "This is my home number."

"Thank you." There was no point in having a policeman standing outside my dorm room or following me around the building—I wanted to be much less visible while I monitored this trial and try not to attract any notice. Having a bodyguard would defeat that objective. I'd take my chances that whoever searched my room was a snoop, not a personal threat.

Chapter 31

LOUISE, SAN, 1950

THE public phone was located on the wall in a small closet with a pocket door at the end of the residence hallway. I dialed the number of the manse and listened to it ring five times. Robert answered, and I was surprised to hear his voice, since he was usually in his church office or on pastoral visits during the day.

"Mary's on bed rest for a few days and can't come to the phone."

"Why?" I had a sinking feeling that I already knew the answer.

"Another miscarriage."

I groaned. "I'm so sorry. How is she doing?"

"It gets harder and harder." He sounded sad.

I paused. "I'm sure it's difficult for both of you. Could you please give her my love and tell her when she is up to it, I'd love to talk with her?" I twisted the coiled phone cord around my index finger. I could picture Mary in the double bed upstairs in the manse. Did she have friends who understood what she was going through? Did the church ladies bring casseroles and fuss over Robert?

"I know she'd love to talk to you. I'll give her the message."

"Give her a hug."

"Will do."

I hung up the phone and sat for a few moments in the dark phone booth. I felt badly for them. I resolved to write her to try to cheer her up. It would be impossible to get away now with the drug trial in progress; I hoped Mary would understand. With any luck, Robert wouldn't be too heavy handed with his explanations of God's will. Mary certainly didn't need to hear that right now.

Whatever I thought about God these days, I knew with a deep certainty that no divine being would intentionally initiate such loss. Nature was just inherently unpredictable, no matter how much people wanted to tame it or pretend they could control it. Robert and I had argued about such things far into the night, but he'd never convinced me of his version of God's will. I pointed out to him that his arguments were mere speculation, since no human had the capacity to know God's mind. I'd seen unexpected deaths, as well as spontaneous healings, and I had to allow for some inexplicable mystery that kept full understanding out of reach of either scientists or theologians. Robert refused to give up his claim to know God—perhaps that was something that resulted from his degree in theology. In the end, though, I needed to acknowledge that we weren't all that different. We were both filled with arrogant certainty that we knew all the answers.

But as I tried to explain to him the last time we had one of our discussions, the longer I practiced medicine, the more I had to admit that the human body was a mysterious creation. My efforts to understand it had to be couched in humility and wonder, not in arrogance and superiority. If God was truly divine and transcendent, then it seemed logical to me that all humans could ever do was glimpse imperfect knowing. To be human was to accept with humility that there were limits to knowledge. If I applied that to my own profession, I'd have to admit that medical certainty had to be guided by both awe and wonder. Robert, needless to say, thought I'd lost my marbles.

I still believed in and relied on science to try to eliminate the suffering caused by illness, but I had to admit that there were holes in my understanding of the bigger picture.

Robert and I had also argued about how religion could mislead people about illness. I'd seen so many patients wonder if their illness was a punishment for something they'd done. I happened to think that illness was random and that no one deserved or earned that kind of trouble. Making God an unpredictable partner in the daily workings of the world meant that no one was safe. How could one develop trust the face of such a mercurial divine will? That sort of question made me grateful to return to research and experiments to find solutions. The "why" of suffering was something was outside of my expertise.

Perhaps doctors weren't any better than preachers, promising cures that couldn't always be delivered. And in other cases, patients healed themselves without any specific medical intervention. Both professions dealt with uncertainty in different ways, but in the end, they tried to claim a certainty that I doubted was humanly possible. Sometimes I wondered if my claims for atheism were more religious than Robert's professed faith in his version of God. But I made sure I didn't say that aloud in his presence. There was no point in provoking him, and Mary didn't appreciate our arguments.

I looked forward to talking to Mary and felt deeply unsettled by the knowledge that she was going through tough times. Even if I could talk to her, there was little I could share with her about all that was going on at the san. She would only worry.

I bundled up and went outside—maybe the sub-zero temperatures would energize me. I was starting to feel the same listlessness I observed in many patients. We needed the flat white and cold grays of winter to be replaced with some sunlight and color, but patients warned me that this would continue for months. I walked east on the property, observing very few footprints in the snow and even fewer walkers on the usual paths. I headed towards the barn, drawn by the familiar sounds and smells. Mary would have found it hilarious, I was sure, but I felt a wave of nostalgia for the farm. I stood at the entry to the barn and watched the men at work.

"Hey, doc, come in."

I smiled and walked into the barn, giving my eyes a moment to adjust.

"Don't suppose you want to do some milking?" the foreman asked with a smile.

"Actually, I'd love that."

He looked at me to see if I was joking, but then realized I was serious. He motioned for me to follow him and showed me where to sit.

I patted the cow's flank a few times and murmured to her and then proceeded to collect the milk in a pail.

"You've done this before?" the man asked.

"Grew up doing this. But it's been a long time."

"You're welcome any time."

I watched the barn cats delicately wander through the barn, alert but uncaring, knowing there was plentiful food to be had. They had reasons to feel secure—the mice and milk offered them a comfortable existence. When I was done, I stood up from the stool and stretched my back. I brought the pail to the foreman and thanked him.

"Come back anytime. We won't tell your boss."

I smiled and waved to the others. I hoped I didn't reek of the barn, but I felt like my feet were more solidly planted on the ground than they'd been for a while. I decided to detour to Rose Cottage and to see if anyone was home. A cup of tea would be the perfect antidote to the cold before I went back to work for the rest of the day and evening.

As I approached Rose Cottage, I saw Jimmy shoveling the snow on the walk, and the snow banks were up to his waist.

"Is this part of your physio?" I asked. "Why do your roommates never help?"

Jimmy smiled, slightly out of breath, as he leaned on the shovel. "They're just lazy. We're supposed to get another foot this weekend. Do you want to come in for some tea?"

"I would love that, but I really need to wash my hands. I've been milking a cow."

"You're a person with many talents."

"I also smell like a barn, but I have to say, it sure felt good to be there."

I followed him inside, and we sat at the kitchen table while waiting for the kettle to boil. "I wanted to talk to you about something, but it has to be confidential."

He nodded.

I continued. "We have access to very limited doses of an experimental drug that has shown promise in other sites. I'd like to enlist a few patients to try this, and I wonder if you'd be interested?"

He blew his nose in a cotton handkerchief that he stuffed into his coat pocket and studied her. "You say this has been tested elsewhere with success?"

"It has gone through trials in a few different settings with good results."

"And what might bad results look like?"

"Some patients might not be able to tolerate the drug and develop an allergic reaction or toxicity. Or the drug might not be effective for their particular kind of TB."

He got up to make tea.

I let him think about what I'd said and waited quietly for his response.

He carefully poured hot water into the pot and brought it to the table.

"If you think this is a good idea, I'm willing to try. I hate to get my hopes up, but you know that I am anxious to get home."

"I understand. I can't guarantee that this will work, but I believe it's worth a try."

"And this would replace surgery . . . if it works?"

"We'll hold off on the surgery and see if we can get the needed results using the new medication. But we'll keep a surgical option in reserve, in case we need it."

Jimmy nodded thoughtfully. "Throughout history, my people have been subject to medical experiments that were not always to their benefit."

I nodded. I knew about some of that history, but I hoped he would realize that this was nothing of that sort. "You know where my office is in the basement of the infirmary. If you could drop by this afternoon, I'll have you sign the release form and do some blood work. I'll explain any potential side effects to you. You'll need to keep this very quiet. We can't afford to let this become public yet. In fact, it would be very harmful if it did. And I only have a handful of doses so I can't expand the trial at the moment."

He looked at her carefully. "I wouldn't want to start a stampede on your office." He paused. "You're going to get me better, right?"

"I'll do my best. I know they're waiting for you at home."

He nodded thoughtfully. "As long as there's a plan. I need to feel that something is happening. Drifting through days and weeks hoping someone will do something is not how I want to live my life."

"I'll explain the rest this afternoon. By the way, although Joe will be invited to be part of this trial, Dan won't be in this round. He doesn't seem to be in any hurry to get out of here. I don't want to create problems with your roommates, but I have limited doses to work with, and I need to have an equal number of men and women."

"Dan will understand. I think he has some romantic reasons to linger."

"He does?" I knew nothing about any romance.

Jimmy smiled but gave nothing else away.

"There's something else I wanted to ask you." I cradled the china cup in my hand and felt its warmth. "Might I ask you for some advice?"

"Of course."

"This place has many secrets."

He nodded again.

I decided to trust him as he had trusted me. He wouldn't be surprised by anything I told him about the san. As head of the patients' council, he probably knew much more about what happened there than I did. "I've been doing some research and there's a lot here that just doesn't feel right. Dr. Clarke warned me away from any investigation, but that only made me more determined. I feel like I'm only seeing the tip of the iceberg, and I'm not sure what to do about it or who to trust."

"I think you need to be very careful. It's important to get evidence if you think something isn't right, but you need to be vigilant. He has eyes all over the place. Just because he's on leave doesn't mean he isn't monitoring things from a distance." He paused. "What are your plans once this fellow-ship is done?"

"I hope to get into a surgical residency. I came here to get some experi-ence and boost my chances of getting into a good program. But I'm also afraid that if I get into trouble here, no one will accept me, and my career will be over before it has even started."

"Do you think that any of the issues you are concerned about could threaten a patient's health or safety?"

I thought for a moment. "No, this is related to reimbursement matters. If I saw a direct threat to patients, I'd be morally obliged to act."

"Do no harm?"

"Exactly."

"Don't let concern for the future dictate how you act in the present. There'll always be work for you to do. Being a high powered surgeon may be your goal, but there might be other options as well."

"Like what?" I looked at him in surprise.

"I wonder if surgery will be enough for you in the long run. You're good with people, and you have an excellent ability to solve problems. Just keep an open mind."

I studied my teacup. I didn't know what to say. I'd had one goal for so long that it felt disloyal to question it. For a long time, it seemed like I'd made steady progress towards getting what I wanted, but in the past year, I'd had some doubts. The operating room had been a safe place where I felt competent and in control. I felt I was awkward in dealing with the emotional complexity of patients and families, and doing surgery eliminated the need for interaction. But some of my illusions about surgery had begun to be shattered when I'd had that miserable experience with the chief of surgery at Yale. I didn't want to become that kind of person. It was hard to let go of a plan that had been so constant for so long. I wasn't the type of person who tolerated that kind of ambiguity of purpose very well.

Jimmy patted my hand. "The answer will reveal itself in time."

"I can't afford to wait too long. I'll need to apply for residencies soon. When this fellowship ends, I'll have nowhere to go."

"Listen to what makes you happy. The road will open."

I was no longer sure of what made me happy. The surgeries I was doing were not that challenging. Only my own research and reading offered me learning opportunities. "Any advice for the investigation?"

"Continue your research, but be careful. And remember, the Bible tells us that the truth can set us free."

I looked at him. "Free from what?"

Jimmy looked at me. "Slavery is very real for some of us, but the lack of freedom can take many forms. The Bible suggests that knowledge can bring true freedom."

"What would that freedom look like and what would it cost?"

"It's hard to know in advance. All you can do is start from the right place with good intentions."

"Are you saying that pure ambition is not a good starting point?"

"We all need some ambition or hope to get us going, but if our only concern is to focus on ourselves, there will always be something missing."

"I'm more confused than ever," I said, putting down my china cup on the saucer. "What am I supposed to care about if not myself? No one else will do that."

"You will find your way. There are causes much bigger than any one person can take on. When our eyes are open, we see the need."

I took a big breath. "I hope I don't disappoint you. I may be too shallow to work from such deep motivations."

"You might surprise yourself. But if you are doing any investigation here, be very careful. There is danger everywhere."

I felt confused. On the one hand, he was encouraging me to take risks, but on the other, he was warning me that some of my choices might not be ultimately satisfying. In the meantime, time was passing, and I was stalled in my decision-making process. If I missed the application deadlines, I would have to find something else to do. I could possibly get a locum somewhere and work for another year to build up my savings, but it seemed like yet another delay.

I walked over the shoveled path towards the infirmary and made a mental list of what I needed to do before this afternoon when the prospective trial patients would arrive at my basement office. I wondered again if the trial was too small to be significant. It seemed I was hastening my own premature departure from this place—even as I had promised myself I would go along with the program to get a good reference. Was trouble following me, or was I choosing trouble? I wanted to turn away from these challenges and just do my job, doing surgeries and admitting patients without a thought to the bigger picture. But that was impossible. If I did that, I would be no better than Dr. Clarke, using the san and the lives of innocent people for my own benefit.

A few days later, I finished my rounds and hurried over to the pharmacy to check with Doug. The pilot project was underway. Doug seemed excited to be part of the research—the work kept him in touch with pharmaceutical companies and government regulators. Although normally a shy, retiring type, he was more energetic and forthcoming than I'd seen. By contrast, Dr.

Patterson had become sullen and noncommittal, withdrawing into himself in ways I didn't understand.

Doug had told his contacts in the drug company to keep the trial quiet until we had some solid results. For most people on the pharmaceutical side, the test sites were numbered, and their researchers didn't have access to the specific location. Even with those precautions, I knew we wouldn't be able to keep this under wraps for long, but I truly hoped we could get some results before things became public or Dr. Clarke returned.

Chapter 32

LOUISE, SAN, 1950

EVERY day I checked on the four patients I'd enrolled in the trial, and so far they were all doing well. I was relieved. Jimmy and Joe represented long-term patients and Sister Claire and Mrs. Collier were more recent admissions.

While I was talking to Doug, Joe knocked on the door.

"Excuse me, Dr. Garrett, you gotta come quick. Jimmy's sick. He's been throwing up and dizzy. I don't know what's wrong. He says he feels terrible and sent me to get you."

I looked at Doug in alarm, grabbed my coat, picked up my stethoscope and hurried to follow Joe.

Jimmy reclined in one of the sleeping chairs on the porch with a bucket on the floor beside him. He looked miserable.

"What's going on?" I felt his brow and found him to be feverish. I checked his eyes for signs of jaundice and saw a yellowish cast.

"Maybe Joe poisoned me with his cooking last night. Please tell me you're not killing me with this drug." Jimmy looked at me sadly, disappointment written on his face.

I gave him a thorough examination, checked his pupils, palpated his abdomen and took his blood pressure. I took off my stethoscope, folded it carefully and put it in my pocket, and looked at him. "I think you're having a drug reaction. I'm so sorry. We're going to have to stop the meds. You can't afford to get liver damage."

"But if you stop the trial . . . what happens then?"

I touched the top of his hand lightly. "There's still the surgical option. I wanted to try this first, but if your body can't handle the drugs, we'll do the surgery."

"Why is no one else having a reaction?" he asked.

"Each person will react differently depending on a lot of factors. You are the only person of your race in the pilot. We can't predict how the body will respond—that will take a lot more research."

"How soon can you do the surgery?" he asked with concern.

"As soon as you're stable, and the drugs are out of your system."

He grabbed her hand. "I need to go home. I've been away too long. My mother-in-law is very ill and my wife needs my help."

"I'll do my best. I promise." I felt badly. This was not how I wanted things to go. "I'll be back to check on you. In the meantime, I'll order some anti-nausea medication, and we'll stop the drugs immediately. I really hope you feel better, and I'll be monitoring you closely."

I turned away and went to consult with Joe, who waited anxiously in the living room. "Keep an eye on him and let me know if there's any change. Although I could admit him, I have a feeling he'll be more comfortable here. I'll make sure that a nurse will check on you. She won't know about the trial but we can act like he has the flu. It's a necessary deception for now—I can't afford for the news to go through the san, if I can help it. I'll be in the base-ment office or in the residence if you need me."

"Do we get to choose which nurse?" he asked.

"I could find a few that would be more than willing to whip this cot-tage into shape."

He held up his hand to stop her. "Never mind," Joe said with a smile. "We'll be just fine."

I walked briskly over the newly cleared path to my office and checked Jimmy's more recent lab work. Some values were slightly elevated. I planned to check with Doug, but I was pretty sure I had to discontinue the trial in his case—I couldn't afford to have anything go wrong. If something happened to a patient while on the trial, Dr. Clarke would have my license suspended. I wanted to live up to Jimmy's trust; I had promised I'd find a way to get him discharged.

As I walked past the corner of the surgical floor, I saw Nurse Benoit, the security guard, and one of the young doctors in a huddle. They were arguing about something, but I couldn't hear what it was. I couldn't linger without being noticed, so I ran up the staircase to the operating room. I wondered if they represented Dr. Clarke's faithful followers. Without his daily commands, his team might be in disarray, unless he was he giving them orders from a distance. I couldn't imagine he'd ignore the state of the san in his absence. Jimmy was likely right about that.

Mary would be horrified if she knew that I'd put myself at risk to pursue this. It was particularly difficult because there was no safe place here—even our rooms were subject to search, and it felt like there were eyes everywhere monitoring what we did. It was an essential part of sanatorium care—to monitor and control every moment of a person's life under the guise of helping them regain their health. That so-called concern had been twisted to give authorities the right to control every aspect of a patient's life, when what they really needed to do was to cure and send people home. And the surveillance extended from patients to staff.

The situation at the moment gave me increased anxiety that made me jumpy and unable to sleep deeply. I even wondered if my chest pain was a heart attack but then decided that it was just panic. Managing my clinical and surgical responsibilities was one thing, but juggling the trial and the research and being on call at night was having an effect on my health. The uncertainty about who was friend or foe made me feel like I was walking on eggshells.

I took the stairs to the operating room and searched the fridge of the doctors' lounge to find a sandwich. I had to eat something before my surgery; it would be very unprofessional to faint in the operating room. If that happened to a man, it would be a joke to be shared—but if it happened to me, it would be seen as a sign of weakness.

I tried to list the things that were making me anxious in an attempt to contain my fretting. I felt like a dog chasing its tail. I was worried about the drug trial, Jimmy, and Mary. Robert had sounded so sad on the phone the other night. I worried about what would happen when the trial was uncovered and what I would do if I were fired from this fellowship. Somehow I had to break this cycle of anxiety—it would undermine all my best efforts if I didn't manage it better. If I had been a praying type, this would have been the time. I admit that I sent up general pleas for assistance; at that point, I needed all the help available. But first, I needed to eat the sandwich and calm myself before entering the surgical suite.

When I focused on the patient in front of me, I realized how much I loved the solemn quiet in the operating room and the sense of anticipation for the procedure ahead. There was no room for distraction when you prepared to cut into a person's body. Other surgeons I'd worked with enjoyed gossiping and chatting with the nurses in the operating room; I preferred silence and focused attention. Maybe it was a form of prayer after all, I thought, wondering what Robert would make of that.

&

After surgery, I was trying to catch up on some work in my office, when Joe knocked on the door. I felt a jolt of alarm when I saw his face. I hoped Jimmy hadn't had another setback.

When he saw my face, he realized what I was thinking.

"He's fine. I just wanted to talk to you."

"Sure, come in."

"I really appreciate what you are doing for us at the cottage. Don't get me wrong. And I don't need to know what you're working on with Penny. She said she promised you that she wouldn't share information because it would threaten the results. But it gets me riled up when I see Penny intimidated and threatened. I don't want her to be put at risk."

"What happened?"

"That guard was following her around and then he told her she better mind her own business or he'd teach her a lesson she wouldn't forget."

"I'm so sorry. Is she all right?"

"Sure, Penny is tough. But that doesn't mean I'm happy that she's in a position to be threatened or that some creep is following her around."

What could I say to him? He looked visibly upset. Penny would never back off—she was tough as could be, and she was determined to do the research. "I'm really sorry that this happened. I can talk to her, but she's got her own mind."

"I know that. I just hope that you two don't get in over your heads. And you better know how to ask for help when you need it."

I nodded. How could I reassure him when I didn't know exactly what we were up against? "I'm really sorry, and I'll talk to her. We'll be very careful, and we'll ask for help should we need that."

Joe studied my face and seemed satisfied for now with my reassurance. "I gotta go. See you."

My heart was pounding in my chest. I didn't want Penny to take unnecessary risks, and I didn't want Joe to worry. Were we really doing the right thing? Maybe if I picked up the phone and called the state, they would come and figure it all out. Why did we need to take all the risks? Why run a drug trial when I could only get four doses of medication? Who would care about that? It wasn't significant enough.

Once I started doubting, the questions wouldn't stop. Why had I come here? Did I really think I could build a reputation using this place and further my career as a result? I was no different than Dr. Clarke, I realized, maneuvering people and events to support my own agenda. I held my head in my hands and let the misery roll over me like a vast frothing wave. I suddenly remembered Pastor Cal in Mississippi who challenged me to be a doctor with a heart—someone who kept the poor at the forefront of my work. Instead, I'd focused on my own success, and in the process I'd created a mess that endangered the people around me.

I was exhausted from worry and work. I put my head on my arm and fell asleep at my desk. When I finally woke up, I felt groggy and sore, as if the anxiety and dread had invaded my very muscles. I wanted to talk to Mary but I couldn't let her know what was going on here. She would be so worried.

The next day I finished surgery and took a cup of coffee to my office, planning to do some reading. I passed the security guard on the staircase, but ignored him. His smirk irritated me to no end. I wondered what he was doing there in the first place. There were two other guards I'd noticed on other shifts, but they stayed in the administrative building and kept an eye on the reception area and the offices.

I unlocked the door with one hand, balancing my mail and coffee mug in the other. When I turned on the light, I froze and almost dropped my coffee. Someone had vandalized the office—papers were strewn around and something sticky had been poured on the floor. On the chalkboard on the far wall someone had written "Go Home!" I stepped carefully over the tacky floor and put my mug and mail on the desk. My hands trembled as I called Doug and asked him to come to my office.

He arrived a few minutes later. "Oh, no. Who did this?"

I looked at him silently. "Let's just say, I don't think we should call security."

"Do you keep any records here?"

"Nothing significant. I don't think anyone could tell much from what's here."

"I think we should call the police."

I sighed. "I'm afraid of drawing attention to our work."

"They don't need to know about that. It's just a matter of safety. Who knows what someone might try to do next? These things can escalate and then the police will ask you why you didn't report the trouble."

He reached over to her phone, got an outside line, and talked to the police in town.

"They'll be here in fifteen minutes. Don't touch anything. In fact, I think we should leave this and wait for them by the front door."

I reluctantly left the mess and followed Doug to the reception area. There was no sign of the guard anywhere. He was probably smoking somewhere and chuckling at his handiwork. I reminded myself that I had no evidence that it was the guard. There might be others who were working on Dr. Clarke's orders.

When the policeman arrived, we showed him the office and he took notes and asked a few questions. There was little he could do. The vandal had left no trace and no fingerprints; it was easy enough to find gloves here. He reassured me that he would file a report, and if we needed additional security he would talk to his chief. When he asked me if I had any idea who might have done it, I said no. There was no point in flinging accusations that I couldn't substantiate.

After the policeman left, Doug helped me to recover lab work and notes. I called housekeeping to clean the floor.

I needed to let Dr. Patterson know. I would hate to think that these acts might escalate and affect others—Joe would not be happy if he heard about this. There was a limited time frame to prove something conclusively or we would be stopped—which for me likely meant being fired. I had saved some money in the past months, and I had my car. I could last for a little while, but it wouldn't take long to run out of funds. Maybe Mary wouldn't mind a houseguest for a few weeks till I sorted out my future. In fact, maybe she and Robert could use some help. She had sounded so fragile in my calls with her.

Chapter 33

LOUISE, SAN, CHRISTMAS EVE, 1950

WITH all the worries of the past weeks, I almost lost track of the upcoming holiday. Luckily, I had mailed my parcel to Mary and Robert a while before, and I planned to call them the next day after their morning service.

I hurried to change for the chapel service. Ambulatory patients were allowed to attend the service this evening followed by a special dinner in the cafeteria.

Wearing black wool trousers and an off-white sweater, I made sure I wore my hair down and applied some makeup to save myself another lecture from Penny. After putting my gifts in a bag, I put on my coat and boots. The weather continued to be bitterly cold with no hope of thaw in the near future. This was not a time to dash anywhere without proper outdoor clothing.

The grounds of the san had turned into a winter wonderland. Some of the cottages had been decorated for the season using strings of colored lights. A few hardy souls had even made snowmen. In the center of the green, a large evergreen was lit up with bright bulbs. It felt magical as the snow crunched under my feet and the cold air grabbed my breath.

Penny was waiting inside the foyer of the chapel. "I hope you're hungry. Joe's been cooking all day."

"What are we having?"

"He wouldn't say, but it's some Italian Christmas Eve tradition from his grandmother."

"I brought some wine."

"That's great. Don't break it on the chapel floor."

"Can you imagine? Look, before we go in, I just need to tell you something."

Penny paused. "What?"

"Joe talked to me and he was really worried about the risks we're taking. He said you were threatened by the guard."

"He worries too much. That creep of a guard doesn't scare me. Let him just try something, and I'll show him. I grew up with brothers and I know how to defend myself."

"I don't want to get into trouble with Joe."

"Don't worry about him. He fusses worse than my mother. Let's go find the guys before the place is full."

Patients and staff were streaming into the chapel. Every time the front doors opened, I felt a blast of cold air.

Jimmy, Dan, and Joe had claimed a pew and covered the empty spaces with their coats, so we hurried over to sit with them. I sat in the middle of the pew, between Jimmy and Penny and Joe sat at the end of the row. It felt good to be there with them. Tonight I was not a doctor, but just another person among friends.

Volunteers had put together a nativity scene at the front of the church. Each window was decorated with evergreen branches and simple white lights. Several Christmas trees were decorated with lights and tinsel near the altar. Even the pipe organ on the left was covered with pine branches. A row of electric candles ran along a rafter at the front.

A small music ensemble gathered from patients and a few staff stood at the front with their instruments. As last-minute arrivals hurried to take their seats, the lights were turned down. Someone lit the Christ candle as the ensemble began to sing "It Came Upon a Midnight Clear." Before the next carol, the director indicated that we should stand and join them. As the voices filled the cozy chapel, I had goose bumps when I heard the familiar carol. On one side, Jimmy's baritone floated effortlessly over us, while on the other, Penny sang the alto line. I felt the richness of the harmony inviting me into the mystery that we had gathered to celebrate. Despite my despair yesterday, a feeling of gratitude surprised me. Although I had celebrated Christmas as a child, in recent years I was often on call. I heard the songs and story in a different way. Not only Mary and Joseph, but also all of us at the san were dislocated. The unexpected gift of the season was to find friends and fellow travellers.

As the service drew to a close, the lights were again turned down until the church glowed with the warmth of the candles and the decorative lights. We sang "Silent Night" accompanied by a violin. As the song moved into the second verse, the congregation slowly and quietly emptied into the cold night. There was something profoundly touching about that quiet exodus from the simple chapel.

As we moved outside, I imagined the difficulties of the journey that Mary had taken and the birth that had put them in a rough place, so far from home. Despite that, perhaps they'd experienced both joy and amazement at the birth and the subsequent celestial recognition.

We walked quietly over the shoveled pathway. Penny and Joe took the lead while Dan disappeared into the crowd, and Jimmy and I followed. We shivered as we took off our boots and coats at the cottage. Jimmy gathered up the coats and took them to the upstairs bedroom. The house was infused with the scents of garlic and wine.

Joe invited us to sit in the living room. "First, I will serve an antipasta course that will be delicious, if I say so myself. If someone could open the wine and someone else could slice the bread and light the candles, we'll be ready to begin the feast."

"It smells incredible." I sliced the bread in perfect slices, thinking ruefully that my surgical training was occasionally put to good use. Penny lit the candles.

It was touching to see the effort they'd put into decorating the cottage. Fresh branches lined the windows and the fireplace mantle. Jimmy started a fire with the logs that had been piled up in advance.

Joe placed the platter with an arrangement of olives, salami, roasted peppers, and cheese on the coffee table. He flipped a record onto a small record player—Bing Crosby.

A small Christmas tree stood in the corner decorated with old-fashioned glass ornaments and lights. I slid my presents under the tree and then joined Penny on the couch.

"Are you sure we can't do anything else?" I asked as I saw Joe working in the kitchen.

Joe held up his hand. "No one is allowed in the kitchen. We're reaching the final and critical stage. I'll join you in a moment, so please go ahead. I have to boil water for the pasta and warm up the sauce."

Jimmy poured wine for us and passed the appetizers. He served himself a glass of water. After his drug reaction I'd cautioned him against having any alcohol.

I leaned back against the couch and looked around, smiling at the coziness of the cottage.

"What kind of traditions did you have at home?" I asked Penny.

"My mother and I always baked cookies for a neighborhood cookie exchange. We usually went to Midnight Mass on Christmas Eve. And then on Christmas Day there'd be a mad opening of presents, and in the afternoon we usually went skating. I had three brothers who were born with hockey sticks in their hands and there were lots of frozen ponds around where we lived."

"How about you, Jimmy?"

"I remember relatives showing up from all over the place. Aunts and uncles and cousins piled into cars and drove from wherever they lived. We played all day until we fell asleep on the floor upstairs. There was tons of food and singing at church and playing in the park down the street. We had so much fun."

We sat and listened to the music while sipping our wine and sampling the food on the platter. After a while, Joe joined us in the living room and lifted a glass. "Merry Christmas. Here's to a happy and healthy New Year! Cheers! And now, I invite you to take your place at the table. Bring your glasses."

I sat down at my designated place and admired the setting. Somehow they had found a Christmas tablecloth and napkins. A wreath of greens with berries was placed in the center of the table with a large beeswax candle in the middle. "This is just beautiful," I said. "Who did all this?"

The men smiled. "It was a group effort. And we talked the Ladies' Auxiliary into loaning us some decorations that they didn't need."

"What's Dan doing tonight?"

Joe shrugged. "No idea."

Joe brought them each a plate and sat down at the head of the table. "Jimmy, would you say grace?"

Jimmy held out his hands and we all joined hands and bowed our heads as he quietly blessed the food and prayed for all our families and friends on yet another Christmas far away from home. I thought of Mary and Robert busy with church services and children's pageants. I hoped she was feeling all right.

"What are we eating?" Penny asked.

"This is a traditional seafood dish. In Italy, the feast of Christmas Eve is called *La Vigilia* and it is observed by a partial fast from meat. Being Italian, they don't fast, but instead they eat several courses of seafood dishes or one stew containing more than one kind of fish. My sources were only able to get me two kinds of fish, so that will have to do. As you know, we are far from the ocean here."

"This is delicious," I said as I tasted my first forkful of the homemade pasta and sauce. "You should open a restaurant," I told Joe.

After second helpings, more wine, and some salad made of a red cabbage and apples, we all slowed down.

"Would you like dessert and coffee now or do you want to take a break?"

"A break, please. I couldn't eat anything more. But just so we know, what's for dessert?"

"Jimmy baked an apple pie. He talked the kitchen into giving him some of their windfall apples."

"You fellows were busy sweet-talking the Ladies' Auxiliary and the kitchen staff."

"It was a charm offensive. It worked."

"I need to move a little so I can enjoy that pie," Penny said. "I'll clear the table and you folks relax."

Penny and I brought the plates to the kitchen, rinsed them, and stacked them on the counter. We sat in the living room while Jimmy sorted through the cottage's collection of board games

"Before we get started on games, I have a few small things that Santa dropped off for you. Would you like to have them now or open them on Christmas Day?"

"Now, of course. We can't wait!"

I walked over to the small tree where I had placed my gifts.

"Joe, this is for you."

He unwrapped it and his face lit up with pleasure when he saw the apron. "This should save some of my clothes in the future. Thank you so much." He put the apron on and tied it around his waist.

I retrieved Jimmy's present and gave it to him.

He carefully unwrapped it and smiled with pleasure. "This is beautiful. Thank you." He leafed through the pages of the art book.

Finally, I handed Penny her present. "Merry Christmas. And thank you for all your help." I looked at Dan's present under the tree. He'd get it eventually.

Penny looked at me with anticipation and then ripped open the wrapping paper. She moaned as she saw the colors of the shawl and ran her hand lightly over the wool. "This is gorgeous. Thank you so much." As she threw the shawl around her shoulders, she beamed with pleasure.

Joe stood up. "I'll make some tea and coffee and I'll take dessert orders."

"Not so fast. I have some little things to give."

Penny handed us small packages wrapped in foil paper. When I opened mine, I found a bar of homemade soap and a bag of lavender bath crystals. "These are lovely. Thank you!"

"Joe helped me make them from an old recipe he learned at home. The soap is made with olive oil and the lavender is from the garden here."

"Now, we have one more surprise for our guests. But we'll wait until the dessert is ready. Excuse me while I serve the pie." Jimmy got up and went to the kitchen. He and Joe whispered something and then got to work. I sat back and watched the candles flicker. I felt a deep contentment as I looked around the cottage. It really was a bit of magic that brought us together in this place.

I didn't think I could eat another bite, but I had to admit that Jimmy's pie was incredible. When we finished our dessert, Jimmy went upstairs. He returned with two boxes wrapped in Christmas paper. He gave one to me and one to Penny.

"This is from us. We hope you like them."

Penny and I shook the boxes but had no idea what they contained. When we unwrapped the paper, we each found a pair of hand-sewn buckskin moccasins lined with sheepskin and decorated with beadwork.

"These are beautiful. Where did you find them?" I asked, as I slipped them on my feet.

"We know some folks up here who practice traditional crafts."

They fit perfectly. "How did you know my size?" Penny asked.

"Last time you were here we drew a stencil of your shoes and took that to the crafters."

"These will be great on those freezing cold floors in the residence. Thank you so much."

"Time for some serious games." Joe grabbed a bottle of bourbon and put it on the table with some shot glasses. "And if anyone needs a digestive, I'm ready to pour. Except for Jimmy, of course."

My toes felt toasty in the moccasins. I wished the evening would never end.

At midnight, Penny and I walked back to the residence arm in arm. The building was dark and we figured the superintendent had gone to bed. We used the fire escape to make our way upstairs, collapsing in giggles every once in awhile. The door was wedged open with a piece of cardboard that Penny had inserted earlier.

"When do you have to work tomorrow?" Penny asked.

"Not until noon. I plan to sleep in as long as I can. Merry Christmas. It was a wonderful night."

"Merry Christmas," she said and then she started to sing a Christmas carol.

"Shhhhhh!! You'll wake up everyone on the floor."

She giggled and left humming and clutching her moccasins. Her new shawl was tied over her coat.

I walked to the window in my room and looked out into the still night. One of the old-timers had told me to watch for the full moon at Christmas called the Long Night's Moon. I could see it angling towards my window and wondered about the people who had lived and travelled through these mountains and over the frozen lakes, long before the settlers had showed up. I thought about the service in the chapel and wondered if one could really hear an old story in a new way, like a sweater forgotten at the back of a drawer that suddenly provided familiar warmth.

After brushing my teeth, I climbed into bed. I placed the moccasins right beside the bed—I wanted to see them when I awoke as if Santa himself had delivered them.

Chapter 34

LOUISE, SAN, 1951

AFTER the fun of Christmas, it was time to get back to work. There were only months left to finish the paper that Dr. Clarke had requested on the surgical program at the san. He had promised to help me get it published—something I thought would be helpful to my applications to a residency. It would be difficult, however, to write anything exciting about the surgical program. Perhaps the san was far enough away from other treatment centers to manage to coast on its reputation, but that would not last forever.

I had started collecting information about surgical residency programs around the country. Sometimes I dreamed of leaving the east coast to try a place like San Francisco, but I knew Mary would object if I went that far away. Jimmy had advised me to keep an open mind about the future, but I clung to the original plan because it was better than having no plan at all.

After taking time to recover from the side effects of the trial medication, Jimmy was scheduled for surgery today. Wheeled to the OR by a nurse and an orderly, he looked drowsy, but valiantly raised his hand in greeting. His huge frame could barely be contained on the narrow stretcher.

"This is going to be my lucky day, right doc?" His speech was slurred from the effects of the pre-operative sedation.

I smiled to reassure him. "This is it. Are you ready?"

"Ready as can be."

"We're going to be sending you home soon," I said reassuringly.

"Just make sure it's not in a box," he said. He raised his hand to wave again as the orderly and a nurse wheeled him into the OR.

I was more relieved than I could say when everything went well with Jimmy's surgery. As soon as he was ambulatory, I planned to send him back to Rose Cottage, knowing he would recover with their help.

When I arrived at the nursing station, the head nurse reported that Mrs. Collier's fever had spiked. I ordered alcohol sponge baths and aspirin suppositories to bring down the fever and increased the rate of the intravenous. It was an effort to concentrate—I'd worked till late the night before, calculating dates and numbers from medical records, and I was exhausted.

I yelped as I rounded the corner of the desk too tightly and hit my hip. My fatigue was causing me to lose my balance. Many nights I fell asleep right away, but then I'd wake up after an hour or two and be wide awake for half the night. This was no time to lose my nerve—there were so many irons in the fire. With all my heart, I hoped that I wouldn't end up jeopardizing people's jobs or the health of the patients in the trial.

I tried to picture a happy ending when patients started being cured and discharged. Some of them were no longer just patients; they'd become friends in ways I never would have anticipated. It was impossible to keep strict boundaries between patients and staff—we were all in it together and dependent on each other. And I had to admit those unexpected friendships went a long way to providing comfort in a challenging situation.

"You OK?" the ward clerk asked with concern, after I dropped a chart on the ground.

"Just clumsy," I responded as I hurried to pick it up.

Besides not sleeping well, I'd been drinking too much coffee and skipping meals, plus my stomach was starting to feel like acid. If I kept this up, I would get an ulcer. I was already tossing back medicine cups full of chalky antacid. Although it made me gag, I hoped it would coat whatever needed coating and allow me to keep going. There was no time to stop now. I thought of those small roads in the mountains where runaway trucks could divert in the case of brake failure—for now, there could be no failed brakes because there were no runaway roads; I had chosen this path and I would have to steer my way out of it. Do no harm, I thought, and hoped with all my heart that I wouldn't.

Chapter 35

LOUISE, SAN, 1951

Although Jimmy did well in surgery, his post-surgical recovery was not without some setbacks. I was happy to tell him that I'd been able to remove a small part of his lung. Fortunately the surgery had been less extensive than I'd feared. I was sorry that he had to deal with the complications, but we tried to work through each one as it came up. When he developed a urinary infection, I treated it with medications. After spending a few days on the surgical ward, he'd been very eager to move back to the cottage. With a nurse monitoring his vitals, and the other fellows helping him with meals, he was definitely showing improvement and getting stronger every day. I tried to drop by daily to check on him.

When I stopped at Claire's room, I was pleased to see that she was sitting up in bed and talking to Mother Maureen. It had only been a few weeks since she enrolled in the trial, but the difference was remarkable.

I smiled. "Look at you! A whole new person."

Claire grinned back. "I feel a lot better. Those medications have really done the trick. The nurses helped me to walk in the hall, and every day I feel stronger. Thank you."

"We really appreciate what you've done for her," Mother Maureen said. "If we can ever be of help to you, please let us know. I mean that most sincerely."

"I'm happy to see her looking so well. If you keep this up, you'll be going home soon."

"That's wonderful," Claire said. "I really want to get back."

"I'll check in tomorrow, but till then, keep up the good work." I left the room feeling hopeful. When things went well, it was such a relief; *and things had to go well.*

As I walked through the hallways, I tried to imagine my own departure from this place. I thought about what I might do at the end of the fellowship. My ambitions and goals had shaped everything I'd done for years—they'd become my companions in a self-absorbed and extremely focused life. When I thought about the primitive attempts at research I'd made here, I realized that I needed different skills if I wanted to continue doing that kind of work. It was no longer enough to treat one patient at a time. I needed to have a broader set of skills to address the challenges faced by populations and by communities.

Mrs. Collier sat in a chair holding the baby who was gurgling in delight. I was so relieved she'd overcome the infection and seemed to be on the road to recovery.

"How's the baby doing?" I asked.

"She's put on a few more pounds. Look at her arms—they're so chubby."

I bent to admire the baby. How I would love to see Mary with a baby in her arms. "Keep up the good work!"

Mrs. Collier smiled from ear to ear. "I can't wait to take her home." Mr. Collier beamed at his wife from across the room.

I went to see an elderly patient, Matthew George, who was dying on the third floor, where they tended to keep the elderly and chronically ill patients who didn't have anywhere else to go. I walked by one of the rooms and saw Nurse Benoit sitting at the bedside holding an elderly woman's hand.

I pulled the head nurse aside. "Is that Nurse Benoit?"

The nurse nodded. "She's here every day. Her mother has been here for three years."

"What's wrong with her?"

"She came in with TB but she also has dementia. Because we couldn't find a home for her, Dr. Clarke agreed to let her stay here long term. That way Nurse Benoit can visit her regularly. Sometimes she comes after her shift or on her lunch."

"I see."

The head nurse nodded. "It's very hard to find a place for these elderly patients. They often don't have family and the nursing homes won't take them. This floor has become home to many of them and they'll likely die here. We also have a population of adults that were institutionalized for various reasons; they have nowhere to go, so they stay here."

I nodded thoughtfully and walked with the nurse to see the patient. Either Dr. Clarke was a real friend to Nurse Benoit or he had found a way to guarantee that she would support any of his schemes.

I examined the patient who was breathing in jagged Cheyne-Stokes respirations and was not conscious. "Keep him comfortable," I instructed the nurse. "Use the morphine as needed if he's restless." I lingered for a moment with my hand on his forehead. His jaw sagged and his toothless mouth made it hard to imagine what he'd looked like as a young man. His bony chest worked hard for every breath. It always surprised me how hard the body fought at the end, trying to preserve life, even while the body's systems were shutting down.

"Do you call a chaplain when someone is near the end?" I asked feeling embarrassed that I didn't know.

"We have some volunteer chaplains who come if they can. Sometimes patients sit with them so they're not alone. If you know Jimmy, he often sings to ease their journey across. We gather whoever we can to form a circle around the bed. If you've never been part of it, it's a moving experience."

I patted the patient's hand and left the ward. I was grateful for the caring nurses on this floor. Surely the san could continue to offer some variation of long-term care to these kinds of patients.

When I finished off writing orders in the chart, I ran into Nurse Benoit.

"Can we talk somewhere private?" she asked.

"How about this conference room?"

She looked up and down the hall and then closed the door firmly.

"I am so angry."

I could see that her hands were shaking. I didn't say anything but I hoped it wasn't something I'd done.

"Dr. Clarke allowed my mother to stay on this ward when I couldn't find a nursing home to take her. Now he has decided that she should be moved because he wants to free up some beds. He promised me! The nurses know her, and I see her every day. If she's moved, it will be so confusing. It's not fair to her."

"I'm sorry to hear it. Just to clarify, he promised that she would be cared for indefinitely and for some reason, he changed his mind?"

She nodded.

"But he's away?"

"He apparently talked to the director of nursing recently."

"And where does he suggest that she go?"

"I don't know. But if he tries to transfer her to that other cottage . . ."

"What other cottage?" I was thinking of Rose Cottage and wondering how a woman who was basically bedridden with dementia would function in a cottage.

She dropped her voice. "People don't talk about it—most people don't know. There's a cottage at the far end of the property. I think they have about twenty beds and it's staffed with workers that have nothing to do with the san. There's even a private road that goes into the place."

I was stunned. There was another infirmary that I hadn't heard about? "I'm sorry, I've never heard of this place. What kind of patients do they care for there?"

"They're long-term stays with chronic illnesses, they don't have family, and often have mental or physical disabilities."

"And what kind of treatment do they get?"

Nurse Benoit shook her head slowly. "I don't know. It's very hard to find anything out about the place."

"Surely he wouldn't put her there, after all, you're a nurse and you'd visit every day and monitor the care closely."

"Well, he didn't exactly say what would happen, but he hinted that I'd better find an alternative or else. . . ."

"Forgive me, Nurse Benoit, I just need to ask this in order to understand, please don't be offended. In exchange for providing a bed for your mother, did Dr. Clarke expect anything from you?"

She sat quietly. The fight had gone out of her. Her shoulders slumped and she blinked to try to absorb the tears that were welling in her eyes. "It wasn't anything like . . . well, you know . . . he just expected that I would help him with things around the san, provide him with information about the staff and things on the ward. He is very worried about whether people like him and what they're saying about him."

"Did he ask you to spy on me? To search my room?"

Her eyes darted up and then looked down again. She nodded.

"What was he worried about?"

"He thought you were working on something that might damage the san and he wanted to know what it was."

"What about the vandalism of my office?"

"No, no, I would never do that."

"Were you spying on me at Rose Cottage or anywhere else?"

She shook her head. "No, but Dan sometimes helped me get information about what you were doing there."

"Dan?" I guess I wasn't surprised, but it was still disappointing.

"Dan and I . . . well, we're going out. He helped me sometimes because it was hard for me to keep an eye on everything and Dr. Clarke kept demanding more information and threatening me if he didn't get it."

"Really? Well, that's something." I had to get over my surprise. Who would have put those two together? "What can I do to help you? Do you want me to talk to Dr. Clarke?"

"No, don't do that. He'll be furious that I talked to you."

"Let me think this over and see if we can make a plan. For now, talk to the head nurse of this floor and ask her if there's been any discussion of a transfer for your mother. Ask her to keep you informed if she hears anything. I'm not sure if it's an idle threat or a way to get you to do something, but keep calm, do your work, and let me know if you hear anything. I'll try to figure something out."

"Thank you. I'm really sorry for the way I treated you. You're a good doctor, and you actually care about the patients, unlike most of the doctors."

"Did you find anything of interest in my room?" I asked her with a smile.

She shook her head. "I'm really sorry. It wasn't fair. But I told him there was nothing there."

"And the spying on Rose Cottage?"

"He was worried that you were getting too chummy with the fellows there. He doesn't like it when the staff and the patients get friendly because he feels threatened by that."

"Why did Dan cooperate with him?"

"He was helping to keep me on the right side of Dr. Clarke."

"What do you think drives Dr. Clarke?"

"He wants this san to be the best in the world. It has enjoyed a world-class reputation for a long time and he wants to keep it that way. He really wants to be a big shot in the TB world."

"But the world is changing. Doesn't he see that?"

"He wouldn't agree. He has given his life to this place."

I nodded thoughtfully. "What about Dr. Patterson?"

"There was an incident a few years ago—before my time. He did surgery while under the influence and lost a patient. He could have been disciplined, but Dr. Clarke covered it up and paid a settlement to the family. Ever since then, he's held it over his head."

I sighed. It seemed like Dr. Clarke had an uncanny ability to read people, find their weakness, and exploit it for his purposes. "I have to get to the infirmary. Are you all right?"

"I have to get back to the ward. They'll be wondering where I went. Thanks for listening."

"Keep me informed. Don't say anything to anyone else, and stay on good terms with the head nurse on this floor. By the way, did you get any idea where Dr. Clarke might be?"

She nodded. "I heard he was in Florida. That's all I know."

Nurse Benoit smoothed the creases in her uniform and left the room.

I waited for a few moments and then left. I wasn't sure what I could do for her, but I couldn't ignore the situation. She had confirmed my sense that something was terribly wrong.

That evening, I stuck to my normal routines in case anyone was watching, but instead of going to bed, I rested on the bed fully dressed and waited till midnight. Most of the nurses seemed to go to bed by eleven and then things got quiet on the floor.

Slipping a piece of cardboard in between the door and the frame, I crept down the fire escape. To blend into the darkness and be able to walk over bumpy terrain, I wore my hiking boots and some dark clothes. After scouting the location of the cottage by studying a topographical map in the library, I knew it would likely be a vigorous walk to the site. I stayed close to the tree-lined margins of the property where I'd be less visible—with the disadvantage that the ground was uneven. At first the dark seemed thick as molasses, but I gradually became able to distinguish the shapes of things in front of me. I told myself it was irrational to fear the dark—most humans and animals accepted that night was for sleeping. At least I earnestly hoped so.

I passed all the buildings that were part of the sanatorium and finally reached a piece of land that was mostly wooded. Fortunately there was a dirt road that I could follow. A gate with a chain and padlock hung across the road with a large sign that said "private." Because I could feel tire tracks in the frozen mud under my feet, I knew that some kind of vehicle had used this road.

If Mary saw me now she'd think I'd lost my mind and perhaps she'd be right. I felt morally obliged to investigate this rumor—if there was a facility in these backwoods that existed without oversight or accountability, I doubted that it was a good thing. There was no good reason to place a facility out here in the woods with "No Trespassing" signs everywhere. I intended to find out what Dr. Clarke was doing. I would march all night if

I had to—I just felt like he had to be held accountable. If no one else was willing to do it, then I had to.

On some level, I'd already accepted the fact that I'd probably be evicted from the San with little to show for the year—no references, no publishable research, and no contacts. According to Jimmy, I had to be willing to accept the loss of worldly success in exchange for pursuit of truth. I wondered what Jimmy would say if he knew I was out here hiking in the dark to pursue some truth. There was no way I could tell him about this. He was scheduled for discharge. I was delighted that he could go home, and I told myself that I was obeying Dr. Clarke's direction to discharge him as soon as possible.

I wasn't sure how this adventure might end, but in the worst case, it might involve being arrested for trespassing or simply being kidnapped and disappearing without a trace. I would regret not saying goodbye to Mary and Robert; I realized they'd been supportive in so many ways and I wasn't sure I'd ever properly thanked them. Of course, Penny and the guys in Rose Cottage would be worried if I never returned. Penny would probably tell the authorities that she'd warned me to leave things alone, but that I was stubborn.

The depth of stillness at night was amazing—with no wind, the landscape was completely tranquil. As a result, I was truly startled when an owl flew out of the tree overhead and swooped over the field. I remembered learning in science class how owls had ocular tubes instead of eyeballs that gave them binocular vision. I started to imagine the vertebrae in their necks but then reminded myself to pay attention to where I was walking instead— a sprained ankle on this road would mean a long and painful walk back to the residence.

As far as I could tell, nothing else moved in the darkness. I hiked past the various buildings and residences of the san. I kept walking at a brisk pace on the dirt road and finally reached a building nestled in the woods. Although most of the lights were off, I could still see the bluish fluorescent light from one of the rooms.

I walked around the house to get an idea of its layout. It was a narrow, one-storey structure. Locating the nurses' station at the front of the house, I watched for a while to see if there was any movement. The other windows were probably patient rooms with the blinds were pulled down. Occasionally I heard someone cry out in the night to which a male voice replied "Shut up."

My heart was pounding loudly. What on earth was I doing here? What was this place? As far as I could tell, there was only one nurse on duty that night, but it would be a rude shock if I went inside and ran into a second staff member.

In circling the building, I tried to find the back door. If the nurse sat at the front of the building, he might not notice if I entered from the rear of the building and crept along the hallway. The building didn't seem to have any of the hall lights or exit lights that were usually required for safety reasons. That didn't surprise me at all—I doubted that anyone monitored this place for compliance to fire and safety codes. And what would one nurse be able to do if a fire broke out in this wooden structure?

I watched the nurse through the window as he yawned and read a magazine with his feet up on the desk. The radio played rock and roll—a good source of cover. He obviously expected no one to visit or to see what he was doing. I wondered if he made patient rounds during the night. He probably left the patients unattended and then made a quick check in the morning, leaving the worst messes for the day shift. I felt angry just thinking about it.

I pushed gently at first and then a bit harder against the back door, and it opened—they obviously felt no need to lock the place. I stood for a moment and held my breath. If a second staff member appeared, I needed to have a story to explain my presence. I couldn't think of anything that made sense.

I walked softly along the corridor. Although he sat in a front office, the charts were kept separately in a room behind him. It must have been a kitchen because there was a long counter with a sink and cupboards over the counter.

I went into the chart room and took the first chart with me to an alcove that wasn't immediately visible from the hall. There would be no time to take notes, so I'd have to rely on my memory. The chart described a sixty-five-year-old male with physical and mental disabilities. He'd been diagnosed with TB and had been kept at the san for several years until he was transferred to this facility. According to the notes, he had no relatives. When I checked the doctor's notes, I was shocked to see that both Dr. Patterson and Dr. Clarke had signed orders during the time that this patient had been there. And the orders made no sense at all. Why would they give this man electro-convulsive therapy for tuberculosis?

I returned the chart to the rack and pulled the next one. There was just enough light from the fluorescent lamp under the cabinet to allow me to read. The patient was a fifty-seven-year-old woman who hadn't spoken for years due to autism. After being a patient in the san for five years, she had been transferred to this place two years ago. Dr. Clarke had signed the transfer.

In her case, she'd been given a variety of therapies, but what really shocked me was that she'd been injected with live tuberculosis bacillus.

Later, they'd injected her with other drugs, including insulin. The medication records tracked the various treatments she'd undergone and the clinical notes observed that there was no change or improvement in her condition. I was starting to feel nauseous at the thought of these vulnerable patients being subjected to such arbitrary treatment with no family or friends to protect them. Suddenly, the phone rang, and the nurse woke up. I almost dropped the chart in surprise.

"Hello," his gruff voice said. "Oh, it's you," he said, his voice softening. "What you doing up?" He paused. "Yeah, nothing happening here. Everyone's asleep. They all take their sleeping pills, cause if they don't, they know we'll put them where the sun don't shine." He chuckled at his joke. "Are you off tomorrow? Good, that's great. I'll sleep for a few hours and then pick you up. Maybe we could head to the diner for some grub and then see what else we want to do? See you tomorrow. Or today, I guess, since it's past midnight. Can't wait!"

He put the phone down and I didn't dare move. What if he had to give some midnight medication or get something out of the fridge? I was partly hidden by the alcove but if he turned on the lights, he'd find me. I thought maybe he'd do rounds, but he didn't bother. He moved his chair to get comfortable, and within a few moments was snoring again.

I pulled out one more chart. A thirty-year-old male had been diagnosed with TB five years ago. He'd had a series of surgeries but didn't respond to treatment. The history mentioned that he had Down syndrome and had resided in an orphanage before his admission. His treatment regimen was similar to the first patient with a combination of electric shock and medications. Although I wanted to keep reading, partly because I simply couldn't believe what I was reading, I knew I had to get away. Knowledge of this place would put me at great risk.

There were likely around fifteen to twenty patients here judging by the charts, and it seemed the place had been in operation for several years. I was certain that no state inspector realized that the facility existed. Anyone who came to the san for inspection and audit was likely whisked around the infirmary and then taken to the boardroom for a specially prepared luncheon without ever seeing this. Someone at the san made sure these patients "disappeared" from the census, and I'd wager a bet that they were selected because they had no family to miss them. Nor could they speak on their own behalf.

I listened to the even breathing of the male nurse and walked down the hall to the back door. I carried my flashlight like a weapon, but wasn't sure if I'd have the presence of mind to clobber anyone who stopped me. When one of the patients called out, I froze and flattened myself against the wall. I needn't have worried. The nurse didn't appear and continued to snore loudly. I slid out the back door, closed it quietly, and took a few breaths. My hands were shaking so hard that I almost dropped the flashlight.

I walked around to the front of the house and back down the dirt road. I kept the pace steady and tried to concentrate on the road beneath my feet. I hiked as fast as I could, breathing hard from the exercise and perspiring despite the cold night. Although there was no moon, the night sky was populated by an incredible number of stars. I wasn't too proud to send up a prayer for safety as I half walked and half ran back to the san.

After about twenty minutes of fast paced hiking, I saw the porch light of one of the cottages at the far edge of the property. I'd never been so happy to see the place. When I confirmed for myself that nothing was moving on the grounds, I made my way to the residence.

I stood near a tree and watched the residence carefully before moving forward. I crept up the fire escape and exhaled with relief to find the cardboard paper still in place. As quick as I could, I entered my residence floor and made sure the fire door closed quietly behind me. Everything was still, and I hoped I wouldn't run into any nurses going to the bathroom.

When I got to my room, I found a piece of paper pushed under my door. "Where are you?" I recognized Penny's handwriting. She must have come by to tell me something. I didn't want to admit to her that I'd been to the cottage. She had begged me to leave it alone when I'd told her what Nurse Benoit had said. But how could I do that? I'd make up some story about being called to the ward for some emergency, and hopefully she'd accept that as an explanation. I hated to lie to Penny but it was safer if she didn't know about this.

I wrote down everything in my journal that I could remember from the patient charts in the woods and then got ready for bed. After all the fear and adrenaline, I thought I'd be up all night, but the minute my head hit the pillow, I fell asleep and didn't wake till six. When I opened my eyes and saw my dark clothes draped over the desk chair and my hiking boots by the door, I remembered where I'd been. What would I do with the information and who would believe me?

I got dressed and knew that I would have to keep this secret until I sorted out my next steps. I couldn't imagine how I might keep myself alive if anyone knew I had visited that facility in the woods. And yet, it was urgent to find a way to save those people from further experimentation.

Chapter 36

LOUISE, SAN, 1951

I WALKED from the residence along a path to the cafeteria, relishing the sensation of the warm sun on my face. That moment of pleasure was, however, overshadowed by the burden of knowledge I had gained in those woods. Knowing I couldn't share the knowledge with anyone made that burden heavier. I had to be strategic, rather than impulsive, in order to get the information to the proper authorities. But who could be trusted? Dr. Clarke's networks of influence reached deeply into various state and health agencies; I had no such connections.

Remembering my first days at the san, my initial homesickness was minor compared to the misery I felt now. Perhaps Penny had been right—I should have left it alone, because now that I knew, I couldn't turn away. I remembered a picture in the children's story Bible back home, where Eve stood in the garden, cowering with fear and trying to cover her nakedness. I was exposed and alone—soon I would probably be expelled from this place as well. Not that it was in any way my idea of Eden.

I had to figure out how to reveal what was happening in a way that would still protect the patients in the woods. I hoped that I would have the courage to make the right choices.

Of course, the chief at Yale was only one example of where my choices had led me in the past. He knew that I would never openly accuse him, because no one would accept my word against his. Perhaps it was a long-standing aversion to being classed as a troublemaker—I generally felt that my only choice was to keep silent. I could hear Ma's voice as if it were yesterday, instructing us to be ladies and to respect our elders. She never gave any hints about what to do if those in authority were too corrupt to obey—perhaps because that possibility had never crossed her mind.

I entered the cafeteria to get some breakfast. A buffet table had been set up to one side with coffee and a continental breakfast. All the tables had been moved out of the way to create a dance floor for the party. Volunteers stood on ladders to hang streamers and white lights. Local funeral homes had donated flowers, and some of the patients were taking them apart and creating new arrangements to decorate the room and the stage of the auditorium. The room was buzzing with excited energy.

It felt like a graduation—Jimmy planned to leave the next morning. In fact, all of the patients enrolled in the pilot were stable and ready to go home. Dr. Patterson had made them stay a few weeks longer, just to make sure they were cured and didn't relapse.

I had written up the findings of the trial and given them to Dr. Patterson for review. Even with the limitations of such a small sample, the evidence supported the use of a combination of drugs as the most effective way to cure the infection, in most cases. There would still be clinical indicators for doing surgery instead, as in Jimmy's case, but those times were limited and certainly the invasive procedures of the past had to be eliminated from the treatment options. I had made a strong argument for that in my report; I wondered what Dr. Patterson would make of that.

I stopped by Michelle's office to see how she was doing with the gala preparations.

"Have you heard the news?" Michelle asked.

"What news?"

"Dr. Clarke will be back soon. Someone saw him in town."

"That was a long leave of absence. I'm surprised he managed to stay away from the job so long."

"I heard he took his wife to Florida for a while but who knows what the story is? He'll be eager to return to work."

"I can imagine." I had a sinking sensation in my gut—trouble was coming. This fellowship might wrap up early, I thought, once Dr. Clarke returned. I hoped again that Mary would be willing to take me in if necessary.

Leaving the medical library in the late afternoon, I hurried towards the nurses' residence. I had declined Michelle's offer of tickets for the pre-concert event—with Dr. Clarke back, I just wanted to stay out of his way. I did need to change out of my operating room clothes before the concert. Penny would never forgive me if I didn't put some effort into dressing up. Lipstick, I reminded myself, I had to make sure I wore lipstick.

When I slipped into the back row, the auditorium buzzed with excited chatter. The week before the gala, Michelle had arranged for two thrift shops in town to send boxes of used clothes to provide patients with dress clothes for the event. Some patients had been at the san so long that they had very few decent clothes—tonight, however, they were decked out in a variety of evening clothes and hats and gloves. The hair salon in the san had been booked for days and volunteers helped with shampoo and makeup. Although the gala sponsors took over a block of seats at the front, patients and staff filled every other seat in the auditorium and wheelchairs lined the sides and back. Large flower arrangements decorated the stage.

As the curtains slid open, Dan emerged in a tuxedo. "Friends, we are honored today by the presence of a great performer. Without further ado, I give you the one and only Janine Letts."

The crowd roared as the band started to play and Janine moved with elegance across the stage in a bright red silk gown. She was a large black woman and her stage presence was even bigger. "Hello y'all. I'm so happy to be here with you today." She paused. "Some of you know that my sister had TB. I helped care for her and thank God she survived. We will not rest till this disease is seen no more." She paused. "There'll be a time when there'll be no more tears and no more children dying. I tell you, we want that time to start now!"

Applause filled the auditorium.

Janine nodded to the bandleader and the room fell silent. Her rich voice filled the room and brought to mind worlds far from this place. Janine sang old standards and new songs and the audience loved every one of them. They called her back for two encores. "There's one special person I'd like to invite to come up with me on stage to do our final number. Jimmy, are you out there?" Janine looked at the crowd and waited.

I sat up in my chair so I could see what was happening. The crowd began to chant, "Jim-me, Jim-me," until he stood up and went forward. He kissed her cheek and she whispered something to him and then gave the bandleader a nod.

"We're going to do a spiritual that we learned when we were kids in the choir and I hope you'll join in on the chorus. We've all seen hard times but we got a hope that's bigger than all those tears." She started slowly with the first verse of "There is a Balm in Gilead." She took her time with every syllable, caressing the words. When Jimmy joined in, the sound become even fuller, as the saxophone and the piano played in the background. When they reached the chorus, the entire band played, and the audience sang along. When they finished, Jimmy kissed her cheek, gave a quick bow, and left the stage.

"I had a great time here with you, God bless and good night." Janine waved to the audience and bowed. They applauded and shouted but she didn't return for another encore.

I sighed with contentment and slowly stood up, waiting for the crowds to move out of the auditorium. The patrons and board members were guided out of a front exit so they wouldn't have to mingle with the patients.

What a great concert! Patients headed to the cafeteria for refreshments. Michelle told me there was a reception for elite patrons in the boardroom where wine and scotch would be served with a buffet.

When I walked into the cafeteria, I felt like I'd been transported to an old fashioned dance hall. The overhead lights were turned off, and strings of white lights decorated the ceilings. Tables had been pushed against one wall and covered with white tablecloths and small flower arrangements. A Duke Ellington standard rang through the room, followed by Cole Porter's "Ev'ry Time We Say Goodbye." I saw Jimmy dancing with one of the cafeteria ladies and he bowed at the end of the song. He spotted me, took my hand, and led me to the dance floor. I couldn't remember the last time I'd danced with anyone. It took me a little while to relax but he led me easily and deftly around the floor.

Joe took the microphone. "Good evening, ladies and gentlemen. Let's give a round of applause for all the staff and volunteers who put together such a great party." He paused while the crowd erupted with applause. Penny stood near to him and looked splendid in a black dress with spaghetti straps.

"I've got a brief announcement and then we can get back to dancing and eating the great food. You may know that I've finally got my discharge papers and I'll be heading home sometime in the next weeks. You know I'm going to miss you." The gathered crowd cheered. "But I'm taking a souvenir with me. I asked our Nurse Penny if she would marry me and she said yes." He put his arm around her and they kissed to the whistles and shouts of the crowd.

Michelle stepped forward and the crowd again applauded and cheered. She put up her hand to quiet them. "Congratulations to Joe and Penny." The crowd clapped enthusiastically. "I want to thank everyone who participated in the gala and helped make it happen. Tonight I received two major gifts—one check is from the Sydenham Foundation that will provide fifty thousand dollars for pulmonary research and another check from a private donor who has offered thirty thousand dollars. We haven't yet counted up the rest of the donations. You've all done a great job supporting the future work of the san. Congratulations!"

The crowd applauded wildly and raised their drinks. I was happy for Michelle and the volunteers that the evening had been a success, but I wondered what would happen to those donations. I wanted to believe in the cause, but too much had happened to allow that.

Jimmy and I headed over to hug both Penny and Joe. "Congratulations, you two. I'm so happy for you."

I turned to Jimmy. "What time will you be leaving?"

"First thing tomorrow," Jimmy said. "Joe has a pass to take me to the bus station in Penny's car."

"I guess it's time to say goodbye," I said as I held out my hand. "I wish you all the best. I can't tell you how much I appreciated your wisdom."

He took her hand in his. "Thanks for all you did for me. You are a good doctor. Continue to do good work."

"Have a happy reunion with your wife and family. The discharge letter is at the front desk with your name on it."

He smiled and I turned and walked out of the cafeteria. My friends were leaving, and soon I would be very alone here.

The haunting sounds of a Miles Davis song followed me down the hall.

Chapter 37

LOUISE, SAN, 1951

LAUGHTER and music from the party went on through the night, making it hard to sleep in the residence.

When I got up early, the san was quiet. I grabbed a coffee and a piece of toast in the cafeteria and went downstairs to my office to do some work. As I sorted articles to read and made some notes on a new surgical procedure that one journal described, someone knocked on my door.

The security guard leaned against the door with an insolent look on his face.

"What do you want?" I asked.

"Dr. Clarke wants you in his office at ten."

I nodded, but he didn't leave. "I'm quite capable of getting there on my own."

He shrugged and parked himself outside my office. He flipped through a sports magazine he'd had rolled up in his back pocket.

I closed the door and continued to work until I saw that it was almost ten. When I gathered up my notebook and closed the door, the guard followed me all the way to Dr. Clarke's office.

"He's not here," the receptionist said. "Go to the boardroom."

The guard walked a few feet behind me, never letting me out of his sight.

As I walked down the hallway to the boardroom, I wondered why Dr. Clarke had changed the venue. I nodded as I passed Dan in the hall but didn't pause to chat—it was unfortunate, but ever since I'd run into him in town, I didn't quite trust him.

I opened the door of the boardroom and stopped in my tracks. I glanced back and the guard was smirking at me with unconcealed pleasure.

The room was filled with board members who were talking and drinking coffee from china cups decorated with the logo of the san. They looked up at my arrival and the room fell silent.

"Come in and take a seat, Dr. Garrett. We're ready for you," Dr. Clarke said with a phony smile, enjoying the fact that I was completely taken off guard by the summons. He nodded to the guard, who took his position outside the door. I glanced at Dr. Patterson but he refused to meet my eyes and stared steadily at the pages in front of him.

"What is this?" I asked.

"This is an emergency board meeting, and you are our guest. Take a seat, we're ready to begin."

I sat at the table and nodded to the board members beside me. They just stared back and didn't look the least bit welcoming. I wondered what they'd discussed before my arrival; I had the feeling Dr. Clarke had done a thorough job of character assassination.

Dr. Clarke stood up and cleared his throat. "I called this emergency meeting to deal with some important matters that took place while I was on a leave of absence. I asked Dr. Garrett to attend so that she can hear the charges against her. First of all, Dr. Garrett has run unapproved drug experiments with our patients. She has conducted unauthorized research on patient records against my expressed wishes. And finally, she has been socializing and consorting with patients in violation of the professional code of behaviour. Any one of these would be serious, but the combination leads me to present the case to you today so we can make a swift intervention before Dr. Garrett does any more damage."

"I'd like to respond to those charges," I said pushing back my chair and standing.

He raised his hand to stop me. "You'll have a chance to speak when I invite you to do so. Till then, sit down and show some respect for the proceedings."

I sat as ordered and tried to keep my growing sense of panic under control. I kept my face expressionless even though my mind was racing. How could I respond to these allegations? He planned to fire me, and I had no doubt the board would do whatever he suggested. I didn't have a single ally in the room. I was relieved to know that Jimmy was on his way home and two more patients were scheduled for discharge this afternoon. Joe had voluntarily decided to stay until Penny was ready to leave, but soon they would pack up her car and head to Buffalo.

My heart was beating fast, and my face was flushed. I wanted a drink of water but there was no way I was going to walk to the trolley in the back of the room to pour myself a glass—Dr. Clarke would likely order me to sit like a school child on detention. I wondered if he knew that I'd made a visit to his secret cottage facility in the woods. It was a necessary humiliation, I told myself, and it was likely important to leave this place in order to be able to report what I'd seen.

Dr. Clarke distributed two pages of typing that detailed my actions with dates and times. I wonder what his secretary had thought when she typed them up.

"I'd like you to review these documents for a few moments, and then we can discuss them. I'll circulate an envelope of photographs that support my third claim concerning the inappropriate interactions with patients. And then there's a document that Dr. Garrett herself has written that describes her unauthorized medical experiments with unapproved drugs."

I glanced over as the board member on my left took the photos out of the envelope. I saw a photo taken through the cottage kitchen window showing Jimmy and me having tea at the kitchen table when I reviewed his treatment options. The second one showed me standing close to Joe and Dan outside the cottage. The report documenting the medical experiments was the one I'd sent to Dr. Patterson. I looked at him in alarm but he refused to meet my eyes. Had he really encouraged me and then sold me out to Dr. Clarke? Why would he do that? I had worked so hard and he had encouraged me the whole way. What a fool I'd been! Trust no one, I thought to myself. If only I had followed that rule.

Dr. Clarke waited for the board members to read the document and to study the pictures. I wrote comments in the side margins of the copy of the report.

"Let's start with the first point," Dr. Clarke said. "This concerns the unauthorized experimentation with drugs on our patients."

The board members nodded and underlined some of the statements on the page.

As he droned on with his lies, I knew they'd already reached a conclusion. The hearing was merely a formality. He had them eating out of his hand. If the rumors were true, he was guaranteed of their loyalty by generous rewards, golf weekends, and dinners. Why wouldn't they support whatever he said? And in a contest of his word against a woman, I would lose for sure.

"We are ready to meet *in camera*. Dr. Garrett, please leave the room and wait in the consultation room across the hall."

I walked to the back of the room without looking at any of them, took a moment to pour a glass of water, and left the room.

The guard stood in the hall. He watched as I entered the room across the hall.

I ignored him and sat in the small room with my back to the door. There were no windows and no magazines to read. I tried to picture Jimmy on a bus heading towards the city. How excited his family would be to welcome him home. The thought gave me courage. When I imagined the discussion happening in the boardroom, I was surprised how calm I felt. There was no point in continuing to work in a place that didn't value what I had to offer. No amount of ambition justified putting up with this kind of treatment. I concentrated on taking deep breaths. "The courage will be there when you need it," Jimmy had said.

Dr. Clarke planned to punish me by taking away my privileges—but he didn't realize, nor did I fully realize until that very moment, that I was prepared to leave it all behind. He thought he had me in a vulnerable position, but I knew I would manage, even without a reference. In surrendering my ambitions, I'd finally cut myself free from the power he had over me.

Jimmy was right—pursuing the truth had begun to set me free. I closed my eyes and imagined that I was a hawk soaring upwards and then floating on the drafts and currents far above the earth. I flew over the mountains and towards the east where the open waters of the ocean were visible. The blue-gray water, topped with whitecaps, was dotted by sailboats bobbing on the waves.

Below, I saw the hands of my parents, my teachers and professors, Pastor Cal and Bessie, my friends at the san waving to me with encouragement. I realized something I'd never known before—I was not alone and never had been.

Chapter 38

LOUISE, SAN, 1951

WHEN I heard my name called, I got up and smiled at the guard, no longer concerned about his slovenly appearance or his unrelenting surveillance. He was just a paid flunky who jumped when Dr. Clarke said jump. His opinion did not matter to me.

I entered the room and felt the resolve among the board members. I sat in my appointed chair and looked around, daring these men in their suits and ties to look me in the eye. Most of them avoided my gaze and kept their eyes on the reports in front of them, leaning left or right to whisper to someone next to them.

"We have reached a decision. We have decided to suspend your fellowship. You'll be accompanied to your room to pack up and then walked to your car. You are no longer allowed in either your office or the clinical areas."

"I demand the right to speak." I felt pleased my voice was calm and even. I was determined to keep emotion out of this.

"There's no need. We've reached a decision."

"So you said, but justice demands that I have the chance to speak." I stood tall and looked him in the eye, daring him to refuse me this very basic right to respond to the accusations.

Dr. Clarke shook his head to disagree, but another man spoke up. "Let her speak." The chair of the board nodded his head in agreement.

I walked to the front of the room where an oak lectern stood, choosing my location carefully to project authority, despite Dr. Clarke's attempts to undermine me. As I took a breath, I reminded myself to take my time and speak clearly.

I opened my notebook to the page I'd worked on just that morning. "Gentleman, thank you for the opportunity to address you. According to the contract for my fellowship, I am allowed to make a presentation to the board, and I will use this occasion to do so. I have appreciated the time I've spent here to learn about the sanatorium and to work with some of the fine staff." I looked at Dr. Patterson without irony. I might never know what pressure had been put on him to betray me. He'd have to live with his conscience. "My remarks today concern the future of the san. We can no longer ignore the evidence that a major change is underway that will affect the treatment of tuberculosis. Patients will be cared for at home and in community clinics and will no longer spend months and years in buildings such as these. New and effective drugs and drug combinations, such as those piloted here at the san in the past months, will allow patients to continue treatment at home. These changes offer opportunities to those willing to read the signs and make strategic choices for the future."

I outlined my proposal to transform the sanatorium into a community based facility offering a mixed menu of services, including rehabilitation, chronic care, and hospice care, with a research arm to make sure that the staff were educated in the latest developments. I also suggested that they might include a wing that offered boutique care for affluent and international patients. I pointed to the areas of lung disease that I thought were possible growth areas, including smoking-related diseases, chemical exposures, asbestos, and other occupational hazards. The sanatorium could take the lead on expanding their mission while providing hospitality to international researchers and clinicians who were doing research in those areas. I argued that it would be important to encourage research that would inform clinical practice.

"There is no need to focus so narrowly on one disease, nor to fear the changes that will certainly accompany advances in medicine. Embrace them and make sure that the treatments offered here are proven to be effective by tracking the results and valuing statistics. Engage all staff in a regular program of continuing education, encouraging them to use their initiative to learn and to pursue quality improvement."

Although I knew they were listening, I could sense their resistance. Dr. Clarke looked like he was about to have a stroke. I certainly hoped I wouldn't have that on my conscience. "As a board, you are morally and legally responsible to give oversight to the programs offered here. Let me remind you of the description of your task from the last board statement, where it states the following: 'when you accept a position on a board of directors, you are agreeing to help run the organization to the best of your ability. You are also agreeing to learn about the organization so you can make sound decisions that are needed to run it effectively. This means you agree to fulfill certain responsibilities that are common to all governing boards. In addition, you are to preserve the public trust by accepting the obligation to implement programs and services for the benefit of the public and to provide for the responsible governing and management of the sanatorium resources.'"

I looked around the room slowly in an attempt to make eye contact with each one. Their resistance was embedded in the silence. I closed my notebook and walked out of the room. I had said what I wanted to say and had not traded my own authority for compliance with Dr. Clarke's evil plans. It was not my job to judge or punish anyone, but simply to speak the truth. The question of the cottage in the woods would have to be addressed once I was safely out of this place.

The guard followed me out of the building and into the residence. He stood outside the door while I pulled my suitcase from the closet and threw my things into it. I made sure I packed my journal and my notes. Doug still had the data and drafts of reports in his pharmacy safe. I'd leave it to him to find a way to keep those safe.

When I finished packing, I took a last look around the room and closed the door. The guard did not offer to help. I struggled to balance the suitcase and my book bag. The superintendent sat at her desk and also watched me struggle. She didn't bother to say goodbye.

We walked towards the parking lot. As we approached my car, I felt someone behind me take the suitcase out of my hand. I was surprised to see Joe. Penny took my book bag from me.

Dan, Nurse Benoit, and Doug waited by my car.

"News travels fast," I said with a smile.

"We decided to throw a little going away reception," Joe said. "And you can just get lost," he said to the guard who looked around uncertainly, but then backed away with a shrug.

I unlocked the trunk. Joe handed me a large package wrapped in brown paper. "Jimmy wanted you to have it," he said.

I peeled back some of the wrapping and saw the stormy sky and the ray of light. I was so touched that Jimmy had remembered how much I'd admired that work.

I blinked away tears and carefully taped the wrapping paper back in place.

Joe picked up my suitcase and my book bag and put them in the trunk. We all fell silent as a Cooper's hawk flew overhead, circling silently, dipping towards us, and then taking off. I smiled when I saw the bird. It would guide me out to safer places. I'd already had the vision.

Penny handed me a small package. "I talked the cafeteria into packing a lunch. Millie, the cook, told me to tell you good luck."

"Promise me you'll stay in touch," I said to her.

"I have your sister's address. That's the best for now, right?"

I nodded, my throat thick with emotion. "Did Jimmy get away?"

"He was in fine form. He serenaded me all the way to the station."

"And you two. Any plans?" I looked at Dan and Nurse Benoit.

They looked at each other fondly. "No plans yet."

I shook Doug's hand. "I hope I didn't get you in trouble," I said. "Good luck with everything."

"It was the best time I've had at this job," he said with a smile. "Those folks in New Jersey offered me a job if I get bored here. We'll see how things go. There's one more thing you should know." He took me aside so that others wouldn't hear. "My friend at the drug company told me something interesting. Apparently Dr. Clarke contracted TB late last fall and headed to Florida to be treated there. Dr. Patterson encouraged the trial on his orders—he wanted the trial to test the drugs before he took them. Then he ordered the company to send enough meds to treat him. Thanks to you, he recovered and was quite happy to use your research for his own purposes. You can bet they won't be sharing that with the patients here. They'll likely distribute those drugs to the highest paying patients."

Although nothing should surprise me anymore, that truly did. He wanted the trial to run for his own eventual benefit. I felt sorry for Dr. Patterson, who had agreed to this. But that was his problem. I was glad to leave. I kept my emotions in check and said my goodbyes.

"Thanks, all of you. I wish you all the best. And good luck planning the wedding," I said to Penny. "I trust the bride will wear white?" I asked.

"Of course," Joe said. "I wouldn't dare offend my mother."

I rolled my eyes at Penny. "Just try get along with the mother-in-law. He's probably the favored child."

I got in the car. It was dusty from standing in the parking lot but it still looked pretty grand to me. I waved out of the window when I passed through the stone gates. I drove in a state of numbness until I reached the main road that led south to Albany.

I could not longer control my emotions. Rage, grief, confusion made me nauseated. I felt consumed by that rage that I could only describe as murderous. How dare he use my work for his own purposes? What an evil man!

I pulled to the side of the road and clambered into the dry ditch where no one could see me. I threw up in that ditch until there was nothing left in my stomach. When I felt calmer, I climbed back into my car and drove away. I knew I had to leave that rage behind me or it would poison me forever. And I wouldn't give Dr. Clarke that victory.

PART III

Therefore, when you go to your physician, go to him in the same spirit in which one should approach a confessor. You may be certain he will divulge nothing that you tell him. You may rest assured that his advice, based upon a full knowledge of your case and condition and upon what you have done and will do, will be thousands of times more valuable to you than advice based upon insufficient knowledge of the past history of your case . . .

—DR. LAWRASON BROWN[*]

[*] Lawrason Brown, *Rules for Recovery from Pulmonary Tuberculosis* (3rd ed. Philadelphia: Lea and Febiger, 1919).

Chapter 39

NORI, LAKE HOUSE, 1980

Nori realized that someone was shaking her. She untangled herself from the afghan and sat up, blinking at the light.

"Rough night?" asked Belinda, the health care aide.

Nori groaned and ran her fingers through her hair. "I think I fell asleep at six."

"Get back to bed and sleep some more. I'll call you if I need you."

When Nori hesitated, Belinda pointed to the stairs. Nori shuffled away with the afghan around her shoulders. She clutched the diary in her hand.

When Nori woke up a few hours later for the second time that day, she headed downstairs to see if Belinda was still there.

Belinda was folding laundry in the kitchen.

"Good sleep?" she asked with a smile.

"I can't believe I slept this long," Nori said. "Can I do anything?"

"I'm going to make a fresh pot of coffee. We finished with morning care, so she's likely going to sleep for a while."

"That sounds good."

She had so many questions for Louise that she started to jot them down in her notebook. While she wrote, Belinda brought in a mug of fresh coffee.

"Thank you so much."

"Why don't I whip up some pancakes? I'm kind of hungry myself."

"Oh . . . that sounds so good. I'm starving."

Later that afternoon, Nori heard Louise coughing and went into her room. She'd been waiting eagerly to talk to her. "I stayed up all night reading your diary. I can't believe what you went through in that place."

Louise nodded. "I haven't read it for a long time. It's hard for me to read it even though I know the story and how it ends."

"I can imagine. I can see why you weren't surprised when I told you about Ada's sister and her letters from the san. That was only one of Dr. Clarke's many schemes."

"He definitely had his own views about right and wrong."

"If you feel up to it, I'd love to hear what happened after you left. When the diary ends, you stopped at the side of the highway when you were a safe distance away from the san."

Louise was quiet as she looked at the view of the lake. "I'm glad you read the diary and I hope it will help you in your research. There's still another part to the story. I think you're ready to hear it. We can stop if we need to, but I think I need to tell this in an uninterrupted fashion. When we're done, you can ask me any questions you might have."

Nori nodded her agreement and settled into the chair. She was curious where the story would go. The story of the san had been dramatic enough—Nori couldn't imagine there was anything more to tell.

Louise took a breath and began to talk. "Once I collected myself, I drove to Albany to stay with Mary and Robert. I was glad they could take me because I didn't have anywhere else to go."

LOUISE, ALBANY, 1951

It had been a long drive to Mary and Robert's house, and I was relieved to get there.

I sat in a stunned state at the dining room table while Mary ran back and forth to the kitchen. She refused my help and ordered me to rest. Robert indicated that I should let her be—clearly she wanted to make a fuss.

I'd called from a truck stop on the highway to let them know my situation. Robert had not hesitated for a moment. He invited me to come and stay for as long as I needed. I was so grateful.

Watching Mary carefully, I had the feeling that something was off. She was as cheerful and pleasant as ever, but I felt disconnected from her. She refused to make eye contact and kept busy in a somewhat manic way. Robert didn't comment and may have become accustomed to her behavior, but I was uneasy. Mary also surprised me by being completely uninterested in the reasons for my sudden arrival on their doorstep. I felt almost relieved when she excused herself for a ladies' club meeting at church. Robert and I washed the dishes and then sat on the front porch with some coffee.

"Do you want to talk about it?" Robert asked.

I nodded.

"Just a moment," he said. He went inside and returned with two glasses of brandy.

I smiled with gratitude and lifted my glass in a silent toast.

"What happened?" he asked.

I told him about my time at the san, the long work hours, the investigation of things that didn't quite fit, and then the discovery of the experimental cottage facility. He was a good listener and didn't interrupt. I told him about being forced to appear before the board and fired publicly. And I recounted to him how my research had been appropriated for Dr. Clarke's own purposes. When I reached that point, I got emotional, and he waited quietly till I regained control of my emotions.

We sipped our brandy and watched the tree-lined street where children played games after supper and people walked dogs. Against such a backdrop of ordinary life, it was hard to imagine that such distorted attempts at care existed. If I hadn't seen it with my own eyes, I wouldn't have believed it.

"What do you plan to do?" Robert asked.

"I'm not sure, but I have to do something. Every day I don't speak is another day that innocent people suffer."

"That's a heavy burden. But I think you are wise to consider carefully how to report this in a way that will be effective. I'm grateful you didn't try to say anything at the board meeting, because you might have ended up in jail. He would have done anything to silence you; it was wise to leave and let him think you were intimidated into silence."

"One of the patients talked to me about the text, 'You shall know the truth and the truth shall set you free.' Finding out that truth has put a burden of responsibility on me. I don't feel free."

"Your patient picked an interesting text. In the Bible, Jesus teaches about the difference between being enslaved to untruth or the freedom that can be attained through belief. That same text is often quoted or etched on buildings to encourage various types of freedom. I think most would agree that maintaining secrets could make one live a fractured life. You have found out a secret and you feel you can't be free until you find the proper place to reveal it."

I took another sip of brandy. A light breeze moved around the porch, but it was still much warmer in town than it had been in the mountains. I wondered what everyone was doing this evening—Penny and Joe, Dan and Nurse Benoit, my patients in the infirmary. "What do you think I should do?"

"You said you were writing something? Where would you send a report like that?"

"I'm not sure. I can't just send it to a medical journal or to the department of health because it might fall into the wrong hands. If Dr. Clarke heard of it, he would close the place and hide all evidence before any investigator could get there. I don't want to think what he might do to those vulnerable patients."

"You are right. You need to be strategic about who and what to tell and hope that the recipient has the authority and the integrity to act on the information." He paused. "There is a man in my congregation who works for the state. He's a senior officer of some sort in the Department of Health. I think they created a new body for accreditation but I don't know the details. If you like, I could see if he would agree to meet with you. I believe he is a person of integrity. And in the meantime, I imagine you need to get it all on paper as fast as you can."

"I would appreciate if you could set up a meeting. And yes, my plan is to write as fast as I can, if you can put up with my presence for a while. I need to figure out what's next for me."

Robert nodded. "Of course, you should stay here. As long as you need to."

We sat for a while in silence, each lost in thought.

"Robert, if you don't mind me asking, what's going on with Mary?"

Chapter 40

LOUISE, ALBANY, 1951

THE next day, Mary wanted to go out. I had been up since five working on the paper, and I probably needed a break anyway. My hand was cramped from writing, but I wanted to finish this before I met with Robert's friend.

Mary and I drove to the shopping center she wanted to visit. As we travelled up and down the escalator, I followed her enthusiastic march through women's wear, shoes, and makeup counters. After spending so many months at the san and only shopping on the rare occasion when I was in town, I felt like I'd entered a foreign country.

Mary had always been a good sale shopper with a deadly instinct for discounted items. She found a nice dress for church and tried to convince me to buy one too, but I resisted. I needed to be able to fit my belongings in the suitcase that was currently stowed under the guest room bed. In order to afford my tuition and room and board, I would have to be very careful with my savings.

When we finally finished the shopping portion of our outing, I was relieved to rest in a vinyl booth at the new Howard Johnson's restaurant. The waitress served us enormous glasses of ice water and brought us large plastic menus. People were smoking at almost every table, and the conversations were loud. We ordered clam chowder and lobster rolls and some clam strip appetizers. It seemed like a lot of food, but Mary insisted.

"How have you been feeling?" I asked Mary.

"I'm fine," she replied. She didn't want to discuss her health.

I persisted. "Are you taking anything?"

"You mean medicine?"

"Yes." Mary looked out the window. "My doctor gave me something called Milltown after the last miscarriage. He said it would lift my mood enough so I could get through the day and help me sleep at night. The insomnia was getting me really down."

"I'm glad you talked to your doctor, but remember that your system can become dependent on those drugs. Sometimes you need more and more to get the same effect. Plus, getting off them can be a painful experience."

Mary shrugged. "I'm not planning to get off them anytime soon. Several of the women in my ladies' group are on the same pills."

"I was sorry you had to go through those experiences and even more sorry I wasn't able to be with you."

Mary shrugged and took a drink of her cola. "Well, you had your career."

I looked at her but she avoided my look. I wasn't sure what she meant— that my career took precedence or that I had a career and she did not. "Are you working these days?"

"You mean for money?" Mary shrugged. "I teach Sunday school and do things around church, but that's volunteer work."

"Have you ever thought of working somewhere part-time? You're so good at retail and design, and you have a natural flair for color and textiles."

"It's not like I have any experience or training in any of that."

"Train on the job. I think you could learn anything you want—you could work your way up. You have degrees from Smith and Yale, and you are a born creative."

"You're one to talk. And you just got fired. That's pretty creative."

I was again startled by the edge in Mary's voice. It seemed unfair that I was the target of her anger. I felt like Mary had returned to the pouting girl she'd been when she'd had polio—assuming everyone was there to serve her. I was irritated at her and then angry with myself for feeling that way.

"Do you blame me for things—the miscarriage, or your lack of paid employment, or anything else?"

Mary sipped the ice water through a long straw. "It has nothing to do with you. It's just something I have to figure out."

"But I really want to help. I can go with you to doctor's appointments and to job interviews."

"Why should I rely on you? Next thing I know, you'll be off to Boston or New York to do something fabulous. Everyone will forget about the trouble you made in your last job. You're the golden girl—I'm the disappointment."

"To whom? Robert is proud of you, and I am proud of you. Where do you get the idea that you're a failure? You do realize I've left my last two posts in less than ideal circumstances and am currently unemployed?"

"Just watch—you'll get a great job, and everyone will forget all that. You may be broke now, but someday you'll be earning big money and won't have a care in the world."

I looked at her in surprise. Mary had never been one to express jealousy. She'd been quite content to pursue her studies and leave me to what she called "the nasty realities" of medicine. "Help me to understand this, Mary, because I am not sure what is going on here. If you're disappointed that you don't have a career, let's work on figuring out what you want to do. I'm pretty sure Robert would support anything you decided."

Mary shrugged as if she didn't care. She pushed away her half-finished bowl of chowder. "I don't know what I want. I thought I wanted a baby, but that's not working. I thought I wanted to work in church education, but there's no budget to pay me. I thought I would make friends in the church, but I never stop being Robert's wife. I'm always watched and judged."

"Maybe you need a part-time job not connected to the church. You could make a little of your own money and meet people who are not part of the church."

Mary looked at me with a slightly hopeful look and then pushed her food around the plate with her fork.

She didn't even dare to dream, I thought, and that made me sad. "On Monday, we're going to that big department store and we'll pick up the application for part-time work. We'll type up your resume and hand that in with the application. After that, maybe we'll go to a movie."

Mary had to laugh. "You sure are bossy. Some things never change."

I didn't think she minded; in fact, she looked relieved. "You know what else? We're going to look for some courses you can do at night or by correspondence in interior design. It's time to put your good taste to work. You've done lots of free interior design work for other people, and now it's time to get paid. Except for me, of course. I get free consultations for life."

She laughed. It was the best sound I'd ever heard. I planned to finish my paper, even if it took all night, and then I was going to focus on Mary. She seemed to be seriously adrift, and Robert had confessed that he didn't have a clue how to help. If she wanted to have a baby someday, she had to get off those medications. Having some purpose might be just the lift she needed; I certainly hoped so, because if my plan didn't work, she might be in a worse state than when we started. It seemed to me that her single-minded focus on having a baby had affected her ability to engage fully in her life and made it difficult to make plans. I wasn't about to point that out to her now—it was going to take a lot of work to repair the rift between us. I hoped with all my heart that it could be done.

I missed the Mary I knew, and I imagined that Robert did too. Healing a broken heart was not one of the medical skills for which I'd received training. Looking back, I felt ashamed of my childhood jealousy of Mary. I thought she was perfect—only because I was so imperfect. There was a risk in living one's life constantly comparing oneself to others and not realizing that we all had imperfections, whether or not we chose to acknowledge them.

I heard a faint knock on the door. "Come in," I said.

Robert opened the door a crack and asked if he could deliver a mug of coffee. "I think you were up late?"

"I just had to get this done. Thanks for the coffee."

"Breakfast will be in about half an hour. I'm going to get Mary up now." He handed me the mug and closed the door behind him. I felt sad for him. I could tell he was a bit mystified by Mary's behavior and was cautious around her. Her bursts of anger were unpredictable and harsh.

At the coffee hour in the basement after the service, he introduced me to Peter Allan, who worked for the state in some kind of accreditation capacity.

"There's a diner around the corner we could walk to. Would that that suit you?"

"That would be great."

As we walked, I glanced at him. He was a middle-aged man who looked at ease in a suit. He told me he had three daughters with his wife, who worked part-time as an obstetric nurse. He opened the door for me at the diner and followed me to the far corner where we took our seats in a booth.

In record time, plates filled with eggs and hash browns and warm toast were placed in front of us. I felt really hungry when I smelled the food.

"You've been working at the sanatorium up north," he said.

"I was on a fellowship there last year."

"Robert said I should tell you something about my work. He didn't tell me why, so I will just give you a brief overview and you can ask anything you like."

I nodded while devouring my breakfast. I was grateful that he was going to talk first.

"I work with a new body that provides accreditation for hospitals, which originated with the American College of Surgeons. We do regular inspections and develop quality standards for health care. We also respond to complaints about patient safety or quality care by initiating a confidential investigation process."

I looked up at him. "And the names of complainants are kept completely confidential?"

He took a sip of his coffee. "Yes. Is there something that concerns you?"

I took a big breath. "This has to be off the record. I just want to see what you think."

He nodded.

"While I was doing my fellowship, I stumbled on what appears to be fraud in relation to the discharge and death status of patients. I compared records at the san to vital statistics at the local town hall and found that the numbers didn't match. It seems that patients were admitted and then sometimes languished there for years because they were told they had active TB. For most of them, there was no treatment plan in place. Some of the records of patients who had died were altered to look as if the patients had been discharged. Then, at the end of my time there, someone told me that there was a secret facility at the edge of the property. I hiked there one night. When I looked at some of the charts, patients had no signed consent in their charts, nor did they even have the ability to consent due to physical and mental disabilities. Those patients had been subjected to a variety of medical and surgical experiments. None of the treatments have any scientific validity in current practice."

He rubbed his chin. "That's pretty serious. That place has a stellar reputation, but we always approach things with a degree of skepticism. Was your fellowship terminated?"

"I was fired in front of the board and escorted to my car. The administrator was afraid I was getting too close to his fraudulent schemes, but he wasn't aware that I had found the secret facility. At least I am pretty sure he didn't know, because I doubt I'd be sitting here now if he had."

"We would have to do our own investigation because I suspect yours would not stand up to legal process." He smiled to soften his words. "And what about the facility? How did you find out about that?"

"One of the staff told me about the rumors. When I went to visit at night, I got into the place while the only employee was fast asleep at the desk."

He nodded slowly. "Only a minor case of breaking and entering?"

I smiled sheepishly. "I guess so. The san uses completely separate staff to work at the facility that's located on a private road. Even though the place is technically on the grounds, it seems to exist as an independent unit with minimal oversight. Because there's no signage, people passing might think it was a private home, if they didn't look closely."

"I suggest that you write up your findings and provide us with dates, locations, and names. We can initiate an investigation and see what we find—the less warning they have, the less chance they have to cover things up. We will use the utmost discretion in our initial inquiries. The conditions of your firing will have to be investigated. It will take some time, and it will be complicated, but I think you were right to come to me with your observations. This kind of thing can't be tolerated. Experimentation without consent on vulnerable people is unacceptable. I commend your bravery but hope that you'll stay on the right side of the law in future."

I decided to trust him. Robert would not have made the introduction if he didn't think the man was trustworthy. I pulled the report I'd written out of my handbag and gave it to him. I had provided as much detail as I could.

He glanced at it and then looked up. "This is excellent. You might want to consider a career with us. Of course, our methods have to be a bit more above board than sneaking around at night. . . ."

I smiled. "I've applied to public health programs. But thanks."

"I'll do some initial work and I'll get back to you if I need any more information. I understand you'll be staying with Mary and Robert for a while?"

"I'll eventually move to whatever university accepts me, but they'll know how to reach me."

"I'll do my best to get some answers. This can't be allowed to continue."

The waitress came to offer more coffee, but I declined. I felt like my pulse was racing fast enough.

"Just the bill," Peter said.

I reached for my purse, but he held his hand up.

"Save it for your textbooks. Those colleges get pretty expensive; I should know with three daughters."

"Thanks," I said. I felt like a weight had been lifted from my shoulders. And with my stomach full, I also felt like I could put my head on the table right there and go to sleep.

I went home after that meeting and slept for three hours, got up for Sunday dinner, and was in bed again by nine. I was so tired I could hardly stand. But on Monday morning, after Robert left to go to his office at the church, I told Mary we had to get to work.

"Work?" she asked as she looked at me over her mug of coffee.

"Where's your typewriter? I assume you're still the better typist?"

"Of course I am. You were the one who refused to take the commercial courses in high school."

"We're going to update your resume and then we'll drive to that big department store and talk to the HR person."

"So bossy," Mary said, but she put her cup down and went to get the typewriter. After I took notes on a pad, she typed them into a resume format.

"Wow, you're pretty good. Maybe *you* should get the job at the insurance company."

She punched my arm playfully and then put the kettle on for more tea. "What am I supposed to wear?"

"Wear the dress you wore yesterday. That looked great."

"What about my hair?"

"Looks fine. If we go now, we can do this, have lunch, and maybe even go to a movie."

Mary looked excited. "Are you sure my hair is all right?"

"It's fine. I'll proofread this and then get dressed. You go first—takes you longer to put on all that makeup and stuff."

She stuck out her tongue at me—something that reminded me of the old Mary. She went upstairs, and I could hear the water running in the bathroom. After proofreading the resume, I put it in a folder and placed it on the hall table next to my purse.

When Mary emerged, she looked radiant in her new dress, low-heeled shoes, and carefully applied makeup.

"You look great!" I said, grateful to see something of the old Mary back. I hoped that my plan would work, because if it didn't, her disappointment might be crushing. Think positive, I told myself, and I kept my fingers crossed that a door would open for her.

That night Mary and I picked up some Chinese takeout for dinner because we'd gone to a movie and didn't feel like cooking. I was glad I'd checked with Robert before I hatched the plan about helping Mary to get a job. He smiled as she enthusiastically described our visit to the store and her meeting with the head of the design department. He glanced at me with obvious gratitude.

Although there was a risk to getting her hopes up, I felt it was important to help her figure out what she wanted to do with herself. I didn't know whether Mary was down in the dumps after her miscarriage or whether she was struggling with a clinical depression, but having some distraction and a worthwhile project of her own, outside of Robert's church work, seemed like a good place to begin. I would have to talk to Robert before I left and make sure he knew what to do if it seemed Mary was not moving forward. I really wasn't comfortable with the prescription she was taking, but it was hard to convince her otherwise when her friends all seemed to be taking it too. I just didn't know enough about that area of medicine, but I wasn't convinced her doctor did either. It was all too easy to reach for the prescription pad and medicate women to be quiet and go away.

Chapter 41

LOUISE, BOSTON, FALL, 1951

As I left Harvard's medical library, it felt so good to enjoy the last of the afternoon light on a gorgeous fall day. I still couldn't believe I'd been accepted to Harvard to do a master's in public health. I heard from Mary occasionally and it seemed she had moved forward with her plan. She enjoyed working part-time and taking a correspondence course on design. It was gratifying to realize that we'd both made plans and were busy pursuing them.

Not a cloud was in sight, but the shadows were already growing long between the brick buildings. On the steps of the public health department, a small group of male classmates smoked cigarettes and talked loudly with each other.

"Hey Garrett, come on over and join us for a smoke."

I walked over to them. "Thanks for the invitation. I'll be sure to be around when you need surgery for lung cancer."

They all laughed loudly—they were so certain that nothing like that would ever happen to them. How they believed their privileges would insulate them from trouble—*foolish lads*, I thought.

I could hear them mocking me as I walked away. I wasn't going to be intimidated by any of them. I'd been through enough to realize this was just another version of tribal bullying. Someday it might be different, but for now, this was the culture at the school. I doubted change would come soon.

Their crude behaviour no longer surprised me—my best defense was to focus on my goals and to ignore them. The few women at the school tried to support each other—last week I'd met a woman doctor doing research on premature infants with respiratory distress syndrome. She'd told me to focus on my research and not let anything distract me.

Even though my room was a bit rustic, I decided to invite her over for dinner. I went to the fish market and bought some fresh fish and cooked up some greens and rice and we had a lovely dinner. But those kinds of things happened rarely—most of us were too busy to socialize. We found cheap cafeterias and sustained ourselves with peanut butter sandwiches and apples. Sometimes I went to the hospital cafeteria for a meal—it was odd to see the doctors and nurses in uniform, talking about their patients and their work. Sometimes I wondered if I'd lost my skills—it had been months since I'd been in an operating room. I felt this impulse to sit with the medical staff and tell them that I was one of them, but I knew they'd think I was crazy.

Harvard was an interesting place. I loved walking past the old buildings and along the Charles River. Cafés were usually filled with students reading or talking. I had to remind myself how far I'd come since growing up on the farm. I just wished I had some extra money to enjoy the finer sides of life in this city.

On the down side, I found it unfortunate that the atmosphere at school was rife with suspicion and secrets. Accused of being a member of the Communist Party a decade before, one of my professors had been forced out of the school. I'd taken a course with him and found him to be a fascinating teacher and an expert in the history of public health. When Harvard didn't defend him, he left for a teaching position on the west coast.

These days everyone looked over their shoulder and gossiped about who might be next. I didn't think it served universities well to become pawns in the political game—they needed to stand up for the truth and protect the freedom of their students and professors. When they caved in to government or corporate interests, they surrendered their right to shape the nature of academic inquiry. Public health involved political choices, and when that power got into the wrong hands, decisions on funding and policy were compromised. It was one thing to have someone like McCarthy setting the tone for politics, but I wished the university would keep his ideas out of the system. The unsettled political environment only increased my determination to graduate from Harvard as soon as possible.

Dr. Roberts, who taught courses on social science and health, wanted to discuss the research paper I had written for his class. When I sat down in his office, he unwrapped two enormous sandwiches from the deli down the street.

"I thought you might be hungry," he said. "Go ahead."

I'd never tasted anything so good. I'd missed breakfast and was starving.

He seemed to really like my paper. Because he'd been awarded a grant, he wondered if I would be interested in being a research assistant—running focus groups and helping with data analysis. He offered me the second sandwich and said he wasn't hungry. I accepted.

The assistantship would give me job experience, as well as a small income. "I'd love to do that."

"I thought your paper was very good." He took the time to show me his comments and to explain how I might tighten the argument and clean up the conclusions. And then to my surprise, he suggested I send it to a journal for possible publication.

I walked home that afternoon feeling optimistic that things might finally fall into place. Having one supporter in this large and unwelcoming university made all the difference. I knew I would never be a Rockefeller-funded scholar, running health programs in South America and Asia, but I believed that the health of rural communities in America was just as important. When our own citizens lived in primitive conditions and lacked the basics of nutrition, sanitation, and immunization, it reflected badly on the nation as a whole. *It was so easy to ignore the needs of the poor*, I thought, *because they simply didn't have the clout to make politicians listen.*

I thought of Pastor Cal in Mississippi. He'd probably look at me with a slow smile and tell me that I was finally starting to understand.

Funding at the school determined the priorities in hiring and research. The previous decades of community-based orientation had been underfunded and, as a result, marginal to other, more popular programs. In my opinion, research needed to support social and economic reforms that would result in changed practice in the field. None of that would happen without education at the local level. Research had to be applied to practice, or else what was the point?

When I got home that night, I unloaded my bag of groceries into the small fridge. The prospect of some funding had inspired a more generous shopping trip than usual and I was looking forward to cooking up a nutritious meal. Having such a substantial lunch in my professor's office only made me hungrier.

When the phone rang, I thought it might be Mary, but instead, it was a male voice.

"This is Peter Allan from the accreditation commission. I'd like to update you on our investigation. Is this a good time?"

I sat on the couch trying to make sure I didn't pull the phone right off the table. "Yes." I felt breathless, as if I had run a mile or two. I hadn't expected him to call, but as the days passed, I wondered if there would be any results. In my worst moments, I imagined Dr. Clarke, in a rage, chasing me down the sidewalks of Boston.

"Our team investigated the medical records, reimbursement procedures, and other issues at the san. We transferred patients to a long-term care facility from that secret place in the woods. They're all being cared for now. An interim administrator will keep things running at the san until they appoint a new management team. They'll work to discharge patients who are well enough to go home and they've hired a discharge planner to help with that. The state is looking into potential uses for the building and they're talking to a private buyer as well."

"That's incredible."

"We wouldn't have been able to get it done so quickly without your report. It gave us a good indication of where to look. I'm grateful to you for that. And remember, if you are looking for a job in the future, don't hesitate to contact me. We'd be happy to talk to you about joining our investigative team."

"That's very kind. I'm hoping to find a small department of health that needs a director in the state. But I appreciate the invitation."

"We managed to keep your name out of this. The state was overdue for a visit to the san; we presented it as a routine visit and then "accidentally" uncovered the things you'd mentioned."

"Do you know what happened to Dr. Clarke?"

"I heard that he had found another job running a small hospital in Florida. And Dr. Patterson took early retirement."

"What do you think will happen to the building?"

"The state will be happy to sell it if they find a buyer. It's difficult to adapt those institutions to modern health care, and the cost of doing that would be prohibitive. Although some of the buildings were advanced in their time, today's hospitals are built in a way that allows for greater efficiency. I don't get involved in that side of things. How are your studies going?"

"I was offered a research assistantship today. I really like some of the courses and I'm learning more about research methods and statistics. I'll be happy to finish here and start work. I've been a student long enough. I think I'm ready to leave the city for a quieter setting. My hiking boots haven't been used in a long time."

"Good luck with everything and thanks for making my job so much easier. Let me know the next time you plan to be in Albany and perhaps you could come over for dinner. My wife would love to meet you. She and Mary have been friends through the women's group at church."

"I will. Good luck to you."

I put the phone down and stared at the wall. Dr. Clarke had moved on without any disciplinary action or penalty. Dr. Patterson had chosen retirement. I had to admit I felt disappointed that they both got away with it. But

I had done what I could. Patients were being discharged. Soon the place would be empty—a memorial to a disease that was on its way to complete eradication. There were probably a lot of people who would lose their jobs at the san—but hopefully they'd find something else. The entire industry that supported the disease would be dismantled or adapted to something new.

I returned to the task of making dinner by putting some garlic cloves and a lemon inside the cavity of the chicken and covering it with herbs and oil. I'd have plenty of meals from that and even soup from the carcass.

While I was waiting for the chicken to roast, I wrote a letter to Penny. She and Joe had settled in Buffalo, where they established a construction company. Penny helped him with the books and continued to nurse part-time. I was glad she made an effort to keep in touch—most of the others had disappeared into their lives as if the san had never happened. Penny occasionally forwarded clippings, so I knew that Jimmy had an art show in Harlem and Dan had joined the circus school. I missed them and knew I had been lucky to have their friendship during that difficult chapter. I didn't expect to find such fellowship again anytime soon, but I told myself to keep an open mind and treat each moment as an adventure. I was more than ready for the next one to begin, even though the exact outlines of it were still unclear.

Chapter 43

LOUISE, BOSTON, SPRING, 1952

SITTING at the small maple desk in my rented room, I struggled to edit the paper I'd written. Upstairs, the young couple was in the midst of their daily argument—suddenly, something shattered against their wall followed by an eerie silence. I forced myself to stop listening and turned my attention back to the page. As long as they didn't set the place on fire, they'd have to sort out their problems on their own. Occasionally, I took the broom and thumped the ceiling to express my anger at their rowdy behavior, but it wasn't very effective.

In my paper, I examined smoking habits of middle-aged women and demonstrated a clear causal link between smoking and lung cancer. Our findings confirmed those of the well-known researchers Horn and Hammond and lent strength to the anti-smoking literature. Working with my professor, we conducted research in different communities around Boston, something I found truly fascinating because I had the chance to encounter people from different walks of life. I worked hard to establish trust with participants when I did interviews and focus groups. I thought, or at least hoped, that I was learning to overcome some of the awkwardness I'd always felt in public. Whether I was shy or inept, I wasn't sure, but I wanted people to feel comfortable sharing their thoughts with me.

After presenting my initial findings to the American Public Health Association meeting in Washington two weeks before, I was preparing a final draft of the paper. I was thrilled when they asked me to help draft a report to send to the president urging him to form a national commission on smoking.

My fellow graduate students in the program resented the attention I received as a result of this research. They would never admit, however, that research had for years ignored women, even as women were smoking in increasing numbers across the age spectrum. It was just a matter of time before we'd see a jump in lung conditions and cancer. To make women such a low priority for research seemed to me to be such a blind spot and one that would hurt those women who continued to be the target of advertising.

Watching Mary smoke had given me pause—she claimed it soothed her nerves and kept her weight down. I thought that was ridiculous. Mary seemed high-strung and thin as a rail, but she would not listen to any warnings. When I invited her to come to Washington to be with me when I received an achievement award, Mary decided she couldn't leave Robert with all the extra work generated by Easter celebrations in the church. She said she was excited for me and sent a card with money for a new dress. I was touched by the gift, especially because I knew that finances were tight in the parsonage. Realizing that Mary would be disappointed if I didn't use the money, I spent a Saturday shopping. After trying on many dresses, I found a black dress with delicate beading at a consignment shop and some black suede dress shoes to match.

When I checked the mail, I was happy to see a letter from Mary on the hall table. I decided to take it to the park to enjoy some fresh air before settling in to work for the evening. I would put the chicken in the oven when I returned. I didn't mind eating late for a change. The days were slightly longer as spring beckoned.

Mary wrote that she was enjoying her job in the department store and had finished one interior design course by correspondence. But the big news was that she was pregnant. She had passed the critical time and now felt like she could tell people. She sounded delighted despite the fatigue and nausea.

Watching the children play on the swings, I tried to imagine Mary taking her child to a park like this and chatting with the other moms about their nap schedules and food challenges. I felt a familiar feeling deep in my stomach and I knew it was my old companion, jealousy. Mary's life was moving in directions that I knew I would never experience. I thought I'd fully accepted that, but hearing this news unsettled me. It was the price of my career, I told myself for the hundredth time.

Peals of joyous laughter rang up from the playground as one mother pushed a swing high into the air. I thought about how that sound would finally fill the parsonage with welcome joy. Robert would be a proud and attentive father. I hoped that Mary would be up to the challenge. They'd have to share the work of raising a child. Robert would need to set some limits to his church work or Mary would become too isolated at home. But I trusted them to figure that out—they'd come a long way since I had turned up on their doorstep after being thrown out of the san.

One young toddler ran to his mother who had been talking to another on the park bench near me. He threw his arms around her and gave her a hug and then ran off to play again. Even though it would never be the same as having my own child, I realized that as an aunt, I could still have a role to play. Would it be a boy or a girl? Would the baby look like either of them? I'd call Mary the minute I got home and tell her how happy I was for them. If she delivered in the late fall, perhaps I could drive there and help over Christmas. I hadn't held a baby since Mrs. Collier was a patient in the san. The memory made me smile as I tried to picture how big that little girl might be now.

Chapter 44

LOUISE, BOSTON, SPRING, 1953

I SAT on the edge of the stretcher in the student health clinic, having been taken there by one of my friends.

The doctor examined me and ordered some blood work.

"I've been trying to finish my graduate work. I think I'm just worn out," I told him.

"I think a visit was overdue. Let's see what the blood work shows, but in the meantime, I want you to go home and rest. Make an appointment for Monday so we can review the lab work and make a plan. No work. Do you understand?"

I looked at him like he was mad and then pretended to agree. In my final weeks of my program, I had a tight deadline to submit the corrected copy of my thesis to the graduate studies office. If I worked the rest of the weekend, I might finish and then I could finally rest.

Visiting with Mary over Christmas had been such a special time. I hadn't been sure how it would feel to hold her baby, but in two minutes, I was completely smitten. When I got my first smile, I thought my heart would burst. She was a good baby, content and full of chuckles and laughter. I couldn't wait to see her again.

I walked home from the doctor's appointment on Monday and had to stop several times to rest. After reviewing the lab work, the doctor told me I was suffering from extreme exhaustion. I was somewhat relieved. In the back of my mind, I was afraid that I had contracted TB, so exhaustion seemed like a much better diagnosis. Still, I knew I couldn't push any more. I needed to listen to him.

"Your whole immune system is tottering on the brink, and if you don't take a break now, I promise you, you will be admitted to a hospital with something that will be much more serious. I want you to figure out where you can go for total rest for at least a month."

There was no way I could go to Mary—she had her hands full with the baby and she didn't need one more dependent. I couldn't think of anywhere else to go. I thought about Penny, but they were so busy with the construction business, and time had passed, making that kind of request seem awkward.

As I crossed the street, I passed two nuns that were talking quietly as they walked in the opposite direction. I stopped and watched them. *Mother Maureen*, I thought. I would call her and see if I could stay there. She had told me to call them if I ever needed help.

When I got home, I slowly dialed the number with the area code for New York State.

"Mother Maureen speaking," she said.

"This is Louise Garrett. I'm sorry to bother you."

"Dr. Garrett. What a pleasure it is to hear from you. I'm happy to tell you that Sister Claire is doing well. How can I help you?"

"I've been ill, and my doctor feels I should take a month's rest. I just finished my thesis, and I got run down in the process. It's nothing infectious, but the doctor insisted I find a place to rest for a month. I remembered that you said I should call if I ever needed help. I don't know where else to go."

"Of course you can come here," she said without any hesitation.

"I'm happy to pay whatever you normally charge guests."

"We can work something out. We simply don't have enough hands to do the work of the farm. And we could always organize a baby clinic for the locals. The only doctor up here should have retired a long time ago. Anyway, we can discuss all that when you are here. When can we expect your arrival?"

"I need to tie up some loose ends here in Boston and move out of my room. I could be there in a week. Would that work for you?"

"Of course. We'll have a room waiting for you. Till then, we'll pray for your health and wish you a safe journey."

"Thank you so much." I put the phone down and thought about Mother Maureen and Sister Claire and how happy they'd been the day she'd been discharged from the san. But now, I really had a deadline and I would have to push hard to finish up the details and pack up my room. Luckily, everything I owned would fit in the trunk of my car.

The prospect of working on a farm and being outside in fresh air made me happy. I needed to get away from this city and take a break from everything. Hopefully, my next steps would become clear in the weeks ahead. If I could pay for lodgings by doing some work, it would really help. My bank account was getting very low and I was reluctant to ask Robert and Mary for help.

IMMACULATE MARY CONVENT, UPSTATE NEW YORK, 1953

I slipped on a pair of green rubber boots that stood ready at the back door of the convent kitchen. The men's work pants that I'd found at a church thrift shop were perfect for garden work. Because I'd lost weight in the past year, I needed a belt to keep my pants from falling down. A large flannel shirt and a red bandana completed the outfit.

I threw some wilted lettuce to the hens in the courtyard; they pecked at it with enthusiasm while I gathered eggs in my basket. Sister Ginette would be delighted to receive a dozen eggs, which she would turn into a quiche or omelets for lunch. Her ability to stretch the ingredients into a meal big enough for all twenty of them was nothing short of miraculous. I sometimes kidded her that Jesus himself couldn't turn loaves and fishes into the feasts that she made. She would throw her head back and laugh in the most infectious way.

I'd been a guest there for a month. The first two weeks were a blur—I slept twelve to fourteen hours a day and had no surplus energy. Gradually, I started working in the garden to help with the planting. It was hard at first—I wasn't used to that kind of physical labor, and my back ached. Blisters lined the inside of my hands. Despite the discomfort, being outdoors surrounded by the calls of red-winged blackbirds around the farm brought me back to life—that and the hearty food that was served.

I was happy to care for the sisters when they were sick and to offer medical services to the local community. We invited them to attend a free clinic at the convent on Fridays. When word got around, there were long lines for appointments. One of the sisters helped weigh the babies and talked to the mothers about feeding and sleep routines.

Some days I went on house calls with Mother Maureen, who loved an excuse to drive the Oldsmobile along the country roads at breakneck speeds. She shifted the gears smoothly and laughed in delight as the car cruised at top speed. The farmers in the area knew enough to pull out of the way when they saw her coming. I was quite surprised that she also had a fondness for rock music and was a big fan of Elvis. She sang along with the radio as the dust pursued us down the gravel roads. I remembered driving with Pa in the pickup truck and watching the dust rise up behind us in similar ways.

The rural women gave what they could to pay for the medical care. They brought gifts of potatoes, apples, and freshly butchered meat—the kitchen accepted these offerings with gratitude. Many of the patients had never seen a woman doctor, or any doctor at all, and I felt their initial reluctance shift when I gave them practical advice and listened carefully to them. I immunized their children and checked blood pressures and abdominal girth and discussed development issues and infections. The children sorely needed preventive dental care—I wrote one of my colleagues from public health to see if she could make any contacts with dentists in training who could come up and do a clinic. The needs of the community were overwhelming and far beyond what I could deliver—the children needed eye care as well.

Although it had been years since I'd worked on a farm, other than my brief escapade of milking at the san, the routines of farm life felt so familiar and provided a welcome change from the intense mental focus of my research in the past years. I felt such simple satisfaction at the end of the day—whether in the kitchen, garden, barn, or infirmary. The nuns were pleased that I actually knew how to milk a cow and turn cream into butter with their old fashioned churn.

Even though I'd never really enjoyed cooking, I was happy to learn from Sister Ginette. She taught me to bake whole-wheat loaves, quiches and pies. I'd always relied on the hospital cafeteria to feed me during my long shifts, but there was a satisfaction to the preparation and serving of food that surprised me. Somehow this was much more fun than the obligations to help in my mother's kitchen—Sister Ginette loved food and made it an adventure.

Sister Ginette had honed her cooking skills on the family farm in Quebec. Her collection of dried herbs provided that extra complexity of flavors to all she cooked—roasted sage, fresh thyme, and oregano infused her casseroles with intriguing flavors. I only then realized how bland my mother's cooking had been.

Mary would be surprised when I told her that I'd actually learned to cook a few things. I tried to call her once a week from the convent phone. She was getting worn out from feeding the baby night and day, and she wanted to switch to formula. I persuaded her to keep at it for a few more months so that the baby could get all possible benefit from breast milk. I promised to come and see her after I left the convent. After being so focused on my goals, I was strangely content to drift along with the current and follow the comforting routines of life in the convent.

Chapter 45

LOUISE, CONVENT, NY, 1953

I SAT outside Mother Maureen's office feeling like I'd been called to the principal's office in elementary school. Despite the chill of the convent halls, I felt nervous sweat moisten my armpits. I knew I'd successfully avoided thinking of the future, but I sensed that Mother Maureen was about to push me to move forward. Usually fairly practical, my ability to plan ahead had deserted me completely. The thought of leaving the simple routine of this place terrified me. I'd surprised myself by attending prayers; it seemed natural to join the nuns in their worship life as they moved through the rhythms of their day. Rather than feeling confined, I felt supported by such daily devotions and was hungry for that sense of order.

Just that morning I'd listened to Sister Claire practicing a new piece of music in the chapel. Her voice was sublimely suited to the chants and plainsongs that were part of the community life. She'd put on some weight since leaving the san, and her skin had a lovely translucence—what a difference from her condition on admission when she was too weak to respond to questions.

Mother Maureen often told me how grateful she was that I had saved Claire's life. I teasingly reminded her that she needed to give God credit for healing, but she replied that God used all kinds of instruments to do that work.

As I sat in the straight-backed chair in the study, Mother Maureen asked me what my plans were.

"I'm not sure," I replied.

"I think it's time you make a plan. I can't imagine that you're ready to take vows here, and although we welcome your medical training, I suspect that you might find a better place to use your talents."

"But I'm happy here and I like working on the farm and seeing the local people at the clinic."

"I'm afraid staying is not an long-term option. Perhaps you can find a way to identify the things you've come to love here and look for them in your next situation, but I cannot let you continue to stay here indefinitely. We are a community, after all, and although we welcome guests, we don't offer long-term options."

"Don't I work hard enough or give enough back to the convent?" I felt irrationally hurt that Mother Maureen was showing me the door.

"You give plenty, but those who live here take vows and this becomes their home. We can't be that for you."

I started to cry. All the comfort and security I had found here would now be stripped away. I couldn't imagine where else I might go. What if there was no place for me? What if I'd invested all my savings in a road that was simply a dead end?

"I'd like you to think about it. Someone with all your talents can't afford to retreat from the world. The world needs you. Let's talk again in a few days. You can do some research into employment and then report back to me. It's time to make a plan."

I nodded and wiped my eyes. I felt so sad I couldn't even look at her. Although I knew she was right, that didn't make it easier to imagine what might be next for me.

I spent all day at the public library in the closest town investigating public health agencies and employment possibilities. I looked at a map and drew a circle around Albany. I wanted to be no more than two hours' drive from Mary and Robert. I typed up my resume and addressed envelopes to departments of health in the geographic area that I had identified. I'd sent letters to my former professor at Harvard and to the dean of the school of public health, asking them if they could let me know if they heard of any suitable jobs. I used Mary's address as my permanent one in case anyone chose to respond.

Finally, I went to a phone booth and called Mary.

I was so startled by the hoarse voice that answered the phone, I wondered if I'd dialed the wrong number. "Is that you, Mary?"

Mary cleared her throat. "I was just having a nap. Robert's at regional church meetings in New York."

"But you're feeling OK?"

"Yeah, sure. What are you doing?"

"I've been up at the convent and it's time for me to move on. I've started looking for a job but I was wondering if I could stay for a little while at your place in the meantime?"

"Of course, when will you be here?"

"Could I come next week? Maybe Thursday?"

"I'll make up the guest room. The Albany library is good for doing job searches and Robert always knows people in the area."

"How's the baby?"

"She's good. I wish she would sleep more, but other than that she's fine."

"Thanks so much. I can't wait to see you next week." I hung up the phone and stared at the wall. Something didn't feel right.

Chapter 46

LOUISE, ALBANY, 1953

While I was working at the desk in the guest room of the manse, I heard Mary trying to soothe the baby. She knocked on my door and handed me the infant who was swaddled and whimpering.

"Take her. I need a break. She's been fussing since six this morning."

"Sure." I put her over my shoulder and walked around in circles, patting her back gently. I was getting more proficient at this. I looked at Mary who had thrown herself on my bed. "Have you had any sleep?"

"Not much. I'm going for a walk. If she screams, just put her in her bassinette. I'll be back shortly."

I walked around with Nori on my shoulder and patted her back and sang songs to her. I felt her body relax into my shoulder as she fell into a deep sleep. I carefully transferred her into her bed. She startled as her back contacted the cold mattress, but luckily she fell asleep again.

Although Mary seemed exhausted, I wasn't sure what to do about it. If I made any suggestions, she became furious. Last night she raised her voice at me. "I don't want to hear your public health theories," she'd said. "When you've had a child yourself, you might know how it feels. Till then, just assume you know nothing." Robert had tried to calm her but that only made her angrier. She stomped away from the table and went to her room. I tried to talk to her later, but she wasn't having any of it. I had the feeling that I both irritated and disappointed her. Sometimes I wondered if what she wanted was Ma's kind of attention—it wasn't my place to cater to her like that. I wanted to help, but she needed to carry her part of the bargain.

"Mary, listen, if it's too hard to have me here, I can leave. I know you have so much going on with the baby, it might be better if I found another place to stay."

"That's ridiculous. Where would you go? It's not a problem. I'm just tired and I'll be better tomorrow. You need to find a job and that's the only thing you should worry about."

"Let me do whatever I can to help you."

Mary shrugged and walked away.

I went back to my room to do some more work on cover letters and resumes. I felt that I was an additional burden to them at a time when they were still trying to adapt to the baby. Robert had assured me that I was more than welcome, but I had my doubts. The trouble was, I didn't have the money to go anywhere else, and until I got a job, we were stuck there together.

That night I got up when I heard the baby cry and I held her after Mary had nursed her so she could go back to bed. She mumbled thanks and shuffled back to bed.

I'd asked Robert earlier whether he thought Mary was suffering from postpartum depression. He wasn't sure and was afraid to talk about it in case talking about it made it true. I explained some of the symptoms, and he nodded slowly. This was more than he'd bargained for, and I could see the weight of it on his shoulders.

"How can I care for her and for our daughter," he asked, "and continue to serve the congregation? There's not enough hours in the day to do all that."

"Is there someone you could hire as a housekeeper? If she could keep the house and meals going and help with the baby, that would give Mary some support and allow you to do your work."

"There's one lady in the congregation who is widowed. She is very kind. Although her children are grown now, she enjoys working in the nursery at church."

"She sounds perfect. You will need to impress on her the need to be discreet. Just because she works in the manse doesn't mean she can talk about everything she sees. Do you think you can manage that additional cost?"

"I think so."

"As long as I am here, I'll pay you for room and board and you can use that to help with her salary. And when I get a job, if you need some help, I'll be happy to contribute."

He shook his head. "That's very kind but if this is what she needs, I'll find a way to make it work."

"You could always ask for a raise," I suggested.

He smiled. "I'm happy to see you still believe in miracles. I thought science had erased that possibility from your mind."

"You never know until you ask the question. That's true for science as well."

A week later, Mrs. Miller came to work at the manse. She was a quiet woman who managed the housework and cooking with efficiency and relished her time helping with the baby. Mary seemed to relax in her presence and was less volatile.

I accompanied her to her doctor's appointment. Mary flipped through magazines impatiently.

"What's the matter?" I asked.

"I hate being in these places. They're so confining. And they don't let you smoke."

I tried not to say anything about her smoking as I read through the classified section of the newspaper.

"You'll just get a job and leave again, won't you?" Mary asked.

I put the paper down. "I do need to get a job, but I'm looking for something in this area so I can be around when you need me."

Mary studied her nails, scratching the varnish off the nail on her index finger. "I don't know if I can do all this," she confessed.

I grabbed her hand. "You can. And we will help you. And hopefully the doctor will help as well. You're not alone in this."

"I feel alone. And to think I wanted a baby so badly, I thought I'd die if I couldn't have one. And now, I don't know how to look after her and sometimes I don't even know if I have what it takes to do this. Robert must be so disappointed in me. I'm not sure I'm fit to be a mother."

"Listen to me. Robert is proud of you. And I know you love your baby. We talked the other day about postpartum depression, and it can happen months after delivery. Maybe that's the problem."

"I asked him the last time I was in and he just said I was having some post-baby blues and they would pass."

"We'll try again today. Not all doctors know the signs. You will get through this, and I'll try to help in any way I can."

Mary pulled her hand away from mine. She seemed to be thinking about what I'd said. Every once in a while, I'd glance over at her but she seemed frozen in place, unlike the irritable and jumpy person she'd been earlier this morning. My heart hurt for her. I had watched the other mothers at church admire the baby last week. They assumed so much about how a mother was supposed to feel that there was no room to admit when things were difficult. The minister's wife was expected to be exemplary in her standards of mothering. I knew Mary felt the pressure.

I shouldn't have been surprised that Mary's doctor made little effort to listen to her and instead spent his time patronizing her and telling her to buck up. I could see her body sag under the pressure of combined expectations. When we got home, she went straight to bed saying she needed a nap.

That afternoon, I was reading on the front porch when the mail arrived. A letter was addressed to me! The return address was a public health unit in New York State. I carefully opened it and unfolded the letter. I realized I was holding my breath.

They said they were delighted with my qualifications and invited me for interview. I wanted to share my excitement but I was pretty sure Mary would feel that I was deserting her. Perhaps I was, but I needed to earn some money and move on with my career. Mary would never know that I'd turned down a prestigious fellowship in Washington. What was the point in telling her? I'd made my decision to try to stay physically close. And it wasn't just for her sake—I had grown so fond of the baby, I couldn't imagine going for months without seeing her. I would miss all the milestones and feats of her young life. But I did need to find something quickly—it wouldn't look good to have an extended period of unemployment on my resume. I knew I couldn't continue to take space in this household; they needed to be a family without me.

I called the human resource manager and booked an appointment for the following week. If I drove there and back in a day, I'd save money on hotels. Luckily, I'd just filled the gas tank of the car. And I had one good dress suitable for interviews. Sitting on the front porch, I wrote out some ideas about how I imagined myself in that position and what I felt I could offer. I dreamed of depositing that first paycheck into the bank to repay some of the student loans. It had been a long process, but I felt like I was on the cusp of an adult life, ready to take on adult responsibilities.

Chapter 47

LAKE HOUSE, 1980

Nori helped Louise take a drink of water and then sat back down. She felt dizzy and didn't know what to say. "I.. . . ."

"I know it's a lot to absorb. I want you to know the whole story. And I'm not quite finished yet."

"Why wasn't I told this stuff? Why did it have to be secret? After all, postpartum depression is a common enough diagnosis."

"Perhaps it is now, especially after well-known people and actresses have shared their stories, but in those days, it was difficult to give it the attention that it deserved. Women's health was an undeveloped area."

Nori shook her head. "I feel so badly that she had such a hard time. I hope it wasn't because I was such a demanding infant."

"You were the most beautiful baby and as happy as could be. I loved to hear your laughter. When you arrived, they were so grateful to finally have their longed-for child."

"And my father?"

"I can't say enough about Robert. Men of his generation were not generally expected to help with childcare, but he did as much as he could to help Mary. As sole pastor in a large church, he had plenty of pressure at work, but he always put you first. I think that fatherhood brought out the best in him."

Nori sat in her chair trying to fit the parts together. She gently massaged her temples.

"I think we should take a break now, and we can talk more later," Louise said.

Nori stood up. "Would you like anything to eat or drink?"

"I'm just going to rest. We can have tea later."

Nori tried to read the local paper, but she had lost her ability to concentrate. She walked from room to room, staring out the window and trying to make sense of what Louise had told her. She'd resented her father for so long, it had become as familiar as her own name.

Something rang true in what Louise had told her. Suddenly she felt completely exhausted—it was too much to absorb. She decided to have a nap on the couch, and if Louise needed her, she was close enough to hear her call. She wrapped herself in the afghan and curled on her side, facing the fireplace. It was too bad that Jazz had plans for tonight. She'd love to talk to her about all this.

Nori slept deeply for an hour and then woke up, startled to find herself on the couch. She checked on Louise and then went into the kitchen to make tea.

She brought the tray with the pot and cups and a small plate of cookies into Louise's room and placed it on the bedside table.

"I hope I didn't upset you," Louise said.

Nori shook her head. "I don't know what to think. When you've lived with one story for a long time.. . . ."

"Most people refuse to revise their old stories. It takes a great deal of courage."

"I'm not so sure I have much courage. You wanted to share stories, and I have one from childhood. Just to know what you think. I'm not sure I remember anything correctly now, but I'll tell you what I remember. And maybe we'll need to revise it afterwards."

"I'd love to hear it."

"My dad was determined that I attend a sleep-away camp, just like he'd done as a child."

NORI, CAMP SHALOM, 1965

When we drove up to the lodge on the mainland in time for registration, I didn't know any of the other campers, but they all seemed to be well-acquainted with each other from their home churches and schools. After my parents drove away, I hung at the edges of the group of girls who squealed and hugged each other as each new camper appeared. I wished someone would realize how alone I felt. I moved into the corner to read my book.

As we settled into our daily routines on the island camp and into the subgroups in cabins, I felt so homesick. The counselor assigned to my cabin wasn't very sympathetic. She had little patience for me, it seemed, and didn't like it that I had to be coaxed to participate in the group activities. She joked with the other girls and ignored me completely.

If I'd had just one friend, it all might have been tolerable, but I never found someone who wanted to hang out with me. My misery increased as the week went on and the girls found that I was a convenient target for pranks. One night, to my shame, I wet the bed and soaked my sleeping bag and pajamas. My clothes were rinsed in the lake and the sleeping bag was hung out to dry. I watched those pajamas flap in the breeze and felt completely humiliated.

The fact that the camp was on an island made me feel worse—there was no way to get away from the place. There were no phones and no understanding people. I thought about stealing a canoe or trying to swim to shore, but when I looked at the dark waters surrounding the island, I knew I was too afraid to try. That only added to my misery—even Nancy Drew would have found a way out of this mess. The days went on endlessly with programs and lessons and campfires. At night, the girls whispered and giggled in their bunks, but I was never invited to share the fun. I tried to make myself invisible.

When my parents picked me up the following Saturday at the camp lodge, I burst into tears.

"What kind of welcome is that?" Mom asked.

Dad passed me his handkerchief with no comment. He looked around for the counselor, but she was occupied with greeting other groups of parents. He was impatient, and he took my hand and led me to the car.

I climbed into the back seat. I could tell he was annoyed. He put my knapsack on the seat beside me and slammed the door.

"What's wrong?" my mother asked.

I shrugged. How could I ever explain? Maybe they didn't deserve to know. Why had they put me in that camp anyway? Perhaps they felt I was too much trouble and they wanted a break from me.

My father slid into the driver's seat and started the car.

"I hated it," I sniffed, "I'm never going back."

"What exactly didn't you like?" Dad asked with his arm over the back of the seat as he turned to look out the rear window to back the car out.

"Everything," I said quietly. What did he know about how mean girls were? He probably thought that because it was a Christian camp, everyone would be kind and loving. What a joke that was. My parents were so dumb sometimes.

I watched as my mother reached her arm back to console me. When Dad gave her a warning glance, she turned it into a quick pat on the arm and then turned to face forward. I knew he wanted me to be tough; I'd heard that lecture often enough.

From the back seat, I watched the familiar stores on the main street pass by. I wished we would stop for an ice cream at the dairy, but my father seemed to be in a hurry to get to my aunt's house. I knew he wasn't happy with me, so there wouldn't be a chance of persuading him that we deserved a treat.

When we arrived at the house, I grabbed my knapsack, ran into the house, and went directly to my room, where I stayed for the rest of the afternoon. No one even came to check on me—that made me feel even more dejected. I read one of the Nancy Drew books I'd read several times before, but it didn't grip me because I already knew the ending. I had the feeling I'd done something wrong and was being punished. But I knew it wasn't my fault that I didn't fit with those girls.

Eventually, Louise knocked on my bedroom door. I'd expected my mother to turn up, but at this point I'd settle for any attention. It was getting boring being in my room, but I wasn't about to come out and act as if nothing had happened. I knew I was being stubborn but I couldn't help myself.

Louise sat on the side of the bed and rubbed my back. "Do you want to talk about it?"

Her kindness made me feel bad again and I began to sob. "The girls were mean, and they made fun of me. One night they put peanut butter all over my hands while I was sleeping and then they tickled my nose with a feather. Another time they put a snake in my bed. And the counselor wasn't nice at all. She told me to stop being a baby. And . . . I peed my bed." I rolled onto my stomach with my face pressed into the pillow and cried.

"I'm so sorry." She paused. "That sounds like it was a terrible experience. Those girls had no right to bully you like that. I'll talk to your parents and see if we can lodge a complaint with the camp. As far as I am concerned, you never have to go back there."

I stayed where I was with my face in the pillow, but my whole body gradually relaxed. Being taking seriously made all the difference. After a few moments, I rolled over and looked at Louise. I was getting hungry but wanted to be persuaded.

"Your parents have gone away for a week or so and you can stay with me. We're going to have spaghetti for dinner and I picked a movie for later."

I still didn't respond. I was surprised my parents had left. I didn't know they were going anywhere, but part of me felt relieved, even though I tried not to show it.

"Does that sound okay?" Louise asked.

"With meatballs?" I asked. I wasn't going to give in that easily.

"Of course," Louise replied, "and you're going to help me make them. I thought we could also make a fairy house for the willow tree, if you can get out of bed."

I'd hoped to build a fairy house for a long time, but I decided to be skeptical. "How are we going to do that?"

"Maybe you should come downstairs and see. Go wash your face first."

I splashed some water on my face and patted it dry and then hurried downstairs to the sun porch where Louise had arranged some paints, moss, and glue on the table. As we worked to decorate the small wooden house, the afternoon sun angled through the western-facing windows in the kitchen and then through the sun porch, until it dropped below the pines.

"Did my dad want a boy instead of me?" I asked while I glued some moss to the base of the platform.

"Why would you think that?"

"He thinks I should be tough like him. I'm a girl and I can't be like him."

Louise knelt beside her chair and put her arm around Nori's shoulder. "Girls are tough in more ways that I can name. I think that's why women have babies—men would never survive."

I snickered. "Is it all right if I didn't like camp? Those girls were so mean."

"I'll talk to your mom about it. But we'll have to work on ways that you can fight back when you meet bullies. Sometimes you just have to stand up to them and pretend you're not afraid."

I nodded and began to glue tiny stones around the fairy house. Was I too old to believe in fairies? Maybe it didn't matter—Louise seemed to believe in them, and she was a doctor. I couldn't wait to show Jazz what we had made. She was going to want to make one too. Maybe Aunt Louise wouldn't mind if she used some of the materials to build her own fairy house.

Nori fell silent and studied her hands in her lap.

"I remember that time," Louise said. "What did you feel as you told me that story?"

"Looking back on it, I still feel like those girls were mean. My parents should have listened to me when I told them how miserable it was. I felt like my father was disappointed in me. He was so annoyed when they picked me up. And then, when we got to your house, I was in my room all afternoon hoping that someone would come and talk to me, but no one did. That made me feel like I'd done something wrong, and that feeling stayed with me. I remember how you came to my room to talk to me. You ended up saving the day, but my parents had disappeared, and we never talked about it again. I guess you were the one who told them I shouldn't go to that camp again, so I can thank you for that. At least after that, they let me come up here for summer vacations, instead of being sent to sleepaway camp."

"It's amazing how clear our memories can be of days filled with so many complicated emotions. Let me tell you a little bit about the things your parents were dealing with at that time. As you've already heard, your mother had challenges. Her undiagnosed postpartum depression led to continued struggles with anxiety and depression. On that day, your parents were supposed to be going on a vacation to Quebec. They were planning to pick you up from camp, spend the night at the lake house, and then set off in the morning. However, your mother had a setback and they had to drive back to Albany that afternoon. She was admitted to a clinic where she stayed for a few weeks. During that time, you stayed with me until they came back to collect you."

Nori sat in silence watching wisps of clouds surround the peak of the mountain and then drift away. That was what it was like, she thought, when a memory seemed so real, but then changed form just when you tried to reach for it. What was actually true about what she'd experienced that day? She could re-experience the feelings—anger, abandonment, and isolation— but she'd never given any thought to what the others might be feeling, nor the possibility that they were attempting to do their best for her in trying circumstances. Her own views of the events had been so one-sided and she'd clung to those hurt feelings over the years.

"Couldn't they have told me something about what they were going through? I feel so badly about it now."

"They wanted to keep your life as normal as possible, and that led to secrets and lies. There was a stigma attached to those kinds of problems. A minister and his family were held to a high standard."

"Was my father actually held responsible somehow for his wife's condition and his child's behavior? That seems so unfair."

"I think it was much more subtle. And your father didn't talk about that sort of thing because he had such a sense of loyalty to the church. He might have been asked about it by his consistory, but on the whole, I think most people supported him."

They fell silent for a while.

"I think I need to test another story on you," Nori said. "Do you have the energy to hear it?"

"Of course, dear."

"When I was a senior in high school, I used to hate Sunday mornings. The whole house was filled with tension because my dad would be working on his sermon till the last minute. Meanwhile, the phone would ring with people asking about hymns and readings, and I just wanted to stay in bed till it was over. I usually woke up in a bad mood just because it was Sunday. I can imagine I wasn't pleasant to be around. I had this feeling that I was caught up in all this drama that I hadn't asked to be part of, and I was constantly dragged to events and gatherings that didn't interest me at all."

NORI, MANSE, ALBANY, 1971

While I spooned cold cereal into my mouth, I read the Sunday cartoons at the kitchen table. Slouched on my chair, I had stretched my legs to the chair opposite me. The kitchen smelled like soup; I knew without checking that it was the usual Sunday vegetable soup with tiny meatballs. When I'd announced in high school that I was vegetarian, my mother just scooped the meatballs out of my bowl and gave them to my father. That sort of defeated the purpose, but one look from her stopped me from saying a word.

My father entered the kitchen and poured himself a cup of coffee. In his black preaching suit with formal striped trousers and polished black oxfords, he was ready for the morning service. His hair was carefully combed with a side part that was held in place with a liberal amount of hair cream. I could smell it from where I sat—the hair cream that smelled like almonds or coconut. I'd tried it once on my hair and hated it. He leaned back against the counter and took a sip of his coffee while studying me.

Feeling his eyes on me, I glanced at him and then turned my attention back to the comics. He looked like he wanted to say something, and I wasn't sure I wanted to hear it, but it would be hard to escape at this point. I thought he looked like a rooster all decked out for his Sunday performance. The gray haired parishioners always listened attentively to his sermons and would cluck together over the latest gossip afterwards. He'd be flattered by their attention. Later, in the car, I wouldn't be able to resist telling him the sermon had been way too long. He would be annoyed and ignore me the rest of the way home.

While I continued to pretend to read the comics, my shoulders edged up with tension and I started to gnaw at one of my fingernails. I knew it didn't make sense, the way I both wanted his approval and pushed him away. It had always been that way between us. It sometimes felt like he tried too hard to make up for my mother. But I wasn't stupid—my mother wasn't someone who could deal with being a mom full-time. She needed a lot of space and time for herself; I was never sure whether I took so much energy from her or whether my mother had low tolerance for my behavior. I'd become used to it and often made excuses when other kids had their mothers present for school activities. Still, it always felt awkward when my father tried to make up for her absence. He meant well, but he could never quite separate his minister's role from just being an ordinary dad, and that irritated me to no end. Maybe he didn't know anymore where his role began and ended, but I saw through it and it irritated me.

He cleared his throat and tried to pull out the chair opposite me, but it didn't move because my legs were still resting on it. He raised his eyebrows and I slowly slid my legs to the floor.

He put his coffee down and looked at me. "I know you've been procrastinating on your college applications, but you really need to get them done. Otherwise, you might find yourself living at home next year and looking for a job at the mall."

I rolled my eyes. I really didn't like that preaching tone he used that made me feel like I'd disappointed him again. And I knew I didn't have a good explanation for why I hadn't followed through with the applications— it had something to do with feeling that I wasn't good enough. Sometimes it seemed better not to try than to be disappointed or rejected.

I could smell the coffee on his breath mixed with the scent of his aftershave—English Leather, or something like that. I noticed that he had a small cut on the left side of his chin from shaving. I wished my mother would come down and intervene. I wasn't ready for this lecture—wasn't there a rule against lecturing to your child on the Sabbath? His need to connect with me made me want to reject him. He could never fill in for my mother, so why did he try?

"You're lucky your aunt is willing to help support your studies, but you still need to show some initiative to get the ball rolling. It would also help if you had some idea what you wanted to study."

I put the newspaper down and looked at him. I didn't like the sense of being judged in the way that he did so easily. "I know what I want to study."

"You do?" he said with obvious skepticism.

That made me angry, but also made it difficult to speak openly about my interest. I mumbled, "Design and buildings."

"You mean architecture?"

"Not exactly," I said with an impatient shake of my head. "More like the history of how buildings were designed and how that affected the way people did things, like in health care."

"I see," he said, obviously not understanding what I meant. He tried again. "A combination of history and architecture?"

I nodded. At least he was trying. I had to give him that. He usually preferred lecturing to listening. It was hard to explain how interdisciplinary the subject was—I'd need to learn about design and the history of medicine and the history of public health too. But I didn't have the confidence in the topic to be able to elaborate; no one at school knew what I was talking about, except my history teacher, who thought it was a great idea. He said he understood that I wanted to combine disciplines to get a broader perspective—I didn't want to be limited to history or design. He told me there were graduate programs that encouraged that kind of interdisciplinary study and for a few days I'd felt encouraged by the idea, until the doubts returned, and I felt unable to tackle the work of application.

"If you really want to do that, you need to get those applications finished. Your mother can help this afternoon with your statement. And I'm available if you need me."

"OK," I mumbled. I couldn't explain why I hadn't finished them. It wasn't as if I wanted to stay home—I couldn't wait to go away to college. But I sometimes wondered if I'd fit in or if I'd even pass my courses. Some of the people who had graduated from my school had returned for homecoming and talked about how hard it was and how nobody cared if you skipped classes or failed papers. What if I totally flunked out? It was one thing to be smart in high school, but in college, it was a different matter. It was hard to admit that you were afraid when all everyone talked about at school was getting away from home and having fun at college. Sometimes the possibility of failure felt so much greater than the chances of success. I didn't know whether it was even worth trying.

"It's going to be a really big change for us when you go. But you can do this. Don't doubt yourself."

I snorted in disdain, but I was also secretly pleased. Sometimes I felt like nothing I did was ever quite good enough for him—but then other times, it seemed like I was never good enough for myself. I looked at the newspaper on the table without seeing it because it was easier than making eye contact with him. I felt vulnerable and didn't like the feeling. I didn't know what else to say. "I'll do it," I said with a shrug, as if it were the last thing on earth I wanted. It was always better, I thought, not to show that you cared.

I had to admit, he wasn't so bad when he just dropped the official tone and was himself. But maybe that was too vulnerable for him—kind of like a priest going without a collar. *Maybe we weren't so different after all*, I thought, as I fingered the metal studded leather collar I insisted on wearing every day.

"Good." He stood up. "We'd better get ready for church. We can't have them waiting for the show to begin. What if they all walked out because they didn't think we were coming?"

I snickered at the thought of people sitting in the pews, checking their watches and whispering to each other about the tardy minister.

He started to leave the kitchen.

"Dad?"

"Yes?" He looked back at me.

"Thanks."

"You're welcome."

I poured the rest of the milk down the sink, running the tap to make sure the soggy flakes went down the drain. I rinsed the bowl and put it in the rack. I felt some excitement as I started to believe that it might happen—I'd go to college and start my real life. And hopefully not fall flat on my face.

He looked back at me. "Your mother won't be going to church today."

"Why not?"

"She's not feeling well."

"I can stay home with her in case she needs anything. And work on my applications."

"Nice try, but you can do that this afternoon. She'll be fine. Just needs to rest."

Nori fell silent and looked at Louise.

"I can picture the kitchen, the table, and the Sunday morning mood," Louise said with a smile. "What does telling that story bring up for you?"

"It's such a mix of emotions. I remember feeling stubborn and not wanting anyone to tell me what to do, but also being afraid to try, in case I might fail. I was afraid to move forward and afraid to get stuck, and it felt like a really complicated time. I knew my father was pushing me to get things going, and I sometimes wondered if he wanted me out of the house. I hated the Sunday thing, the pressure, everybody watching to see what I was wearing, what my mother was doing, and what my father was saying in his sermon. I felt like we were exposed for all to see, and I hated that."

"I can imagine how complicated that was for you."

"When you tell me that my mother was dealing with her own challenges, it makes me feel guilty for creating more problems for them. If they could have told me what they were experiencing, I might have tried to be a bit more cooperative instead of fighting everything all the time."

"Sometimes rebellion is the only choice, so I wouldn't feel guilty about that. Rebellion can also be a way of signaling that you feel something important to you is not being heard."

"I just don't know how to process all of this. When I look back, I feel guilty about being a problem, and I feel sad about not knowing more, and I feel miserable that I can't even go back and tell them I'm sorry for all they went through."

"You did what you could in a difficult situation. Robert wanted you to go to college, to find your passion, and to be able to support yourself once you graduated. He felt that it was your best hope to be independent. I think he realized that he couldn't give you much and you would need to be able to sustain yourself. Some of Mary's treatments were costly and used up their reserves."

"But you helped with my education."

Louise nodded. "Without children of my own, I was more than happy to do that. As you might imagine, I am a supporter of women's education. And I was more than prepared to allow you to figure out what you wanted to study, even if it took a few wrong turns, because I knew that once you found your way, you would commit fully to it. Robert had some traditional notions about women becoming nurses or teachers, partly because he felt there were solid jobs available to them."

"Was he disappointed when I didn't choose those professions?"

Louise smiled with a twinkle in her eye. "He couldn't say much—I was paying."

"Thank you for doing that. I really hope I haven't been a disappointment."

"Hush, child. I'm delighted with all that you've done. And I suspect you have some amazingly creative work ahead of you."

"I don't know. I feel like so much is going on that it's hard to keep the focus."

"You have to believe that it will come together. As a historian, your own story isn't separate from the stories you assemble about other people and other times. There are many sides to any story, and the challenge is to try to get as full a picture as possible."

"But is it ever possible? Even when we're present at an event, our perspective is so limited. And emotions are tricky—they can lead to illusions, not truth."

"We are always 'looking through a glass darkly,' but that doesn't mean we shouldn't try to tell it as best we can."

"When I think of our family, it's so hard to tell the whole story, especially with my mother and father gone. I can try to imagine what they went through and I can try to revise my own version of those things, but is that any more true than my childhood misconceptions?"

"It's hard when the story line comes to an end and one loses the chance to make revisions or to check one's version against someone else's story. But with humility, I think one can acknowledge the limits and never try to impose one single understanding on events. My truth about the past is a combination of perspectives and observations and mixed up emotions—they are, at best, limited, and at worst, completely flawed."

"In that case, if you're up for it, I have one more story. This one is more recent and still really bothers me because I can't find a way to settle it in my mind."

"I'm listening."

"This happened last summer. I'd been dating Kevin for a while. He was trying to make it in the music business but had to work as a bartender to cover some of his expenses. His parents had split and were living in different parts of the country. Kevin had been self-supporting for a long time."

NORI, LITCHFIELD COUNTY, 1979

Kevin had convinced me to go camping. It had been years since I'd slept in a tent or done anything outdoorsy like that. After my disastrous experience of sleepaway camp on the island, my parents had agreed to let me spend summers at Louise's house. Those were great summers. We took long day hikes in the mountains and kayaked on lakes, but we always ended up sleeping at the lake house. I felt secure in my little room there and was always happy to return to it after a day away.

"I don't even own a flashlight," I told Kevin.

"I'll take care of the equipment and food. You just ride along," he said.

"But where are we going?" I asked.

"Don't worry about the details. I'll pick you up Friday night after work. Be ready by six."

I put down the phone and went to the bedroom to dig up my knapsack from the back of the closet. I rolled up a pair of jeans and a turtleneck and stuffed them into the bottom. On the floor, I made a small pile of things that I would need. I wondered where we were going. Kevin was always unpredictable and ready for adventure. It was something I was trying to learn from him, but I really preferred to know the details in advance. I added a small flashlight, my toiletries, and a paperback novel to the pack and put it by the front door.

During that day, I watched the clock until it was time. I went home to change into jeans and a sweatshirt. It was still early in the season to be camping, and I figured it might be very cold that night. I warmed up some leftovers in the microwave so I wouldn't be starving on the trip—or end up eating in some greasy burger joint that Kevin picked.

When Kevin arrived in his ripped up jeans, a t-shirt, and a short leather jacket, I hugged him and smelled the unmistakable odor of beer and smoke. I almost asked him where he'd been all afternoon, but bit my tongue—he didn't like that sort of scrutiny.

"Are you ready, nature woman, for the adventure of your life?"

"I think so. Are you sure you can't tell me where we're going?"

He walked over and kissed her. "Now that would be no fun at all. Trust me."

"Yeah, that's what I'm afraid of," I said with a laugh. I turned off the lights and followed him out to the car.

As we drove, Kevin sang along to his favorite classic rock station and drummed on the steering wheel as we made our way out of town to the highway that headed north.

I leaned back into the seat and relaxed. In the days before dating him, I would have spent the whole weekend doing schoolwork; I was glad to forget about it and do something else. Although I had several papers due, I hoped that if we got home on time on Sunday night, I could finish things before the Monday afternoon class when the first paper was due. Everything was coming together at the end of term. Although the timing was tight, I hoped I could manage things.

I fell asleep for a while and woke up as the car slowed and bumped down a dirt road.

"Where are we?" I asked, peering into the darkness. There were no lights or orientation points—the headlights of the car illuminated a gravel road filled with potholes.

"Just down this road, our palace awaits." Kevin pulled up in front of a cabin. Two red reflectors had been stuck into the gravel on either side of the drive. I still had no idea where we were. I could hear spring peepers in the dark behind the cabin. We got out of the car and I grabbed my pack from the back seat.

"What is this place?" I asked, as Kevin opened the front door.

"Just a cabin."

"Whose is it?" I asked.

"You ask too many questions. Why don't you put your stuff on that bed there and then we'll collect some firewood? I'll get a fire started so we can cook. You must be hungry."

"Starving," I replied. I was glad I'd eaten something before we left.

I put my pack on the bed and then went outside to help Kevin find kindling. A stack of cut wood was lined up beside the front porch of the cabin; I carried a few logs over to the fire pit. Soon Kevin had a roaring fire going. He took two beers from the cooler and sharpened two twigs so we could roast the sausages that he pulled out of the same cooler. I sat on the small camp chair and sipped my beer while roasting the sausage. The sky was filled with stars—there were more stars than I'd ever seen. There were no other lights anywhere and no sounds of traffic or other people.

"What do you think?" Kevin asked.

"Very nice. Whose is it?"

"We're just borrowing it. Keep turning that sausage or it'll burn."

Kevin handed me a paper plate with a roll on it. We demolished the sausages and cooked more. Kevin finished his beer in a few swallows and helped himself to another. I looked at the dark woods and was grateful I'd brought Kevin's flashlight. The cabin had no running water, so we'd be using the outdoors for a latrine.

We watched the fire burn as sparks travelled straight up and then disappeared into the darkness. The smell of wood smoke mingled with the pine trees around us. I could smell the smoke in my sweater and hair, and it reminded me of summers at Louise's house. I felt a twinge of homesickness for those summers with Louise. It had been a while since I spent any time up there.

I yawned and then yawned again in rapid succession. "I'm ready for bed," I said. "How about you?"

"I'm going to sit up for a while."

I put the flashlight on the ground while I squatted by a tree hoping that no animal would appear.

I shook out my sleeping bag on the double bed and fluffed the pillow I'd brought. Turning off the flashlight, I stared into the darkness—it was amazing how thick it was. I was curious to see what the place looked like in the daylight—it seemed like a pretty rustic setup, but obviously someone had made a woodpile and kept the place clean. At the moment I was so tired, I just needed to close my eyes and sleep. I smelled the scent of the joint Kevin was smoking and heard him open another beer. Much later, I sensed when Kevin came to bed, but I was so tired I couldn't even speak.

In the morning, I was momentarily disoriented as I looked at the unfamiliar pine walls of the bedroom. Kevin was fast asleep; he looked much younger when he was sleeping. I stayed in the sleeping bag for a while, but then I got restless and quietly slid out of the bag and down to the end of the bed.

I went outside to squat by a tree and washed my hands and face in a small amount of the water from the plastic jug. Kevin had even included a bar of white soap in a plastic bag. I looked through the canvas bag of food he'd packed to see what I could make for breakfast. There was an old-fashioned percolator pot and some ground coffee. Since the kitchen had no working stove, I filled the coffee pot with water and loaded the basket with ground coffee and brought some matches outside. Because the ashes were still glowing in the fire pit, it wasn't too hard to get the fire going with some dried hemlock needles and twigs. I placed a well-used rack over the fire pit and waited for the water to boil and the coffee to start bubbling. I hoped Kevin wouldn't sleep too long, because I was starving, and he was far better at cooking over a fire than I was.

I poured a cup and sat on the small beach chair. The cabin seemed to be fairly isolated. Thick woods surrounded the place and no other cottages were visible. The morning sun illuminated intricate spider webs that hung between the branches. A heavy layer of dew coated the grass.

Kevin came out carrying a cast iron pan. "Ready for some breakfast?"

"Starving. I was about to wake you up." I poured him some coffee.

Kevin cooked the strips of bacon and then cracked the eggs into the bacon fat. They sizzled as they hit the hot pan.

I watched him work. "You're good at this."

"Scouts," he replied.

We ate breakfast sitting on the two chairs with blue jays calling noisily from the trees around them.

"Where exactly are we?" I asked. "Is this still Connecticut?"

"We're in the back woods of Goshen. If you drive that way you end up in Washington, and if you go that way you'll be in Litchfield and Torrington."

"How did you find this place? I couldn't see anything last night."

"Someone told me. Plus, I have great night vision. All those carrots I ate as a kid."

I was startled when a truck drove up the dirt road and pulled up beside the cottage. A man got out of the truck, and I was even more shocked to see that he was carrying a rifle.

"What do you think you're doing here?" he growled.

Kevin stood up. "Hey, man, take it easy. We were just here for a night."

"You got no business being here. I know the owner. That road is private property and it's marked. Now get your stuff out of here and don't come back."

Kevin held up his hand. "Just put the gun down. We're going."

He slid past the man as I looked on in shock. I followed Kevin into the cabin. We threw our things into the bags and I rolled up the sleeping bags, grabbed the pillows and took them out to the car. My hands were shaking. Kevin took the dirty dishes from the campfire and threw them into a plastic milk crate.

The man with the gun did not move, nor did he take his eyes off us.

I got into the passenger seat and closed the door. I slumped down in the seat, hoping that the man wouldn't take the opportunity to take aim at the back of my head. Kevin put the milk crate into the trunk, slammed it closed, and got into the car.

The man walked over to the driver's side of the car. "Don't bother coming back or you might get a surprise."

"It's cool. Don't worry. See you around." Kevin started the car and drove down the road away from the camp. When they had driven for a few miles, I asked Kevin, "What was that?"

He shrugged with feigned nonchalance.

"Do you even know whose place that was?"

"Someone told me about it and I figured since no one was using it, they wouldn't mind if we made ourselves at home there for one short night."

"Are you kidding? You just decided to invite yourself? We could have been charged with trespassing. Or the guy could have taken your head off instead."

"Don't make such a big deal out of it. If he hadn't come along, no one would have known."

"I don't believe this. You don't even feel bad." I looked at him in amazement.

"I only feel bad that we got caught. If someone never uses it, why shouldn't we borrow it?"

"That's ridiculous. Have you ever heard of private property? What if you owned a cabin and people came along and decided to use it without asking?"

He shrugged. We were silent for the remainder of the drive. Kevin dropped me at my apartment. I took my pack out of the car, as well as the pillow and sleeping bag, and slammed the door. I didn't say goodbye but marched up to the front step of the house. Kevin squealed the tires as he took off without looking back.

"Asshole," I muttered as I went inside.

The next evening, Kevin showed up at my door. Behind his back he was holding a huge bunch of flowers. I was glad they weren't roses—it always seemed like such a cliché when men gave roses to make up for bad behavior. He must have gone to the farmer's market, because the bunch was filled with tulips and irises.

"Look, Nori, I'm sorry. I thought it would be fun, and my friend said no one was ever there."

"It's the principle of the thing. It just wasn't yours to take, and I didn't like being part of that."

"Do you forgive me?"

I looked at him with the flowers in his hand. He hadn't acknowledged any principle or wrongdoing. He just wanted to be forgiven and get out of the doghouse. But then, he looked vulnerable, like a little boy, instead of the tough guy he usually tried to be.

I sighed. "Come in. Are those for me?"

He hugged me and followed me into my apartment.

LAKE HOUSE, 1980

"Thanks for sharing that story with me. You've mentioned Kevin but I think you said you broke up with him?"

"We're done. He got involved with a waitress and I think he'd been seeing her for some time without telling me."

"What feelings does that story bring up for you as you tell it?"

Nori sighed. "It's complicated. The camping story was just one of many adventures with him. I think I was attracted to him because he was spontaneous and good at making things happen. But his loose interpretation of what was right and wrong made me very uncomfortable. I think I hoped he would make me more fun and spontaneous, but it wasn't his job to turn me into somebody else. It was hard because I was at school and working part-time and the whole academic thing didn't interest him at all. In order to keep up with his band and his schedule, I got to bed late, after going to clubs at night, and I fell behind in my work. We just lived such different lives, it was hard to make that work."

"After this camping disaster, you made up with him?"

"We went through quite a few cycles of breaking up and then getting back together. But when I found him with that waitress, I'd had enough."

Louise nodded and waited.

"The thing is, my friend from school, Jenna, said that I wasn't fair to him and that I tried to make him into something he wasn't, and in the end, I was the one who pushed him away. She said I shoved him right towards that waitress and I needed to take responsibility for my actions."

"How did that feel?"

"Terrible. She told me not to call her until I had figured myself out. The thing is, I miss her. We were really good friends."

"Do you think there's any truth to what she said? Do you feel that you push people away?"

Nori sighed and was silent for a while. "I think there might be some truth to it. I have trouble accepting that people might care about me. I always feel like I want to break it up so it's on my terms, before they get wise and push me away."

"And if you do it first, it will hurt less?"

Nori nodded.

"I have to believe that when we value ourselves fully, it is possible for others to value us as well."

Nori sighed. "I think you're saying that we can't expect our friends to affirm something we don't believe about ourselves?"

"I knew you were ready to swap stories," Louise said with a smile.

Chapter 48

NORI, LAKE HOUSE, 1980

How was she supposed to understand all this? All her life she'd worked on the assumption that her father didn't really love her and that her mother, no matter what Nori did, was just unavailable. Why hadn't they shared their challenges with her? Even in high school, she would have tried to understand—at least she thought so.

Louise had said she had to forgive herself. But how did one do that and really believe it? It wasn't a magic wand that you could wave over the past to make it right.

While the aide was busy with Louise, Nori left the room to sit at the kitchen table but found that it was impossible to concentrate on anything. Feeling restless, she went outside and walked to the small strip of sand that comprised Louise's beach. She felt the need to do something active—her mind was jumping all over the place and making her feel like she was spinning. Nori walked back to the sun porch to grab the paddles and life jacket and then pulled the kayak from the grass into the water. She needed to think and she wanted it to be somewhere where no one would interrupt her.

Memories were coming together with the things Louise had told her, but they weren't fitting back in the usual ways. Her brain felt like a kaleidoscope with a host of images changing by the second. Splashes of color, of conversation, of argument, and dropped sentences ran through her mind. She was sorry her mother had experienced so many challenges at a time when there seemed to be few options and minimal support. She had no memory of that, but she did know that she'd been a challenge as a pre-teen and teenager. Even when her father had tried so hard to pick up the slack, she'd pushed back and punished him.

Louise had done all she could to support her and to offer her summer escapes from the emotional uncertainty in the manse. Things were coming together in ways that had not made sense before. But now, just as she was starting to understand, Louise was moving beyond conversation into the next stage of her journey. The imminent ending of their story and time together was more painful than Nori could express.

If any of the adults had taken her aside and explained some things openly, she would have done her best to behave better. Despite the stigma attached to mental health issues, she would have been grateful to be invited into full understanding. Their conspiracy of silence had made her feel excluded. But then, she reminded herself, she'd resisted getting help when her friend Jenna had insisted she go to the counseling center at Yale when she fell apart towards the end of the semester. Were things really any different? Didn't people still judge those who struggled with challenges? Hadn't she judged herself?

Louise had turned down opportunities to advance her own career, deliberately staying close to provide support when needed. Nori remembered how Louise had driven to Albany to attend recitals and games—Nori had taken that for granted. She hadn't even thought about how Louise must have juggled her work hours with trips to attend those events at Nori's school.

Without noticing where she was, Nori realized she'd paddled to the far end of the lake. She stopped and caught her breath, letting the kayak drift with the current. She felt the wind pick up and then noticed small whitecaps appear on the surface. Huge clouds were gathering and moving quickly in her direction. A bolt of lightning zigzagged its way out of the sky in the north to strike the earth a few miles away.

By the time she decided to head back, the wind acted like a strong hand pushing against her chest and keeping her tethered in place. Having used up so much adrenaline on the way out, she had few reserves left. She fought the wind and gritted her teeth as she dipped the paddle into the waves and tried to find her rhythm. There was no one else on the lake as the rain began to fall with increasing intensity, pelting against her face like shards of glass. Nori knew she had to dig deep to find the strength to get back to the lake house. She tried to steady her breath and concentrate using more effective strokes to point the kayak in the general direction of the house. She couldn't see a thing. She imagined her father's voice, as he'd instructed her so long ago: *"Paddle into the wind with a low stroke that will lessen wind resistance, and do NOT lose your paddle."* She focused on what he'd taught her as a young girl and used his calm voice to guide her kayak back to Louise's beach. She bowed her head over her paddle and tried to catch her breath. Funny to think he was still guiding her now.

When she looked up, she saw the outline of the roof of Louise's house. All the outside and inside lights were turned on. When she clambered out of the kayak, she saw Ben sprint across the lawn.

"Are you all right?" he asked with obvious concern. He helped her pull the kayak onto the grass, tipping it over so the water could drain out. He took her arm and walked with her towards the house. The wind was howling so hard, it was impossible to talk.

"Is Louise okay?" Nori asked when they made it inside the porch.

"She's the same. Belinda was worried about you and she called me. She noticed that the kayak was gone from the beach. I was just talking to the police to see if we could get a boat on the lake to look for you."

He handed her a beach towel that hung over a chair in the porch and guided her into the kitchen. He directed her to sit while he put the kettle on.

"Brandy?" he asked.

"Hutch," she said and pointed to the living room.

He poured a shot glass for her and then turned his attention to making tea. She watched him and felt numbly grateful for his help. "I'm sorry. It wasn't this bad when I went out."

"Why don't you change?" Ben suggested, "And I'll make the tea and let the police know you've been found. Then, if you want, you can tell me what's going on."

Nori nodded and kept the towel around her while she headed up the stairs.

When she returned, Ben poured the tea. He'd lit the beeswax candle on the table and the kitchen filled with its honeyed wax scent.

He sat quietly while Nori tried to organize her thoughts.

"Louise and I have been swapping stories about the past. It's hard to realize that the things you thought were true were actually quite different." Nori looked at Ben and he nodded. "I never knew that my mother had undiagnosed postpartum depression and problems with anxiety and depression. My father tried to help as much as he could. Louise stayed near us so that she could provide support. And being a self-centered little brat, I assumed that no one really loved me or had time for me, so I acted out."

"How do you feel now?"

"I feel ashamed for being such a nuisance. And I'm still a bit angry that they didn't feel they couldn't talk to me about it."

"Louise believed it was important for you to know the whole story now."

"But I can't change any of it." Nori felt some large tears run down her cheeks.

"Maybe knowing those things will allow you to live the rest of your life differently."

Nori sat silently, trying to hear what he was saying. "Why do you think Louise wanted me to know all this?"

"Perhaps she believed that you were entitled to have the whole story."

"But I feel so badly," Nori said. "How can I repair the damage?"

"I think the challenge is to live in the present with a better sense of who you are."

"And what if I just hang on to my old stories?"

"Many people do. That would be a choice you'd make. Louise might give you a talking to that would turn your head."

Nori smiled.

"I'm sorry, but I have to go now. Please call if you need anything. Give yourself time to absorb all this."

Nori watched him leave. She got up and poured herself another mug of tea and walked to Louise's room.

Sleeping in the hospital bed, Louise's pale skin was as white as the pillowcase on which her head rested.

It won't be long, Nori thought, as she saw how fragile Louise looked. The thought made her heart feel unbearably sad.

Chapter 49

LAKE HOUSE, 1980

A FEW days later, Nori sat in her usual chair beside the bed. She'd spent the past nights on the couch in case Louise called, even though they had around-the-clock nursing care now. Although she thought Louise was asleep, her eyelids fluttered open the minute Nori sat down, as if she'd been waiting for her. Her breathing was labored, and she wore the oxygen mask almost constantly. The nurses were giving her regular amounts of morphine; it was clear that Louise was nearing the end.

Nori sat quietly beside her aunt and held her hand. Although she'd appreciated her presence in her life, she'd never fully realized how steadfast Louise had been. Those summers with Louise had been a cherished time for both of them, but it had also allowed Mary to have time to deal with her challenges. How often Nori had thought it was her fault that her mother wasn't feeling well. She had never voiced those thoughts out loud, absorbing the message that some things had to remain unspoken. There must have been many whispers around the congregation about the minister's wife being high-strung and anxious. In good times, Mary had been a leader in many church activities, but in her challenging times, she withdrew and people were offended. How little understanding they'd had of her struggles.

Looking at Louise, so frail and near the end of her life, it was impossible to understand everything that the previous generation had experienced. If she'd thought she could sort out that history in a definitive way, Nori realized that there would always be things that she couldn't understand because they hadn't been part of her experience. Still, she had to admit that things made a lot more sense after the conversations with her aunt. Louise's generosity in telling her stories and in sharing her diary was no small matter—Louise could have destroyed her diary and kept her secrets. Nori was grateful that she'd decided to share them with her.

Louise had always maintained a steady faith in her; soon, that would be gone forever. She imagined Louise telling her that she had all the tools she needed to move on with her life. Nori sincerely hoped that was true. Maybe no one ever felt ready to take the reins from the older generation. She watched Louise struggle for breath and hoped that Louise's spirit was moving away from this physical suffering.

Could she be waiting for some sign from Nori that it was time to leave? Ben had told her to keep communicating with her. Was she ready to let her go?

Nori glanced at the photograph of Mary and Louise sitting on the chairs by the lake with herself as a young child balanced on the armrests between them. They had loved her and she'd been richer because of it. When her mother couldn't cope, Louise had stepped up to provide loving companionship to her, with no attempt to usurp the rightful place of her mother. Without children of her own, it might have been tempting to claim a larger portion of Nori's affection, but her boundaries had always been clear. Love, Nori realized, took many forms. As she sat at the bedside, she could hear Belinda moving around in the living room. At some point Ben had entered the room and stayed discretely by the door.

"I'm here," Nori said, "and I won't leave. I love you. Thank you for telling me about your life. I think you've been so brave, but it's time to let go. We will never forget you."

Her breathing was increasingly irregular—it paused for a moment, and then resumed with jagged edges.

Ben moved forward to stand quietly beside Nori.

Nori found herself holding her breath every time Louise stopped, wondering if it was her final moment, only to exhale when she started again. It was hard to concentrate on anything else. Keeping vigil, Nori thought, was a task far outside of ordinary time. If Louise was setting out on a journey, it felt like they needed to stay close to her as long as they could. Time meant little while they waited.

Nori massaged Louise's feet; her legs were mottled as death claimed her body inch by inch. She'd been restless earlier, but after the visiting nurse had given her more sedation, she had settled.

Nori thought of the summers she'd spent with Louise, reading books, playing with Jazz, and baking with Louise. She'd taken so much for granted. She vowed to do better—to try to realize the potential that Louise had always supported.

Ben reminded her that love had surrounded her from her very first moment. Even when all her elders were gone, she hoped she could live up to the faith they'd had—Robert and Mary and Louise.

As the spaces between breaths grew longer, Ben stood up and moved towards the head of the bed opposite Nori. "Louise, we're here to say our goodbyes. We trust that we'll see you again someday. We're going to pray for your journey towards those you loved. We will stay with you through this time."

Nori closed her eyes and listened to the gentle sound of Ben's voice. She was so grateful for his accompaniment and support.

Brenda sobbed quietly as she stood against the wall near the door. Nori brought her closer to the bed to join them. She made Belinda sit in the chair and kept her hand on her shoulder.

Louise's respirations continued to be ragged.

Nori felt that something essential to her aunt had already left the room.

Ben spoke again. "We thank You for the gift of life, for the treasures we received, through those who loved us and those who we've loved. Give us all peace as Louise begins her journey to a new life free of pain and suffering. Ease the sorrow of those she leaves behind, knowing that she will always live on in our hearts. Take her hand and lead her now beside still waters."

The room felt silent.

A small shudder passed through Louise, followed by a long, slow sigh, and then her breath ceased. They all waited and wondered, but after a few seconds, the nurse moved towards the bed, checked her pulse and nodded to them.

Nori took off the oxygen mask and placed it on the pillow beside Louise. She deserved to feel the breeze on her face as she set out on her journey. Nori hoped that she could see them gathered there, in her room, in her beloved lake house.

The wind swirled lightly in through the open window, fluttered through the lace curtains, and disappeared.

Chapter 50

NORI, LAKE HOUSE, 1980

A WEEK later, Nori remembered little of the funeral service except how the light had glowed through the stained glass of the church windows. She recalled how Ben's quiet voice led the congregation through the liturgy. Louise would have appreciated his leadership. She had organized every detail of the funeral service, including the choice of hymns, so that Nori didn't have to worry about any of it.

Nori continued to feel numb in the days following Louise's passing. People in the community continued to bring regular offerings of food and helped around the yard. Someone had even planted Louise's favorite herbs in the kitchen garden beside the porch. She felt their support even though she had a hard time expressing it in words. The house felt so empty without Louise's presence—it felt as if all the lights had gone out and Nori couldn't find a way to turn them on again. Sometimes she stood at the entry to Louise's room but was reluctant to enter. The hospital bed and equipment had been removed and the room cleaned, but it felt strange to linger there.

Nori had not realized how many people in that community had known and admired Louise—the small church had been packed with people of every age. They told her stories of how Louise had cared for them or their family members; how she had driven out in darkness or inclement weather to help out with a sick family member.

Jazz had come with her little boy, all dressed up in shorts and a shirt with a bow tie. He looked just like her and held her hand as he looked around at all the people.

"I'm really sorry," Jazz said. "Louise was the best."

Nori nodded as her eyes filled up. She thought she'd have no one left once Louise passed, and here she was, surrounded by community made up of friends both old and new. It was overwhelming, and she wished she could tell Louise about it.

Sitting at Aunt Louise's desk in her study, Nori read the condolence cards and bills that had accumulated in the past weeks. In her aunt's filing cabinet she'd located a file with Penny's letters and she sent her a brief letter telling about Louise's death.

Belinda cleaned and scrubbed and helped bring things to the thrift shop in town. Although Nori realized it was silly, she couldn't imagine sleeping in her aunt's bed, so she stayed upstairs at night. She still woke up in the middle of the night and had to remind herself that Louise was really gone. It had become such a habit to wake up and listen for her.

Belinda was going to start another job in a few days. It would be strange when she no longer came to the kitchen door with the latest news from town or with some purchase she'd made at the dollar store in the next town over. Nori would miss her.

Jazz sat on the cedar chest in the attic, sipping coffee out of her stainless steel travel mug. The windows were open as far as they could shove them, and they were kept in place with a piece of wood. A breeze helped to cool down the attic and to fill it with fresh air.

"Try that one, that looks amazing!" Jazz exclaimed in response to a black dress with subtle beading on the bodice.

Nori shucked off her t-shirt and shorts and pulled the dress over her head. She gave a twirl and looked at Jazz to see her response.

"You have to keep it because it fits like a glove. You may not think you'll use it, but just watch, something will come up and you'll be so glad you have it. You have no idea what something like this would get at a vintage clothing sale. And didn't we find some black suede heels in another box?"

Nori touched the beads. "They don't make clothes like this anymore." She thought about how Louise had spent the day in Boston going to consignment shops to find something to wear to the award ceremony using Mary's gift money. She must have looked great in the dress.

"Exactly. It's one of a kind and if you don't keep it, I'll never forgive you. Now what else is there?"

Nori took the dress off and pulled on her shorts and top. She took some more dresses and skirts that were well-worn and serviceable out of the moth bags, but Jazz shook her head and pointed to the bag that was waiting for the thrift shop.

"You're very bossy, but you do have a good eye," Nori said. "I would never have been able to sort out through all this."

"I've always loved vintage clothes. Used to drive all over the place to go to shows before I had my kid. Now it's hard to get him to put up with all that." She sighed. "They were so elegant in the old days."

Nori held up some jackets and coats for her evaluation.

Jazz shook her head and pointed to the bag. They sorted through some table linens and towels, keeping only the ones that were of linen or good quality cotton, with tatting or embroidery on the edges.

"People love to buy this stuff at the flea market," she said, "I don't know if they ever use them, but they buy them anyway. Probably donate them back to thrift shops as soon as they realize how much work they are."

"Take whatever you think you can sell," Nori said. "I'm not going to use any of it and there's no point keeping it up here in the attic."

Jazz opened up another drawer of the old wardrobe that stood in the corner. She held up a small wool blazer with braid around the edges. "This yours?"

Nori walked over and took the blazer. "I remember this. There's a picture with me in this wearing a small beret and sitting on my tricycle."

"Do you want to keep it?"

Nori shook her head. "If I kept all the stuff that had some kind of memory attached to it. . . ."

"I can't believe you cleaned out your folks' house too. You must feel like you're drowning in people's stuff."

"When I get back to my apartment, I'm going to sort through all my things. After my dad died, the church ladies helped me clear the manse. They were really great—like a swat team they packed things up, delivered them to the shop, washed the cupboards, and floors."

"You're saying they were way more efficient than I am?"

"This takes a little more thought," Nori said. "I'm really glad you're here."

"Where would I rather be on a gorgeous day than up in a dusty attic breathing moth ball fumes and inhaling dust? Besides, once you've got a kid, you'll take any offer to get out for a morning."

Nori folded the blazer that she'd been holding and placed it carefully into the bag. "Do you think I ever will?"

"Ever will what?"

"Have a kid."

"Of course you will. First you have to find a decent guy. Then the rest will fall into place."

"What if I always pick losers?"

"You mean, just because one guy didn't live up to his potential, you're doomed to pick losers? Don't be ridiculous. On the other hand, who am I to talk?"

Nori reached into a box and pulled out a hat with an attached piece of netting. She placed it on her head, rolled down the netting, and struck a pose for Jazz.

"That looks really fabulous. I dare you to wear that to the inn."

"Get real."

"I'm serious. You wear it and I'll give you fifty bucks."

Nori studied her to see if she was serious. "And my reputation in town will be secure. The crazy lady who lives in the white house that used to belong to doc. Keep your fifty bucks. I want to be able to come back here."

"Do you ever wonder who's going to clean up after us? You know, when we're old and die and people have to come in and trash our junk?"

Nori ran her fingers around the formed shape of the felt hat at the hat and then placed it carefully into the hatbox.

"I guess it won't matter much who does it once we're dead."

"But don't you worry about all that racy underwear you've been saving up, and all your other secrets?"

Nori laughed. "Are you kidding? That's the first thing I'm going to pitch when I get home. The old ratty underwear."

Jazz reached into the second drawer of the wardrobe and pulled out a white cotton bra from another era. She slipped the thick straps of the bra over her t-shirt. "Speaking of which . . . what do you think of this one?" she asked as she strutted around the attic with her chest pushed forward.

Nori started to giggle and then both of them escalated into hysterical laughter.

"Look at these cones!" Jazz said as she struggled to get the words out.

"I don't get the point," Nori said choking with laughter and finally slumping to the floor, gasping for breath.

"There's more," Jazz said, as she reached into the drawer and pulled out a girdle with stocking attachments. "I hope you're feeling well supported," she said, gasping for breath, "because otherwise . . . we have just the thing for you."

When they'd finally stopped laughing and gasping for breath, they wiped the tears from their eyes. Jazz put the rest of the granny panties and corsets in the bag. "You know, I was thinking . . ."

"Uh-oh," Nori said.

"There's a place about an hour away in Janesville that has a burlesque night where they teach women how to dance. No men are allowed during the class time. We could go and give it a try." She swung the bullet bra over her head seductively and swayed her hips suggestively.

"Absolutely not. You're out of your mind."

"I'll take that as a yes. Thursday night. I'll get my mom to stay over. We need a night out." She waved her hand over the bags of discarded clothes and the open drawers of the wardrobe.

Nori had her hand on her hip. "Listen, there's nothing in this body that reads burlesque. I can't do it!"

"Still waters run deep. We'll soon find out." She turned her back to Nori and emptied out the rest of the drawers, ignoring her protest. "I'll take these bags down so we have more space. And if there's anything you might want to wear on Thursday night, just set it aside." Jazz picked up one of the green bags and started to go down the stairs.

Nori picked up a flannel shirt, rolled it up, and threw it at her head.

"Hey, watch out, it took me an hour to do my hair this morning." Jazz started to snicker which set Nori off again and soon they were howling with laughter and throwing clothes at each other.

"Girls, girls, what's going on up there?" Belinda asked.

"She started it," Jazz accused.

"Surely you realize it's just been a short while since we buried Louise. I think you could show some respect."

Nori and Jazz looked at each other. Jazz started to move towards the stairs to apologize, but Nori put her hand on her arm to stop her and went instead.

"Belinda, I'm really sorry. We meant no disrespect. I think we were just letting off a little steam. It's been a long summer."

Belinda sniffed. "When you're done cleaning all that up, I've made some lunch." She turned away from the stairs.

Nori went upstairs. "She's really pissed at us."

Jazz shrugged. "She'll get over it."

They continued their task of sorting but talked in whispers, not wanting to aggravate Belinda again. After all, they were looking forward to the sauce and pasta Belinda was making—the scent of tomatoes and garlic was wafting up to the attic.

"Look, Jazz, I think we better do your proposed field trip another time. I really don't think this would go over well."

"Wimp! Who's gonna know?"

"Are you kidding? You live here and you don't think that reports of our misbehavior wouldn't get back to this town before we did?

Jazz sighed loudly. "I still think it was a good idea."

"Another time," Nori said. "Let's get this clean up done. That will make Belinda happy."

Jazz pitched another green garbage bag of clothes down the opening to the floor below. "I'm going to get rid of all my stuff."

"You got any good stuff, like diaries?" Nori asked.

"Nope, burned all that a long time ago. Although . . . I have one diary that describes in glowing detail what a total jerk you were. That one I'll keep for future reference. Maybe even blackmail."

"You do not!" Nori objected, hitting her with a pillow.

"Girls, are you misbehaving again?" Jazz said in a mock whisper, imitating Belinda's stern tone.

"Lunch," Belinda called from below.

"Saved by the meatballs," Jazz said. "I plan to sell it someday."

Nori glared at her with her hand on her hip.

Jazz climbed down the ladder, chuckling out loud.

Chapter 51

NORI, NEWTON'S CORNERS, 1980

Nori visited the lawyer's office in an old Victorian house on Main Street. He was a kind man who had known Louise from her first days in the town. He carefully explained the bequests Louise had made to her church and some local charities and then revealed that she had left Nori the house along with funds to help maintain it. She'd also set up an educational trust for the son of Nori's friend Jazz.

Apparently Louise had wanted Nori to decide whether she wanted to keep or sell the house, but suggested she rent it for the winter while she went back to school. She could deal with the house later.

The lawyer gave Nori a personal letter from Louise. She tucked it in her purse and drove to the picnic table by the bridge in town to read.

The early maples had already turned to deep crimson. She couldn't believe it was the end of August. The small park was covered with pink milkweed, white and purple asters, and goldenrod, interspersed with white and yellow daisies. Late summer had saved its most brilliant presentation for last.

She'd called Jenna yesterday and apologized for her behavior. She hoped that her group would forgive her for not showing up for the seminar. Jenna told her they had all gotten a decent grade in the end. When she'd told her she was coming back to New Haven to finish her degree, Jenna offered her a place in a three-bedroom apartment they'd rented. Nori was ready for a fresh start and accepted the offer.

"I'm not a finished project," Nori warned, "but I've really tried to change. And I'm truly sorry for hurting you and others."

"Thank you," Jenna said. And then she told her about the third roommate who was a studying to become an Episcopal priest. "She works as a chaplain at the Veterans' Hospital and is a rock climber in her free time. But best of all . . . she loves to cook."

"That sounds really promising. Do you need any furniture or kitchen stuff?"

"We have most of that. When you get here we can deal with your apartment and move whatever you want to bring to this place. I know someone who has a van."

"I talked to the woman who is subletting and she's happy to keep anything I don't want, so that should be easy. I'd rather travel light for now."

Boats crisscrossed the lake as the cries and shouts of children playing in the water travelled across the lake from the camp on the other side. Soon they would be back in school and memories of their summer days would fade along with their tans. Perhaps that would be the case for her as well, but she doubted that she'd forget one moment of this summer.

She was reluctant to open the envelope but finally carefully slid her finger under the glued triangle of the envelope and unfolded the paper. She read the letter slowly, knowing that this would be her last direct communication from Louise. From this point on, she'd have to rely on the stories they'd shared this summer.

> *Dear Nori:*
>
> *Thank you for spending this past summer with me. I am grateful for your time and care. Although my story is ending, yours is still being written, day-by-day and page-by-page. Fill it with laughter, with friends, and with deep purpose.*
>
> *You may wonder at the unfamiliar handwriting—I no longer had the strength to finish the letter. Fortunately, Ben was willing to be my scribe. I must confess that asking you to sort my papers was a bit of a ruse to get you up here. Ben said a holy fib is permissible if it's for a good cause, but I just want to clear my conscience on that. I needed to convince you to come up here at any cost.*
>
> *We have talked a great deal about stories and I am grateful for those conversations. The thing about stories, that I am only beginning to understand, is that they are an imperfect rendering of the past. We can never claim that our version is the truth, since our memories are flawed and our understanding of any event is only partial and biased.*
>
> *But still, we persist in trotting out tired stories, those ragged and moth-eaten cardigans that carry in their pockets the heavy stones of hurt and disappointment. This cargo is so familiar we don't even feel the weight of them as we carry them through our days.*

When we tell stories, it's as if we take out those stones to show them to others, hoping that they will confirm the pain they represent. We never get tired of doing that—holding those stones and showing them to others. They continue to define us decades after the events have happened or hurtful words have been spoken.

I realize now that it is not necessarily the "facts" of those stories that are important, but it is the telling of them that is significant. When we share them, over and over again, we ignore the toll this repetition takes on our ability to live in the present.

While we may think those stones, and the wounds they stand for, are our prized possessions, they are actually a burden we continue to carry. We may beg for some accountability from those who passed so long ago, but it is not their job to take those stones from us. We turn to the next generation, eager to transmit our pain to them. We ask them to trust our accounts, to share our pain, and to sympathize, as if they'd seen it with their own eyes. But it is not their job to walk in our shoes—they have their own path to walk.

I don't include here those who have had truly evil things done to them. For them, the pain is written in their very being. Some of this cruelty lies beyond the capacities of storytelling. They need help to roll the enormous stone away from their lives and from those of their children.

I write instead of the transgressions and hurts that are part of our daily life. These turn into the river stones, worried smooth by hurt.

Now that I am at the end of my life, I wonder, what it would take to let go of these stones. I have befriended them, these memories, these grievances, and I reinjure myself by refusing to let go. My shadows have been welcomed as permanent residents of my soul. And I realize that letting them go involves two steps—forgiving others and forgiving myself.

I have one task left. I must chase those shadows from my soul. They are not my truth, but only by grace can I walk past them, fearless and searching for the light. But how can I? My body is frail; I am confined to this bed, this room.

When all is stripped away, I have the freedom to choose how to walk this last mile. I turn my pockets inside out and let those stones fall where they will. I regret I waited so long to do this.

There is much about forgiveness I have struggled to understand. Sometimes those who offend us are not able or willing or even present to meet us face to face; still, we have the chance to find peace without them.

That day I drove away from the san and faced the reality of Dr. Clarke's actions—the lying, the use of my research, and the distortion of my work relationships—I was overwhelmed by anger. I felt like I might drown in it. On the side of that highway, I felt every emotion from rage, to anger, to despair. I threw up. I feel ashamed, even now, to confess that I felt a murderous rage. For me, who had promised to preserve life and do no harm, this was something I regret. I wanted to strangle that man until he had no life or breath in him.

When I finally got out of that ditch and looked at the landscape, I saw how the road angled gently down from those mountains where I'd lived for the past months. I noticed how it ran beside the river as it cut through the valley, descending into the flat land as far as I could see. Even in my disheveled state, I had to acknowledge the beauty of it. I saw that I had a choice. I could look back at the mountains, those unmoving towers of strength, where so many secrets had been buried. Or, I could focus on the vista ahead, watching the bends and turns of the river.

I did what I had to do as a professional. I reported what I'd seen and I passed the information to those who could take action. I knew that my job was to move forward and to focus on my work. And I did just that. But I did carry a sense of failure and shame about this episode at the san, and I kept that diary buried all these years. I am ready to finally let that go, forgiving myself for all that was wrong, both in what I did, and what I left undone.

I hope that the stories we have shared will ultimately lead you alongside that river that brings healing. Give yourself time, and find wise mentors and companions who can correct your direction when you go astray.

You have mentioned the idea of doing something with your research for the community once your thesis is complete. I am sorry I will not experience that, but I heartily support the plan. There are many people who still carry the secrets and hurt of the sanatorium experience—the lingering shadows of that place inhibit the necessary healing. Perhaps enough time has passed that those who remain might be willing to share their stories and release some stones.

Forgiveness is a task requiring courage. It has taken my lifetime to realize how essential it is, and here you are, at the portal of this undertaking, with so many more tools with which to work.

You have asked me if I am ready. Are we ever ready to face the end of our lives? I feel as ready as I can be, realizing that one might always dream of one more hiking trail or one more sunrise lifting the blanket of fog from over the lake. Perhaps we always leave something undone, while taking comfort in knowing that others are there to continue the journey.

The night has been long, but even now, the slightest hint of light rises up in the eastern sky, a thin pencil line of hope that divides the night from day and the dark from light.

With love,
Aunt Louise

Nori folded the letter carefully and placed it back in the envelope. She looked over her shoulder at the bridge that arced over the point where the lake turned into a river. She had kayaked under that bridge and followed the river into the wetlands filled with lily pads and marsh grasses that made a rich habitat for many birds.

She watched a woman walk over the bridge and head out of town towards the camp that was on the opposite side of the lake from Louise's house. Nori studied the bridge and knew that when she walked over the river of her grief, she had to trust that solace waited on the other side.

She checked her watch and realized it was time to head home. Ben and Jazz and J. J. were coming over for a campfire and early dinner. She was looking forward to spending the evening with them. It was a farewell to summer—soon she'd be heading back to school.

They sat in the Adirondack chairs in a circle around the fire. She watched as Ben built a fire in the fireplace pit. Jazz and her son were curled together under a blanket. Ben had brought some beer and sausages to grill in the fire, and Jazz had brought two kinds of salads. Nori had picked up the necessary ingredients at the store for their s'mores.

She planned to finish her thesis and to dedicate it to Louise. She'd worked as much as she could over the past weeks, taking advantage of the early mornings when the house was quiet. She sent a final proposal to her advisor, making sure to follow every step of the guidelines.

When a letter finally arrived from the department that afternoon, she'd saved it for the campfire. If it were bad news, at least she'd have Ben and Jazz there to commiserate. One way or another, she planned to do the project.

As they settled in to enjoy the campfire, Nori pulled out the letter from her hoody pocket and opened it. "OK folks. Here we go. This is from Yale." Ben and Jazz looked at her expectantly while J. J. tried to open the bag of marshmallows.

Nori cleared her throat. "*Dear Nori. We are pleased to receive your thesis proposal as requested. We approve the proposal as submitted and have set the date of your doctoral supervisory committee meeting for the second week of September. Your graduate assistantship will be reinstated and you will meet with your advisor to finalize courses and teaching for the year ahead.*"

At the bottom of the letter, her advisor had added a brief note. "*I've been out of town on research and apologize for the delay. The proposal looks great and I look forward to working with you.*"

Ben came over and hugged her and Nori got up and gave Jazz and her son a collective hug.

"I told you," Jazz said.

"Congratulations," Ben told her.

"Can we make s'mores now?" J. J. asked.

"After dinner. But wait a minute, I'll be right back," Nori said.

She ran inside and grabbed Louise's precious brandy from the hutch and three shot glasses.

By the fire, she poured a glassful for each of them. "To Louise," Nori said.

"To Louise," they echoed.

Over the trees a full moon rose, illuminating the landscape and cutting ribbons of reflection on the lake as far as the eye could see. Twilight had morphed into darkness as the fire crackled, sending flames up into the night sky. Silver strips of light danced with waves that collapsed and then retreated from the tiny beach.

They sat mesmerized by the fire and listened to the crackling of the wood. Sparks flew up into the air with abandon. Out on the lake, a loon sent a plaintive call into the night. Across the lake, Nori could see some lights from the camp.

Learning to see, she thought, took a lot of sitting and waiting in the darkness, imagining and hoping to find the light.

Acknowledgements

I WOULD like to thank my managing editor, Mathew Wimer, as well as Jim Tedrick, Daniel Lanning, Emily Callihan, George Callihan, Joe Delahanty, Shannon Carter, and the production team at Wipf and Stock for their work on this book.

Heartfelt thanks to the staff at Lake Pleasant Public Library (Speculator, New York) and the Museum on Blue Mountain Lake (Blue Mountain Lake, New York).

Thanks to students, staff, and colleagues at Emmanuel College, Victoria University, and the University of Toronto. Conversations in classrooms, hallways, and the kitchen on the second floor were essential to the story.

Friends in various locations provided hospitality and laughter. With gratitude to Martha Smalley, Anne Howland, Emily Walzer, Emily Fine, Jeanne Thomsen, Nancy Thompson in Connecticut, and Linda Van Damme, Hei Wai Kwan, Candace Pulver-Taylor, Sangun Oh, Jennifer Batt, and Mel and Jill Sauer in Canada. Thanks to Celeste Roney, who provided a key to the cabin in the Adirondacks. I remember fondly conversations with Jack Leadley (1927-2018) of Speculator, New York who shared his tales and artistry. Far away friends, such as Sander Adelaar, Diane Howard, and Hannah Bowman, kept in touch by email and visits when possible.

With gratitude to Toronto Women's Housing Cooperative and St. Andrew by-the-Lake Anglican Church (Toronto Island), for housing and community during most of the writing of this project. I am grateful to the medical staff and alternative health practitioners who taught by example. Thank you to Jayne Davis, MD, Heather Atkinson, RMT, and staff at St. Michael's Hospital and Princess Margaret Hospital of Toronto.

Thanks to Diane Terrana who suggested the title and so much more. I encountered similar hospitality from writing teachers, including Genevieve Appleton, Helen Humphreys, Susan Olding, Kim Eichlin, Lauren Winner,

Pat Schneider, and Kathryn Kuitenbrouwer. Setting aside one's own work to mentor students reflects an admirable generosity of spirit that builds creative community. I'd like to thank the artists in my life who also provide essential nourishment to the creative process, including Dee Van Dyke, Florida; Michele Miller, Ontario; and Geraldine Ysselstein, Hope River, Prince Edward Island.

I would like to acknowledge Professor Alison Prentice and classes on the history of women's higher education at OISE/UT. Her classes sparked my curiosity about women's colleges, professional training, and the challenges to those early women pioneers in social movements, education, and policy. Her ongoing support over the years has helped to bring the realities of the history of education into the fictional realm of the characters described in the story.

My family are distributed throughout several provinces and two states and I grateful for the support of siblings and their partners and families: Marian, Rein, Geraldine, John, and Otto. Special thanks to Isabelle Selles whose help arrived at just the right time.

All of these people, and many others who are not named here, are a part of the story and contributed in ways they may not realize. I thank them for believing in Louise and Nori and in the practice of story sharing that builds community in the most unlikely places.

Appendix

Reading Questions

PART I

1. A common saying is that "trouble comes in threes." Nori experiences trouble on multiple fronts. What is your experience with trouble? What wisdom were you taught about expecting trouble or inviting it into your life?

2. Nori chooses escape from her personal troubles and travels to her Aunt Louise's house for a holiday. She hopes to recreate some of the happy experiences of summers spent with her aunt. Have you ever tried to recover something from the past, only to find that the reality doesn't match your cherished memories?

3. Caregiving is often described as a burden. How does Nori react when she realizes that someone needs to coordinate her aunt's care? Have you found yourself in this situation? Was the experience of caregiving a burden or did it have unexpected elements of joy?

4. When Nori sorts Louise's personal papers, she is disappointed. Have you ever been in the position of sorting through your own or someone else's belongings? What emotions did you experience?

5. Louise is increasingly confined to bed as her illness progresses. She initiates a story exchange with Nori. Louise's stories include

memories of her youth and growing up on a farm. How did those experiences shape her ambition and determination?

6. As a young person, Louise is jealous of her sister, Mary. Why do you think she feels that way? Have you experienced those kinds of feelings in relation to siblings, friends, or colleagues? How does Louise arrive at a fuller understanding of her sister and of herself?

7. Louise works to excel academically as a way to escape farm life. When her mother takes her along on a visit to a sick neighbor, Louise doesn't hide her disgust. As they drive home, her mother chastises her for not caring. Have you ever experienced an absence of caring or empathy in yourself or from someone else? Describe this experience.

8. Louise experiences harassment in medical school. Why couldn't she report this to anyone? Has this changed for workers today?

9. How does the experience in Mississippi affect Louise? Describe an experience that was pivotal or transformational for your future direction.

10. Nori and her old friend Jazz have followed different trajectories in life, but they manage to reactivate their friendship. Have you reconnected with old friends? How does Jazz support Nori? How have your friends influenced your choices?

11. Nori's research sparks her interest in the history of the local sanatorium. How is historical research similar to detective work? What role does curiosity play in the process?

PART II

1. When Louise arrives at the san to start her fellowship, she is disappointed in the welcome. How is her arrival similar and yet different from Nori's arrival at the lake house in Part I?

2. What features of the institutional culture does Louise notice in her first days at the san? Have you encountered aspects of an institutional culture or design that struck you as unusual or different in a new situation? How can design affect function in a building/office/institution?

3. Louise experiences a low moment after losing her first patient. How does Jimmy's presence console her? How have you been consoled in challenging moments?

4. From the patient's perspective, what impression do you have of daily life at the san?

5. Until she arrives at the san, Louise had has limited interaction with patients. At the san, she befriends the patients at Rose Cottage. In what ways was Louise made to feel like an outsider at the san and how did she find other sources of belonging? Describe your experience of feeling like an outsider.

6. When Penny joins Louise's research, what advantages are gained?

7. Despite the regulation of patient life by the institution, there is evidence that patients also had a lively subculture outside of the official rules and regulations. What evidence can you find in the story to support this?

8. In the story, patients have limited rights. They are expected to comply with the regimen assigned them with little information about their health or eventual discharge. What is your sense/experience of patients' rights today? How do you imagine that individual rights can be balanced with the rights of a community in the face of a real or perceived threat?

9. Louise is drawn into exploring the discontinuities she observes at the san. Wouldn't it have been safer to just ignore the evidence and keep quiet for the time left in her fellowship? What are the risks in taking a moral stance?

10. Penny and Louise discuss the cover story they prepared in case they are discovered doing unauthorized research. Is this untruth justified for the greater good of the project?

11. Louise starts a research trial using drugs that have been tested elsewhere and have shown promise for curing patients with TB. She takes advantage of Dr. Clarke's absence to do this, knowing he will be furious. Is this a reasonable risk?

12. Louise sneaks out of the residence at night to investigate the secret facility in the woods. Is this a good plan?

13. When Dr. Clarke returns, he gathers the board to fire Louise. Does he have grounds for this firing? Louise carries herself with dignity,

demands the right to speak, and leaves the san. She delays her true reaction until she is on the road away from the san. Can you imagine how she felt at that point?

14. When Louise arrived at the san for her fellowship, she discovered that many of their practices were outdated. During her fellowship, she acknowledges that there is an aspect of mystery to healing. What is her response to the contradictions she encounters?

PART III

1. After reading the diary, Nori struggles to fit new information into her previous understanding of her family story. Why is this challenging? Have you ever had to revise your understanding of the past when new information came to light? Describe that process as you experienced it.

2. Mary expresses jealousy of Louise's career and work. How have things changed since their childhood days on the farm? How does Louise encourage her?

3. Louise decides to study in Boston. Why has she chosen to focus on public health? What challenges does she face at school?

4. Louise is diagnosed with extreme fatigue and told to find a place to rest. How does she react to convent life?

5. When Louise visits her sister, what does she discover? What do you know about the treatment of postpartum depression in the past and in the present?

6. Nori is shocked to find out about her mother's postpartum depression. She felt that she should have been told. Are family secrets ever justified?

7. Louise suggests a story exchange because she is genuinely interested in how her niece experienced events while growing up. Nori recounts her experience at summer camp. What strikes you about her story? When Louise fills in the blanks of another summer, Nori feels badly that they didn't share their struggles with her. Why is Louise telling her these details now?

8. What does Nori learn from telling her stories to her aunt? When we tell stories or write them down, sometimes we gain a new

perspective on the past. Have you told/written/illustrated your perspective or stories? What have you learned from this?

9. Did Louise have a "good death"? What do you imagine as a "good death"?

10. What is Louise's final lesson to her niece in talking about stones? Are there stones you are carrying that you would like to put down? Describe these.

11. Summer has ended and Nori says goodbye. What aspects of her transformation strike you as interesting? In what ways has she changed? Have you experienced a season of transformation? Write/reflect on your memories of that season, naming the factors that made it possible and the emotions you experienced.

A Note on Sources

THE author gratefully acknowledges the following works for their help in writing the book: *Living in the Shadow of Death. Tuberculosis and the Social Experience of Illness in American History*, by Sheila Rotman; *Portrait of Healing: Curing in the Woods*, by Victoria Rhinehart; *Doc: Orra A. Phelps, MD, Adirondack Naturalist and Mountaineer*, by Mary Arkaleian; *The Wounded Healer: Body, Illness and Ethics; The Illness Narratives*, by Arthur Frank; *Suffering, Healing and the Human Condition*, by Arthur Kleinman; *In the Company of Educated Women: A History*, by Barbara Solomon; *The Immortal life of Henrietta Lacks*, by Rebecca Skloot; *William Alphaeus Hunton: A Pioneer Prophet of Young Men*, by Addie Waite Hunton and John R. Mott; *How the Light Gets In*, by Pat Schneider; and *The Solace of Fierce Landscapes: Exploring Desert and Mountain Spirituality*, by Belden C. Lane.

CPSIA information can be obtained
at www.ICGtesting.com
Printed in the USA
FFHW011930271019
55768457-61642FF